LEGEND OF THE FIVE RINGS

The realm of Rokugan is a land of samurai, courtiers, and mystics, dragons, magic, and divine beings – a world where honor is stronger than steel.

The Seven Great Clans have defended and served the Emperor of the Emerald Empire for a thousand years, in battle and at the imperial court. While conflict and political intrigue divide the clans, the true threat awaits in the darkness of the Shadowlands, behind the vast Kaiu Wall. There, in the twisted wastelands, an evil corruption endlessly seeks the downfall of the empire.

The rules of Rokugani society are strict. Uphold your honor, lest you lose everything in pursuit of glory.

BY THE SAME AUTHOR

LEGEND OF THE FIVE RINGS
Poison River

ARKHAM HORROR
Wrath of N'kai

WATCH DOGS LEGION
Day Zero (with James Swallow)

ADVENTURES OF THE ROYAL OCCULTIST
The Whitechapel Demon
The Jade Suit of Death
The Infernal Express

EXECUTIONER (as Don Pendleton)
Border Offensive
Arctic Kill
Murder Island
Final Assault

JIM ANTHONY, SUPER DETECTIVE
The Mark of Terror
The Vril Agenda

WARHAMMER 40,000
Deathstorm
Primogenitor
Clonelord
Lukas the Trickster
Apocalypse
Manflayer

THE HORUS HERESY
The Palatine Phoenix

WARHAMMER FANTASY
Knight of the Blazing Sun
Neferata
Road of Skulls
Master of Death
The Serpent Queen
Return of Nagash
Lord of the End Times

WARHAMMER: AGE OF SIGMAR
Skaven Pestilens
The Black Rift
Fury of Gork
The Undying King
Plague Garden
Spear of Shadows
Soul Wars
The Mirrored City
Black Pyramid
Dark Harvest

NECROMUNDA
Sinner's Bounty

Wake the Dead
Dracula Lives!

DEATH'S KISS

A Daidoji Shin Mystery

JOSH REYNOLDS

First published by Aconyte Books in 2021

ISBN 978 1 83908 080 7

Ebook ISBN 978 1 83908 081 4

Cover art by Merilliza Chan

Rokugan map by Francesca Baerald

Distributed in North America by Simon & Schuster Inc, New York, USA

Printed in the United States of America

9 8 7 6 5 4 3 2 1

ACONYTE BOOKS

An imprint of Asmodee Entertainment Ltd

Mercury House, Shipstones Business Centre

North Gate, Nottingham NG7 7FN, UK

aconytebooks.com // twitter.com/aconytebooks

For Elodie. Without whom I would have gotten this book done much faster. And for Sylvie, without whom I might not have gotten it done at all.

Unicorn Lands
CITY OF THE RICH FROG
Rokugan
HISATU-KESU
GATHERER OF WINDS CASTLE
CASTLE OF ORGANIZATION

CHAPTER ONE
Foxfire Theater

Daidoji Shin raised a cup of tea to his lips. A sudden clatter of falling wood interrupted him mid-sip, and the hot liquid scalded his tongue. Sighing, he set the cup down carefully. Around him, the interior of the Foxfire Theater echoed with the sound of labor. Tradesmen moved back and forth across the stage, carrying tools and planks. Above them, laborers maneuvered new roofbeams into place. Down in the benches, artisans argued over the placement of various cosmetic additions.

Shin sat in his private box, on a cushioned bench that still smelt slightly of smoke. The theater no longer resembled the burnt-out ruin it had been only a few short months ago. Nor did it look as it once had. Instead, the theater's new owner had decided to make some – in Shin's opinion – long-needed improvements, including an extension of the stage, an expansion to the changing areas and a complete refurbishment of the backstage area. It was all very expensive – but necessary for future success.

Or so Shin assured anyone who cared to ask about such

things. In its heyday, the theater had been infamous for its ribald performances and riotous patrons. More recently, it had fallen on difficult times, hosting a succession of largely uninspiring kabuki troupes for dwindling audiences. After it had been gutted by a sudden fire, Shin had purchased the smoldering ruin from its previous owner and set about renovating it.

The idea of owning his own theater, which had seemed positively brilliant at the time, had lost some of its luster in the interim. But he was confident that his enthusiasm would be rekindled once the renovations were complete.

His eyes flicked down to the stack of ledgers that sat before him, on the small writing table he'd had brought up. The ledgers contained the financial records for the theater, and he'd been working diligently to make sense of them for the better part of a month. So far, he'd made little headway. The theater was suspended in a web of debt that kept it unprofitable and yet somehow functional.

Despite his best efforts, Shin yearned for a distraction – something, anything, to take him away from the mess he'd made for himself. Preferably somewhere far away, and for long enough that the matter would sort itself out. Sighing again, he opened the uppermost ledger and began to scan the page.

"I simply must protest, my lord. It is not fitting that a man of your station be seen in such surroundings." The statement was delivered with modest and subtle venom, as was appropriate for a courtier speaking to one who was nominally his superior. Shin looked up, gave a thin smile and fixed the speaker with a heavy-lidded gaze.

Junichi Kenzō was a narrow needle of a man, dressed in blue, with a face like a hatchet and the pinched expression of one who expects only disappointment. He'd been sitting quietly, if impatiently, since he'd been ushered into Shin's box moments earlier. Shin, somewhat unkindly, had decided to let him stew for a bit.

Shin closed the ledger, and deftly squared it atop the others before him. Similar to his guest, he was clad in a kimono of the finest blue silk, though his was emblazoned with a pattern designed to draw the eye of even the most casual observer. His white hair was pulled back from his narrow, handsome features, but a few strands were left free so as to frame his face just so. He took great pains to ensure that he cut an attractive, if somewhat rakish, figure. "And what surroundings might those be, Master Kenzō?"

He picked up his fan and snapped it open. The spokes were made from steel, and they made a pleasing hiss as he extended them. If Kenzō noticed, he gave no sign. Then, being a courtier himself, perhaps he was familiar with iron fans and their myriad uses.

Kenzō frowned deeply. "Forgive me, but the air is full of dirt and noise, my lord. Why, I even overheard one of the laborers cursing a few moments ago."

"How dreadful for you," Shin said, in his most sympathetic tones. He paused. "Though I do believe the individual in question had dropped something heavy on his foot only a moment prior."

"That is no excuse!"

"Indeed not. Sadly, standards are not what they were."

"If that is the case, might I ask why you insisted on meeting here, my lord?" Kenzō indicated their surroundings with a twitch of his chin. Shin wondered if Kenzō had ever been inside a theater before. Though the Crane prided themselves on being patrons of the arts, not all of them appreciated such things.

Shin sat back, fanning himself. "I confess, Master Kenzō, that I find being amidst all this clamor somewhat invigorating. There is something poetic about the sounds of tradesmen as they set their shoulders to the wheel of progress, don't you agree?"

Kenzō had no reply to this. Shin took the opportunity to study him more closely. He knew Kenzō's type well – a petty man, looking for any opportunity to impress his betters and amaze his subordinates. Not a bully. Just officious and somewhat obnoxious.

Unfortunately, he was also seneschal to Shin's grandfather. As such, he spoke with the voice of the Daidoji Trading Council. Shin took a sip of his now-cool tea, grimaced, and signaled for the servant lurking at the door to refresh the cup.

Kenzō placed his hand over his own cup as the servant made to do the same for him. "Be that as it may, surely you have others capable of dealing with such matters." Disapproval punctuated every word as he spoke.

Ever since his arrival almost a week ago, Kenzō had made clear his feelings – as well as those of Shin's grandfather – about this latest business venture. Since no directive to cease in his current preoccupation had accompanied Kenzō's arrival, Shin had decided to endure the other man's displeasure with all the good grace and humor he could muster – though it was waning fast.

He fancied that Kenzō would eventually wander home, to report on what would be deemed Shin's latest foolishness. It was simply a matter of weathering the storm. He laid his palm flat on the topmost ledger and said, "Is that an offer, Master

Kenzō? I have heard that you have quite the head for financial matters. Indeed, I am told that my grandfather often seeks your advice on such things."

Kenzō, as Shin had hoped, swelled slightly at this. "It is true, my lord, I am quite familiar with the pecuniary side of things. That is why I am here, after all. To inspect your finances – with your permission, of course, my lord." He ducked his head, as if suddenly recalling that Shin was his superior – an affectation, but one Shin appreciated.

"But of course you have my permission, Master Kenzō." Shin spoke as if it had never occurred to him to consider otherwise. In fact, it was something of a nuisance. Kenzō was ostensibly acting on behalf of the council. In reality, he'd been sent to spy on Shin and find out why he was no longer drawing on his allotted stipend.

As spies went, Kenzō wasn't the worst he'd ever encountered. Nor, however, was he the best. That particular title rested with the bald, round man sitting to Shin's left. Master Ito met Shin's gaze and gave a knowing, if surreptitious, smile. He had been quietly observing Kenzō since the other man's arrival, and Shin wondered what he made of the courtier.

Ito wore the plain robes of a merchant. Allegedly, he was merely one of the trio of such whom Shin oversaw on behalf of the Daidoji Trading Council. The three were the sum total of the Crane's interest in the City of the Rich Frog.

All three paid a portion of their profits in return for protection, and while they were not family, they were considered vassals. This gave them some advantages when it came to import fees, annual tithes and the like. Of the three, Ito was the only one whose name Shin could recall without being prompted.

There was good reason for that. While Ito endeavored to look soft and unassuming, his guileless demeanor was but a mask hiding a mind sharp enough to draw blood. He'd been of some help to Shin in a previous affair – enough to earn his patron's trust. He knew everything about the city's trading networks, both legal and otherwise, and on his advice Shin had made several private investments in various local businesses – including the Foxfire Theater. He was also a spy for the Crane, though he had never admitted it in so many words.

At Shin's glance, Ito cleared his throat. "Perhaps, my lord, Master Kenzō is the man for the moment? After all, while I have given you what small help I am able, I am but a humble merchant. Surely a man of Master Kenzō's reputation might be able to untangle this particular fiscal knot with ease."

Kenzō looked sharply at Ito and said, "What knot might that be?" Despite his lingering frown, there was an undercurrent of curiosity in his voice.

Shin indicated the ledgers. "As I'm sure you might have guessed, the finances of this theater were in quite the state when I took on ownership. A tangle of debts, payments, contracts and such – all of which are now my responsibility. I find such matters tedious, but it must be done."

Kenzō's gaze sharpened, and there was a light in his eyes that told Shin he'd read the man right. "Oh yes, certainly, my lord. But you must have more important matters to attend to, as I said."

"Yes, but needs must. I fear I shall be occupied with this matter until it is resolved."

Kenzō licked his lips. "Perhaps… I might be of service?"

Shin's eyes widened. "You, Master Kenzō? Why, I wouldn't

dream of inflicting such a conundrum upon you. Not when you have other duties..."

"My lord, it would be my privilege. I have often conducted similar audits on behalf of your grandfather, though never, I must admit, for a business such as this."

Shin sat back, and Ito gently nudged the stack of ledgers towards Kenzō. The courtier practically rubbed his hands in barely restrained glee. "Never fear, Master Kenzō. I am assured that one business is much like another, when it comes to money."

Ito coughed politely, and Shin nodded. He rose smoothly, smoothing his own blue kimono with a practiced gesture. "Please, make yourself at home here. I must speak with a certain tradesman regarding a shipment of lanterns. I will return shortly."

Kenzō, his mind already on his task, barely remembered to bow as Shin and Ito left the box. Once safely out of earshot, Ito said, "Well played, my lord. Kenzō has something of a reputation as a keen problem solver. Overly keen, in fact."

"Easily distractable, you mean?" Shin asked. He snapped open his fan and gave it a twitch, to better disperse the smells of pitch and sawdust that permeated the theater.

"Even so, my lord." Ito bowed low, almost obsequiously so. "If you will permit me, I must return to my own labors. I have deliveries to arrange and shipments to contract."

Shin waved him on, and Ito departed. He turned to address the figure lurking unobtrusively nearby. "A clever man. I'm glad I realized it before it was too late."

The young woman leaning against the wall snorted. "And it only took you a year." She straightened and fixed him with a disapproving eye. "Kenzō?"

Shin gestured with his fan. "Happily plying his trade for the moment."

"You tricked him."

"Me? Don't be absurd, Kasami. Such a thing is beneath me." He started down the creaking stairs towards the stage. Kasami, trotting in his wake, snorted indelicately. Then, there was little delicacy and even less tact in Hiramori Kasami.

A daughter of the Uebe marshes, she had been born into a vassal family but now served the Daidoji directly, her skills honed to murderous lethality. She was also his bodyguard, something she complained about often and at length. "That won't keep him occupied for long," she said, her mouth a thin line. It wasn't quite a frown, but neither was it a smile. "Eventually, he's going to remember why he was sent here in the first place."

"We'll burn that bridge when we come to it," Shin said, watching the laborers haul a joist into place above the stage. "For now, perhaps we can get some use out of our guest."

"Cross," Kasami corrected.

"What?"

"Cross the bridge. Not burn it."

Shin fanned himself. "Is there a difference?"

"Ideally."

Her tone bordered on disrespectful, and Shin quirked an eyebrow. "Well, as I always say, a day without learning is a day wasted." He paused, waiting for her reaction.

She didn't look at him. "To my knowledge, you have never said that."

"Maybe you weren't listening," he countered, teasingly.

Kasami grunted, but didn't take the bait. Shin sighed. "Still, you are correct, I suppose. I had hoped my grandfather might be content to leave me to my own devices, but I see that I have once more piqued his interest."

"It's because you're spending too much money."

"Technically, I'm not spending any money – well, any of his money at any rate." Shin assumed an air of aggrieved innocence. Kasami gave him a level look.

"He's probably curious as to where you're getting it."

"And I have informed him many times–" Another level look from Kasami compelled him to correct himself. "Fine, I have informed him at least once of my various investments. It is hardly my fault that he ignores my existence save for when I suffer some unforeseen and undeserved embarrassment…" He trailed off as he noticed her expression. "What?"

"Nothing."

Shin peered at her in suspicion. "Are you implying something?"

"I would not dream of doing so, my lord," she said, her tone bland and respectful. Shin made to reply when he caught sight of Wada Sanemon, master of the Three Flower Troupe, the troupe-in-residence for the Foxfire Theater, hurrying towards them across the stage.

"My lord, my lord," Sanemon called out. He was heavyset, with broad shoulders and a hesitant, nervous manner. He was sweating profusely, as was his custom, and his cheeks were flushed. "My lord," he wheezed, as he reached them. Bending over, he braced his hands on his knees, panting.

Shin waited politely for him to catch his breath. When Sanemon straightened, Shin said, "How might I be of service, Master Sanemon?"

"You have a guest, my lord," Sanemon said. "A… ah… a lady. She wishes to… ah… speak with you, in private. I… I took the liberty of showing her to one of the dressing rooms backstage. Just in case, you understand."

"A lady?" Shin perked up. "Did she give a name?"

Sanemon lowered his voice conspiratorially. "Iuchi Konomi, my lord."

Shin's eyes widened.

"Well now. Isn't that interesting?"

CHAPTER TWO
Iuchi Konomi

Shin strolled backstage, Sanemon hurrying in his wake, and Kasami trailing behind them both, at a respectful distance.

"How goes the day, Master Sanemon? Is the Three Flower Troupe ready for the new season?" Shin asked, throwing the questions over his shoulder.

"Fortunes willing, my lord," Sanemon said. He hesitated, then added, "I cannot thank you enough for this opportunity, my lord. Without your patronage we would surely have had to disband. Especially after… well." He gestured somewhat helplessly.

Shin nodded in understanding. Sanemon and his troupe had been involved in a recent incident that had nearly upset the delicate balance of power in the city. Shin had extricated them from the situation and had become their patron in the process.

"Yes," he said. "And have you… heard from her at all?" He paused. "Okuni, I mean," he added, more artlessly than he'd intended. Okuni was the lead actress of the Three Flower Troupe, as well as a shinobi of no small skill. She had been at the center of the incident in question, and Shin had only managed to resolve it with her aid. She'd vanished in the aftermath, a wise decision given all that had gone on.

Sanemon didn't meet his gaze. "Not for some months. I believe she's returned home."

"Ah." Shin forced a smile. "A shame. What is a troupe without its principal actress?"

"I wanted to ask you about that, my lord." Sanemon licked his lips nervously. "Might we… undertake auditions for a replacement?"

Shin glanced at him. "You don't think she's coming back."

Sanemon shrugged. "I know nothing, save we that we need a lead actress."

"I'm sure Nao would disagree," Shin said, referring to the company's lead actor.

"Nao overestimates himself."

Shin chuckled softly. "Perhaps, though I will not be the one to say it." He stopped and turned to face Sanemon. "Very well. Hold your auditions, with my compliments."

"Would you like to attend them, my lord?"

Shin briefly considered, then dismissed the idea. "I think not, Master Sanemon. You are the master of the troupe, and it must be your decision." He allowed himself a small smile. "Else what am I paying you for, after all?"

Sanemon blanched slightly, but mustered an appreciative laugh. He was still unsure of his new patron, and Shin often had to restrain his more playful urges. Changing the subject, Sanemon said, "I showed the lady into Nao's dressing room – he's out, for the moment – as I thought it would give you the most privacy."

"Well done, Master Sanemon. Your forethought does you credit."

Ahead of them, a pair of bodyguards in the livery of the Unicorn occupied the narrow corridor. Both were armed, though they wore no armor, and their swords were peace-knotted to show that their intentions were peaceful. Sanemon paused. "I'll just leave you to it, shall I, my lord?"

Shin nodded absently. "Yes. Oh – and Master Sanemon?"

"My lord?"

"There's a gentleman in my box, attempting to unravel the theater's finances. Would you send someone to see to his needs? Not immediately, but by and by. I'd hate for him to think that we'd forgotten him."

Sanemon bowed low. "Of course, my lord." He retreated with as much speed as dignity allowed, and Shin watched him go with a smile.

"He's getting better," he murmured.

"Still too jumpy for my liking," Kasami said. She looked at him. "He knows more than he's saying. About Okuni."

"Of course he does. But I see no reason to press the matter. When she is ready, she will return – or not, as fortune wills."

"But you hope she does."

"We need a lead actress."

"And that's the only reason, obviously."

Shin ignored the insinuation and said, "Two guards. She's practically travelling incognito." He indicated the bodyguards with a jerk of his chin. Kasami studied them for a moment before replying.

"She doesn't want to draw attention to herself."

"Interesting, don't you agree?"

"Dangerous," Kasami said.

"She is a friend, you know."

"Even worse." Kasami frowned. "Why do you think she's here?"

"Maybe she wishes to chat."

Kasami peered at him. Shin fluttered his fan dismissively. "Fine, yes, she probably wants something." He tapped his chin with the fan. "Still, we won't find out what it is by standing here, will we? Come on."

The taller of the two bodyguards, a woman, bowed shallowly as Shin approached. She kicked her companion in the ankle and he hastily followed suit. Shin inclined his head politely, acknowledging their greeting. "Kasami – wait here, if you please."

Wordlessly, Kasami took up a position opposite the two bushi. Shin was relieved to see that she kept her hand away from her swords, instead folding her arms over her chest. Shin snapped his fan shut, and the first bodyguard slid open the dressing room door. Shin entered to find that he was late to the conversation.

Iuchi Konomi sat demurely on a hard bench across from a tall, effete man, clad in an ornate kimono the color of sunset. The man was in the midst of telling an amusing story, and Konomi was giggling raucously behind her fan. They fell silent as Shin entered, and both pairs of eyes swiveled towards him.

"Lady Konomi," Shin said, with a polite bow. He inclined his head to the room's other occupant. "And Master Nao. I'd heard you were out for the day."

"I was. But I returned to find her ladyship ensconced in my poor excuse for a dressing room." He clucked his tongue in disappointment. "Sanemon has no sense of decorum. To leave a lady such as this here, and with no company to entertain her…"

"You have performed in that regard remarkably well, Master Nao," Konomi interjected. She was a tall woman, and sturdily built. The sort of woman made for arduous rides in full armor across hostile terrain. Shin had heard that she'd once stabbed a particularly obnoxious suitor with a paring knife, though he was not so gauche as to ask her about the incident. She gave a polite twitch of her lips. "We have been having a most fascinating conversation while we waited for you, Lord Shin."

Nao tittered. The actor was, for the moment, the most skilled member of the Three Flower Troupe. He often played multiple parts in plays, and had achieved some small celebrity for his aptitude for shifting from one role to the next in full view of the audience, as well as his ability to transition seamlessly from the more popular bombastic style of acting to a gentler, more realistic performance.

Shin, who had spent many hours in conversation with Nao over the preceding months, found him good company. Though he made no claim to noble birth, the actor was clearly more than familiar with the rules – enough, at least, to flout them in a most charming fashion. "You flatter me, my lady," he said. "I am but a humble thespian, doing his best to entertain his betters."

"There's something I never thought to hear – you referring to anyone as your better," Shin said. Nao glanced at him, eyes narrowing slightly. Shin's smile did not slip, and Nao looked away, the picture of insulted dignity.

The actor rose and, straightening his kimono, made for the door. "On that note I shall take my leave, my lord and lady… with your permission, of course."

"And with my compliments," Shin said, taking over Nao's seat. Nao gave a sharp laugh and slid the door shut behind himself, leaving Shin and Konomi alone. They sat in silence for several moments. Shin studied her, and she returned the favor. He restrained a smile. Conversation with Konomi was often much like a duel – it began slowly, with a wary circling of the participants. Whoever spoke first was often at a disadvantage.

Finally, Konomi broke the stalemate. "It has been some time since last we spoke," she murmured, softly, her mouth hidden behind her fan.

Shin leaned forward, so as to better hear her. "I regret that my responsibilities have kept me from fulfilling my social obligations of late, my lady. Now that you have reminded me, I shall endeavor to correct my failing."

Konomi gave a throaty chuckle. "It was not a criticism, Shin. Merely an observation. And you may dispense with formality, unless it pleases you to do otherwise."

Shin grinned. "I forget sometimes the value you Unicorns place on plain speaking."

"It depends entirely on who's doing the talking." Konomi snapped her fan closed and made a show of looking around. "I like what you're doing with the place."

"I'm pleased it meets with your approval."

"I look forward to attending the first performance."

"I shall ensure your customary box is waiting for you."

Konomi inclined her head in thanks. "Still, it must be quite arduous, overseeing all of this. I've heard it said that theaters are but cities in miniature, with their own laws and factions."

Shin scratched his chin. "There are frustrations, to be sure. For instance, at the moment we are lacking a manager – which means that I, myself, must play the role, unfit as I am for a position of such responsibility."

"Could you not simply delegate the more onerous duties to some trustworthy individual?" she asked, and Shin detected a second, unspoken question shadowing the first. He paused before replying.

"It is possible, though it would require such an individual to be found."

"A not insurmountable task, for one as resourceful as yourself."

"No, not insurmountable. Though I would have to have good reason, I fear." He tapped his chin with his fan. "And while an escape from tedium is an excuse, it is not a reason." He studied her openly, waiting for her to make the next move.

"Just why did you buy a theater, Shin?"

The question took him aback for a moment. "A good investment," he began.

Konomi twitched a finger. "A terrible investment, whatever the context. Theaters do not fill purses, they empty them. Even the meanest hinin knows this. I find it strange that you would burden yourself thus."

"Perhaps I like a challenge."

"That I believe. I also believe that you are bored."

"And why might that be?"

"When was the last time Tetsua called for you?"

Shin frowned. "A few weeks ago. A small matter of a stolen jade shipment."

Konomi nodded, and from her expression Shin knew that she was fully aware of the incident in question. There was little in the city that escaped her notice. Her spies were, if not superior to Master Ito, then certainly more numerous. "And since?"

Shin sighed. "You are correct. Of late the city has been somewhat… quiet."

"Boring, you mean."

"Not the word I'd use." Shin gestured. "Sedate, I'd say. Calm."

"Peaceful?"

Shin laughed. "Never that." The City of the Rich Frog was theoretically a tripartite assemblage. Three clans – the Unicorn, the Lion, and the Dragon – claimed mastery of it, and had divided it between themselves, using the Three Sides River and the Drowned Merchant River as natural borders. The other clans had their representatives, of course, but mostly kept out of the affairs of the city, where possible. An imperial governor, Miya Tetsua, had been installed by the Emperor to keep the peace, where possible. So far, despite a few hiccups, the city had not drowned in blood.

Shin had made himself indispensable to the governor on several occasions. Mostly the sort of innocuous puzzles that any major city provided to the observant. Though some had been rather less harmless than he cared to recall – the affair of the poisoned rice, for instance. Or that rather ghastly incident involving a missing delivery of sake barrels and a dissected corpse. He pushed the thought aside.

"I admit," he went on, "my recent ventures might have been somewhat motivated by a certain… boredom. But some might say that boring is good. Especially in this city."

"You are not some."

Shin acknowledged the point with a dip of his head. "That is very true, though modesty prevents me from saying so myself."

Konomi did him the courtesy of laughing – a real laugh. It

was an interesting laugh. Low and jolly, with a great warmth to it. She twitched her fan as if to chide him, and took a deep breath. Shin waited until she had regained her equilibrium and said, "Very well. You have me. I am bored. But are you here to relieve my tedium, O daughter of the Unicorn?"

Konomi ducked her head. "That depends entirely on you." She did not quite meet his gaze. "Would you say that I was of some help to you, in that unfortunate matter that led to our introduction?" They'd met during the same affair that had led him to make the acquaintance of Sanemon and the Three Flower Troupe. Konomi's information had led, if somewhat indirectly, to the successful resolution of the matter.

Shin sat back, somewhat surprised by the question. It was fairly blunt, even for Konomi. "I… would, yes. Yes, you were of great help to me."

She gave a small smile. "Then you will not think me impertinent to ask for a favor in return."

"A favor?"

"A small one."

"What sort of favor?"

"I require your services."

"In what manner?" he asked, intrigued.

"As an investigator."

His smile sharpened. "Ah. And what am I to investigate?"

"Then you will do it?" she asked.

"As you said, I owe you a favor." He grinned. "And I'm bored. So what am I investigating? Something interesting, I hope."

"I believe so." She lowered her fan. "Hisatu-Kesu," she said. "You know it?"

Shin frowned. The name rang a bell, though only dimly. A

city, he thought. Somewhere in Kaihi Province. "There's a rather nice hot spring there, I believe."

"Even so."

"It is also in Unicorn lands." Kaihi Province was under the control of the Iuchi family, and was, to his knowledge, mostly rice fields and mountains.

"That as well."

Shin leaned forward. "What about it?"

"I wish you to go there."

He raised an eyebrow. "With you?"

"No. As my – our – representative."

Shin tilted his head. "Our?"

"The Iuchi."

Shin paused as he digested this new information. "And why might I be taking this unscheduled trip? You still haven't mentioned exactly what I'm supposed to be investigating."

Konomi smiled.

"It seems, my Lord Shin, that there has been a murder."

CHAPTER THREE
Rivers and Mountains

The three-masted sloop made its way laboriously upriver, accompanied by the creak of oars and the rustle of the folded blue sail. The crew bent to their arduous task with commendable good humor. Shin suspected that was partially due to the bonus he'd promised their captain on the assurance of an uneventful trip.

Shin sat on a stool on the upper deck, well out of the way of the crew as they went about their duties. He fanned himself gently as he took in the sights. They were a day out from the city, and closer to their destination than they might otherwise have been, had they taken the trade-road. He congratulated himself on his foresight.

At the time, Kasami had complained of the expense. But they had shaved many pointless hours off their journey. Besides which, it was so much more pleasant to travel by boat. While he could ride a horse as well as any bushi, he found them largely disagreeable beasts, prone to biting and bouts of flatulence. Much like some samurai he could name.

He smiled at the thought, and turned his attentions to the river. It was little more than a tributary of the Three Sides River, and small enough that no one had bothered to name it – at least officially. It didn't even appear on most maps, and he'd been somewhat surprised when the vessel's captain had known of its existence. Then again, Lun was a former river pirate.

The boat rocked slightly and the deck twitched beneath him in a disconcerting fashion. He swallowed a sudden, familiar rush of bile. "Smell that river breeze," he said, inhaling sharply to cover his sudden discomfort. "There's nothing like it." He gestured loosely. "It's as if the air is somehow cleaner here, away from the city."

"It is," Kasami said. She sat on another stool nearby, running a whetstone carefully along the length of her katana. "The city smells of fish and dung. The river just smells of fish." She looked up. "This is a mistake. Getting involved in the affairs of another clan–"

"Is what the Crane excel at," Shin interjected.

Kasami shook her head. "Surely they have their own magistrates in Hisatu-Kesu."

"Oh, I'm certain that they do. But this particular situation calls for an outside party – one not aligned with either faction, and with no stake in the solution."

"And what is this particular situation?" Kasami peered down the length of her sword, then went back to sharpening it. "You mentioned something about murder."

"A murder," he clarified. "Singular." He sat back. "On the face of it, it is an exceedingly dull affair. One Zeshi Aimi was to wed one Shiko Gen, thus strengthening the fraying bonds between the two families – and by extension, the bonds between the Iuchi and the Ide."

Kasami paused and looked out over the river. "I know one of those names. The Shiko; they're a forge family, aren't they?"

"Yes. Both families are Juhin-Kenzoku." The forge families, as they were more commonly known, were tasked with crafting the weapons and armor of the clans. Without the resources they provided, a clan's ability to wage war was curtailed. Most were quite wealthy, though often not well known outside of the lands of their patrons, so it was no surprise Kasami had not heard of the Zeshi. "For some reason, Gen took it into his head to accost his bride-to-be while she was out one evening, and subsequently provoked her devoted yojimbo, Katai Ruri, into defending her. Ruri killed Gen."

"As is to be expected," Kasami said, not looking up.

"Yes, well, it's what happened next that upset the rice barrel. Ruri attempted to abscond the district and was caught by the local magistrate."

Kasami grunted. "Why did she attempt to flee?"

"Likely because she did not wish to take her own life – which is the penance the Shiko demanded, as is their right as the aggrieved party."

Kasami frowned. "Was the fight fair?"

"Insofar as a fight between a trained killer and a hot-headed fool can be, presumably." Shin sighed. "You know as well as I do that in a case like this, the law is not on the side of the yojimbo – especially one who is a clanless ronin, besides."

Kasami raised an eyebrow. "They had not adopted her?"

"Apparently the Zeshi did not consider it a matter of great importance – or perhaps they were waiting to see whether she was a suitable candidate," Shin said. "Either way, I doubt she'll be adopted now. She might have been defending her mistress, but she killed a member of a high-ranking family, in their seat of power, during a period of diplomatic uncertainty. She almost certainly realized her fate the moment she drew her sword."

Kasami turned her attentions back to her own blade. "So she ran."

"That is what I'm told. We'll see what she has to say for herself when we arrive."

Kasami looked up. "They haven't executed her yet?"

"No. Apparently Zeshi Aimi is a favored cousin of our own Iuchi Konomi, and as daughter of Iuchi Shichiro, who is well placed in his family, she prevailed upon familial bonds to ensure that there was some… delay in sentencing."

"Why do the Iuchi care?"

It was a good question. Fondness alone did not explain Ruri's continued survival. Shin had wondered at it himself. "I have no answer for that. Theories, plenty – answers, none. Would you care to hear one?"

"No."

"Too bad. There are deep currents in motion here. A rift between vassal families can easily lead to the same between the great families of the clan. The Iuchi, with great foresight, wish to head this off, if possible."

"Then why send you?"

"Who better? The Crane and the Unicorn have long been allies. And if there is one thing a Crane is good at, besides meddling, it is family politics."

Kasami frowned. "Is this a favor for the Unicorn – or for Lady Konomi?"

"A favor for one, in repayment of a debt to the other," Shin said, blithely. "A satisfying arrangement for all concerned." He watched the afternoon light play on the water. "Besides, it is always good to get away from the city for a bit."

"And what about Lord Kenzō?"

Shin smirked. It hadn't been difficult to talk Kenzō into acting as the temporary theater manager in his absence. The courtier had seemed almost giddy at the prospect of such a challenge. "Master Ito assures me that he has the dutiful Kenzō well in hand." He'd left Ito to watch over Kenzō, and make sure he did nothing save straighten the books and ensure the rebuilding continued on schedule.

"Besides," Shin went on, "there is no need for us to be present while he sniffs about our finances. It is better for us both if I do not hover over him. If he finds anything untoward, well, he knows where we'll be." He smiled faintly. "And anyway, it is not as if we can turn down this opportunity to strengthen the bonds between Crane and Unicorn. I'm sure my grandfather would agree."

"Convenient," Kasami said.

"It is, rather, isn't it?" Shin gestured at her with his fan. "Cheer up. It's not as if we're heading into enemy territory, after all."

"These are not our lands, and Unicorn ways are not our ways."

"Then we shall simply have to adapt." Shin tapped his lips with the fan. "What do you know of Hisatu-Kesu?" It wasn't the largest city in Kaihi Province, but it was the most interesting, to his way of judging such things. It climbed the mountains, stretching from the peaks to the foothills, and was somewhat famous for the quality of its hot springs.

"It's a city."

"What else?"

Kasami shrugged. "A Unicorn city. Is there anything else to know?"

"Context, Kasami. Context is key. We must know everything in order to judge what has bearing on our investigation, and what does not."

Her eyes narrowed. "Investigation? What investigation?"

Shin's eyes widened in mock-innocence. "Why, the investigation Lady Konomi asked me to undertake, obviously."

"They've already got the killer," Kasami pointed out.

"So they say. But we both know that these matters are often more complex than they seem on the surface."

"I do not know any such thing." Kasami sounded affronted by the thought. "It would be unseemly to overcomplicate this matter for your own amusement."

"Which is not what I'm planning to do at all, I assure you," Shin said, easily. "But if one is to do a thing, one must do it well. As the duly chosen representative of the Iuchi, I must bend my shoulder to the wheel, and push it along the track." He placed his hand over his heart. "Wherever said track might lead."

Kasami's expression was one of consternation. Somewhat to his disappointment, however, she chose not to press the matter. "Context," she said, finally. "What is the context?"

"The Zeshi and the Shiko have been competitors for some time, and the Unicorn have made numerous attempts through the years to quell that rivalry. While the conflict is largely inoffensive in general, in Hisatu-Kesu it has become something of an issue."

"Bloodshed?"

"More than once. As well as accusations of sabotage, bribery, and the like."

Kasami was silent for a moment. She lowered her gaze back to her sword. "You're even more of a fool than I thought, agreeing to this."

Shin was about to reply when he heard a sudden commotion from the deck below. He looked around. "Where's Kitano?"

Kasami paused. "Where do you think?"

Shin sighed and rose. "I'll just collect him, shall I?"

"Let them cut off one of his fingers," Kasami called after him. "He might finally learn his lesson if he loses another one."

Shin ignored her and descended the rough wooden steps to the deck below. Most of the crew were busy with their own tasks – rowing or otherwise. But some few were off duty, resting up for their next turn at the oars.

A small knot of them had gathered near the bow, and were crouched over something on the deck. Shin ambled towards them, fanning himself, his free hand tucked behind his back. When he heard the telltale rattle of dice in a cup, he smiled. The smile widened when he heard the curses of the crew, and the harsh tones of his manservant.

Kitano was all rough edges and shifty looks. In a previous life, he'd been a sailor and a gambler and had tried to kill Shin once. Shin had shown mercy, disappointing Kasami no end. Despite her misgivings, Kitano had proven himself useful – if somewhat incorrigible.

Shin waited for them to notice him, but they were too wrapped up in their game. A game that did not seem to be going well. Hands rested on the hilts of knives, and faces were set in expressions of anger. Hoping to head off any violence before it started, Shin cleared his throat. He was forced to do so a second time before he caught their attention.

Kitano looked up, his expression neutral. Shin took in the guilty looks of the sailors and the small pile of coins by his manservant's feet, and said, "I trust all is in order?"

"Yes, my lord," Kitano said. He scratched his chin with a wooden finger. He wore a half-glove of silk and leather straps over his hand, holding the prosthetic finger in place. An affectation, but one Shin was willing to tolerate in return for the services Kitano provided. "Just a few friendly wagers is all."

"Very good. Sadly, I must pull you away from your entertainments. I have need of your services. Collect your winnings and let us be off."

"As you say, my lord," Kitano said, scooping up his take and hastily hiding it away about his person. He trotted after Shin as the latter headed back for the upper deck.

"How much did you win?" Shin asked, idly.

"Twenty koku, my lord."

"A bushi's ransom." Shin held out his hand. "I'll take my percentage now, I think."

"Percentage?" Kitano asked.

Shin clucked his tongue in a chiding fashion. "I am your master, Kitano. As such, I am entitled to a percentage of your winnings. It's a very old tradition – think of it as a sign of gratitude from a loyal servant to his master."

"It's not a tradition I've ever heard of," Kitano muttered, handing over the money. "Why did you need me, my lord?"

"Ask Kasami if you don't believe me. And I didn't. I just wanted to keep Lun's crew from feeding you to the river kami."

Kitano fell silent. Shin smiled benignly. He caught sight of the vessel's captain watching them, and gave Kitano a swat with his fan. "Go on. Stay out of trouble until I call for you."

He turned to greet Captain Lun as Kitano hurried away. "Ah, captain."

Lun dressed like a common sailor, despite her rank – bare feet, bare arms and her hair cropped short. Her most arresting feature was a missing eye, and the scars that marked her cheek like cracks in porcelain. A short, heavy blade with a sharkskin-wrapped hilt hung low on her hip, a streamer of blue silk knotted about the ring pommel.

She grunted a greeting at him. "My lord," she said. "Still feeding that street cur, then?" She indicated Kitano's retreating form with a jerk of her chin.

"Kitano has his uses. And he is in my debt."

"As am I," Lun said.

"No. You are in my employ – a different thing entirely. You owe me nothing save an honest day's work, captain." Shin looked at her. "Thus far, you have not disappointed me. Speaking of which, are we still on schedule?"

Lun grunted. "If the weather is good, and the kami kind."

Shin smiled. "And how are things otherwise, captain?"

Lun squinted at him with her good eye. "Business has been good."

"So I hear. Master Ito has nothing but good things to say about you."

Lun gave a sharp smile. "He's a sneaky one."

"He would consider that a compliment, I think." Shin looked her up and down. "All recovered from your injuries, then?"

"Save the parts that don't grow back." She thrust a finger beneath her patch and scratched the socket. Shin winced and averted his gaze. That particular habit of hers always made him a bit queasy. From her smile, he suspected she knew that.

She'd been a soldier once, he knew. A marine aboard a Crane vessel, to judge by the faded tattoo on the inside of her wrist. He did not know for certain how she'd come to her current profession, nor did he think it polite to inquire. What he did know was that she had little liking for bushi – of any clan. Given what he'd seen of the day-to-day behavior of most of his peers, he could not fault her for that.

"Can't take you all the way, you know," she continued. "Boats and mountains don't mix. You want to climb a mountain, you can do it yourself."

"Of course." The tributary would take them close to the foothills where the city of Hisatu-Kesu began. There were a number of small fishing villages dotting the river's length. Most of them served as small merchant ports, for the loading and unloading of goods. "How long until we arrive at our port of call?"

"Tomorrow, maybe the day after, then we'll be at Two Step Village." It was the largest of the villages and supposedly quite a disreputable little hamlet. Konomi had assured him that the local Iuchi magistrate would be waiting to meet them there, and would escort them the rest of the way to the city.

"Good. It's been a lovely trip, but I am looking forward to a change of scenery."

Kasami kept one eye on her sword and one on Shin. He laughed at something Lun said – a joke, maybe, though Kasami had never known the former pirate to demonstrate anything resembling a sense of humor.

She tried to distract herself by watching the river. In a way, it reminded her of her childhood in the Uebe marshes. She'd grown up around boats – flatboats, mostly. As a girl, she'd watched the fishermen at their work, and learned the art of hunting marsh-hens. It had been a simple time and good, though it hadn't lasted long.

Her training had begun early, like that of every Hiramori. Up at the Hour of the Tiger, down with the Hour of the Boar. Mundane tasks had filled her mornings – servants' tasks. Humble work, intended to instill humility and discipline.

She still remembered scrubbing the barracks until the wood glowed and her skin cracked. Then, hands still raw, she would start her lessons – the ones she liked best. She'd felt so alive then, with a blade in her hand. She'd dreamed of what it would be like to wield it in truth, in the name of the Crane and the Daidoji.

The reality of it had come as something of a shock to her. There was no way to teach someone how a sword felt, striking living flesh. No way to describe the tug of a dying man's gaze and the sound of his last exhalation. And no way to explain how, all too soon, such things ceased to have any effect on one whatsoever.

Kitano shuffled past, looking smug, interrupting her train of thought. She was tempted to pitch him over the rail on general principle, but refrained. She would only have to fish him out again. Shin was too lenient with the gambler, probably because he found him amusing. Shin was always on the lookout for things that amused him, be it books or people.

Once, she'd feared amusements were his only interest. She knew better now, though there were days where the old doubts came back and she once again found herself wondering whether he was truly a wastrel after all. That he'd bought a theater had been a bit startling, but at least it was a business of sorts. If nothing else, it would keep him occupied.

She held up her sword, watching the sun glint along its edge. It was a good blade and had served her well. She caught a flash of motion in the sword's polished length. "Stop lurking, Kitano, or I will take the rest of your fingers."

"You look unhappy, my lady," Kitano said, appropriating Shin's stool. He scratched his unshaven chin with his wooden finger and smiled obsequiously. Kasami didn't acknowledge him. Kitano had been trying to slither into her good graces for months. She knew she frightened him, and felt an unworthy satisfaction at the thought.

Though she didn't trust him, she had to admit that he had fallen easily enough into the role of servant. A special sort of servant – one with a particular set of duties – but a servant nonetheless. Then, some people were born to serve.

"I am neither happy nor unhappy," she said, finally. "I exist in a state of harmony – something you would know nothing about, gambler."

"You'd be surprised," Kitano said. Kasami glanced at him and his smile wilted. "My lady," he added, quickly. Kasami grunted and ceased her efforts to further sharpen an already sharp sword.

"You want to say something. Say it, and go elsewhere."

Kitano swallowed. "Northern Owari," he said, hesitantly.

"We are nowhere near Ryokō Owari."

Kitano shook his head. "Not Ryokō Owari – Northern Owari. The slums of Hisatu-Kesu. Dangerous sort of place."

"Yes. And so?"

"Lots of… temptation."

Kasami's eyes narrowed. "Speak plainly or stop talking."

Kitano glanced in Shin's direction. He cleared his throat. "A few days ago, he asked me to find him a game. You know the sort he likes."

Kasami stiffened. "I was not aware of this."

"He told me not to say anything."

"Then why are you telling me now?"

Kitano looked at his hands. "I don't… He's better than most, as masters go." He clenched his fists, and she read the sudden tension in his broad shoulders. "But if he gets himself killed…"

"You should have more confidence in him than that," she said, but she knew what he was feeling. "After all, he handled you, didn't he?"

Kitano shot her a glare before he remembered himself. He glanced at his hand, and then out over the water. "He's bored. And bored noblemen are dangerous noblemen. Both to themselves and others."

Kasami settled back on her stool. "I am aware." She sighed. "Did you?"

"What – find him a game back before we left?" Kitano looked at her. "Of course! But he didn't go. Said he was too busy planning for this trip."

"That's something, at least." She paused. "How often has this occurred?"

Kitano shrugged. "A few times. He never goes, but… he wants to, I think. And Northern Owari is a pesthole – games, geishas, the lot." He frowned. "I think that's why he brought me."

"You've been there before?"

Kitano hesitated. "Once or twice. Never for very long." He scratched his chin again, an unconscious indication of his nervousness. "It's a dangerous place."

"So is the city."

Kitano tapped his prosthetic finger against his knee. "Not like Northern Owari. There's a reason they call it that – it's… rough. Nasty. They're a different breed in the mountains. Not reasonable, like river folk."

Kasami snorted. "Reasonable."

Kitano shrugged. "Practical, let's say."

"Cowards, you mean."

"Unwilling to provoke their betters," Kitano said. "But up there? They'll leave you for the crows, noble or common. They don't care."

"I will keep that in mind."

"You should, my lady, for both our sakes and his."

Kasami jerked her head. "Go away."

Kitano rose hurriedly and departed, leaving her alone with her thoughts. In a way, it was heartening to think that he feared for Shin's safety. A loyal cur was still a cur, however, and still likely to bite the hand that fed it.

But, despite her distrust, she could not dismiss his concerns. Not when they so closely mirrored her own – that this outing was nothing more than an excuse for Shin to indulge himself somewhere where his proclivities were not the stuff of gossip.

He was bored, despite his protestations. And, as Kitano had said, that was dangerous. A bored Shin was a Shin who went looking for trouble. She did not know what she hoped for more, that the matter was already settled when they arrived, or that it was not, and required Shin's particular attentions.

One thing was certain either way – if there was trouble to be had, Shin would find it. And that meant she would have to be ready to get him out of it.

Kasami carefully sheathed her sword and laid it across her knees.

CHAPTER FOUR
Hisatu-Kesu

Iuchi Batu sighed softly as his servant announced his visitor. The clan magistrate set aside the letter he'd been writing and sat back to receive the newcomer. "Welcome, my lord Shijan," he said, in mild tones. "It feels as if it has only been a few scant hours since we last saw one another."

Zeshi Shijan was a slim man of moderate years, and fashionable by the standards of Hisatu-Kesu. While he might not have made much of an impact at the Winter Court, in the mountains he cut quite the dashing figure. Worse, he knew it.

Shijan was the current head of the Zeshi faction family in Hisatu-Kesu. Ever since the disappearance of his uncle Hisato, the younger man had diligently applied himself to his responsibilities. Though he had let his position go to his head somewhat, Batu thought.

He bowed low, though not so low as he should have. Though the Zeshi were a vassal family to the Iuchi, Shijan had a high opinion of himself and acted accordingly. Batu, keenly aware of the practical limits of his authority, let it pass. Shijan was a bad enemy to have, and things were tense enough as it was. "I would not have come save that it has been brought to my attention that we are to have a guest."

Batu, who knew full well what Shijan was referring to, decided to play dumb. "A guest? And who might this guest be?"

"You tell me." Shijan knelt in front of Batu.

Batu gave him a few moments to stew before he replied. "I might ask how you came to be informed of such a thing."

"The Zeshi are not without ears," Shijan said, stiffly.

"Or perhaps you received the same missive I did, informing you of the imminent arrival of a special representative." Batu was rewarded by a flinch. Though Shijan prided himself on his poise, he was not so composed as he imagined.

"The Iuchi have taken an interest," he continued, carefully. Gently. "The Shiko are vassals to the Ide, and the Iuchi wish to make certain that this matter is handled with the utmost consideration and discretion. Surely you understand?"

Shijan flushed. "I am not a fool, Batu. Provincial, perhaps, but not an idiot."

"Forgive me. I merely wished to impress the seriousness of this matter upon you."

"I am well aware of the seriousness of the situation. It is my family's fortunes that are on the line here, not yours. If this matter is not settled soon and to the satisfaction of both families, things will go poorly for everyone."

Batu tensed. "I would ask that you counsel the others to avoid any rash action."

Shijan frowned. "It is not the Zeshi you should be concerned about, Batu. It is the Shiko who are the cause of all this trouble, and you well know it. Hisatu-Kesu has always belonged to the

Zeshi. That these upstarts think to take it for themselves ..."

"They are vassals of the Unicorn, the same as your family," Batu said, firmly. "In public, you will accord them the respect due them, whatever feelings you might express in private. Out of my hearing."

Shijan ducked his head, visibly abashed. His mouth often got him into trouble, especially when he was upset. "Forgive me, Lord Batu. I forget myself sometimes, despite my best efforts."

"I have noticed," Batu said, drily. He was rewarded by a twitch of Shijan's cheek muscles. Otherwise, the man gave no sign he'd noticed the chastisement. "The representative will arrive tomorrow. I am meeting them in Two Step Village myself. Once I have made the facts of the matter clear to them, they will no doubt leave, satisfied."

Shijan took a deep breath. "That would be for the best, I think. The Shiko are looking for any excuse to cause trouble. The less opportunity we give them, the better." He paused. "Once they've left ... what then?"

Batu was silent for a moment. "I have not yet made any decisions in that regard."

"I should have thought the answer would be obvious. The ronin must die."

"I have not yet made my decision," Batu repeated, more firmly.

"You can only avoid your responsibility in this matter for so long, Batu. If this is to be settled amicably, a certain amount of blood must be shed – better hers than ours. After all, she is no one. A hundred such can be had for a few koku in any major port. What is one less in the world?"

Batu's expression hardened. The role of magistrate required a certain amount of callousness, but there was a fine line between knowing a thing and speaking it out loud. His hands curled into fists on his writing desk. Carefully, he set it aside and rose, gathering his authority about himself as he did so.

"I will take that under consideration, my lord Shijan. As I hope you and the rest of the Zeshi will consider this – I am clan magistrate for this part of the province. I speak with the voice of the Iuchi, and the Unicorn. I will not be rushed into any decision, regardless of the reason. Now, if you will excuse me…" He gestured to the door.

Shijan stared at him for a moment, his expression tight and his cheeks flushed. Then, he stood and bowed – again, not as low as he ought to have – and departed. Batu released a long, slow breath as his servant slid the door shut.

He sank back onto his cushion, a familiar pressure building behind his eyes. The headaches had been with him since childhood. They came without warning, and left him out of sorts for days. He rubbed his temples and called for tea.

In a way, the headaches were to blame for his current situation. They prevented him from riding a horse for an extended period, as well as other activities expected of a bushi. But he could sit and listen, and make considered decisions. He could weigh a situation on the edge of a knife, and cut it correctly – or as correctly as circumstances allowed. The Unicorn were a pragmatic folk, and never let anything go to waste if they could help it.

Thus, he was a magistrate – but not a provincial magistrate, no. He had only a city to his name, but sometimes he thought even that was too much for him. Hisatu-Kesu was an ugly little onion of a city, with more layers than one could take in at a glance.

Shijan had been right, in a sense. The city had always belonged to the Zeshi. They were one of the preeminent forge families of the Unicorn, famed for their leatherworking skills. They provided the bulk of the clan's riding armor, as well as tack and harness. As such, they had a certain amount of quiet influence, as well as the wealth to back it up.

Unfortunately, so did the Shiko. The Shiko were also a forge family, though smaller. Like the Zeshi, they made their fortunes in leatherwork – a distasteful occupation, but a necessary one. The families acted as patrons for numerous low-caste leatherworkers and tanners, making a profit on their hard labor.

But where the Zeshi made armor for men, the Shiko made it almost exclusively for horses. Even so, they were firm rivals and always had been. But in the city, that rivalry had recently erupted into something fiercer.

The Shiko had come to Hisatu-Kesu looking to use the waters of the hot springs for their leatherworking. Batu supposed that the vast amounts of heated water allowed for the easy mass boiling of leather, though, like most right-thinking people, he had an instinctive distaste for anything that involved dead flesh.

Despite his aversion to the process, it seemed only sensible to Batu that both families make use of the hot springs to the greater advantage of the Unicorn. The issue was that the provinces of the Ide were traditionally on the other side of Iuchi Pass, and that some – the Zeshi in particular – saw the city and its surroundings as wholly the property of the Iuchi, and by extension, themselves.

Of course, the matter was not so simple as that. In point of fact, the border had drifted back and forth across the mountains for centuries. At one time or another, both the Ide and the Iuchi had laid claim to Hisatu-Kesu, whether in part or in whole.

The Zeshi and the Shiko had all but gone to war over the matter. The Iuchi and the Ide had done their best to ameliorate the situation in the most expedient manner, but, for their vassals, the fire still burned. Violence was only one misstep away. Indeed, only luck had prevented it from breaking out already. Especially here, at the focal point.

The negotiations over water rights, import duties, and the like had been going on for years. Almost since the first month of his arrival. Just when things seemed to be settled, some new disagreement would crop up. The Zeshi would accuse the Shiko of undercutting their efforts to purchase unworked leather, or the Shiko would complain that the Zeshi had hired all the carts in the city – on and on. A new problem every week.

Not to mention the brawls between servants and hangers-on. Fights in the street, or worse, in the bath houses, which led to gossip. Gossip which inevitably got back to the Ide and the Iuchi, who then wondered – pointedly – what Batu was doing to keep the matter under control.

The recent incident had almost been the spark that set everything alight. Had he not acted as swiftly as he had… well. He hesitated to think of the consequences. Even so, perhaps he had not acted quickly enough. If he had, Gen might still be alive. Batu frowned.

His eyes fell on the letter he'd been composing – a formal protest. That the Iuchi had decided to send a special representative to investigate the matter, despite his assurances, could only be seen as an insult. Perhaps it had not been intended as such, but there it was. And if one did not answer an insult, how could one call oneself a samurai?

He paused. Yet perhaps there was an opportunity here. One he had not considered initially. Whatever decision he made in this matter would have consequences. Why not let someone else suffer them? He smiled, despite the dull ache now throbbing in his temples.

Batu carefully shredded the unfinished letter and fed it into a nearby brazier.

Shijan stood outside Batu's home and gnawed on a thumbnail. His servant coughed discreetly, and Shijan jerked his thumb out of his mouth guiltily. Such displays were indecorous in a man of his rank. Thankfully, he could always count on the ever-faithful Yo to correct him in a polite and respectful manner.

He cut his eyes to the man, and saw that Yo's gaze was downcast, as was only proper. Yo was slim and effete, a bland slip of nothing. The perfect servant; invisible and all-seeing. Shijan turned and looked up at the gabled tile roof of the magistrate's house.

It was a tradesman's home. Little more than a farmhouse, though perhaps a good deal larger than the average commoner could ever afford. And his servants were even worse – only two of them, and neither were particularly well trained. The one who'd collected his sword at the door had barely seemed to know what to do with it.

"It is a poor sort of home for a magistrate," he murmured. Then, Batu was a poor sort of magistrate. Everyone knew that the Iuchi had not so much assigned him to the city as banished him. He could not even ride a horse. What sort of Unicorn samurai couldn't ride a horse?

That he had to show respect to such a man aggravated him to

no end. Batu himself seemed to feel no need for any displays of courtesy. He hadn't even offered Shijan tea. Shijan sighed and smoothed his kimono. "Come, Yo. Let us return home and see if my recalcitrant cousin has come to her senses yet."

"As you wish, my lord," Yo murmured softly, unfurling a sunshade to protect his master's fair skin from the harsh mountain sun as they made for the street. The quartet of purple-armored ashigaru that served as Shijan's escort fell into step with their master. Shijan paid them little heed. Like the sword thrust through his sash, they were more ceremonial than practical. A reminder to any commoners who might be watching of the strength of the Zeshi.

Batu resided at the heart of Hisatu-Kesu, rather than at a remove, as one ought. Another sign of his unsuitability, as far as Shijan was concerned. The air here stank of tanneries and smoke. There was too much noise, and not even enough room for a horse to trot. What sort of place was this for a nobleman?

Shijan extracted a scented handkerchief from inside his sleeve and pressed it to his mouth and nose, somewhat moderating the stink of boiling fat. The handkerchief was left overnight in rosewater to absorb a more pleasing scent. He found it to be a necessity in this part of the city, with all its putrid odors.

In its layout, Hisatu-Kesu tended towards chaos. It had grown from a minor trading post into a village, then a town, then finally a city. Each successive generation added a new layer to the onion, expanding the reach of the city up into the heights and down into the foothills. Unlike many cities, however, the central district was still much the same rancid trading post it had always been, however large it had grown.

The noble district was farther up in the mountains, where

access was more easily controlled and the residents could avoid the worst odors thrown up from the tanneries. Below, in the foothills, were the entertainment districts and commoner districts. The local population jestingly referred to the expanse as "Northern Owari", as if the rundown sake dens and geisha houses were any patch on the illicit pleasures of Ryokō Owari, the City of Lies.

Shijan, who only rarely descended into the foothills, suspected that there would come a day when someone – not himself, of course – would take a torch to it and cleanse Hisatu-Kesu of its infestation. Then, and only then, might the city begin to take its place among the great urban centers of Rokugan.

He flinched as the sudden bellow of a heimin merchant echoed through the tangled street. A hinin urchin scampered into an alleyway, clutching something – likely stolen. The streets were becoming crowded as Lady Sun continued her stately promenade across the sky. The spicy aroma of noodles mingled with the gut-churning stench of the tanneries.

Higher up, the air was cleaner and the streets wider. Here, near the foothills, the city was all but a tangled slum – cramped and ugly. An affront to every sense a man possessed. He wouldn't come down here at all, save that it was necessary.

Yo coughed lightly, and rang the bell he carried. Ahead of them, a heimin peddler hurried to haul his cart from Shijan's path. At Shijan's gesture, one of his guards hurried forward to lend the peddler some stout encouragement. The cart toppled with a crash, and fowl squawked in their wicker cages. Shijan picked his way through the detritus, eyes firmly fixed on the street. Behind him, Yo dug a zeni from his purse and compensated the peddler. Shijan pretended not to notice.

It was all Aimi's fault, of course. If she had merely done as was expected of her all could have been avoided. Instead, she had made a mess of it, as usual. She had always been troublesome, even as a child. It was why her parents had brought her to the mountains, hoping that life in Hisatu-Kesu might break her of her unruliness.

Once, he'd found that rowdiness attractive. Nowadays, it was less so. It was true what they said – the more responsibilities one bore, the less entertaining one found disruption and disobedience. And Shijan bore many responsibilities indeed.

For many years, the Zeshi contingent of Hisatu-Kesu had been led by Aimi's father, Hisato. But he had vanished some weeks ago, on an annual trip to Shiro Iuchi. Though Batu had dispatched riders, no sign of the man was to be found. Though no one wished to say it, the truth of the matter was plain: Hisato was dead, the victim of bandits or worse.

Shijan frowned at the thought. He had warned Hisato, had offered to make the trip in his place, but the man hadn't listened. None of them ever listened. Or they hadn't. Now they had little choice. In Hisato's absence, his responsibilities had fallen to Shijan.

The prospect was not as pleasing as it might once have been. He had always longed for some important duty, but he was beginning to feel as if he were stuck in the sand with the tide was coming in. He was holding on, but barely. If the situation in Hisatu-Kesu deteriorated any further, the Zeshi daimyo might send someone to replace him. As frustrating as the current state of affairs was, it was infinitely preferable to such a disgrace.

Another discreet cough from Yo pierced his reverie. Shijan glanced at his servant in annoyance, and then followed the man's gaze. Another party of soldiers in Zeshi heraldry was heading towards them, escorting someone. Shijan signaled for his group to halt, curious as to who might be out and about without his knowledge.

When he caught sight of the individual in question, his eyes widened. "What are you doing out, girl?" he barked, shoving past his ashigaru to confront the newcomers. They crashed to a halt in the face of his anger, and parted before him. "Well? Answer me, cousin." he demanded, glaring at the small form before him. He gestured sharply as he spoke.

"I wished to visit Ruri," Zeshi Aimi replied carefully, her eyes fixed on his mouth and fingers. His cousin was short and willowy, but with a certain leanness of muscle that bespoke constant, hard training. Aimi had always been diligent about such matters; more so than Shijan. She gestured in a similar fashion to himself as she spoke, speaking more quickly with her hands than she could her mouth.

She had been partially deaf since birth – enough to make communication difficult, though not impossible. She could read lips, but her voice lacked inflection when she spoke. Fortunately, her hands made up for it.

"And how would that look? The Shiko have spies everywhere. What if they were to see you? What might they think?" He gesticulated, ensuring she caught every word of his chastisement.

Her eyes flashed, and her fingers stabbed at the air. *I do not care what they think.*

"You should," Shijan said, fighting to keep his voice level and the motion of his hands steady. "Because of you – because of that worthless ronin – relations between the two families are worse than they have ever been."

I should have thought that would please you, cousin, Aimi signed. *You were never in favor of peace between the families.*

"I am not in favor of an equal peace," Shijan said, drawing close to her, so that she could more easily read his lips. He waved her guards back, and they turned resolutely away, facing outwards. Once they had done so, Shijan gave them no more thought. "But peace is survival. A war between the Zeshi and the Shiko will only result in the destruction of both families – or worse, our penury."

Aimi's gestures became sullen. *You would think that is worse,* she signed.

Shijan bared his teeth in a smile, so that any observer might think he was merely sharing a joke with his cousin. "You are acting like a child, so I will treat you as such. An alliance between the Zeshi and the Shiko only benefits the clan. A healthy competition is infinitely preferable to a bloody war. Especially a war that we might not win."

Another flurry of signing. *Are you afraid then, cousin?*

Shijan stiffened. Once, he'd entertained the idea of marrying her himself, if only to further cement the bonds between their sides of the family. But these past few months he'd come to realize how lucky an escape he'd made – she was obstinate, disrespectful, and troublesome. "Fear is not in me, girl," he said, flatly. "But I am not a fool, either. I am responsible for the Zeshi holdings in Hisatu-Kesu, and I will do as I think best–"

"You are only responsible for so long as my father is away," Aimi said out loud, her signs becoming sharper. She wanted any bystanders to hear, to embarrass him. Pink patches glowed on her cheeks, and her eyes narrowed dangerously. Shijan hesitated. She was correct, of course. "When he returns–"

"And how long has it been, then?" he said, sharply, interrupting her with a flick of his fingers. "Since he was due back?"

She fell silent. Her eyes slid away, but only for a moment, signaling her surrender. Shijan nodded in satisfaction. "Yes. You begin to understand, I think. Before he left, your father arranged your marriage to poor, unfortunate Gen – now, thanks to your bodyguard, I must find some other arrangement, and swiftly, else all that we have worked towards these long months will be for nothing."

She gestured. *What will you do?*

"Nothing, for the moment." Shijan glanced around. No one was paying them much attention, thankfully. "The Iuchi have sent a special representative, who is due any day now. Until the matter is settled to their satisfaction, we can do nothing save wait."

Aimi's eyes widened slightly and she made the sign for surprise. Shijan read the guilt in her gestures, and felt a sudden flush of anger burn through him. "This was your doing, wasn't it?" He didn't wait for her to reply. "Bad enough it was your detestable bodyguard who killed that idiot, Gen, but you had to go and beg the Iuchi to send someone else to interfere? Do you understand what you've done?"

She gestured frantically. *Ruri was defending me – and herself. To condemn her for that is not justice, no matter what you and the Shiko claim.*

Shijan stared into her eyes and felt his anger evaporate as quickly as it had risen. "No, but it is as close as we will come." Then, a thought occurred to him. "Have you spoken to her at all since Batu arrested her?"

No. Her hands dropped.

He smiled sadly. "Speak to her, cousin. I cannot make you see sense, but perhaps she can." He stepped aside. "If not, I am certain we will have this conversation again."

Aimi stared at him for a moment. "Thank you, cousin," she said, out loud.

"Do not thank me yet," he called after her, as she hurried away, trailed by her guards. He sighed and pinched the bridge of his nose. "Yo, the sun is giving me a bit of a headache. Let us return home, so that I might relax."

"As you will, my lord," Yo said.

CHAPTER FIVE
Two Step

Shin's first impression of Two Step Village was that it smelt strongly of river mud and horse dung. His second impression was that the houses seemed to have been made from a combination of both. He descended the sloop's gangplank with stately care, a sunshade held protectively over his head. Lady Sun beat down fiercely this time of year, and he had no intention of braving her wrath unnecessarily.

Kasami followed him, in full armor despite the heat of the day. Indeed, she seemed more comfortable attired for war than she did in a kimono. He hoped their hosts would not take offense – though, knowing the proclivities of the Unicorn, they likely wouldn't care one way or another. They had their own standards of etiquette which often only barely resembled those held by the other great clans, but which they upheld with no less severity.

The creak of rigging and the slap of water against hulls was omnipresent. Carts trundled down dirt lanes heading to or away from the scanty docks that mushroomed off the shore.

Houses crouched along the water's edge, growing smaller and more inoffensive as one drew further away from the river.

As one might expect, there were people everywhere. River birds swooped and circled, crying out to one another, and stray curs yapped and snarled over piles of refuse near the docks. Shin paused at the foot of the gangplank to take it all in. His eyes missed nothing, filing everything away for later study.

If he'd seen one village like this, he'd seen a hundred. But each of them was unique and worth some study, however brief. "I should have brought my paints," he said. He glanced at Kasami, and was rewarded by a surreptitious roll of her eyes. He allowed himself a thin smile. She had been remarkably courteous all trip, and it was quite satisfying to breach the armor of etiquette once in a while.

"I thought you said the magistrate was meeting us," she said.

"I was told they would. Perhaps they were unavoidably detained." Shin fluttered his fan, stirring the muggy air of the river bank. Summer was on the prowl, and the heat would be oppressive by the afternoon. He could taste rain on the breeze. Nearby, a wandering musician plucked at the strings of a battered shamisen with her bachi.

Kasami shifted her weight slightly. "We're being watched."

"Of course we are. We wear the colors of the Crane and these are Unicorn lands. The local heimin have probably never seen our like before." He let his gaze roam freely, noting the cargo being loaded nearby. Heavy wicker crates, containing deliveries of armor and barding bound for Shiro Iuchi. He considered a bit of innocent snooping, but refrained. That deliveries were still being made implied that the situation had not grown any worse. Then, in his experience, there was little that could dissuade a merchant from trying to make a profit, even in a time of war.

He heard the sudden thud of hooves and saw the streets near the docks clear. Merchants, sailors, and beggars made way for a small but impressive column of eight riders bearing the livery of the Iuchi. The horses slid to a halt at the edge of the docks. Shin waited patiently for the riders to announce themselves.

"Yoriki," Kasami murmured. Shin nodded. Lesser-ranking samurai, often found in the entourages of their betters. Though they wore Iuchi colors, they were no more of that family than Kasami was a Daidoji.

One of the riders urged his mount through the ranks. Unlike the others, he wore no armor. Rather, he was clad in the official robes of a clan magistrate. He dismounted with some awkwardness, helped by one of his followers. Something about the way he half-fell to the ground seemed familiar to Shin.

As the dust of their arrival cleared, allowing Shin to see the newcomer's face clearly, his face split in a wide smile. "Batu!"

"You." Batu stared at him in what Shin judged to be mingled shock and horror. Shin felt a flicker of disappointment at the thought. He forced an easy smile.

"Me. I was not aware you had become a magistrate, Iuchi Batu."

"I did not see the need to inform you, Daidoji Shin."

Shin lowered his fan. "How long has it been, then? A few years?"

"Ten."

"Forgive me. One loses track of these things."

"It is to be expected. You were always quite self-involved." Batu looked away. "You have your travel papers, I assume."

"Of course. Would you care to inspect them?"

"That won't be necessary. Later, perhaps." Batu spoke stiffly. "My cousin did not say you were the chosen representative."

"Of course, she's your cousin." Shin shook his head, feeling somewhat annoyed with himself. If he'd been half as observant as he liked to pretend to be, he would have realized it earlier. In all the months he'd known Konomi, he'd never thought to ask if she knew Batu. "Well, if it helps, she didn't mention you either."

"Why would that help?" Batu asked, icily.

"I sense a certain hostility." Shin arched an eyebrow. "Don't tell me you're still angry with me. I did apologize for the misunderstanding."

"There is no need to discuss the matter," Batu said, flatly.

"Are you certain? I'd hate to think you've been angry with me all this time."

Batu flushed. He'd always been easy to read – and provoke. He lacked a courtier's sheen, like many provincial bushi. Shin had done his best to tutor the other man in their short time together, but some lessons were easier to learn than others. "I confess, I have not thought of you at all," Batu said, as harshly as courtesy allowed.

Shin kept his smile fixed in place. "Well, I'm sure you've been busy. It is fortuitous that you are here, however. It will make this whole affair so much more pleasant."

"Pleasant," Batu repeated, his tone implying that it was anything but.

"Well yes, of course. Three years or ten, it has been too long since we have spoken, and I look forward to catching up with you. I'm sure you feel the same."

"Of course. Nothing would please me more. You can still ride a horse, I assume."

Shin frowned. "I can."

"Good. My subordinates will oversee the collection of your baggage. Horses will be procured. We will ride to the foothills and then ascend on foot. I trust that will not be too tiring for you."

"I think I can manage." Shin was somewhat startled by Batu's attitude. While they had not parted on good terms, he had not expected this level of vitriol.

"Good. You will be escorted to my residence. I have other business requiring my attentions and so must leave you until tonight." Batu's face might as well have been a mask as he spoke. Shin, startled by this rudeness, could only nod mutely.

Batu promptly remounted his horse as awkwardly as he had dismounted, and rode back the way he'd come. His subordinates glanced at one another in apparent concern. One cleared her throat and said, "If you will wait here, my lord, I will see to acquiring horses."

Shin smiled at her. "Please do not rush on our account. We are in no great hurry, I think." She returned his smile hesitantly, as if uncertain as to whether it was proper to be on good terms with someone her master clearly disliked.

"Thank you, my lord." She turned to confer with the others, leaving Shin to endure Kasami's level, unyielding stare.

"You know him, then?" Kasami murmured, after a moment.

"So I thought." Shin watched as one of the samurai broke away from the group and hurried back into the village, likely to look for horses. He settled himself in for a long wait. He doubted there were any steeds worth the name here.

"I wasn't aware you knew any of the Iuchi."

"Possibly because I have never mentioned it." Shin glanced

at her. "On occasion, the families of the Unicorn will send their sons and daughters to train with the families of the Crane. To learn those arts that we take for granted. Batu was sent to the Daidoji."

"And?"

"And we became friends."

"He didn't look very friendly to me."

"Times change. People too."

Kasami was silent for a time. But Shin's hope that she'd let the matter drop was in vain. "What did you do?"

"Why do you think I did anything?"

"Because I know you. What did you do?"

Shin sighed. "I'd rather not discuss it, if it's all the same to you."

Kasami looked as if she might press the issue, but he was saved by Batu's subordinate. She joined them. "The horses will be here shortly. Again, I must apologize for the wait. Two Step is a large village, but still a village. It took time to locate suitable mounts. Most of the horses here are unfit for riding."

"So I suspected. Still, your efforts are most appreciated…?"

"Nozomi, my lord. Kenshin Nozomi." She bowed her head, and Shin gestured for her to straighten up. "I am pleased to meet you. I was sent to train with the Daidoji as a girl."

"Then I must apologize in advance, for I am something of a disappointment to my family." She blinked, uncertain how to respond, and Shin took pity on her. "Tell me, how long have you served as Batu's – Lord Batu's – bodyguard?"

"Since he became magistrate, my lord. The Iuchi felt he required a trusted blade at his back, and I volunteered."

"A volunteer? Do you hear, Kasami – she volunteered. They didn't have to order her to do it. Unlike some."

"I heard," Kasami said, with equanimity. She studied Nozomi, as the latter studied her in return. They were of similar height and build, but there the resemblance ended. Nozomi had the look of the plains about her, an almost foreign cast to her features – a reminder of the Unicorn's wanderings outside of Rokugan.

"Hiramori," Nozomi said, after a moment.

Kasami frowned. "Yes."

"I trained under a Hiramori. At Kosaten Shiro." Nozomi smiled. "He was quite popular, though I confess that I could not quite understand his accent."

"It is quite peculiar," Shin interjected. "I often find myself at a loss when Kasami speaks." He was saved from Kasami's rejoinder by the arrival of their horses, as well as a cart for Kitano and his luggage.

The ride into the foothills was uneventful, if a touch longer than Shin might have liked. He questioned Nozomi as they rode, and she answered readily and respectfully. She had obviously been ordered to provide him with any help he might require.

"Tell me," he said, "what has the mood of the city been like since the death of Shiko Gen?"

She pondered the question for a time before answering. "Uncertain. Hisatu-Kesu is a largely sedate city, compared to some. Parts are more troublesome than others, and those parts have grown worse since the killing. The commoners smell war, though that word has not so far been uttered by either family."

"The heimin often notice what we refuse to see," Shin said. "And what of you, Nozomi? What do you make of it all?"

Her face became a mask. "I would not wish to bother you with my humble thoughts on the matter," she said.

"No bother. I asked, after all." He peered at her. "Tell me, if you would."

She looked away. "It was inopportune."

Shin hid a smile. "A curious word."

"The negotiations between the families have been ongoing for several years. The marriage would have been the culmination of those efforts." Her eyes slid towards him. "Now, it might all be undone because of one rash decision."

"Then you believe the yojimbo is guilty."

"She confessed."

"There are many reasons one might confess."

Nozomi eyed him. "To protect her mistress, you mean?"

"I have no doubt that Kasami would do the same for me."

Kasami gave a sudden, sharp bark of laughter, followed by a moment of mortified silence. Shin smiled at the perplexed expression on Nozomi's face. "See?" he said. "The very thought fills her with joy."

Nozomi gave him a hesitant smile in return. "I had considered that, my lord. That the yojimbo might have taken the blame for her mistress."

"And yet it does not give you pause."

"Is it not a yojimbo's duty?" Nozomi shook her head. "There must be consequences. Who better to suffer them?"

Shin had no reply. Instead, he merely nodded. After a few moments, he turned his attention to their surroundings. There were houses and farms scattered throughout the rugged foothills for miles in all directions. "It must be quite arduous to keep the peace in such a scattered community," he said.

Nozomi nodded. "It poses its own challenges, but Lord Batu has risen to meet all of them. When he arrived, he gathered us all together around a map of the city and divided it into patrol-districts. For every yoriki, there are a dozen heimin vassals trained in arms and ready to serve, and we alternate routes so that none of us get too comfortable."

"Wise," Kasami murmured.

"Batu always did have a head for that sort of thing," Shin said. "You mentioned challenges – is it dangerous, then?"

"Parts of it. In the foothills especially. The families see to the security of their own residences in the heights, but in the foothills there are brigands and worse." She glanced at Shin. "I'm sure it's nothing you haven't witnessed yourself, in the City of the Rich Frog."

"Indeed," Shin said, suddenly conscious of Kasami's eyes on him. He changed the subject, remarking on the scenery, and Nozomi happily fell into a discussion of the natural steam vents that were spread throughout the mountain and under the city.

As they rode, he studied the mountains looming above them. The craggy peaks were imposing towers of rock that rose well into the sky, higher than he cared to look. The thought of those vast heights made his stomach twitch in a most uncomfortable manner.

He had never made an attempt to cross the Spine of the World Mountains himself, but he had read about those who had. It seemed a perilous undertaking, unless one was wise enough to take Iuchi Pass or one of the other cut-throughs.

Shin preferred the river to the forest, and the forest to the mountains. A mountain seemed to him an untrustworthy sort of thing, prone to rockslides and other assorted dangers. While a bit of risk was the spice of life, there was a such a thing as too much spice. And the mountains seemed a great deal of spice indeed.

But he let none of this show in his voice, or on his face, as they rode along the narrow, dusty trails up into the foothills and then through narrow streets winding ever upwards. Clumps of mountain cedar and cypress dominated the foothills, giving way to maple and beech as they ascended. His stomach settled as he lost sight of the high peaks amid the rooftops rising about him.

Eventually they came to the mercantile district, where heimin townhouses rose narrow and deep. Storefronts glared warily at one another across the street. That Batu had chosen to make his home here did not surprise Shin. Batu had always had a good sense for finding the center of things.

His residence proved to be as humble as Shin expected. It sat at an awkward angle to the street, not quite facing it. A low stone wall had been erected around it, with a tall, narrow gate overlooking the street. Past the gate, the building rose tall. It had been a farmhouse once, he thought, built in the true-ridge style: three stories, shuttered windows, square plan, and a massive gabled roof that sloped down to either side of the building. It was engulfed in a copse of beech trees, which mostly hid the scattered outbuildings that crouched at the gable-end of the house.

A pair of servants were waiting on them, clearly having been given orders to see to their needs. Kasami handed over her sword to a nervous-looking youth, and Shin made himself at home. Soon enough, he had acquired tea and a light midday meal of rice and soup. Kasami prowled the residence alongside Nozomi, the two women seemingly quite comfortable with one another. Kitano was dispatched to the guest quarters, there to make himself useful in an inconspicuous fashion.

Shin knew that Batu would eventually make his appearance, once he'd gotten over his snit. He simply had to be patient. When he'd completed his meal, he wandered into Batu's study – a small, boxy room with large windows and shelves holding the papers that every magistrate seemed to collect.

He perused the shelves and the papers, looking for anything of interest. He found a copy of *Winter*, by Kakita Ryoku. Somewhat surprised, he pulled it down. Flicking through the book, he wandered to a window so he could read by the fading light of dusk, and to wait for his host's return.

CHAPTER SIX
The Blind Woman

Gozen Emiko listened to the call of the night birds as she climbed the steep peasants' route into the foothills. Bachi in hand, she plucked at the strings of her shamisen, providing brittle accompaniment to the birds.

The road was clear this time of evening. Few peasants were brave enough to enter the foothills after dusk without a good reason. But Emiko did not fear ghosts, hungry or otherwise. The night held few terrors for one who had lived in darkness since birth.

That she could walk and play without being able to see the path was a result of years of hard practice – and not a few hard falls. But a blind woman had to learn how to walk without fear, else she would never get anywhere at all.

Her bamboo cane was nestled in the crook of her arm as she played, providing a sense of comfort. She owned only two things of any worth – the shamisen and the cane. Everything else was negotiable. Her clothes, her pack, all of it could be and had been replaced many times. But the shamisen was the only way she could earn the koku that kept her from starving or selling something other than her voice. And the cane – well, the cane had other uses.

Hers had been given to her by an old teacher – a masseur of some distinction. As blind as she, but without her talent for singing. He had earned his money with his hands, and had taught her to do the same.

The bird calls changed, became shrill and aggressive. Emiko stopped, head tilted, listening. Though her eyes saw nothing, her ears still worked, and so too did her nose. She sniffed the air and caught a whiff of unwashed flesh and soiled clothing. She stilled the strings of her instrument and carefully slung it over her shoulder, where it would hang safely out of the way. She gripped her cane in both hands and set the tip on the ground.

Pebbles shifted beneath poorly made sandals. Brush dragged at the hems of tattered clothing. She swung her face towards the sound, calculating the distance. "Hello," she said, letting the word quaver on the air.

Laughter was the only reply. Someone whistled, and she followed the sound. Another voice barked like a dog, drawing her back the other way. Three, perhaps four of them. Five at most. "Who are you?" she asked, softly.

"Can't see us at all, can she?" a voice grunted.

"If she could, she'd have run by now – especially from your ugly face, Tano." Laughter greeted this witticism, and Emiko tried a smile.

"If it helps, I cannot tell if you are ugly or beautiful. Thus, it is of no importance to me." She held her cane close, across her body, and bowed her head. They drew closer. She heard the rasp of steel on leather, and smelled the stink of their night's drinking. "I have nothing for you, my friends. Unless you would like me to play a song?"

"Play us a song, she says," the first one said. Tano. "Want a song, lads?"

"Maybe after we see what she has on her. I hear these musicians hide the day's take in their rags, like some filthy eta." She felt the heat of the nearest man, his sweat stinking of cheap booze and spicy noodles. "Take her arm, Higo."

The grip on her arm was light – not gentle, but tentative. She did not protest. Instead, she let her cane slide through her grip and gave the upper section a quick twist. With a clack, the shikomi-zue slid free with a serpent's hiss, and she slashed upwards and out. She had positioned the cane so that the edge of the blade was facing the one called Higo, and she was rewarded with a splatter of warmth and a strangled scream.

She pivoted, following the string of curses that exploded from the lips of the next closest man. She brought the blade around in a horizontal slash, and felt something part. More wetness spattered her front and legs. There was a squawk, like that of a dying chicken, and then she was turning towards the sound of running feet.

She did not cease moving, did not slow or pause. Once begun, the dance of death had to continue until its end – hers, or her opponent's. To stop before the last blow was to invite disaster. Crouching, bent forward so as to make herself a smaller target, she turned and twisted, blade darting in all directions with a speed that might have appeared heedless to any onlooker, but was in fact agonizingly precise.

Tano was the last. He came at her slowly, warily. She could

hear the trepidation in his footsteps. Felt it in the air of his blow as it passed by her face. She turned into it, and her blade chopped into something – he gave a grunt, and the gravity of his fall nearly pulled the blade from her hand. She waited, head cocked to the side. Then, flicking blood from the blade, she slid it into its hidden sheath and straightened.

A rock clattered. The smell of familiar perfume on the air. "Tashiro," she murmured. "Did you enjoy the show, ronin?"

"Most truly, Emiko. Your performance is, as ever, unmatched." His voice was smooth and easy, like honey. She heard the rustle of his kimono as he approached, and the rattle of his swords in their sheaths. "Though, this may cause trouble with our esteemed comrades."

"Then you know them?"

"Some of Honesty-sama's men. New ones, I should think. Else they would have known better than to bother you." The name of Northern Owari's undisputed criminal master never failed to make her smile. A blatant lie, and yet with some truth to it – for he was honest, and honored by those who served him. A daimyo, though not titled as such.

"He should thank me. They were too foolish to live."

"I am not certain he will see it that way, but hey-ho – a problem for another day. Take my arm, and I will guide you the rest of the way."

"A ronin guiding a blind woman may attract notice."

"A lone woman covered in blood will attract more. At least this way, I can take the blame for this little… massacre."

"As ever, I am in your debt, Tashiro."

"What is a bit of debt between friends?" He took her arm in his. Beneath the perfume, he smelled of sweat and foreign spices. Not a bad smell, but a comforting one. Tashiro claimed to have journeyed across the Burning Sands, and sometimes she even believed him. Despite his origins, Tashiro was a firm believer in the great work – just as Emiko was. Along with their brothers and sisters they would set right the wheel of heaven, and impose justice upon an unjust world.

He leaned close. "So, did they arrive, then? As our contact warned us?"

"Yes. By river." She had not seen the Crane envoy arrive, but she had heard him. A nice voice, as smooth as Tashiro's, but with a far greater warmth to it. She had enjoyed listening to it, and looked forward to hearing it again.

"Trust the Crane to take the easy route," Tashiro sniffed. "I still don't understand why that fool is even here. What is the magistrate thinking?"

"It was not his doing. The Iuchi wish there to be an investigation."

"If it were one of us, I doubt they'd bother."

"Why should they? We are half-people, Tashiro. The great unwashed, whom the nobility barely notice save when we impede their triumphal progress." She spoke without bitterness. It was simply a fact, and an indisputable one. One did not argue with the stump in the field – one merely uprooted it and got on with one's day.

That was what the great work was all about. Uprooting the stump that hindered the ploughing of the fields of progress.

"They will notice us soon enough," he said, and his grip on her arm tightened. She could hear the righteous anger in his voice, and smiled. She patted his arm. Toshiro hated the Celestial Order more than she, for he had once thought it the truth. Now that he knew otherwise, he could not help but feel anger towards those whom he had once served.

"Yes, but not now. Not because of this. We must tread carefully, my friend."

Toshiro laughed. "So counsels the blind woman."

Still smiling, she dug her fingers into his forearm. She felt him flinch. "That I am blind does not mean I cannot see what is plain. There is only one way the investigation ends – only one way it can end. The wheels of Rokugani justice have but one track, and they follow it without remorse or pity."

"It does not sit well with me," he said, after a moment.

"It does not sit well with any rational person," she replied. "But sometimes a sacrifice must be made for the greater good. I console myself with the thought that she would have struck any one of us down without a thought, had her masters ordered her to do so."

"You do not know that," Toshiro said. "She is a ronin, like me."

"Not like you, dear Toshiro. Having slipped the leash once, she chose to go back. You were wise enough to see that for the trap that it is."

"Some of us see little choice," he said.

"And some of us choose to take the unmarked path," she countered. "Why did you come to meet me, really? I do not think it was merely curiosity."

"There is talk, among the others. A worry that we have overplayed our hand of late. We – they – fear that the war will not happen. That we have forced them to a point where they have no choice but to make peace. The Unicorn will not allow them to do otherwise."

"How would the Unicorn stop them? The clan is not all-powerful. They do not control the hearts of people, however much they might believe otherwise." Emiko shook her head. "And anyway, war is not the optimal result of our gamble."

Toshiro grunted. "I thought..." he began.

"War is like the bursting of a boil – it hurts, but soon enough the pus leaks out and the wound heals. Better that the boil... fester. That it swells painfully, causing distraction and discomfort to the afflicted."

"How poetic," he murmured, in revulsion. She chuckled.

"But apt. We must think long term. We are seeding the field, not for this year's harvest, but the next and the next after that." She patted his arm. "This affair has already served us well. If we are careful, it will yield great dividends at some future time."

"What about this Crane? What if he causes trouble?"

"If it becomes necessary, we shall clip his wings. But I do not think we will have any trouble with him. He seems a dull sort – kind, but foolish. The sort of man who would weep for trampled grass."

"That doesn't sound like a Crane at all."

"Perhaps he is an odd sort of Crane." She decided to change the subject. "Those men – you are certain they belonged to Honesty-sama?"

"I have seen them around," Toshiro said. He ostensibly worked for the criminal cartel that controlled most of the illicit activity in Northern Owari. He was Honesty-sama's man, if he could be called anyone's. But it was only a mask.

They had needed someone to keep an eye and an ear on the cartel, and Toshiro had been the obvious choice. A ronin who, to all appearances, had the usual bad habits of that breed – strong drink, games of chance, and no respect for human life.

He had done well, so far. Through his efforts to ingratiate himself into Honesty-sama's confidence, they had managed to steer the crime lord in the necessary directions and funnel a sliver of the cartel's profits into more deserving hands. Namely, theirs.

"Then it will be up to you to see that they are not missed. If Honesty-sama should come to know of us before we are ready, he may well prove our undoing."

"A low-born criminal like that?"

She sighed. Sometimes, Toshiro still fell prey to the biases of his upbringing. "Low born or not, he has welded together a formidable organization in the years since his arrival. And save for you, we have not been able to successfully infiltrate his ranks."

Toshiro grunted. "Do not fear, Emiko. They will not be missed."

"It would be for the best if he thought bakemono were responsible. He will not bother to investigate, or seek vengeance, if he believes they were slain by goblins." There was no profit in hunting the creatures, at least not for a man like Honesty-sama.

"I will see it done."

Emiko patted his arm. "I know."

"Where will you go now?"

"There is to be a luncheon at the magistrate's house tomorrow, for the Shiko and the Zeshi – his guards were speaking of it in town. He might be in need of musicians, and I can listen as I play."

Toshiro inhaled sharply. "Isn't that dangerous?"

"No. I am a blind woman, remember?" She smiled. "No one ever sees me."

CHAPTER SEVEN
Katai Ruri

Lanterns had been lit by the time Batu returned. Shin, engrossed in the book, had barely noticed the passage of time. Batu paused in the doorway. "I was not aware I had given you leave to come in here."

"I was not aware you had denied me the option." Shin snapped the book closed and tapped it with a finger. "A curious book. One I did not imagine to find in your possession."

"I am capable of reading, Shin."

"It's not your ability I question, but the material. I was not aware you were interested in such things, though I am heartened to see that you finally took one of my suggestions. Albeit at a remove of ten years or so." Shin set the book down on the window sill and gave Batu a frank look. "Feeling better, then?"

"No."

"A shame."

The two men stared at one another for long moments. Batu yielded first. "You have something to say to me?"

"You were surprised when you saw me."

"I was."

"Displeased?"

Batu hesitated. Shin could see hospitality warring with honesty on his face. Finally, he said, "I was not expecting you. That is all."

Shin nodded. "I was told I would be residing here for the duration. If that is no longer the case, I will make other arrangements."

"Like what?" Batu asked, in a pugnacious tone.

"Your city is famous for its ryokan. Perhaps I will partake of their hospitality, since yours is lacking."

"Did I say you could not stay?"

"I do not wish to impose."

"Yet here you are."

Shin sighed. "Have I offended you somehow, my lord?"

Batu stared at him. "Do you truly not recall, or is this more of that obfuscating stupidity of yours?" The words hung etched on the air for long moments.

"I have offended you. Tell me how, so that I might make restitution."

"That ship, as they say, has sailed." Batu's hands curled into fists. "I truly loved her, you know. Kaiya."

"Kaiya?" Shin frowned. Sluggish memories percolated to the surface. A daughter of the Kakita, and troublesome besides. A notorious flirt – she still was, in fact. "Kakita Kaiya?"

"I would have wed her, had you not interfered."

Shin laughed. "No, I do not think so." Batu had followed Kaiya around like a fool for months, hanging on her every utterance. She'd found it highly amusing, and made something of a game of it. Shin had not approved.

"She loved me!"

"Is that what she said?" Kaiya had never loved anyone but herself. She was lovely, true, but that beauty was a shallow pool. When Shin had confronted her, she'd laughed the matter off as if it were of no consequence. He'd almost challenged her there and then, but had restrained himself – something he still regretted.

Batu hesitated. "It doesn't matter now, does it?" He was silent for a moment, lost in his memories. Flawed memories at that, Shin thought. "You will stay here. You are a guest of the Iuchi. My home is yours."

"I am glad to hear it."

"Nozomi will show you to your room."

"Not yet. Though it is late, I would like to speak to the prisoner, if I might. Where is she being held?"

Batu was silent a moment. "Here, on the grounds. I suppose you want to hear her confession for yourself."

Shin nodded slowly. "If that is agreeable to you."

"Nothing about this situation is agreeable to me. But you are here to judge the correctness of my decision. So let us be about it." He stepped into the hall and called for Nozomi, who came hurrying into view, trailed by Kasami.

"My lord?"

"Show Lord Shin to the cells. He wishes to speak to the prisoner."

"Of course, my lord."

Batu turned away as they left. Shin saw that he'd picked up the book as Nozomi pulled the door shut. She led them through the house and out by a rear door, towards the outbuildings he'd noted earlier.

"Tell me, what are your impressions of the prisoner?" Shin asked, as they walked. He forced his mind onto the matter at hand, and away from thoughts of a younger Batu and a Kakita noblewoman.

"She is well trained. When we arrested her, I thought she might resist – and I was not looking forward to it." Nozomi colored slightly. Such an admission might be considered a tad too self-effacing, but Shin thought it was the truth.

"But she did not resist?"

"No. She seemed… relieved." Nozomi shook her head. "That may not be the right word, forgive me. Resigned, perhaps."

"Either way, it seems a strange reaction from one who fled."

"I thought the same at the time, my lord. I believe she panicked after she struck down Lord Gen. She knew what would be required of her, and fled."

"That does not sound well trained to me," Shin observed.

Nozomi shrugged. "Nor to me, but it is what happened."

Shin pondered this as they walked. The evening was largely silent, and what noise there was from the street was muffled by the trees. Past them, and over the top of the walls, he could make out the red glow of paper lanterns.

Like many cities, Hisatu-Kesu came alive in the early evening. He hoped to make time to sample the city's delights, but it would have to wait for later. Indulgence was all well and good, but denial made the meal all the more savory.

He felt Kasami's eyes on him and slowed his pace so that she was forced to walk beside him. "What is it?" he murmured, fan raised before his face.

"You still think there is something here?"

"I will not know for certain until I speak to our murderess, but… yes, I suspect so. It is plain to anyone with eyes and ears that there are holes in the fabric of the thing."

"But that does not mean that you have to point them out."

"Someone should, else greater embarrassment might ensue."

Kasami grunted. "Nozomi told me that Batu thinks the same – but he believes an investigation will only cause more trouble than it's worth."

"Batu's sense of propriety has always been a thing of iron."

"Whereas yours is more like straw," she said, curtly.

"I prefer to think of it as a thing of water – bending and flowing to fit the shape of the moment, rather than adhering to a single, brittle form."

Kasami grunted again. Further conversation was curtailed by Nozomi announcing that they had arrived. The cells were in one of the outbuildings. Like the house, it had been converted from a storage building into something altogether less pleasant. Through the windows, Shin could see that animal stalls had been turned into cells, with iron bars and thick doors. "Lord Batu had it altered not long after his arrival."

"Another of his improvements," Shin said. Nozomi nodded.

"Before this, prisoners were rare, I'm told." She pulled a torch from a wicker stand and lit it with the provided kindling and starter.

"The previous magistrate was lenient, then?"

"Not as such," she said, simply. Shin caught her meaning. For many bushi, justice was akin to a sword; a thing to be wielded swiftly, and surely. There was no room for hesitation or mercy. No room for thought or investigation – only judgment, especially when the crime struck against the social order.

"And Batu?"

"Some would call him lenient, my lord."

"He always did have a soft heart," Shin said. Nozomi wisely refrained from replying. Instead, she handed him the torch and gestured.

"There is only one occupant, currently. She is in the middle cell on the left."

Shin acknowledged this with a nod. "Thank you. If you would stand outside, I will be but a few moments." He looked at Kasami. "You as well."

Kasami frowned mulishly. "Are you sure that's wise?"

"She is unarmed and locked in a cell. I doubt she poses much of a threat."

"Ronin are tricky…" Kasami began.

"As am I. And I suspect that of the two of us, I am a good deal more so." He twitched his fan. "Go. I wish to speak to her alone." They went. Grudgingly, in Kasami's case, but they went, nonetheless. Only when the outer door had shut did Shin stroll down the corridor between the cells, fanning himself.

It was dry inside, but still stifling. He could only imagine that it was intentional. Heat and a lack of air would engender a useful lethargy in the prisoners. Or perhaps he was giving Batu too much credit.

When he reached the cell, he at first thought Nozomi had been mistaken. That there was no one there. But then, something moved, far back in the corner. A lean shape unfolded and a rusty voice said, "You are not the magistrate."

"I am not."

"You are not a Unicorn, either. Not with hair like that."

"Thank you for noticing. One tries one's best to make an impression. It is good to know that the effort was not for naught."

She was a tall woman, but not elegant. There was a stubborn grace to her movements as she came forward into the light. Round features, pale skin, eyes like green agates. Her dark hair was cropped short and without style. It looked as if it had been done by a knife, rather than the shears of a trained barber. Her kimono was filthy, and the color of the stones on the river bottom. Her face and hands were dirty as well, as if she had been grubbing in the mud.

Her gaze fixed on his face. "A Crane. Why is a Crane here?"

"To see a Lion in a cage is a rare thing," Shin said, letting an edge of mockery creep into his tone. He wanted to see if she was the sort with fire in her veins – or ice.

"I am not a Lion. Merely a woman tossed on the waves of fate."

Shin nodded. Ice, then. "My apologies." There were many reasons a samurai might forsake their family and clan, and choose the life of a masterless ronin. Some even kept their names, though it was often frowned upon. He considered asking the obvious question, and then decided against it. He saw no reason to add insult to injury, as it were.

Instead, he considered her for long moments. She did not flinch from his inspection, or grow otherwise impatient, and he raised his estimation of her a few notches. "You were yojimbo to Zeshi Aimi."

"I am yojimbo to Zeshi Aimi," she corrected.

"Of course. For a few days more yet, at least." Shin tapped his fan into his palm. "I am told you killed Shiko Gen."

"I did."

"Why?"

"He would have killed me."

"Self-defense?" He gestured. "Never mind. Of course it was. You would not have drawn your sword, save that he threatened you or your mistress. Why did he attack you?"

She hesitated. "I do not know."

Shin frowned. "That is your first lie. I give you three. You have two more. Use them wisely. What happened afterwards?"

"I fled."

"Why?"

"I knew what the price for my actions would be." She looked at him meaningfully. "I did not wish to die. If I had, it would have been simpler to let that fool kill me."

"Why was he a fool?"

She bowed her head. "A slip of the tongue."

"Second lie," he said, swatting the bars with his fan. "One left. You did not resist when you were caught. Why?"

She looked up at him, expression guarded. "Who told you that?"

"No one. It is an extrapolation. You are uninjured, and being treated with comparative equanimity. If you had killed any of Batu's people, you would have been executed on the spot, or at least badly injured. So you ran, but did not resist when caught. Why?"

She said nothing. Shin waited, but she remained silent, eyes downcast. Finally, he cleared his throat and said, "You understand what must happen."

"Yes."

"You are content with this?"

"Yes."

"Third lie," Shin said, sharply. She looked up, her gaze hot with sudden anger. Shin bore on, relentless, giving her no chance to speak. "If you were content, you would have waited for Batu to pass sentence. Instead, you ran. Why do that, if you were only going to surrender at the first obstacle?"

She lifted her chin. "I do not draw my sword against those who have not given offense," she said, stiffly.

"That is the truth, at least. Might I hazard a guess?"

"I cannot stop you."

Shin's smile was cold. "Your mistress ordered you to run."

Ruri's face became as unreadable as a waxen mask. Shin paused, satisfied that he'd hit the mark. "I wonder why she did that? Surely she knew that it would only make things worse for everyone. Yet she did it, nonetheless. Curious, don't you think?"

Ruri didn't reply. Nor did she meet his gaze. Shin felt a twitch of frustration. He leaned close. "Do you know why I am here?"

Nothing. She might as well have been a statue. Shin sighed. "Zeshi Aimi wrote to her cousin, asking for a special investigator to come and – one assumes – ensure that you are not executed. I can but conclude that this killing is not as simple as you have insisted."

At this, the mask slipped. A look of consternation crossed her face, so swiftly that Shin almost missed it. "I confessed," she said, softly. "Let that be an end to it."

Shin paused, studying her. "I am afraid I cannot. It is a flaw of mine, a refusal to accept these things at face value. I think you are innocent of this crime, and I intend to prove it. This will be easier with your help."

"I killed him," she snapped. "What more is there to know?"

"The reason for this senseless act," Shin said. "And I think you know it."

"I know nothing, save that you are tiresome." She bared her teeth at him and returned to her corner. "I am tired. I wish to sleep."

Shin watched her for a few moments. When it became clear that she had nothing more to say, he turned and left her alone in the dark once more.

Nozomi and Kasami turned as he left the building. He handed the torch to Nozomi, who doused it in a nearby bucket. "Well?" Kasami asked.

"She holds to her confession."

"Then we are done here."

"Maybe." Shin glanced at her. "Maybe not."

CHAPTER EIGHT
Preparations

Kitano Daichi leaned against the doorframe, a stalk of barley between his teeth. He'd risen at the Hour of the Tiger, as had become his habit. Earlier than he preferred, but the mornings were quiet. At least at home. Here, the servants were already hard at work, making breakfast for their master and his guests.

There were only the two of them. Both younger than him, and born into service. They'd never known a life that didn't involve being at the beck and call of a samurai. He didn't know whether to pity them, or envy them.

He watched them with a calculating eye. He knew they were doing the same to him. Probably wondering why he wasn't helping. He smirked. Let them wonder.

He scraped his cheek with his wooden finger, eyeing the young woman preparing Lord Shin's tray – Yuki was her name. She colored slightly as she noticed his attentions, and he let his smile lengthen. She hastily turned away, and he relaxed, somewhat disappointed, but not greatly so.

So far, the trip was proving less onerous than he'd expected.

He'd even had a chance to test his skills at hanafuda and dice – a rare opportunity these days. Before coming to serve Lord Shin, he'd made his living as an itinerant gambler. While life was easier in some ways now, there was something to be said for living by one's wits.

When the meal was prepared, Kitano carried it to his master's room. He knocked and waited to be invited in. Closing the door behind him, he found Shin already bathed and dressed. Lord Shin did not require help in those matters, something Kitano was thankful for. Bringing a man food was one thing. Washing him was another.

"You slept well, my lord?" he asked, as he laid out the food.

"Tolerably, Kitano. And yourself?"

"As can be expected, my lord."

Shin nodded and said, "You were out late last night."

"Getting the lay of the land, my lord. As you requested."

"And what did your efforts yield?"

Kitano smiled. "The expected, my lord. Northern Owari is as I remember." He'd slipped out after everyone else went to sleep and had spent much of the evening scouting the city's underbelly, looking for the local action.

Sake houses and opium dens abounded, most of them small-time operations. There were a few gambling dens located at the edge of the foothills, but he'd steered clear of them for the moment. He wasn't certain whether his face would be remembered, but he didn't want to take the chance until he had to.

"Is that a good thing, or a bad thing?" Shin inquired, tasting his soup.

"Depends on what you're hoping for, my lord."

"Your old contacts?"

"Some are still around. There's a new cartel in control of things, though. The old gangs are broken up or, well, dead." That had been something of a shock, but in retrospect it shouldn't have been surprising. Whoever Honesty-sama was, he was tough and smart. He'd whipped the local bakuto ikka into shape, and taken over the rackets. "Gambling, loan sharking, it all goes through one person now."

"How convenient," Shin murmured, still seemingly concentrating on his food.

"Do you… wish me to find you a game, my lord?" Kitano asked, hesitantly.

Shin paused for a moment, then shook his head. "No. At least not immediately. Business before pleasure. Speaking of which, what of the prisoner?"

Kitano had been waiting for that question, and he answered quickly. "Three meals a day. Decent, not exceptional. Better than I got fed, when I was… well." He shrugged.

"Yes, well, Lord Batu is a more kindly jailer than most." Shin looked at him. "Things proceed apace in the kitchen, I trust?"

Kitano bobbed his head. "As far as I can tell, my lord." Preparations were underway for a gathering in the afternoon. Both of Batu's servants were in a state, nervous and excited in equal measure. Kitano got the impression that they didn't often entertain company.

"Good. We are to play host to the representatives of two noble families today, Kitano. Their servants will also be in attendance. I trust I do not have to ask you to keep your eyes and your ears open for anything of interest?"

"No, my lord. Whatever I hear and see, you will know."

"Excellent." Shin paused, and Kitano paused with him, waiting. He had grown to recognize the signs of a forthcoming request or comment. Shin arranged his thoughts like game pieces, and every word was chosen with care – especially those that seemed the most careless. "How are you getting on with Lord Batu's servants?"

"Who? Hiro and Yuki?" Kitano scratched his cheek. "She's a fine girl. From a local family. Her father is a baker, I think."

"And Hiro?"

Kitano frowned. "Bit full of himself for a servant."

Shin accepted these observations with a tilt of his head. "What do they think of this matter – if anything?"

Kitano paused, considering how best to reply. He'd known the question was coming, and so had made some effort to find out an answer. "Yuki is worried. She thinks the ronin will try to escape and kill her master. Hiro wonders why she isn't dead yet. The ronin, I mean. He thinks it's unfair."

"Unfair? How so?"

"Well, it is, isn't it?" Kitano said, hesitantly. "If it were one of them, they'd have already lost their head. But this ronin, just because she's a samurai, people are trying to save her from punishment."

"They think it's because she's a samurai?"

"Isn't it?"

Shin paused, and Kitano feared for a moment that he'd overstepped himself. Then his master gave a wan smile and he relaxed. "I fear that it is so. I like to think I might make the same effort for anyone, but the fact is, she is a samurai – disgraced or not. As I said, you will speak to their servants. Insinuate yourself, as I know you are capable of doing. Share stories about my embarrassing adventures, if you like."

"I have never known you to be embarrassed, my lord." Kitano gave an internal sigh of relief. The whole matter seemed nonsense to him. Nobles had their code, but he wasn't a noble so he saw no reason to concern himself with the particularities of it. That said, even he thought it a bit strange that they'd expect a bodyguard to kill herself for doing her job. Lord Shin, thankfully, was more sensible than that. Kitano's master was never one to let a good tool go to waste – which, Kitano knew, was the only reason he himself was still alive.

Shin smiled at that. "Nor will you, if things go as I hope." He bent to his food. "Be about your duties, there's a good fellow."

Recognizing a dismissal when he heard one, Kitano bowed low and saw himself out.

Batu stood before his window, considering the pale fingers of morning now clutching at the sky. He had slept, but not well, and risen early, as was his wont. Shin was still asleep, of course. No early mornings for Daidoji Shin.

He rubbed his head, feeling the beginnings of a headache take root. It was going to be a long day. He was certain that formal protests from both the Zeshi and the Shiko would be delivered later today, after they'd politely attended the luncheon he'd invited them to. Batu sighed and leaned his head against the wall beside the window. Eyes closed, he tried to think of something pleasant.

Seeing Shin standing there had been something of a shock to his system. The last time they'd seen each other had been the day that Batu had finally been sent home in no small disgrace. He'd accompanied Shin on one too many of his hare-brained exploits and paid the price. He'd known it was always a possibility, but in the arrogance of youth he'd assumed that possibility would never come to pass.

For people like Shin, it never did.

And yet… it was as if they'd picked up where they'd left off. He thought of Shin standing in his study as if he owned the place. Shin cajoled, Batu surrendered. It was just so blasted hard to say no to that Crane. He'd never been able to resist Shin, and he had a feeling he wasn't going to be able to start now.

"My lord?"

He turned. Nozomi stood attentively in the doorway. "You called for me, my lord?"

"Yes. You did well yesterday. I am pleased."

"Thank you, my lord. Though, if you had business, one of us should have accompanied you, surely…" She paused. "Two Step is not safe for a man such as yourself. If Honesty-sama thought he could rid himself of you, he would take any opportunity, no matter the risk."

"I am aware. I was not thinking. I apologize if I worried you."

She flushed slightly, disconcerted by the apology. Hastily, Batu added, "Have the servants fed the ronin yet?"

"I saw to it myself, my lord."

"And her mood?"

"Sullen. Angry."

Batu almost laughed. "Lord Shin does have that effect on people."

Nozomi nodded. He read the question on her face, and though he knew she would never dare ask, he answered it regardless. "No, I do not care for him." The words tasted like a lie, and he hoped Nozomi didn't notice. "He is a preening fool, and I find his company tedious. But he is here now, and at the request of the Iuchi, so we must play the good host. I trust the room was to his liking?"

"He was very complimentary, my lord."

"Of course he was." Batu blew out a ragged breath. "He will cause us much trouble, you know. If I had known it was him, I might have written that protest after all." He paused. "Not that it would have done any good, probably."

"My lord?"

"Nothing. Never mind. Tell the servants that I will take my morning meal here. I wish to go over last night's reports while I eat."

Nozomi bowed low. "As you wish, my lord." She saw herself out without another word. Batu seated himself and began going through the papers. He was interrupted by a light knock at the door. Thinking Nozomi had forgotten something, he said, "Enter."

"And a good morning to you, Batu."

Batu looked up at Shin. "You're awake."

Shin smiled and closed the door behind him. "You sound surprised."

"I am."

"I often awaken early when there are matters to be dealt with." He paused, as if listening for something. "Also, I'm hiding from my bodyguard. She has taken it into her head that I have been avoiding sword practice, and has become annoyingly diligent in shoving a practice blade into my hand first thing in the morning."

Batu shook his head. "You work hard to avoid your responsibilities."

"Such labor is its own reward."

"You still wear your swords on the wrong side, I noticed."

"Left, right, I get them confused so easily." An obvious lie. Shin didn't get confused. At first, Batu had thought Shin's propensity for wearing his swords on the right was a jape, to better annoy his Daidoji kin. But soon, he'd realized it was more akin to a gambler's sleight of hand – obvious evidence of his foolishness. A way of gulling his opponents into thinking him a simple-minded fop.

Shin leaned over his writing desk. "What are you looking at so intently?"

"Reports." Batu slid the papers out of sight. "What do you want, Shin?"

"To talk."

"We spoke last night."

"We argued last night. I wish to speak, one investigator to another."

Batu snorted, but gestured for Shin to continue. Shin sat before him. "This will be easier with your assistance. But I am aware of the political tightrope you must walk, as I am aware that any further investigation will only irritate those involved."

Startled, Batu looked at him. "If you know this, why do it?"

Shin answered his question with a question. "Why did you not protest the dispatch of an outside investigator?"

"How did you know I hadn't?"

"I didn't. You just told me." Shin smiled.

Annoyed, Batu turned his attentions back to his reports. "Same old Shin."

"Same old Batu." Shin paused. "How are the headaches?"

Batu frowned. "They come and go."

"I hope I will not be the cause of them while I am here."

Batu felt the muscles in his shoulders tighten. "Too late for that."

"Ah, well, one can but apologize."

Batu waited. "Well?"

"Well what?"

"Apologize."

Shin smiled again and made a placatory gesture. "I will. I find it best to save my breath until the end. Apologize for everything all at once." He paused. "Batu, have you ever studied the investigative techniques of Agasha Kitsuki?"

Batu frowned. The name was familiar. He wondered why Shin was bringing it up now – though he feared he knew the answer. "I might have heard of them," he said, carefully. "Some nonsense about studying the body or some such, isn't it?"

"The collection of physical evidence is part of the method, yes. I have added my own refinements to the process. A form of analyzation that I think is far superior to the more commonplace observational methodology espoused by the Kitsuki family. There is only so much one can learn from a bit of ash or dried blood, after all."

Batu shook his head. "It sounds like you've just added more nonsense to the other nonsense, but fine. Pray, enlighten me."

"The Kitsuki observe and develop their theory based on that observation. But I find that mere observation is not enough to truly plumb the depths of such matters. Facts are important, but the framework in which the facts hang is equally vital. One must see the whole picture to appreciate it."

"Murder is not art, Shin."

"In this case, no. But even here, the facts do not explain why the event occurred. And the why is as important as the how."

Batu rolled his eyes and sighed. "What does this have to do with anything?"

"I am attempting to explain why I am here. It is not to cause you grievance, but to solve a crime."

"The crime has been solved. You spoke to the culprit yourself."

"She was singularly unhelpful."

Batu looked up. "I did warn you."

"You did. I did not listen."

"You were never very good at that, as I recall."

"Luckily, my other talents compensate. She's not guilty, by the way."

Batu stared at him. "She murdered a man."

"In self-defense."

"Even so, someone must be made to pay for it. The Shiko demand it. Otherwise I would let her go. You know that."

"She's clearly protecting someone," Shin said. "Her mistress, I suspect. There's more going on here than is immediately apparent. She ran because she was ordered to run. Why would her mistress do that, unless something else was going on?"

"Zeshi Aimi is well known for her soft heart," Batu said, but even to him the explanation sounded weak. This whole affair had bothered him from the start, but he'd seen no way forward save to do what duty demanded. "The bodyguard admits her guilt. That is enough for the families."

Shin dismissed this with a wave of his hand. "Even so. You're not blind, or deaf, Batu. You have a brain. You can see that something else is going on as clearly as I can. There were other witnesses, I assume."

"Yes," Batu admitted, grudgingly. "Gen's cousins. From his

mother's side. Drunken louts." He toyed with his stylus, staining the tips of his fingers with ink. He looked at Shin. "What do you intend to do?"

"I thought I'd made that clear – I intend to investigate."

"Investigate what, exactly?"

"We don't know why Lord Gen attacked Lady Aimi – what prompted him to do something so idiotic?"

"Well, Gen was an idiot," Batu said, without thinking. He saw Shin smile and flushed as he realized what he'd said. "Smile all you like, but you know nothing of this place or these people. These are not Crane lands, and these are not Crane vassals. Things are handled differently here. Justice is rough and delivered swiftly. You would be wise to remember that fact, before you find yourself in a situation you cannot talk your way out of."

Shin looked away. "Crane lands or not, some things are always the same."

"What is that supposed to mean?"

"The scales of justice are weighted towards expedience. Why bother to find the real perpetrators if there is a convenient one already to hand?" Shin gestured. "Everyone wants the matter settled, and yet so long as the truth is hidden there will never be a real peace."

"What do you care?"

Shin frowned. "It offends me."

Batu sighed and ran a hand through his hair. He'd heard that argument from Shin before. It never led anywhere but to trouble. He composed himself before continuing. "I follow the path set before me. I always have. You, on the other hand…"

"I make my own path."

Batu inclined his head. "Even so." He was silent for a moment. This was the Shin he remembered, and yet not. Something had changed in the other man. Whether it was for the better or not, he could not yet say. "The families will not like it. They will complain."

"Yes, I expect so," Shin said. "I will need to speak to the members of both families, as well as the matchmaker." He paused, considering. "I assume there was a matchmaker?"

"Yes, of course. We are not bumpkins."

"Good. I should like to speak to her today, if possible."

Batu frowned. "Why?"

"Why not?"

Batu's frown deepened. "A less flippant answer, please."

Shin sighed. "The matchmaker will have spoken at length to both Gen and Aimi, as well as their respective families. If anyone noticed anything untoward or suspicious in the behavior of either, it will likely be them."

Batu grunted. "Maybe."

"And if not, we are no worse off than before. It is a good place to start, at least."

Batu rubbed his face. "You make me very tired. The matchmaker is named Suio Umeko. She is the personal matchmaker for the daimyo of the Ide family, Ide Tadaji. As such, she is beyond reproach."

"I do not intend to reproach her, Batu, just ask her a few middling questions."

Batu fixed him with a wary look. "See that you remain pleasant, at least. An insult to her is an insult to the Ide, and that is the last thing we need at the moment."

"I will be on my best behavior, I assure you."

"Is there anything else you will require?" Batu asked, somewhat sourly. He was annoyed with himself for agreeing so readily. But it all sounded so reasonable. Almost dutiful, in fact. Maybe Shin had changed after all.

"I'll let you know as soon as I think of something." Shin rose. "For the moment, all I ask is that you give me the opportunity to do as I was sent to do."

"The Iuchi did not send you to solve this mystery – if there is a mystery here at all," Batu said, warningly. "You know that."

"I disagree. I think that is exactly why I was sent." Shin smiled down at him. "Whatever the Iuchi as a whole intended, Iuchi Konomi knows me better than that. She sent me here to help her cousin, and I intend to do that very thing – one way or another."

CHAPTER NINE
Bitter Welcome

The preparations for the afternoon's meal were minimal, despite Shin's helpful suggestions. Indeed, Batu seemed almost determined to make the affair as dull as possible. The magistrate had shut himself in his study to complete his work for the day before the arrival of his guests. Shin was left to entertain himself as best he could.

This he did in the traditional Crane fashion, by taking the preparations in hand and overseeing the whole affair to his satisfaction. As Batu's servants bustled about, setting out ceremonial tatami mats and adjusting the internal walls to make room for the guests, Shin busied himself with decorations. Nothing ostentatious or out of balance. Tasteful, and in the colors of the Unicorn and the Crane.

He'd brought a Daidoji banner and hung it beside the Iuchi one directly across the room from the entrance. He positioned the blue banner somewhat lower than the purple, so as not to imply equivalent status, or cause offense to their guests. The Crane had no authority here, save what the Unicorn allowed.

When he'd finished, he stepped back from the banners, hands

clasped behind his back. "What do you think? Too much?"

"I was wondering why we brought that," Kasami said, from behind him.

"I like to be prepared for any eventuality."

"I wish you put as much effort into sword practice."

Shin turned. "And I wish you'd cheer up a bit. This is supposed to be a social occasion. How will it look, you glowering at our guests?"

"Am I to be in the room, then?"

"Do you wish to be?"

"Not especially." Kasami stepped past him and adjusted the Daidoji banner slightly. "They'll be bringing their own guards. Nozomi and I will keep an eye on them."

"You're quite taken with her," Shin observed. Kasami turned.

"She is easy to get along with. We have much in common."

"I expect so."

"We both have difficult masters, for instance."

Shin smiled and turned his attention to the rest of the preparations. After a moment he said, "Keep an eye on the prisoner."

Kasami frowned. "You think she will try to escape?"

"No. But I would be remiss if I did not consider that someone might take the opportunity to bring this matter to an end, regardless of what we intend. She is alone and unprotected."

"Nozomi has already made preparations," Kasami said. "Two men will be watching her at all times. No one will be allowed in or out, unless accompanied by Lord Batu."

Shin nodded. "That will do, I suppose." He ran over the guest list in his head – representing the Zeshi would be Lord Hisato's daughter Aimi, as well as her younger brother, Reiji.

The latter was newly returned to the city, having been away on business. Reiji was reputedly something of a rakehell, even by the standards of the Unicorn. Hisato's nephew Shijan would be there as well. He was somewhat surprised that Lord Hisato wasn't attending, but gave the matter little thought.

The Shiko would be represented by Lord Koji, brother to the slain Gen, and his wife, Lady Himari. Shin knew little about them. Batu had mentioned that Koji was in bad sniff with the local merchants' association, for reasons which were undoubtedly as dull as they were inconsequential. Even so, he made a mental note to learn more, should the opportunity present itself.

His train of thought was interrupted as one of Batu's servants, the boy Hiro, ushered in a young woman clad in plain, but well cared-for, robes. The woman carried a shamisen close to her chest, and with her free hand tapped a cane against the floor. Hiro pointed at a mat set against the side wall and said, "There."

The young woman cocked her head. "Perhaps if you could help me?" She had a lovely voice, low and throaty.

"Against the side wall," Hiro said, brusquely. "Find it yourself."

Annoyed despite himself, Shin stepped forward and cleared his throat. "Very good, Hiro. Please return to the kitchens. I shall deal with this."

Hiro hesitated, and then bowed his head and scuttled away. The woman turned, following the sound of Shin's voice. "There is no need to trouble yourself on my unworthy account, my lord. I am capable of finding my seat."

"I am certain of it. I merely wished to study your instrument more closely. The body – catskin, I believe. And finely treated."

The woman ducked her head. "It is a foolish musician who

treats their instrument with disdain, my lord."

"Even so." Shin studied her. "I am fond of the biwa, myself." She was shorter than Kasami, underfed but not malnourished. She moved with a certain, particular grace. A familiar grace, in fact. His eyes flicked to her cane, noting, among other things, the angle of her wrist and the sound it made as it tapped the floor. "Would you allow me to guide you to your mat?"

She hesitated. The look on her face was one of wariness. "If you wish, my lord."

Shin took her elbow in a gentle grip and led her. She sat, and bowed low over her shamisen, head almost touching the floor. "Thank you, my lord."

Shin gave a shallow bow in return, though he knew she could not see it. "I look forward to your performance."

He left her to ready her instrument and joined Kasami on the other side of the room. "Did you notice that?" he asked, softly. If the woman could hear them, she gave no sign. Kasami looked at him, and then at the musician.

"Notice what?"

"I believe she is carrying a shikomi-zue – a sword cane."

"A blind woman with a sword?" Kasami muttered, peering more closely at the other woman. "That doesn't seem practical."

"Depends on the wielder, I should think."

"She is not a noble. It is illegal for her to carry a fighting blade."

"By all means, arrest her." Shin gestured. "It would be most entertaining, I feel." He met Kasami's glare with a grin. "No?"

"We are not here for that, or have you forgotten?"

"No, but for a moment I thought you had." He motioned dismissively. "It is likely for protection. Blind assassins are the stuff of pillow books, after all."

Kasami blinked, and Shin realized that she hadn't even considered the possibility. He shook his head. "I will keep one eye on her, if it makes you feel better." He gestured. "Go on, join Nozomi. Our guests will be here soon. I want you at the door when they get here." He paused. "Scowl a bit, if you would. We don't want them to think we're not taking this seriously, do we?"

She snorted. "Where would they get an idea like that, I wonder?"

Shin didn't watch her go. Instead, he found his eyes drawn back to the musician. For a moment, from the way she tilted her head, it had almost seemed as if she'd been listening to them. But surely not. He dismissed the idea and went to roust Batu from his lair. It was only right that the host be on hand to meet his guests.

When he got to the study, one of Batu's men was in the process of leaving, a chastened look on his face. Shin got the feeling he'd missed another of Batu's storms. Batu followed the man a moment later. "Something wrong?" Shin inquired.

"They are not coming," Batu said, grumpily.

"To whom are you referring?"

"The Zeshi."

Shin paused. "That is unexpected. Did they give a reason?"

"No. Regrets, but no reason." Batu rubbed his face. "I received word only a few moments ago. I sent my men to remind both families of their obligation to attend."

"But the Shiko are still attending?"

"As far as I know." Batu grunted and shook his head like a fly-stung horse. "Idiot."

"Me?"

"No – wait, yes. But not in this instance. The idiot I am referring to is Lord Shijan."

Shin hesitated, momentarily at a loss. "Lord? What of Hisato?"

Batu looked uncomfortable. "Lord Hisato... disappeared some time ago."

Shin blinked. "Disappeared? What do you mean, exactly?"

"I mean disappeared. We searched – obviously we searched – but could find no sign of him. He was heading to Shiro Iuchi, on business. He never arrived."

"Brigands?"

"Possibly." Batu shook his head again. "There was some talk that it might have been something more, but it was just that. Without a body or witnesses, there is no way to tell what might have happened to him."

"And this Shijan is his replacement?"

"A nephew. The oldest of the next generation. He took over, took Lady Aimi and her younger brother Reiji under his care."

"You do not care for him."

"He is a twit." Batu looked him up and down. "Reminds me a bit of you, actually."

Shin sniffed. "There's no call for insults this early in the day." He gestured airily. "Well, I shall just have to tender my regards in person later."

"I'm sure he will love that."

The Shiko arrived with much pomp and circumstance. On horseback, trailed by a curtained norimono, borne on the shoulders of a quartet of burly servants. Their escort was peeled away in stages as they entered, until finally only the invitees entered the receiving room. There were fewer of them than expected.

Sitting beside Batu, Shin studied them as they were shown

into the room. The current head of the Hisatu-Kesu branch of the family was Shiko Mitsue, a thickset man whose wasted legs required that he be carried into the room by a pair of servants.

Raising his fan before his face, Shin murmured, "Illness?"

"Accident," Batu grunted. "Or so they say." He cleared his throat. "Mitsue, it is good of you to come. I am pleased to see you in good health."

Mitsue gave a jolly laugh as his servant arranged him on his cushion. "And I you, Lord Batu. Your invitation was most gracious – most gracious indeed." His wife joined him. Lady Nishi was a tall woman, angular and thin. Her face was lined, but from grief not age. She greeted them politely, but without her husband's enthusiasm.

The other two members of their party were their remaining son, Koji, and his wife, Himari. Koji resembled both his parents, and his wife was a round woman with a pleasant smile. Koji was nervous. Himari was serene, but alert. They bowed low, heads nearly touching the floor. "Yes, thank you for inviting us, my lord," Koji said, echoing his father. "It is a most welcome diversion." He glanced at Shin. "It is not often that we of the Shiko dine with a Crane, especially one of such high rank."

Shin accepted the compliment with a shallow nod. "I look forward to making your acquaintance, my lord. I have heard much about your family."

"Lies and calumnies, my lord," Mitsue said, with a wide smile. "I assure you, we are a civilized folk. Unlike some I could mention." He made a show of looking around. "Have the Zeshi not arrived yet?"

"They will not be attending," Batu said.

"A shame," Shin interjected. "But we shall struggle on in their absence, I am sure." Mitsue laughed, and a palpable easing of tension followed. As the food was brought out, Shin tried to keep the conversation light. The blind musician had begun to play softly in the background, and he found his gaze drawn to her more than once. It was curious that Batu had not mentioned hiring her. He wondered what her name was.

Twitching the thought aside, he turned his attentions to their guests. He prodded Mitsue with a question about leatherworking. "I understand that your family is one of the preeminent suppliers of equestrian armor, both to the Unicorn, and, to a lesser extent, the other clans."

Mitsue nodded. "That is our privilege, yes."

"The waters of Hisatu-Kesu aid you in the production of said armor, by providing easy access to hot water. That is why the Shiko established a holding here, even as the Zeshi did before them. Am I correct?"

Another nod. "Yes, my lord."

Shin arranged his expression into one of pleasant vapidity. "How vital then is Hisatu-Kesu to the Shiko's financial welfare? You have other holdings, surely. Why is this one important enough to go to war over?"

Mitsue hesitated. Then, "I was told you had some connection to the Daidoji Trading Council. I should have expected such a question."

Shin smiled airily. "I confess, among my vices is an abiding interest in the economics of trade." He took a sip of his tea. "It seems to me that war is largely unprofitable, save in the short term. Even when you are in the business of selling the implements of such."

Mitsue studied him, and Shin could almost hear what the

other man was thinking. Finally, Mitsue said, "Our finances have… increased, of late. But with such good fortune comes new obstacles. Demand exceeds production. If we fail to supply our patrons, they will turn to others to do so, and our coffers will dwindle. So we must continue to produce our goods, and faster than before."

"Having access to a ready supply of hot water eases the production time, I believe?" Shin said. "I am not unfamiliar with the process, but I do not pretend to be an expert."

"You know more than some," Mitsue said, with a crooked smile. "Most bushi have no interest in where the tools of their trade come from."

"Most bushi have other concerns." Shin set his cup down. "So if you were to be driven from Hisatu-Kesu, your finances would suffer significantly."

Mitsue nodded. "Our production capacity would be crippled – at least for a time." He hesitated, and added, "It would not surprise me if the Zeshi are in the same position."

Shin considered this. "It is strange to me that you would be rivals. You provide different things, after all."

Koji interrupted. "But those things require the same resources, my lord. We need leather and thread, dyes and iron. We use the same process, and we take pride in our craft."

Mitsue glanced at his son. "And in truth, it is not just about that. The Zeshi have long had pretensions to a status they cannot claim. They see our sudden wealth as a threat to that status." He shrugged. "It does not surprise me that they wish us gone. Hisatu-Kesu has been their uncontested fiefdom for a generation. It must rankle that the Ide and the Iuchi decided to grant us access without so much as a by your leave."

"You give them too much credit, Father," Koji said. He looked at Shin. "They – the Zeshi – questioned our right to the hot springs from the first. Access to such waters simplifies the leather-making process, as my father said. They do not own the waters, whatever they like to imagine. We protested and they… reacted poorly."

"By poorly, you mean with violence?" he asked.

"Not at first. Threats, mostly. Some sabotage, though nothing ever proven."

Mitsue laughed. "Nothing proven – ha!" He looked at Shin. "They tried to drive us out by choking off our access to Two Step and the river trade. They hired thugs from Northern Owari to attack our caravans. They even bought up all the leather from the merchants in the city."

"And you fought back."

Koji nodded. "Obviously." He glanced at his father. "Not with steel – not at first. We traded like for like."

"We fought like heimin – with insults and money." A look of disgust passed across Mitsue's face. "We should have challenged them from the beginning. Settled it in blood, and for good. Instead…" He trailed off.

"Instead, you tried to keep the peace," Shin said, smoothly. "To fight without shedding blood. There is nothing foolish about using the weapons best suited to the battle. I am curious, what finally brought you to the negotiating table?"

"Money," Koji said. "What else?"

"By which you mean the loss of income both families undoubtedly suffered?"

"Yes. We were informed that to continue the conflict would unnecessarily weaken our standing with the Ide. The Zeshi were undoubtedly given a similar ultimatum. A truce was declared and negotiations began thereafter."

"And how did they go?"

"Fine. Surprisingly well, in fact. Neither my father nor Zeshi Hisato were inclined to continue the conflict – nor had they been in favor of it to begin with. Hotheads like Ikki were the ones causing most of the trouble."

"Ikki?"

Koji grimaced. "My… cousin. One of them, I should say."

"Troublemakers, the lot of them," Himari said. "It is they who–"

"Quiet," Koji said. He glanced at his mother, and Shin followed his gaze. Nishi had remained studiously silent through most of the meal. But her face was pale, her expression strained. As if she wanted to speak, but feared what she might say.

Shin cleared his throat. "But you were satisfied that the matter was settled?"

"We were," Koji said.

"Until they killed my son," Nishi said. She rose suddenly, bowed, and retreated from the room. The others watched her go with awkward concern. Mitsue made to summon his servants, but Shin intervened.

"Please forgive me. It was my curiosity which drove her out, and it is my responsibility to bring her back." He was out the door and on her trail a moment later.

CHAPTER TEN
Concerns

Shin caught up with Lady Nishi as she made for the outside.

Servants fluttered about her like birds, and he caught sight of Kitano lurking attentively nearby. "Lady Nishi, please – allow me to tender my most sincere apologies. Curiosity is among my vices, and I am ashamed to admit that I allow it free rein at the most inappropriate times."

She stopped at the door. In the moments since her abrupt departure she had managed to compose herself. She took a breath and dismissed her servants with a sharp gesture. She turned and gave him a lingering look. "I am told you are a friend of Iuchi Konomi – Lady Konomi is well regarded among many I deem friends."

"I have some regard for her myself, come to that."

"And it is she who asked you to come here?"

Shin looked at her. "You know much."

"I like to keep informed." She took a steadying breath. "May we speak in private?"

"Of course. This way." He led her to Batu's study, and she

sighed gratefully as he slid the door shut. She looked around.

"He does not act as one would expect," she said, finally.

"Batu, you mean? No. He has ever defied expectation."

"You know him, then?"

"We were… are friends. Or so I hope."

"It is good to have friends. You seem to have many."

"As you said, it is good to have them. Better still to have many of them."

She nodded absently. "I know your reputation, my lord. More, I made it a point to learn all I could of you – of your… methods."

"And?"

"My son is dead. His killer has been caught. There is no mystery here. You have a confession and testimony. What more is needed?"

"That is what I am trying to determine."

"To suggest that anything you learn might outweigh the testimony given is inconceivable. It is against the very nature of things."

Shin nodded. "You might be surprised to learn that you are not the first to make such an argument. Yet as well-intentioned as that argument might be, I find it sadly flawed." She raised an eyebrow. Shin pressed on. "Some maintain that truth is determined by the majority. But I believe truth to be like the elephant in the folktale – its form is impossible to determine from one perspective, or even two or three. One must see the whole beast in order to truly describe it."

She laughed softly. "Madness."

"No. Merely a different opinion. There are many who make that mistake, however, and I do not hold it against you." He paused. "You wished to tell me something, I think."

She looked away. "Is that so?"

"Your display at the table. Our conversation here. Hardly an oblique approach."

She stifled a laugh. "They were right about you." She looked at him. "I am not certain that this is a good use of your time, my lord. Surely you have more important tasks?"

"A woman's life is at stake. What could be more important than that?"

Nishi frowned. "I'd heard the Crane were pompous, but I thought them sensible as well. Many things are more important than a single life. The lives of many, for instance."

Shin ducked his head in acknowledgment of her point. "Perhaps. But I am here for the one – the many are for others to concern themselves with."

"Are we so unimportant, then, that you can dismiss us so easily?"

"No. You have importance, just not to me."

"The Iuchi overstep themselves – and you with them. That is why I have written to the Ide, seeking a representative of our own."

Again, Shin ducked his head. Her words were ones of anger, but her tone was sad. "If we overstep, it is in a good cause."

"What cause might that be?"

"The truth, my lady." Shin paused. "Everyone must serve a master – mine is truth."

She fell silent. Then, "A harsher master than some."

"Yes. But fair. What more can one who serves ask?" Shin fixed her with a steady eye. "Tell me about your son."

Startled, she frowned. "What?"

"Your son. Tell me about him."

She was silent for some time, her gaze vague. "Gen was a fool," she said, eventually. She was tense – almost quivering. Shin wondered whether it was due to anger or grief. Perhaps both. "He was my son, but he was a fool."

"You are not surprised by his death, then," Shin said.

Nishi smiled sadly. "No. The question of it was when, not if."

"But you wish his killer punished." Grief, he decided. Nishi was not angry. She was sad. Broken-hearted. He felt a flush of sympathy for her.

"Yes. That is only justice, after all."

"Possibly."

Nishi peered at him. "You think otherwise?"

"I think Gen was provoked into his rash action, though I don't yet know the reason for it – or who might have done it. Why confront his intended in such a manner, and why draw steel on her bodyguard?"

Nishi shook her head. "I have asked myself the same questions. But I do not have an answer for either of us, I fear."

Shin heard the lie in her voice, but said nothing of it. He was not surprised. He decided to try a different tack. "Were you in favor of the marriage?"

Nishi looked away. "No."

"Why?"

She did not reply for long moments. Then, "The girl was… unsuitable."

"Unsuitable how?"

"It is not my place to speak of it."

"Whose place is it? You were the mother of the groom. Who better to know the reason for such an assertion?"

She looked away again, and he knew that she had told him all she wished to tell. At least for the moment. He sighed. "I am sorry. I am sorry that your son is dead, and that I must ask you such painful questions. But I am most sorry that you will not trust me with the truth." He went to the door and slid it open. "Perhaps we should return to the others."

"How dare you?" Koji said, from the corridor. Shin turned, surprised. Koji advanced, face tight with anger. "You will not question my mother, as if she is some – some hinin fishwife! We are an old family – an honored family! And your behavior here towards us is – is intolerable."

Shin stepped back, his face a mask of indifference. "My behavior is not the issue. The death of your brother is. One would think that you would want me to find out if it was the result of misadventure – or something else." Now he fixed Koji with an icy look – the Crane, feathers ruffled and beak sharp. "Then, perhaps you are glad to see him dead, my lord. By all accounts he was an embarrassment to your family."

He heard Nishi gasp behind him, and Koji spluttered in shock. Shin leaned forward, forcing the other man back into the corridor. Koji retreated. Shin saw that his wife stood behind him – and Batu as well, frowning thunderously.

Koji stared at Shin, face like snow. Himari clutched his arm and whispered urgently into his ear. He pushed her aside – not ungently – and said, "I see the Crane's reputation is well deserved. But I will not be threatened."

"Nor do I intend to do so." Shin folded his hands before him. "That is not a threat. None of this is a threat. I was sent to ask questions. I will ask those questions."

"You were sent to embarrass the Shiko," Koji said, stubbornly.

"And who told you that?"

"No one had to tell me that," Koji said. "It was obvious from the outset. Why else would Batu refuse to follow all protocol and simply… deal with that ronin as she deserves?"

Shin shrugged. "The answer to your question, my lord, is simple – extenuating circumstances."

Koji shook his head. "What?"

"Katai Ruri has not been executed for the simple reason that to do so might mean compounding the crime, rather than punishing it." Shin let his eyes bore into Koji. "To kill her for doing her duty is the height of foolishness – how much worse, then, to do so when the fault lies elsewhere?"

"She killed a samurai," Koji said.

"She is a samurai."

"So? Someone must pay for my brother's death. If not her, then who?"

"The correct someone – not the most convenient."

Koji's face flushed. "And what gives you the right… ?"

"Because the Iuchi commanded it," Nishi said, suddenly, from behind Shin. Koji looked at his mother in shock, and she met his gaze, unflinching. "And we obey the great families in all things. Whether we agree or not." Shin glanced at her, grateful she'd chosen to speak up. She turned to him, and he felt a pang as he saw the tears at the corners of her eyes. "Even if you find the answers you seek, it does not bring Gen back to me."

"No, but it might enable his spirit to rest somewhat easier."

Nishi smiled sadly. "Maybe. For what it's worth, I do not wish for the ronin to die. But someone must pay for Gen's death, else his cousins – my kin – will seek restitution in their own way."

"These cousins – they were the ones who witnessed Gen's death?"

"Yes. Ikki and the others were there, but were too slow to intervene. Or so they claim." She frowned as she said it, and Shin nodded in understanding.

Agitators on both sides would see this not as a tragedy, but an opportunity to improve their standing within the clan at the expense of a rival. Alive, Gen might have been a buffoon, but dead, he was a martyr. Perhaps that was the reason for it all – a grim thought, but one that had to at least be considered. "They will spill blood in his name, if that is what it takes," she said. "Whatever my wishes."

"Then it is a good thing that I am here to prevent that," he said, after a moment.

"But for how long?" she said, softly. "How long can you drag this charade out? The yojimbo killed my son – that is a fact. The why of it does not matter, only the deed itself."

"That is where you are wrong, my lady," Shin said. "In my experience, the why matters very much indeed." He looked at Koji. "I intend to see this matter resolved in a timely fashion, and to the satisfaction of all parties. Including myself. The more help you provide, the sooner it will be done."

Needless to say, that ended the meal. Shin watched with some small embarrassment as Batu made the usual apologies and the Shiko departed. When the guests had safely gone, and the musician paid and sent on her way, Batu rounded on him. "Aren't the Crane supposed to be known for subtlety?"

"Are we? I thought we were known for our impeccable taste?"

"No jokes, please. This is bad enough."

Shin patted his shoulder. "I'm afraid it's going to get worse.

During our conversation, Nishi mentioned that she'd written to the Ide, looking for someone to represent them in this affair. Which is, of course, her right. Though I do question the timing."

Batu stared at him. "I wish you had not come."

"So you've said."

"And I will keep saying it. It is a comfort to me." Batu rubbed his brow. "My head hurts. What now?"

"Were you aware that Lady Nishi did not approve of the marriage?"

Batu frowned. "No. She told you that?"

"Yes. Something about Lady Aimi being unsuitable."

"Any clue as to what she meant?"

"Not yet. I'm hoping the matchmaker – what was her name? – will shed some light on it." Shin paused. "She is still coming today, yes?"

Batu glowered at him. "Suio Umeko. And yes, she should be here soon, though she has protested the inconvenience."

"I will make note to apologize most abjectly."

"Why are you so concerned with that? What does it matter now?"

"It is part of the framework," Shin said. "The marriage was a political necessity, but it seems one of the involved parties had concerns. Maybe more than one. Perhaps not all those concerns were aired in a healthy manner."

"What are you saying?"

"Someone might well have wanted to sabotage the arrangement. And this might not be the first time that they've done so, given all the trouble you've had."

Batu stared at him for a moment before looking away. "Turning over such rocks often reveals unpleasantness beneath." He ran his hand over his scalp. "The Zeshi and Shiko are not the only involved parties, you know."

"You mean the Iuchi and the Ide…" Shin began.

Batu shook his head. "Them as well, but I mean the merchants' association. The ones who most profit from the success or failure of the Zeshi and the Shiko. You speak of sabotage, well – we have had plenty of that. Less, of late."

"Thanks to the marriage. But now…?"

"Now they are waiting. The whole of the city is waiting. Holding its breath." Batu pointed in the general direction of the outbuilding where Ruri was being held. "If she dies, they will all breathe easier. But while she lives, everything is on hold. Do you understand?"

Shin was silent for a moment. "I understand. My resolution is undaunted."

Batu looked at him. Then he gave a sad smile. "I did not expect it to be. You were never the sort to admit defeat. I always admired that about you."

"You… admire me?"

Batu frowned. "Aspects of you. Not the whole."

"Still, I was afraid we were no longer friends."

"We were friends?"

"The best of friends," Shin said, ignoring Batu's attempt at humor. "I recall our youthful indiscretions quite fondly. Such as that time we made off with my cousin's prize mare and sold her on to that Ide merchant, then spent the money on an evening's entertainments."

Batu grunted. "I recall that he insulted me."

"Which is why we stole the horse," Shin said.

Batu snorted. "That was unworthy of us."

"Most of what we did was unworthy of us. That was why it was so much fun."

Batu laughed ruefully. "Maybe so. But we are men now, with responsibilities." He looked Shin up and down. "Some of us, at least."

"I have responsibilities," Shin protested. "I am responsible for the activities of two – no, three – merchants. It is quite taxing." He paused. "I also own a theater."

"A… theater?"

"Yes."

"Why?"

Shin shrugged. "Why not?"

Batu shook his head, clearly befuddled by this. "I have not been to the theater in years," he said, finally.

"Then I formally invite you to our first performance. I will set aside a box for you."

"How kind." Batu looked at him. "I might even attend."

They stood in silence for some time after that, listening to the birds. Shin thought of past days, and a stolen mare, and smiled. Finally, he said, "I would be obliged to you if you would speak to this merchants' association you mentioned, on my behalf."

"You wish to talk to them as well?"

"It might not prove necessary. But if it does, your authority will go a long way towards opening those particular doors." Shin smiled. "You are, after all, a well-respected man in the community, and I am just a nosy Crane."

CHAPTER ELEVEN
Iron Sect

Emiko made her way along the rocky path between buildings. Somewhere to her left, she could hear the murmur of running water. Many streams bled down from the heights, and the city had grown in the spaces between them. Hisatu-Kesu was a city of generations; each had added a new layer atop the last.

Beneath the pervasive whisper of the water, she could hear the clatter of cart wheels and the lowing of oxen. The smell of dung and fried food mingled into a fuming pulse that filled the side street. Merchants hawked their wares from storefront stalls, their voices beating at her ears. The midmorning crowd broke around her, the heimin giving her as wide a berth as possible. She ignored their murmurings as she followed the curve of the street.

As she walked, she thought again of what she had heard at the magistrate's house. They had all but ignored her presence, all save the Crane. She'd felt his attention on her more than once, though that might simply have been her imagination.

The whole affair seemed satisfactorily tedious. Despite the Crane's presence, there was no obvious danger to those whom she represented. Both sides wanted a quick solution and to move on, and they would no doubt pressure the magistrate into doing his duty, regardless of what the Crane might intend.

Her thoughts circled him – his voice stayed with her, though she could not say why. There was arrogance there, but not the sort she was used to. Perhaps because it was an earned arrogance – the confidence of an experienced warrior. Though she did not think this Crane was much of a warrior. His hands were soft, and he smelled of paper and perfume rather than weapon oil. An interesting man.

A kind one, as well, if she had judged what she'd heard of the confrontation in the hallway correctly. Few bushi were kind. Considerate, yes. Polite. But not truly kind. It was… interesting to consider.

She walked until the rocky ground gave way to rough-cut planks. With her cane, she located the door of the shop and entered. The musty smell of dried herbs enveloped her. She stopped and waited for the proprietor to notice her. She heard a wheezy chuckle, and someone knocked on the countertop.

"Hello, Natsuo," Emiko said. Natsuo had run his herbalist shop since before either the Zeshi or the Shiko had come to Hisatu-Kesu. She paused, waiting for him to speak the expected words. Though he knew her, and she him, some forms must be observed.

"Their rule is iron," the old man murmured.

"And we are rust," she said, softly.

Natsuo grunted. "Such a silly thing, these codewords and phrases. As if I can remember them all. In my day, we made do with gestures, and were glad of them."

"All well and good, if you have eyes to see them."

"Bah. I have no doubt you would make do." She heard him pull back the curtain that separated the front of the shop from the back. "They are downstairs."

"All of them?"

"All who deign to attend." Natsuo grunted again. "In my day, when the sect met, every member was sure to make themselves available – else *hsst.*" She heard a scrape of skin on skin, and imagined him miming a slit throat.

"Things have changed, Natsuo."

"Not for the better," he sniffed.

"That depends entirely on your perspective, I think."

"Mine is the only one that counts," he said. She laughed and made her way into the back. From previous visits, she knew that the shop's storeroom was bigger outside than in. She went to the back wall and felt along the coarse planks. When she found the loose one, she pushed it in. It was not easy, and when she did so, she heard the soft click of a counterweight somewhere beneath her feet. There was a creak behind her as the hidden trapdoor fell away.

Cautiously, she made her way over to it, and found the uppermost of the steps that led down beneath the shop. The mountains were full of natural caves and this was one such. The story went that Natsuo had discovered it by accident in his youth and used it as a smuggler's hole, before he'd joined the sect. Now it served a different purpose.

The steps were narrow things, barely wide enough to accommodate her feet. Thankfully, there were only a dozen of them, and the passage was narrow enough that she could keep one hand on the wall as she descended. When she reached the bottom, she brushed aside the curtain there and entered the chamber beyond.

It was cool down here, and a breeze whipped past as she let the curtain fall back into place. As she entered, all conversation ceased. She paused, letting them see her. Though she could never know their faces, they all knew hers, for better or worse.

The Blind Woman, they called her. Not the most original title, but evocative nonetheless. Appropriate, given that she was one of the hidden blades of the Iron Sect, ready to draw blood on their behalf.

The Iron Sect had been born in the alleys and sake houses of The City Between the Rivers. The city was the crossroads of trade in the lands of the Unicorn, and the largest city in Ikoku Province. Emiko had been born there as well. Her father had been a collector of nightsoil, and her mother the wife of a nightsoil collector.

Hinin – untouchable and unseen by their betters.

Blind since birth, the first smell Emiko could recall was that of the excrement. It was a smell she associated with her father, for it clung to him most stubbornly even after he had cleaned himself. Her family had reluctantly divested themselves of her, having two other children to care for, and no wherewithal to care for a child who could not see.

At a young age, she had been offered up to the local goze house, where blind girls were taught to sing or give massages – the only employment open to those unlucky enough to be born poor. It was better than collecting nightsoil, she supposed. She did not bear her parents any malice. They had not made the choice lightly, and she could recall the sound of their weeping as they departed. They had loved her, but had no choice.

Society had given them no choice. The poor suffered and the rich prospered. Such was the way of it.

She had been a quick learner, and skilled with the shamisen. One of her teachers, an older man, had taught her to gamble – and to kill. He had been blind as well, and had spent his youth learning how to kill on behalf of criminal masters. As he'd often told her, the blind could not see, but neither were they seen. No one expected a blade in a blind man's hand – or a blind woman's, for that matter.

As he'd taught her the art of the quick draw, and how to listen and identify opponents by sounds and smells, he had also taught her of the crime that had been committed against the folk of Rokugan so long ago. She could still recall the hoarse rasp of his voice as he spoke of the Kami, not with reverence – but revulsion.

The Kami, he'd taught her, had enslaved humanity, bound them to a celestial wheel and instructed the Hantei to keep that wheel turning, so that none might escape. The Great Clans saw to it that this hateful order was enforced, that all people were broken to the role that the Kami had chosen for them – regardless of any skill or aptitude they might possess. Thus were the unworthy elevated beyond reason, and the worthy consigned to collect nightsoil, all by simple reason of birth.

When she had learned all that he had to teach her, she had been sent to Hisatu-Kesu, there to join with others who shared this belief, and take part in the great work. Her teacher had explained it as akin to a bird, chipping away at a mountain. A mountain was an insurmountable obstacle, but through persistence the bird might cause it to crumble into nothing. The

Unicorn was the mountain, and the Iron Sect, the bird.

Little by little, they chipped away at the Unicorn. In Hisatu-Kesu, that meant exacerbating the tensions between the occupying vassal families, so that more amenable individuals might rise in influence – individuals loyal to the Iron Sect.

Emiko had heard that there were other sects like hers, in other lands. That only stood to reason, for she knew that the Hantei would not be crippled by the loss of one clan. Such an undertaking would require a concentrated effort by more than just a few hundred people scattered across the lands of the Unicorn. But she had never been given reason to venture into those distant lands. Nor did she wish to.

She was content here. She had purpose. That was enough.

Emiko followed the curve of the chamber. Conversation resumed, though it was subdued, and she listened to the swirl of voices. She could pick one from the other with ease, for they were as familiar to her as her own, and as she listened she found that she could predict the flow of the conversation. Then, perhaps that was because it was not simply the voices that were familiar – but the argument in which they circled one another like curs in the street.

To act – or not. A familiar dispute. It had been the same since the late, unlamented Shiko Gen had slid off the yojimbo's blade and into the dust where he so deservedly belonged. The others had chewed over that moment and its repercussions again and again. It was beginning to annoy her.

For some time now, their efforts had been directed towards exacerbating the issues between the Zeshi and the Shiko. Little nudges towards an inevitable clash. Outright war was too much to hope for, but an increase in tensions between the families and their patrons would be of invaluable use to the Iron Sect as a whole.

Unfortunately, the negotiations between the families had stalled – not collapsed. As a result, everything in the city had come to a halt. Some wished to take advantage of the lull to further the economic interests of the Iron Sect – money was always in short supply, and the state of the sect's war chest was of constant concern. Others wished to seize the moment and launch attacks on previously chosen targets, using the conflict between the families as cover. The deaths of these certain key individuals would allow the sect to insert their own people into positions of influence within the city.

A third faction wished to wait. To observe and ready themselves to seize whatever opportunities arose as the situation came to a head. There were other opinions, of course. Some wanted to assassinate the head of the Shiko. Others wanted to sabotage the tanneries. One lone voice demanded that they kill the magistrate, Batu.

So, as with every other meeting of late, things had devolved into an argument. She found her mat in its accustomed corner and sat. She cradled her shamisen and began to tune it. A bit of music might be in order, to pass the time until they had run out of words.

She began to play, softly at first and then more loudly. One by one, the voices fell silent as her tune filled the room and drowned them out. When she felt their attentions at last shift towards her, she allowed herself a smile. She stilled her strings and said, "We cannot undo what has been done, no matter how often we discuss it."

"That is not what we are doing," a rough voice said. Eiji. A blacksmith by trade, and a well-respected one. He was coarse and crude, but he took some care not to insult others, especially those lower in status. "And anyway, unless you have something to contribute..."

She plucked at the strings of her instrument. "Would you listen, if I did? Or would you ignore my words, as you did when I warned you of the foolishness of attempting to bridle this particular horse?"

"Impertinence," Fumihiro said. His voice was prim and polished. She sniffed the air, detecting the faint whiff of rosewater, and turned her face towards the merchant. She did not care for Fumihiro. Eiji could be unpleasant, but his offenses were largely unintentional – the result of ignorance. Fumihiro spoke with venom out of preference.

"The word impertinence implies that we are not equals, merchant. I remind you that here, in this room, we most assuredly are." She stilled her strings. "Unless you disagree?"

A sudden hush fell over the assemblage. She heard Fumihiro swallow a retort, and one of the others murmur something – a warning, perhaps. She allowed her smile to widen. "We are not them, my friends," she said, soothingly. "We do not divide ourselves into heimin and hinin, into seen and unseen. We are all children of the world. To forget that is to betray everything we have worked towards."

Carefully, she set her shamisen down and placed her hands upon her knees. "Talking in circles serves only to make one dizzy. I cannot see your faces, but I can read your voices. You are worried."

"And should we be otherwise? Have you something to report that might alleviate our concerns?" Emiko recognized the soft, musical tones as belonging to Ichika, the geisha. She worked in the Jade Hare, a bawdy house in Northern Owari. Many patrons of note passed through that house, and Ichika knew them all by name – something the sect found highly useful. "You attended the gathering at Lord Batu's house earlier today. What did you learn?"

"It was much as we expected," Emiko said. "Much hot air, and little direction." She shifted her weight. The others waited for her to arrange herself, some with more patience than others. "The Crane intends to investigate the circumstances of Shiko Gen's death, over the protests of both families."

"Why?" Eiji again. Several voices echoed his question.

"Because it amuses him to do so, I imagine." She paused. "He spoke to me."

"You? Why?" Fumihiro, sounding annoyed.

"A servant was rude to me. He apologized."

Fumihiro made a sound of disbelief. "The Crane apologized – to you?"

"In his own way."

"Preposterous." Fumihiro laughed, and not for the first time, Emiko wished she had reason to kill him. He made much money, and had familial connections that were useful to the sect, which were the only reasons he was tolerated.

"Possibly not," a new voice intruded. "The Crane. What was his name?"

Startled by the question, Emiko turned. "Daidoji Shin."

A short, sharp bark of laughter followed her words. She knew the laugh. Yuzu. Another merchant, and a more prosperous one than Fumihiro – a fact of no small irritation to the latter. The two men hated each other, she knew, and often clashed in meetings. They were often the poles around which many of the others clustered. It was the nature of some to be ever in want of leadership.

Emiko detested them both, though Fumihiro more than Yuzu. Yuzu was a heimin, and his rapacious nature was a result of the struggles he had endured to get where he was. Fumihiro, in contrast, belonged to a minor noble family – smaller than the Zeshi or the Shiko, but with wealth and influence enough to provide for even one of its less capable sons.

"You know him?" Fumihiro demanded.

"I know of him. How amusing." The way Yuzu said it, it sounded anything but.

"Explain, please," Eiji said. He sounded worried. He often sounded worried these days. She wondered, idly, if she might soon have to pay him a visit – to settle his worries, and keep his fear from infecting the others. She hoped not. Despite his crudity, she bore him no malice, and he was a true believer in the great work.

"Some time ago, I had reason to visit the City of the Rich Frog. Never mind why. While there, I contacted an individual who… shared our hopes for the future, you might say."

"A member of another sect?" Ichika asked. She sounded intrigued. The geisha had ever been curious about such things; more so than Emiko.

"Perhaps," Yuzu said, evasively. "A fellow traveler, at least. They were all a-flutter about the activities of a certain Crane nobleman. It seemed he had inadvertently disrupted a scheme of theirs, though what that scheme was they did not say. I made it a point to learn the fellow's name. It was he – Daidoji Shin."

"What does this mean?" Eiji asked. Emiko heard the creak

of his mat, and knew he was leaning forwards. "What does it matter?"

"It means things will not be so simple as we imagined. This Crane has experience in rooting out secrets. He may well discover our friend among the Zeshi. And if he does, we must be prepared for the worst."

"Perhaps we should all leave the city. Just for the duration." This from Fumihiro.

"A good way to draw attention from anyone who might be looking," Yuzu said. "No, the best thing to do is nothing. We wait, we watch, we let things play out as they will."

Fumihiro laughed. "And then what, Yuzu? What if this clever Crane uncovers some link to us? Would you have us just endure discovery?"

"What can he discover? We do not exist."

"Except we do," Fumihiro said. "We exist in a chain of knowledge. Too many people know about us. There are too many connections."

"And what would you suggest? That we kill everyone connected to us on the remote possibility that they might – I stress might – be discovered?" Yuzu snorted. "Perhaps we should start with old Natsuo, eh? After all, he's right here, in easy reach."

There was a murmur at this. Natsuo was beloved, if not universally. Indeed, he was responsible for introducing many of those here to the great work. Emiko had come by a different route, but she respected the old man nonetheless.

"I am suggesting nothing of the sort," Fumihiro said, acerbically. "I simply believe that we should take steps to ensure we are not exposed by this business."

Emiko spoke up. “So long as the yojimbo insists upon being so foolishly loyal, we have little to fear. Soon enough the magistrate will have no option save to see justice – such as it is – done.”

“And what if she does not remain loyal? What if the Crane pecks away at the matter until a crumb of truth is revealed?”

“Let him,” Emiko said. “What will he find, but the name of the one who set Gen on the trail of his rival?”

“What if that one gives us up?”

“He will not. He fears us.”

“He might fear death more.”

“Then I will ensure otherwise.” She smiled. “As I have always done.”

CHAPTER TWELVE
Matchmaker

"She's here," Batu said, entering the study. Shin looked up from his perusal of the incident report. He'd read through it multiple times that morning, scanning it for any irregularity that might give him a hint as to something untoward. Unfortunately, it made for quite dull reading. Batu was not the sort for narrative embellishment.

"How does she seem?"

"Angry."

"Good."

"Why good?"

"Angry people are less apt to dissemble. Remind me – who is Ikki?" Shin tapped the papers. "He gave testimony as to what occurred between Gen and Ruri. And Lord Koji mentioned him, though I expect it was a slip of the tongue. Lady Nishi spoke of him as well."

"A number of lesser cousins swarm about the Shiko, suckling at their influence. Ikki is one of the greediest. He and his coterie were often seen in Gen's company. Why?"

"I wish to speak to him."

"I have already spoken to him."

"I wish to speak to him as well."

Batu grunted. "If you can find him, be my guest. He and the others were supposed to be here this afternoon with the rest of the family. They never turned up."

"Why is that, I wonder?"

"From what Koji let slip while you were out of the room, they refused to attend, apparently, believing your presence to be an insult to the Ide and the Shiko. Or so they claimed."

"Koji expressed similar sentiments."

"Yes, well, there is something in what they say, unfortunately."

"Some people are eager to see insult where none is intended. I fear Lord Koji is one of those." Shin put the papers aside and rose. "I will need to speak to these cousins regardless. If they were witnesses, they might be able to shed some light on why Gen did what he did."

"As I said, if you can find them, be my guest."

"You know, your people might locate them more quickly than mine."

"My people have other duties to attend to. Our numbers are few and the area we must oversee is large. If you want those idiots found, you'll have to do it."

Shin looked askance at him. "Is this what you call being helpful?"

Batu snorted. "I found you the matchmaker, didn't I? Be grateful."

"Oh, I am. I shall speak your praises to your family when this affair is brought to its happy conclusion." Shin pressed a hand to his heart. "I wager you might even get a promotion out of it."

Batu grunted. "She's in the receiving room. Do you want me to…?"

"No. But – find Kasami if you would and send her to wait for me. I will have need of her afterwards." With that, Shin trotted to the receiving room, arranging his thoughts for the conversation to come. It had been some time since he had last spoken to a matchmaker, and that had been under vastly different circumstances.

Batu had been involved then, as well – to his detriment. He felt a flicker of regret as the memory of that moment – a moment from a simpler time, flowered unbidden. Kaiya had been unsuitable. Batu deserved better.

He had done what was needed, for Batu's sake. Batu, of course, had not seen it that way. He hoped this time might turn out better for both of them, even as he wondered whether Batu was hoping the same. He pushed the thought aside as he came to the door.

He paused there for a few moments before entering. It was always polite to let guests compose themselves before one entered a room. The matchmaker knelt on the provided cushions, waiting patiently. Shin settled himself on the flat dais before her. "You are Suio Umeko," he began. "You were employed by the Shiko as a matchmaker, after some negotiation with the Zeshi."

"Is that a question?" the old woman asked. There was a sharpness to her voice that Shin found admirable. Though he was of higher rank, she saw no reason to give him anything but the most basic of courtesies. A calculated insult – or, rather, a warning that she was protected by the authority of the Ide daimyo. It spoke to the influence of the Shiko that Ide Tadaji had sent his personal matchmaker to oversee things.

"A statement," Shin said. "You are quite famous, in certain circles. The Suio are well known for their recordkeeping, and the matchmakers they produce are highly sought after, even outside the Unicorn clan."

"You flatter me, my lord," she said, in mild tones. He studied her carefully. She was older than him, of an age with his grandfather, perhaps. She had never been pretty, he thought, but she was striking in a particular way.

"Merely in service to my own ends," he said, with equal mildness. She paused, momentarily taken aback by the bluntness of his admission. Then, she smiled.

"Good. I would hate to think you meant anything you said."

The tea arrived then. Kitano brought the tray with a blessed lack of his usual clumsiness. He bowed low and retreated without speaking.

"Sometimes I do. A rare occasion, to be sure, but it does occur." Shin passed her a cup of tea. She accepted it politely and bowed her head.

"You wish to ask me something, I believe."

"A few things, actually. If you are willing."

"I am always willing to help in such matters as these."

"You speak as if this is a familiar occurrence," Shin said, taking a sip of his tea.

"Arranged marriages can be perilous things, especially for the inexperienced." She sipped her tea and made a pleased sound. "Delightful."

"I am pleased you like it. It is my own blend."

"Then you are more skilled than you appear, my lord."

Shin gave her a sharp look. Her smile was bland, her gaze

open and unassuming. "Thank you," he said. "Is this the first murder that has occurred as a result of one of your matches?"

It was her turn to frown. "This was not my doing."

"It was unintentional, I am certain, yet… the evidence is before us."

She fell silent. But only for a moment. "The match was suitable."

"But not perfect."

"They rarely are, especially in situations such as this. The tensions between the two families were – are – volatile. There was much riding on both of them. They knew this. Whatever happened, it was not because of the marriage."

"Can you say that with certainty?"

"I would stake my reputation on it."

"That is good to hear, because in a very real sense, you are."

Umeko looked at him. "What do you mean?" she demanded.

"Surely you understand – whatever the truth might be, what matters is what people will say. And what they will say is that you arranged a marriage in which one party attacked the other and died as a result."

Umeko set her cup down. "And I am sure that, as a Crane, you would be happy to promulgate such rancid gossip."

Shin smiled. "I would feel it my duty to warn others of such a possibility. But, if you were to speak freely with me, I would feel myself… bound to ensure the sanctity of your reputation, let us say."

Umeko made a disgusted noise. "I am too old to bandy words with a puffed-up court popinjay. Tell me what you wish to know, and I will tell you what I can."

"I want to know why Gen attacked his betrothed in the street."

Umeko stared into her teacup. "Why would I know that?"

"I do not believe that you do. But you have formed an opinion of our young lovers, and I would know what you think."

"Young is a good word for them," she said, finally. "Not in years, so much, but in thought. You understand what I mean?"

"I do. Naïve, then?"

"Yes. A particular sort of ingenuousness common to the children of vassal families. High enough that the world is at their feet, but low enough that their responsibilities are small. The Shiko and the Zeshi rule here like Khans, though it is only their fiefdom by grace of the Unicorn. Some of them have not yet learned to be suitably humble in the face of this gift." She frowned. "Gen was one such."

"Arrogant?"

"A brat. Spoiled and coddled. A swaggering oaf."

"You did not care for him?"

She smiled thinly. "I did not. Had the families not been so insistent, had other factors not been involved, I would not have made the match."

"You feared for the girl?"

Umeko snorted. "I feared she would kill him in his sleep."

Startled, Shin raised an eyebrow. That was something to consider, though he would need to speak to Aimi before he did so seriously. "She is so fierce, then?"

"Are the women of the Crane not dangerous in their own way?" Umeko asked. "They kill with whispers and words. Our daughters kill with steel."

Shin sipped at his tea. "The latter is, perhaps, more merciful, I think."

"Only if you are of a mind to be quick," Umeko said, absently.

"My sister once.... Well, that is neither here nor there." She looked at him. "The boy was a fool, the girl fierce – but foolish too, in her own way."

"What way might that have been?"

"She was... reserved. Not sullen, but resigned. As if she was carrying a weight on her shoulders. I could read it on her face." Umeko paused. "There was a sadness there."

"For her father, perhaps?" Shin asked. "I am told he went missing, soon after the arrangement was made."

"Possibly. At first I thought it was a result of her deafness – a disconnect with the world around her. It happens sometimes."

Shin interrupted. "She is deaf?"

"You did not know?"

"No."

Umeko flapped a hand dismissively. "She is only partially deaf, and can read lips, and sign – all Unicorn children are taught to sign at an early age. Proper sign, not that genteel fluttering you Cranes use. It was not an issue." She paused. "She was in love. Or had been."

"A lover?" Shin leaned forward, hands clasping his knees. Nishi's concerns about suitability suddenly made more sense. "Did Gen know?"

"No. No one did. I am not certain of it, you understand. But I have been matchmaker long enough to recognize the signs."

"Yes, I suppose that is something one would want to be aware of."

Umeko smiled. "Yes, one would." Her smile faded. "Gen was not a man who would accept such a thing. I wondered myself if he had found out, and... well." She gestured helplessly. "He was that sort of fool."

"Could someone have told him – the mysterious lover, perhaps?"

"A possibility. I have seen it before, in the case of an ill-thought out match. But if you are thinking of asking me, no, I do not know who it might be, if anyone."

"A shame." Shin smiled. "That would have made things so much easier."

"Yes, well, as I often tell people, I can't do it all for you – much as I might like to, on occasion." She sat in silence, as if mulling something over. Then, "While I do not know who it is for certain, I had my suspicions."

Shin waited, enjoying his tea. She considered it a moment more and said, "The bodyguard. Katai Ruri."

"And what makes you say this?"

"A woman's intuition." Umeko paused. "That was glib. I apologize."

"No, it is as good an answer as any." Shin set his cup down. Relationships between yojimbo and their masters were not unknown, though they were frowned upon for the obvious reasons. Especially in a case like this, where the mistress in question had a duty to fulfil. "I should have seen it myself. It explains much that I found odd about the situation. Though it still begs the question – who told Gen what was going on?"

"Why does that matter?"

"Because if you are right, and my suspicions are correct, whoever it was instigated this matter with malice aforethought. That bodes ill."

"Yes. Thankfully, that is your problem, not mine." She gave Shin a frank look. "Tell me, Crane… have you yet considered marriage?"

Shin blinked. "Ah – well, no."

Umeko sniffed. "Of course you haven't. People rarely do, until it is too late. There are several young women – and young men – of my acquaintance I think you might find suitable, should you wish for me to make the introductions."

"I will keep that in mind, thank you." Shin set his teacup down and said, "My thanks for all that you have told me, as well."

At his gesture, Umeko rose stiffly to her feet. "You are welcome, my lord. But do not forget my offer. A clever husband is prized among the Unicorn – but not too clever. You would find yourself a welcome match, I believe." She bowed low and retreated.

After a moment, Kasami entered, a cloth-wrapped bundle in her hand. Shin motioned for her to sit. "You were listening, I hope."

Kasami nodded, somewhat reluctantly. It had taken him no small effort to break Kasami of her habit of not eavesdropping on private conversations. So many people assumed that paper walls were universally respected, that one could learn much if one was willing to ignore such traditions. "Yes," she said. "She's right. It's time you started to consider settling down."

"Not about that," he said, quickly. "Lady Aimi's lover."

"She wasn't certain that the girl had one," Kasami said, doubtfully.

"She was," Shin countered. "She would not have mentioned it otherwise."

Kasami gave another grudging nod. "It would explain things. Gen found out and felt slighted. I've known many men who would do the same as he did."

"And what is your opinion of them?"

Kasami grunted. "In my humble opinion, the world is better off without them. If the girl did have a lover, it was likely someone Gen knew."

Shin gestured. "Go on."

"His reaction was too strong otherwise. He would have challenged a stranger and thought no more of it. That it was someone he knew made the betrayal sting all the more sharply." Kasami fell silent. Shin nodded in satisfaction.

"Excellent. You have been listening, haven't you?"

"You talk so much, it's impossible not to hear some of it."

"Either way, I'm pleased." Shin clapped his hands onto his knees. "Now, I need you to deliver a message for me – to Zeshi Shijan."

"Why not use one of Batu's people?"

"Because I wish it to come from me, not from the authority of the magistrate. From what Batu has told me of Shijan, I believe he will appreciate that more. I am sure Nozomi can tell you how to get there."

"Why not send Kitano?"

"Because I am asking you." Shin paused. "You are more impressive than Kitano. And I wish him to be impressed."

Kasami nodded, frowning. "And what am I to tell him?"

"I will call upon the Zeshi tomorrow." He paused. "I was hoping to get into the city some. Lord Shijan has given me the excuse. Thank him for me."

She nodded again, but did not move. Shin looked at her. "Well?"

"I will go. But first…" She unwrapped the bundle, revealing two wooden practice swords. Shin winced at the sight of them.

"Ah. Must we? There isn't really time, I don't think…"

"You avoided me this morning," Kasami said, sternly. "It is my duty to protect you, even from your own bad habits. Nozomi showed me a space out back that Batu uses for his own exercises. We will be quick." She stood and tossed him one of the swords.

"Up, my lord. Let us see if you remember anything your tutors taught you."

CHAPTER THIRTEEN
Zeshi

The next day, the streets of the middle district were crowded. Business had to be concluded before Lady Sun surrendered the field to Lord Moon, and merchants hawked their wares for the day. Shin could smell spicy noodles and incense beneath the omnipresent tang of the tanneries on the lower slopes. The wind had shifted, dragging the stink upwards.

Carts and horses vied for control of the street, forcing pedestrians onto the narrow paths that wound along the shopfronts. Refuse collectors scurried at the edges of the crowd, trying to keep the walkways free of animal dung and the debris left by careless travelers. Shin wished them luck in their task, though he knew enough about horses to know it was largely in vain.

A yubatake – a hot water field – of impressive size occupied the center of the district, and the majority of the shops and storefronts clustered about it, taking advantage of the pleasant sulfur odor and the warming steam. It was the largest source of hot spring water in the city. A web of wooden conduits surrounded the field, and water spilled through them at great volume. These, Shin knew, served to cool the waters as well as draw them to the numerous ryokan, onsen, and public baths for which the city was famous.

Shin could feel the volcanic warmth of the waters settling onto the street. Even at this time of year, the mountains had a chilly air. The heat from the water nicely offset it. But everything had a pall of dampness and humidity. Banners sagged, water-stained and dripping. Wood inevitably swelled, and brick cracked.

The hot springs that formed where the waters eddied or emerged from the rock were the lifeblood of Hisatu-Kesu. But they would also be its eventual undoing. Century by century they wore away at the outer shell of the mountain, even as the people of the city dug down to meet them. Eventually, there might be nothing left of the mountain. Just water, rising up and falling down, forever.

He glanced up, noting the hundreds of paper lanterns that hung from cords stretched across the street. They were not yet lit, but, come nightfall, the streets of Hisatu-Kesu would look as if a swarm of fireflies had invaded. From what Batu had implied, this was done purely for the benefit of the noble district ensconced on the slopes above. Apparently it gave them something pretty to look at in the evenings.

When he mentioned this to Kasami, she shook her head. "Wasteful. I am surprised."

"Why?"

"I thought the Unicorn above such things."

Shin chuckled. "I suspect that they learned such vices from us. They have always been quick studies. Besides, where is the harm?"

"I said wasteful, not harmful." She paused. "You believe there is something to it, then? What the matchmaker told you?"

Shin nodded. "Yes. Though I do not yet know whether it is the whole of the thing or merely a fragment of some greater conspiracy."

Kasami glowered at a fruit peddler, and the heimin scrambled from their path. "If you find out who it is, what then?"

"That depends on who it is – and what part they played in Gen's death." He swept his fan out, trying to brush aside the noisome smell of horse dung and sulfur. "It is conceivable to me that whoever it is might have alerted Gen in order to bring an end to the marriage, with no thought given to the consequences. Similarly, it might have been someone who knew and thought it wrong for Aimi to wed Gen while still beholden to another."

"Whatever the reason, the end result was the same."

"Yes, but either way, it exonerates Ruri."

"She does not seem to wish exoneration."

"You've asked her?"

Kasami hesitated. "No."

Shin gave her a steady look. "Then how do you know what she wishes?"

"She is a samurai. However fallen, however graceless, some things do not change. They are woven into the fabric of us. She wishes to die. The families wish her to die. Let her die."

"Her mistress does not wish it."

Kasami fell silent. Shin went on, remorseless. "It is Lady Aimi she serves, and it is Lady Aimi who holds the final sanction at bay. It was Lady Aimi who wrote to Lady Konomi, seeking her intervention. And it is only Lady Aimi who can give her the absolution she seeks. Until such time as that occurs, she remains a prisoner."

He looked at Kasami, and saw a familiar mulish expression on her face. "You have been glowering more than usual since we arrived. It cannot simply be your annoyance with the situation."

Kasami didn't look at him. "You sent Kitano into Northern Owari. Why?"

He wasn't surprised she'd figured out what Kitano's errand was. He'd made no attempt to hide it, after all. "To find these Shiko cousins everyone keeps mentioning."

"Is that the only reason?"

Shin paused, and Kasami continued past him for several steps before she stopped and turned. "What are you asking me?" he demanded.

"You're the investigator. You tell me."

Shin frowned and made to reply. But before the words left his lips, he closed his mouth and looked away. Finally, he said, "He told you about that, then?"

"Yes."

"Since when does he tell you anything?"

"He is worried about you."

"That's being charitable. Kitano rarely worries about anything other than Kitano." Shin sighed and shook his head. "You have nothing to fear. I have no intention of seeking such entertainments while we are here."

"And after we leave?"

Shin looked at her. "I cannot predict the future, helpful as such a skill might be."

"You are a fool."

"Yes. I thought you knew that by now." Shin forestalled her

reply with a gesture. "It is nothing more than… practice, you might say."

"Practice?"

"A test of my resolve." Shin watched as a quartet of servants bore a curtained litter across the intersection. The curtains were of good quality and bore the markings of a noble family, though not one he recognized. As everywhere, the lands of the Unicorn were infested with an excess of minor nobility. Provincial retainers and vassals of vassals, all seeking to climb the steps of influence.

"Boredom is a sickness for me," he continued. "You know this. It… insinuates itself in me, and I cannot shake it, save by indulging it. Once, that meant surrendering to my vices. These days, it is not so simple."

"What do you mean?" she asked. There was suspicion in her voice. He didn't blame her. These days, he often asked himself whether he was telling the truth – or rationalizing his decisions.

"Because now I have a new vice." He tapped the side of his head. "A new compulsion, one more satisfying to indulge in than any illicit game of dice." He started walking, and she joined him. "You were right, before. My boredom is what drove me to accept Lady Konomi's request. And it is why I am so… intent on this matter."

"You admit it?"

"Of course." He gave her a stern look. "That my motive is purely selfish, however, does not preclude me from being correct. This cannot simply be about a courtship gone wrong. Something else is going on, I can feel it. And I suspect I am not the only one."

"Batu, you mean."

"Mmm. He would not have surrendered to my hare-brained impulse so quickly if he did not suspect something untoward was going on. He risks much by letting me rampage through his jurisdiction. He would not do so without reason."

"So he's hoping you'll do his job for him."

"He's hoping I can find an excuse to keep him from having to do his job." Shin sniffed the air. The streets were shaped such that the strongest odors of the city were trapped, unable to rise and disperse. They blended and layered, becoming almost solid. The smells of food, of horse dung and boiling leather. Of lard and ash and steam.

Sound too was trapped here, folded back in on itself by the curvature of the mountain. By turns it was too loud and too quiet. One street might shudder with the thunderous clamoring of rushing water while another might be as silent as a tomb.

"This city is odd," he murmured. "It rides the mountains, but not with any skill. Rather, it is like a man barely holding on to a horse that threatens to buck him off."

"All the more reason to finish what we're here for and leave."

Shin nodded. "Perhaps." He smiled mischievously. "Though there is a dearth of Crane influence in this city. Not even a single vassal merchant bearing our feather. Shameful. I wonder if I should talk to my grandfather – see about establishing someone here."

Kasami grunted. "A proper use of your time at last. I am glad to see…" She trailed off and gave him a stern look. "Was that a joke?"

"Only a little one."

"Very little." She blew out a breath and gestured towards a set of wooden stairs, careening upwards between two nondescript buildings. "The noble district occupies the heights – not quite the crown of the mountain, but close. The home of the Zeshi is to the west." She looked at him. "They may not let us in. They did not seem happy to receive your message."

"Were you received by anyone of importance?"

"No."

Shin nodded, unsurprised. "Ah, well. I have no doubt that they are expecting us."

The climb was not as arduous as he feared. The steps were rough-cut and scraped beneath his sandals. Lanterns, bearing the sigils of the families, marked the paths to their homes and estates.

The Zeshi owned a number of houses, all clustered together on the same slope behind a high masonry wall reinforced by timbers. A pair of rearing horses, cast in bronze, stood sentry to either side of the main gate. A trifle ostentatious, Shin thought, but he kept this to himself as he presented himself at the gate.

A pair of ashigaru, clad in utilitarian armor with badges denoting their loyalty, stood sentinel. A servant was waiting with them. He bowed low as Shin came into sight, and gestured for the gates to be opened. "Lord Shijan awaits you in the gardens, my lord. He hopes you will forgive him for not meeting you in the proper fashion, but he wishes to take his exercise while he may."

"Oh, excellent, I always enjoy a bit of exercise," Shin said, blithely. Kasami snorted, but mercifully remained otherwise silent. The servant led them across a garden courtyard to the main house, with its foundations of stone and timber walls. At the top of the outdoor stairs, a second servant waited. Shin and Kasami offered up their swords, as decorum demanded. They were guided through the house to the interior garden.

The garden was a large square of green, centered at the heart of the house. A few carefully cultivated trees provided shade and a home for the songbirds he heard flitting about in the branches. Flowers of unusual lushness and a bright crimson hue clumped in bunches beneath the trees. Bees buzzed among them.

Zeshi Shijan reclined on a bench near the trees, running a bow across the strings of an igil. Shin recognized the instrument, though he'd never seen one up close. It was one of several curious musical instruments that the Unicorn had brought with them on their return to the empire. And though he admittedly knew little about the igil, he knew enough to know that Shijan was not at all skilled in its use.

"A fine tune," Shin said, courteously. He gestured for Kasami to wait near the door, on a mat provided by the servants.

Shijan smiled. "It is, isn't it? I confess, I am something of a composer in my spare time. I fancy I am the finest player this side of Iuchi Pass."

"How modest of you." Shin studied the other man. At first glance, Shijan was every inch the proper bushi, if a touch out of shape. He was handsome, and wore fine clothes. But he wore them without skill, and his good looks were thus wasted.

Shijan snorted. "False modesty is the province of the Crane. If a man is skilled, let him show it, lest the Fortunes reclaim their gifts."

Shin recognized the quote, though he suspected that Shijan had assumed he wouldn't. "A line from *The Ujik Debtor*, I believe. A treatise by Moto Bolormaa. A fine work, though somewhat limited in its appeal."

Shijan stared at him for a moment, and then turned his attentions back to his instrument. "You are well read, my lord."

"My responsibilities are scant, so I have little to do but read." Shin wondered if the invitation to sit would be forthcoming. "I find the work of Bolormaa to be invigorating, I must admit. There's a sort of casual crudity to it which neatly cuts to the heart of things."

"You mean it is simple."

"Simplicity is an art, like any other." Shin let his gaze roam about the garden. "Is it true that the best igils are made from the wood of a mountain larch?"

"Yes. With strings made from the hairs of a horse's tail." Shijan tapped the instrument with his bow. "I plucked these myself."

"I hope the horse was suitably compensated."

Shijan frowned. "Was that a joke?"

"A poor one," Shin said, bowing his head.

"Forgive me, I am not used to courtly humor."

"Neither am I, come to it. I have not attended court in some time."

"But you have attended?" Shijan asked, somewhat hesitantly.

"Once or twice."

"Is it… as they say?"

"That depends on who they are and what they've said," Shin replied. "It is an experience, I will say that much. By turns engaging, invigorating, and disastrous. I was honored to be invited, of course."

"Of course," Shijan said. There was a note of longing in his voice that made Shin feel a flicker of sympathy for the other man. "I must apologize for not being on hand to welcome you yesterday. An unforeseen matter required my attentions."

"I was told you were insulted by my presence. That is why I have come – to make my own apologies." Shin bowed, and

Shijan nodded, nonplussed. He set his instrument aside and stood. He glanced at the servant who'd escorted them in.

"Yo, have my archery equipment set up. I feel like practicing this morning."

The servant bowed and retreated. Shin smiled. "Ah, archery. There is such poetry in the flight of an arrow, don't you think?"

"Ah – yes. Yes, I suppose so." Shijan looked at him. He hesitated, and then said, "I have heard the Daidoji are trained to the bow. Would you care to test yourself as we talk?"

"I would be delighted, thank you," Shin said, smiling.

CHAPTER FOURTEEN
Target Practice

"I confess, I have heard something of you, my lord," Shijan said, as the servants cleared the garden. "You are known to interfere with the course of justice – to amuse yourself at the expense of propriety."

Shin turned as the servants brought out a straw target and a bow and arrows. "Not solely to amuse myself, I assure you."

Shijan whistled, and his servants scattered, leaving the target where it was. He lifted the bow and loosed his arrow. It missed the target by a wide margin. He lowered his bow, a look of annoyance on his face.

"A difficult shot," Shin said, charitably.

Shijan grunted and pulled another arrow from the quiver. He loosed his arrow, and was rewarded by a weak hit. The straw target wobbled, and a servant hurried to reposition it. "Forgive me, but may I speak plainly?"

"I insist."

"Your presence is hardly conducive to our ongoing negotiations with the Shiko."

"Then the negotiations have not ceased?"

"Why would they?"

"The death of Shiko Gen, for one."

Shijan selected another arrow. "A tragedy, but not insurmountable. The marriage was the simplest way of joining the families together. There are other ways, as I'm sure you're aware – I have already spoken to Lord Koji, and he assures me that he has his parents' full support to continue the talks."

"I am told that there are some who do not approve of... well... all of it, really."

Shijan lowered his bow and looked at Shin. "There are always obstacles to progress." Before he could elaborate, they were interrupted by a new arrival. A young man, clad in a garish kimono. Unshaven, hair unruly, he appeared on the opposite side of the garden and stopped dead. He stared at Shin for a moment before turning a glare on Shijan. "What is he doing here?" he demanded. "He has no right to be here!"

Shijan set his bow down and glared at the younger man. "He requested an audience and I granted it. That is within my authority, I think."

"This is our house – not yours," the youth said. His hand hovered over the knife in his sash. It was a curious, curved thing – a foreign blade, and quite old, Shin thought. "You are caretaker here, cousin. Nothing more."

Shijan shot to his feet, his face taut with anger. "Silence, Reiji. You embarrass us both in front of Lord Shin."

"What do I care for Lord Shin?" Reiji replied, giving Shin a sullen look. "What is he to me, save an uninvited guest and a nuisance?"

"Reiji... Lord Reiji, I presume? Brother to Lady Aimi?" Shin peered at him. Reiji was painfully young, and sullen besides. Probably barely past his gempuku. While that made him an adult by the standards of Rokugan, Shin judged that he was still unseasoned.

Reiji paused. "What of it?"

"Nothing, save that it is fortunate you are here. For I wished to speak to you as well."

"I have nothing to say to you, Crane."

"You have said much to me already," Shin said, pointedly.

Reiji flushed. He looked Shin over with an insolent expression on his face. "So you're the one they sent to clean up our mess?"

"Be silent," Shijan hissed. "And if you must speak, do so with respect!"

Shin made a placatory gesture. "I am a firm believer in respect being something one earns. And it was a fair question. Yes, I am the Crane. Daidoji Shin, at your service." He gave a shallow bow. Reiji sneered.

"I doubt that." He looked at Shijan. "I'm going out."

"You are not."

"Watch me, caretaker." Reiji started past them, and Shijan's hand shot out to catch the youth's arm. Reiji was jerked to a halt. Shijan was obviously stronger than he looked.

"You will address me with respect, boy," he said, in a low voice. "After all I have done for you, and your sister, I am owed that much."

Reiji jerked his arm free and stepped back. He gave a mocking bow and stormed out of the garden. Shijan watched him go with a peculiar look on his face. Shin felt a flash of sympathy for him. Shijan turned.

"I apologize, my lord. Reiji has ever been a snappish whelp –

and he has only grown worse since his father's disappearance."

"There is nothing to apologize for, Lord Shijan. Family is as much a burden as a blessing. I know this all too well." He paused. "Speaking of which, your other cousin, Lady Aimi. Is she at home?"

Shijan selected an arrow, and then glanced at Shin. "Why?"

"I wish to speak to her, if that is permissible."

"And if I say it is not?"

"If the road is blocked, one must simply find another route."

"Bolormaa," Shijan said, confidently.

"Mongke, actually. An Ide philosopher."

Shijan frowned. "Ah. That explains why I was not familiar with the saying. The writings of the Ide have never been to my taste."

"A shame."

"Your turn, I think," Shijan said, handing him the bow and an arrow. Shin looked at the arrow for a moment, then thrust it back into the quiver and selected another. Shijan's eyes narrowed, but Shin pretended not to notice.

Shin took aim. "Katai Ruri," he said, loosing the arrow. He was pleased to see it thunk home into the straw figure. "I believe I would have split his breastbone with that shot."

Shijan grunted. "A good shot."

Shin selected another arrow. "There is always room for improvement. What can you tell me about her?"

Shijan hesitated. "Why?"

"Everything turns on her action, or inaction. Therefore, who is she? Where did she come from? How did she come into the service of your family?"

"She was hired by Aimi's father during a period of tension

between our family and the local merchants' association. There had been some threats – all anonymous, of course."

"The best threats always are," Shin said, airily. He took his time selecting a second arrow, letting Shijan talk.

Shijan paused, and then continued. "I do not know how he knew of her, or where he found her. Only that he returned from a trip to Shiro Iuchi with the Lioness in tow."

"The Lioness?"

"That is what we used to call her. The Lioness – a jest, you see."

"Ah, yes. How amusing. And what was your impression of her?"

"That she was competent." Shijan selected an arrow and fiddled with the fletching. "I was not otherwise impressed, I must admit."

"And now?"

"Less impressed than before. I'm glad we never got around to formally adopting her into the family." Shijan thrust the arrow back into the quiver. "A good yojimbo would have known better than to answer the insults of a drunken lout."

"He was drunk, then."

"He was always drunk."

"According to Ruri, she was merely defending herself."

"Then she should have done so in a non-lethal manner."

"Sometimes that is not possible," Shin said.

"And you would know this, my lord?"

"I would," Shin said, almost gently. Shijan looked at him, and then away.

"Be that as it may, she killed a bushi of higher status. Therefore her punishment must be severe. That is the way of things."

"Death is but one punishment. There are others."

"The Shiko demanded death. I do not fault them for that, do you?"

"No," Shin said, after a moment's hesitation. He selected his arrow. "What does Lady Aimi think of it?"

"Heartbroken, of course."

Whether he was referring to Gen or Ruri, Shin could not say. "Two tragedies in such a short span of time. You said her father disappeared?" Shin asked, nocking the arrow. "When was this, if I might ask?"

"Not long after the match between Gen and Aimi was made."

"Curious."

"I don't follow."

Shin loosed his arrow. It punched home next to the first. "An idle thought, of no importance. When you say disappeared, what do you mean, exactly?"

"I mean exactly what I said, my lord," Shijan said. "He rode for Shiro Iuchi on business, but did not arrive."

"And what is the prevailing opinion?"

"My lord?"

"As to what might have happened to him. He had an escort, one presumes. A body of armed, mounted men – especially those led by a minor lord – do not simply vanish. There must be theories. I wish to hear them."

"Might I ask why?"

"You may." Shin selected a third arrow and nocked it.

After a moment, Shijan made a disagreeable noise and said, "Why?"

"Because I am curious." Shin loosed his third arrow and

was pleased when it split the first with a startling crack. Shijan gawped for a moment before quickly recovering. Shin offered him the bow.

"You are an impressive archer, my lord," Shijan said, gingerly taking back his bow.

Shin bowed his head slightly, in acknowledgment of the compliment. "We Daidoji are trained as archers from our earliest years. I do not often get the chance to test my skills in that regard, so I am most thankful to you for indulging me."

Shijan nodded and made to select his own arrow. "I am happy to be of service." He said it somewhat grudgingly, but Shin pretended not to notice.

"Then perhaps you will indulge me further and satisfy my curiosity, however impolite you may find it." Shin pulled another arrow from the quiver and made a show of examining it. "What do you think happened to your uncle?"

"Brigands, perhaps," Shijan said, readying his arrow. His form was sloppy, Shin noted. He was distracted, either by Shin's presence, or something else. He loosed, and the arrow wobbled short of its mark. Biting his lip in frustration, he reached for another. "Or maybe Bakemono. There is a breed of the filthy creatures that inhabit these mountains. On occasion they will attack merchant caravans or travelers, looking for food and plunder."

Shin paused. He knew little of the stunted creatures, save what he'd read in certain rare treatises which described the Bakemono as ugly, corrupted things, largely feral, and dangerous only in great numbers. "I find it hard to believe that any number of Bakemono might prove troublesome for armed samurai, even if they took them unawares."

"These things happen," Shijan said, loosing his second arrow. "Even the most skilled warrior loses his footing on occasion."

"But surely a search was conducted. Was there no sign of such an occurrence? Bakemono are not known for clearing up after themselves."

"Maybe they were smart."

Shin studied the other man. From the set of Shijan's mouth, and the tenseness of his posture, he could tell the conversation had steered into perilous waters. He decided a change of course might be optimal. "Maybe so. As you said, it is of no import. I ask again – might I speak with your cousin?"

Shijan's arrow glanced off the target. He turned, frowning. "I think not."

Shin raised an eyebrow. "No? May I ask why?"

"Because I do not wish you to do so. Aimi has endured enough in this time, and I do not wish her to be further troubled."

"Surely that should be her decision, not yours."

"I am the head of the family."

"For the moment," Shin said, voice mild. Shijan turned, arrow nocked.

"Regardless, I must do what is best for my family. Besides, what could she tell you that you do not already know?"

"I will not know that until I ask her."

"Then you must live in ignorance." Shijan spun and loosed his arrow. It punched into the target with such force that the straw figure toppled over. "My lord," he added, as an afterthought.

Shin bestowed a genial smile on the other man. "That is your prerogative, Master Shijan. As you say, you are head of the family, and I am but an outsider." He bowed and turned. "I believe I have outstayed my welcome. If you will excuse me..."

Shijan stopped him. "I do not wish you to think I am being intentionally insulting, Lord Shin. It is merely that I am protective of my cousins. I always have been."

Shin inclined his head. "Of course. I too have rushed to the defense of kin, on occasion. It is what family does."

Shijan smiled, though it did not reach his eyes. "I am glad you think so."

"Of course, when I did so, it was to spare them embarrassment. Is that what you fear as well? That some embarrassment will come to light if I speak with her?"

Shijan's smile faltered. "No."

"No? Then there is some other reason. Perhaps you think that Aimi is the one who struck the fatal blow, and not her faithful yojimbo. That would be awkward, I think – though I do not doubt some accommodation could be reached."

"The yojimbo killed Gen. She admitted it, and that is the truth and the whole of the truth. Aimi was but a bystander, and she saw nothing save what you have already been told." Shijan spoke harshly, but the words were rote. Practiced. As if it was a story he'd told himself so often that he'd come to believe it. "I think you should leave now, my lord."

Shin bowed and retreated. Kasami fell in behind him as they were escorted out by the same bland-faced servant. "That could have gone better," Shin said, as they reclaimed their swords at the front entrance. They started towards the gate.

"You were diplomatic enough."

"I was politesse personified. Unfortunately, Shijan is determined to be an obstacle." He turned as someone called out behind them. A young woman, in the robes of a servant, hurried after them.

Shin stopped, and when she reached them she bowed low and offered up a folded paper balanced on her palms. "Compliments of my Lady Aimi, my lord."

"I see." He gestured, and Kasami took the paper. She unfolded it and handed it to Shin. It was simple and to the point – Lady Aimi wished to meet him later, at a certain location. She would send a servant to contact him. He folded the paper back and slid it into his kimono. "Pass along my thanks to your lady, if you would," he said, smiling.

As he spoke, he spied Shijan's servant watching them from the front steps. Without a word, or a change of expression, the man turned on his heel and went back inside. He looked back at the servant. "Let Lady Aimi know that I am at her disposal, whenever she wishes."

CHAPTER FIFTEEN
Small Lord

The Shrine of the Small Lord was modest, nestled safely above a mountain fumarole. For most of the day, it was hidden by the thick clouds of gas and steam that vented from the mountain's belly. It could only be reached by a winding path of wooden steps that rose from the uppermost district of the city into the wild, rocky heights.

The upper reaches of the mountain were densely forested, and the steam hung thick amid the trees, like a crowd of silent ghosts. Or so Emiko imagined, for she could not see it. She could feel it on her cheeks and the backs of her hands – a sharp dampness that stung the sinuses when one inhaled too deeply.

She could hear the tinny chiming of the bells strung in the lowest branches. The closer one got to the shrine, the more bells there were and the greater the noise. Like the clamoring of strange birds. It was not pretty, or comforting. Rather the sound was an eerie one – fitting, perhaps, given its purpose.

From what little she knew of such things, the bells were meant to confuse and misdirect the gaki that were said to wander the mountains – the hungry ghosts of lost travelers, or those slain by brigands. She wondered if the ghosts of the men she'd slain in the foothills were among them. The thought made her smile.

She flicked a loose stone from her path with her cane and continued up the steps. The smell of sulfur grew stronger – a sign she was nearing the shrine. She often made the climb, finding it good exercise and an easy way to obtain peace from the raucous crowds that filled the streets of the city in late afternoon. The shrine wardens were quiet sorts, and few in number. They mostly kept to themselves, sweeping the shrine and blessing the grounds.

The shrine itself was not large – Tashiro had described it to her, once. A handful of wooden outbuildings, set atop a walkway of bister-stained beech planks that wound about the fumarole like the coils of a snake. There was no grand worship hall or torii arch, no purification basins – only a large stone sitting beneath a lantern pole. According to Tashiro, the stone was carved to resemble a lord's palace in miniature.

Legend held that the stone had once blocked the fumarole. A passing traveler had heard a muffled voice call from below, and had somehow levered the stone free. The traveler had been rewarded by the kami of the hot springs, though the legend did not go into the particulars.

Emiko often wondered what might happen if one were to, say, put the stone back. Would the kami be angry? Would it make the mountain shake, and spill sulfur into the clean waters? Would it, perhaps, shrug Hisatu-Kesu from its flanks, like a dog shaking off dirt? The thought gave her some amusement.

She had even suggested that they make the attempt, but the others had not been inclined to give her proposal any sort of consideration. Some of them were afraid, others perhaps hiding a secret reverence, and a few, like her, believed the kami was nothing more than a legend cooked up to lend a sheen of credibility to the city.

Regardless, the shrine made for an ideal meeting place. Few pilgrims visited this time of year, and the outer coils of the walkway were well hidden from casual observers by the dense growth of trees and jutting rocks – not to mention the steam venting into the air. As she made her way along the outer coil, she listened for the tell-tale hiss of brooms. When it had receded, and the smell of sulfur had grown overpowering, she knew she was close – and when she could smell him, she knew she had arrived.

She stopped and hugged her cane to her. "You smell of jasmine and rosewater, my lord," she said. A waft of hot air momentarily enveloped her. The wind had shifted, blowing the steam south. The individual she was meeting grunted.

"I know you." He spoke softly, as if trying to disguise his voice. She wondered if he was wearing a mask. She hoped he wasn't too disappointed that she could not appreciate it. Men often took pride in their theatricality. Especially men of this sort.

"Yes, I should hope so. Else we are both in the wrong place."

"No, I mean I have seen you before. In the gambling houses." The words were laced with suspicion. "The blind musician." She could hear the sneer in his words. He was revolted by her. Nauseated to even look at her.

"I am a musician, and I am blind, yes."

"Why were you there?" he demanded. Arrogant, like all his kind. He gave no thought to issuing commands to his perceived inferiors. She was used to it, and the words ran like rain down her back. Even so, she felt a flicker of familiar anger. The same anger that had set her feet on this path in the first place. As always, she tamped it down.

"Why do you think?"

He grunted. "You were spying on me."

Emiko smiled. "No. And yes."

"I will not have it. Is it not enough that you blackmail me? Must you invade my every waking moment as well?"

Emiko tilted her head. She could hear the hiss of steam billowing into the warm, humid air. She could taste sulfur and other, less identifiable things. Beneath her feet, the wood of the walkway was damp but firm. "What you call blackmail, I call reminding you of your debts. I know you are unfamiliar with such, being of noble birth."

"You insult me."

"Yes. As you have insulted me. We have insulted each other. With the preliminaries completed, let us now proceed to business." She felt for the rail and ran her fingers along the rough wood. "You have made a request. We deny it."

"You ... ?" He made a sound that might have been a laugh. "Why?"

"The Crane will find out nothing that troubles us. An attempt on his life this soon after his arrival would only cast light on our shadows. Therefore, he will live."

"He is dangerous. He suspects something."

"That is your problem."

A moment of silence. Had she not heard him breathing, she might have thought he'd left. "I could make it your problem," he said, harshly. "I could tell Batu everything."

Emiko smiled, though she wanted to bare her teeth at him. "Then what?"

"What?"

"After you tell him, what then? Do you think he will thank you, my lord?" She turned her face up. She could feel the warmth of the sun, though only faintly. The fire in her swelled. Arrogant, demanding fool. Just like all of them. Even now, he thought he could bully his way to victory. "More, do you think he will believe you?"

A palpable hesitation. "He might."

"You know better than that. Just as you know that you can still get out of this with your reputation intact. Even if the Crane discovers your part in events, what does it matter?"

"He will wonder why I did it."

"So tell him." She shrugged. "Tell him you were jealous, or concerned, or anything, really. It does not change the facts of the matter. It does not change the end result."

"And once she – the ronin – is dead? What then?"

"Then we will pick up where we left off." She turned her face towards the trees, seeking some relief from the smell of the fumarole. "What we do is not the swift strike, but the slow poison. Little by little, we draw closer to our goal."

"Your goal, not mine."

She shook her head. "You are with us, or you are against us. To pretend otherwise insults us both. We have given you much, and, in return, you help us. A fine partnership."

His laugh was strained – awkward. A strangled sound. She paused, considering what it might mean. She could hear the tension in his voice, the accusation – the suspicion. He was nearing the limits of his cooperation. All men had their limits.

For some, that limit was death. But for others, it was fear. Fear for others, fear for themselves. It did not matter. Once it took hold in them, their usefulness was diminished.

She ran her thumb along the faint line that marked the hilt of her blade. Two steps would take her close enough, she judged. She took the first, and could tell that he had not noticed. She could not tell if he was armed, but imagined he was. It did not worry her. Bushi carried swords the way children carried dolls.

But no. Not yet. His death would help nothing. She lowered her cane and waited. Finally, he said, "So you will not help me, then?"

"We have helped you. We are helping you. But in this matter – no. Leave it. Let justice be done, so that we might carry on our work unhindered."

"Very well. It will be as you say."

She heard the lie in his words, but did not remark on it. If he proved foolish, he would pay the price. Then, perhaps his foolishness might well engender new opportunities. Only time would tell. She smiled. "I am glad to hear it. Now, if there is nothing else..."

"There is one thing."

She frowned. "Yes?"

"Money."

"What about it?"

"I need it. Debts, you understand. With this business – the dowry – I need more."

"You have been paid enough. Your debts are no concern of ours."

"And what happens when those I owe come for me?"

She paused, considering. "Send them to us. We hold your marker."

Another harsh laugh. "Will they believe that?"

"We have someone who will ensure that they do."

"And you will pay them?"

"We will come to some arrangement, yes."

Another pause. Then the rustle of a fine kimono. "Very well. I shall just have to trust you." She could hear the derision in his voice. The frustration at having to lower himself to speak to the likes of her. As if he were polluting himself just by breathing the same air.

Emiko took the second step. The smell of him filled her nose. The cane clicked – with a hiss the blade came free. She heard him gasp and let her arm follow the sound. He gave a choked cry as she put the edge of her blade to his throat.

"You should not trust me," she said, softly. "You should fear me. This is not a game of equals. I have you in my hand, and I can crush you at a moment's notice."

"You… You need me…"

"No. We need someone like you. Bushi are not in short supply, sadly. You can be replaced. As can I – though you more easily than me, I think." She tilted her head, listening to the rapid hiss of his breath. She fancied she could almost hear his heart thudding fearfully. She smiled. "Good. Good. You are a slow learner, but you will eventually come to grasp the lessons we teach. As all your kind will come to understand the truth – there is no order under heaven. Only a thing of artifice, erected by the few on the backs of the many."

"You are mad," he said, his voice hoarse.

"No. But I am angry. And anger is the fire that will light our way forward." She stepped back and sheathed her blade. "Your anger is not hot enough yet. It is a little fire. But with our help, it will swell up and consume all those that deny you."

"Yes," he said. "Yes. I will."

"You will what?"

"I will… I will do as you say."

"Good. When they contact you, send them to us. Your debts will be settled… again." She let a note of warning creep into her words. "But this will be the last time. After this, if you wish to gamble away your money, best to ensure that you have the funds to cover your losses. That is what the heimin do, after all. Can you do any less?"

She heard his grunt, and knew her words had struck home. She heard his footsteps on the planks and listened as he departed. When he'd gone, she took a deep breath and shook her head. She'd come close to making a mistake of her own. Killing him would have served no purpose. It had been fortunate that she'd been able to pull the strike at the last moment – to merely graze his throat, instead of opening it.

For now, he had been frightened into obedience. But the day was coming where his fear for himself would outweigh his fear of her. On that day, she would not pull her blow. She smiled at the thought and gave a soft sigh of satisfaction.

That would be a good day indeed.

CHAPTER SIXTEEN
Northern Owari

Lady Sun had set by the time Kitano found the men he was looking for. Lord Shin had sent him out that afternoon, with strict orders to run the trio to ground. Their trail had, unsurprisingly, led him directly into Northern Owari.

This part of the city was a red lantern district. The crimson light lent it a raw sheen that fit well with the rough goings on. Above him, on the second floors of the nondescript houses to either side of the street, kneeling ranks of courtesans looked down from behind bamboo screens, and touts invited passersby into these houses of ill-repute. Drunks spilled out of sake houses and disreputable onsen, singing raucous songs that echoed through the steamy streets, and somewhere close by a scream ended abruptly.

Kitano smiled. It was like coming home. He wandered down cramped alleyways, his prosthetic finger tapping against the pommel of the knife thrust through his sash. It had taken him most of the day to pick up their trail.

Totara Ikki and his two friends ran through Northern Owari

like the flux. The Totara were a minor – very minor – aristocratic family, and their only claim to influence was a daughter married into the Shiko. But Ikki acted as if he was a Shiko himself, to be accorded all due respect. Mostly this meant he left stacks of unpaid bills everywhere he went and that he was barred from most of the larger gambling establishments.

Kitano had dealt with similar louts in his previous career – indeed, such men had been his fish and rice. As a rule, they wagered heavily and played badly. So long as you had enough muscle to convince them to pay their debts, they were a professional gambler's dream. He himself felt the itch to take them for all they were worth.

He tracked them down to the Jade Hare, a bawdy house that offered a bit of everything to the discerning customer. It was a tall building, leaning tipsily against its closest neighbor. Upstairs, courtesans waited for the well-to-do heimin, while prostitutes of a more common vintage circulated through the crowd on the ground floor, selecting their quarry for the evening with unerring accuracy.

The ground floor was given over to games of chance, like dice and hanafuda. Kitano threaded the edges of the evening crowd, looking for Ikki. When he spied him, a rueful grunt slipped his lips. They were amidst a game, and losing heavily by the looks of it. He took up a position nearby and bought a drink.

As he took a sip of the rice wine, his eyes remained fixed on Ikki's table. The samurai were dressed in rich robes that had seen better days, and armed. That wasn't so surprising – most everyone in the Jade Hare was armed. Ikki was muscular and feral looking. His hair was clipped short on the sides, with the rest bound back in a loose knot. He was unshaven, and scratched at his chest with one hand. He had a jug of sake in the other, and took sloppy swallows from it as he glared at the dice.

His companions were a study in contrasts. One was short and muscular, but already running to fat. The other was a long, lean man, with a face that drooped dolorously. The unfortunate object of their attentions gave the dice a tentative roll – and received a blow across his jaw from Ikki for his trouble. Ikki laughed harshly as the gambler fell from his stool, one hand pressed to his face. "I win," he growled, an ugly glint in his eye. The gambler, no fool, bowed and scrambled away.

That was the danger of gambling with bushi – especially drunk ones. They didn't cheat, because they didn't have to. They could just declare themselves the winners, and unless you had armed men at your back it was wise to let them do so.

Even so, it rankled. Lord Shin, slippery as he was, hadn't resorted to such tactics. He'd cheated, of course, but skillfully and professionally. Kitano hadn't realized it at the time, but it had been a sign of respect in some ways. Shin had beaten him at his own game. Fools like these only won by luck, or because they bullied their opponents into giving up.

He paused. Then a slow smile spread across his face. He made his way towards the table and took over the empty seat. Ikki glared at him. "Who said you could sit down?"

Kitano bowed his head, as if chastened. "I bring you greetings from my master, my lord. He is eager to speak with you."

Ikki snorted. "Who is your master, then?"

"Daidoji Shin."

Ikki took a slug from the sake jug. "Never heard of him."

"He is only recently arrived in the city."

The heavyset man frowned, wrinkles forming on his wide

face. "The Crane. The one the Iuchi sent? Is that who you're talking about?"

Ikki slammed down the jug. "The Iuchi provocateur, you mean?"

Again, Kitano shrugged. The shrug was the greatest weapon in the peasant's arsenal. It conveyed whatever a highborn questioner wished it to convey. The fat man looked at the others. "Maybe we should speak with him."

Ikki snorted. "Why? We already spoke to that fool, Batu."

They talked amongst themselves as if Kitano weren't there. They always did. He listened, as Shin had taught him. They might say something of use, which would be advantageous if they refused to come. "There might be consequences if we don't," the one with the long face muttered.

"Consequences?" a new voice interjected. "Never heard of it." Kitano glanced up and saw a youngish man in a garish kimono saunter towards the table. He grinned at Ikki and the others. "Started without me, then?"

"What are you doing here, Reiji?" Ikki growled. He made as if to rise, but the fat one stopped him. "We've no time for you, fool."

"That's a shame. I came with money."

"Gen's dead because of you – because of your blasted family!" Ikki snapped. The smile was jolted from the young man's face. He stepped back, his expression clouding.

"I had nothing to do with that. He was my friend too."

"Maybe you should go, Reiji," the fat one said. "Find your fun somewhere else for the moment."

Reiji turned and hurried away, pushing through the crowd. Kitano watched him go. He turned back only to find Ikki glaring at him. "Your master can go to hell," the samurai said. "I'll not speak to any Iuchi dog, whatever his colors."

Kitano nodded. "A shame." He paused. "I fear my master will not take this well. He is a hard man, and prone to violent fits. If only there were some way to convince you..." He trailed off and gave his kimono a twitch, causing the koku in his pouch to rattle. Ikki's eyes narrowed, and a familiar gleam came into them.

"I know," Kitano said, voice mild. "Maybe a wager would do it, eh?"

Ikki licked his lips. "What sort of wager?"

Kitano picked up the dice and let them roll across his palm. He smiled ingratiatingly.

"A friendly one, my lord."

The night was crisp. A gentle breeze wafted across the balcony. Shin and Batu stood, looking down into the foothills below. At this time of night it reminded Shin of a swarm of fireflies, rising up out of the dark.

Batu had procured a jug of sake from somewhere, and two clay cups. The cups were crude things, made by unskilled hands. Batu's hands, as it turned out. "I needed a hobby," he said, somewhat defensively.

"I make no judgment," Shin assured him. "I have delved into the arts myself, on occasion." He peered at a cup. "Though your technique could use work."

"Some of us have to work for a living. Not all of us have the leisure time to perfect our skills at the pottery wheel."

"It wasn't a criticism, merely an observation." Shin leaned atop the veranda rail and looked down. "I can see why you chose this place now. The view is stunning. Too high up and you wouldn't see it at all."

"Yes." Batu took Shin's cup and filled it. "I have placed myself at the exact midpoint of the city. Equidistant between high and low."

"Easy to find, you mean."

"That was my hope."

Shin studied his host over the rim of his cup. "I gather from your tone it was somewhat in vain."

Batu took a stiff slug of sake before replying. "The heimin here had their own way of settling things before the clan took an interest. They've held to it over the years, despite the efforts of my predecessors and myself."

"Northern Owari," Shin said.

Batu nodded. "It's been a suppurating boil on my hind end for the entirety of my time here. But there's little to be done about it. I don't have enough people to patrol it effectively, and the families aren't interested in helping – not when they enjoy their vices as much as the commoners."

"Surely the Iuchi would send reinforcements if you requested them."

Batu shrugged. "In theory. I do not wish to put it to the test, though."

Shin sipped his sake. "No, I can see where you might not wish to know the answer to that particular question. It seems somewhat short-sighted, however."

"We are a pragmatic clan. Why discard something useful because it is unsightly?" Batu refilled his cup. "Regardless, at the moment I have no authority save what the clan gives me. And what little authority I have been given is mostly concerned with keeping Hisatu-Kesu afloat – and that includes the bits I don't particularly like."

"It is much the same in the City of the Rich Frog," Shin said. "The wheels of progress roll over the unjust and just alike. Speaking of which – have you made a decision yet?"

Batu looked at him. "Have you found out anything new?"

"Not as such."

"Then no. But I will have to, before long. Already there is talk."

"It sounds as if this matter has united them after all."

"Yes," Batu said, sourly, "Against me."

"It could be worse."

"How?"

"It could have united them against me."

Batu gave a snort of laughter. "I've never known you to be concerned about such things. You always seemed to take such pleasure in making enemies."

"It is true, not everyone appreciates my wit." Shin looked at Batu. He felt a sudden pang as he did so, but forced it aside. The past was the past, and he lived like water – always moving. He swallowed and said, "I do understand – whatever you might think of me. I understand the pressure you are under. And I understand that convenience is a powerful drug. But this sort of thing can fester. A sop to hard feelings might serve in the short term, but the truth is the only thing that can cleanse the infection."

"And what is the truth, Shin?"

"That someone engineered this tragedy for reasons we do not yet know." He paused, considering his next words carefully. "I have a theory, if you'd care to hear it."

"Oh, by all means," Batu murmured, pouring himself a new cup of sake. He set his elbows on the rail beside Shin's. Shin was suddenly reminded of past nights, and past talks, and he felt the pang again. He looked up at the stars.

"Shiko Nishi considered Aimi unsuitable, because Aimi was already in love with someone else."

Batu frowned. "Do you know who?"

"I do. Or at least I have a good idea."

"Who?"

"If you think about it for half a moment, you'll guess it yourself."

Batu made to reply, stopped, and sighed. He set his cup down on the rail. "Ruri."

Shin nodded. Batu had probably known as well, without consciously realizing it. "It's obvious, in retrospect. Why else would Gen try to assuage his honor by killing her? Only Gen wasn't half the swordsman he thought he was."

"Do you think whoever told him meant for him to kill her?"

"I think it didn't matter. I believe the confrontation itself was the point – a rupture in the burgeoning alliance between the Zeshi and Shiko."

"But what would anyone gain from that?"

"What indeed? That is the question, isn't it?" Shin tapped the rim of his cup. "There's something we're not seeing." He chewed his lip for a moment, and then asked, "Was this the first such arrangement between the families?"

"What do you mean?"

"Have they tried to make peace before?"

Batu nodded. "Since the Shiko arrived, practically. The negotiations have been ongoing since almost before my time."

"And none of them took?"

"No, sadly."

"Why?"

Batu paused, cup halfway to his lips. He cut his eyes to Shin. "You think this isn't the first time someone has meddled." It wasn't a question. Shin was pleased – Batu had been paying attention after all. "That someone has been deliberately stoking the conflict. But why?"

"As I said, that is the question." Shin looked at Batu. "I do not know for sure, but it wouldn't surprise me. The Zeshi and the Shiko are relative newcomers to this city. Neither family has been subtle about their intentions to control the flow of trade. Someone might well resent their growing influence, and hope to undermine them."

"But it would have to be someone close to the families," Batu said.

"Social proximity is an obstacle that can be easily overcome, if one but has the wit."

Batu shook his head. "I knew you were going to overcomplicate this."

Shin laughed. "Admit it, you're having fun."

"You're having fun. I'm enduring it." Batu upended the sake jug. When nothing came out, he peered into it. "What now?"

"Now, I take the mood of the city." Shin leaned over the rail. "Someone down there knows something – and I intend to find out who, and what, in that order."

"Is that why you sent that scruffy servant of yours into Northern Owari without telling me?" Batu asked, drily. Shin glanced at him, somewhat guiltily.

"Ah. You know about that."

"I know everything that goes on in my city."

"Clearly not, else I would not be here."

"You know what I mean," Batu said, testily.

Shin nodded. "I sent him to find the cousin, Ikki."

"Why?"

"He was with Gen when he made his ill-fated challenge. He might know who told Gen there was something to be mad about."

"Has your man come back yet, then?"

Shin shook his head. "Not yet, but I am confident he will return soon."

"You have a lot of confidence in such a disreputable looking character." Batu paused. "I have already questioned Ikki and his cronies, you know."

"But did you ask the right questions?"

Batu was silent. Then he set the jug down on the rail.

"I'm going to get another jug."

CHAPTER SEVENTEEN
Lady Aimi

Dawn's light danced among the trees as Kasami stepped inside the outbuilding. She had awoken early, to practice in the quiet hours before the rest of the household awoke. It had been her habit for some time, and she saw no reason to change it simply because they were not at home. She had dismissed the men on duty with a nod, wanting to be alone with the prisoner. That they had listened to her was somewhat surprising, but she supposed Batu had given orders to that end.

Her feet made barely any noise as she moved down the line of cells. She did not know why she was here, only that she felt it important to see the woman they had come to save. No, not the woman – the ronin.

Even the word repulsed her. There was a fundamental wrongness to it, a repudiation of all that was certain. Everyone had their master. That was the way of the world; masters and servants; order and purpose. But ronin were outside of that order. They had no master and no purpose. Some, she knew, found it by choosing a new master. Those, at least, were better than the sort who turned to brigandage.

But even in choosing to serve, there was an implied disloyalty. If one could select a master, what stopped one from doing so again? How could you trust such an individual, especially with your life, or the lives of those most precious to you?

And yet, many samurai did. And many ronin prospered from such alliances, clawing back the honor they had forsaken, one generation at a time, until their sins were forgotten and they were simply another loyal retainer.

Most, she knew, did not keep their names when they left the path. They chose new ones, or went without. What was a name worth, after all? But some did not. She did not know why the Katai had allowed Ruri to keep her name. Perhaps her sin had not been great, or maybe they were hoping she might return. Or maybe they did not care.

Katai Ruri did not look up as Kasami stopped outside her cell. "It is not time for my meal," she said, after several moments had passed. Still, she did not look up. Kasami studied the prisoner, then turned her attention to the straw floor of the cell.

Shin's opinion of her skills at observation aside, she knew what to look for. Signs of disturbed straw, of exercise and practice. Even here, the habits of a lifetime were hard to break. Her gaze fixed on a curious shape beneath the rough tatami mat that served Ruri as a bed. "What is that beneath your mat?"

Ruri froze. "It is nothing. An amusement."

"Let me see it."

Ruri looked up. Her gaze was flat, her face stiff. Slowly, she reached out and flipped the mat aside. A sword lay there. Not a sword of steel or wood, but one of straw. Woven into shape over the length of her imprisonment.

Kasami stared at it, trying to imagine the patience and coordination it had taken to complete such a project. She was surprised Shin hadn't noticed it. Maybe Ruri had known better than to leave it in such an obvious place when she'd spoken to him.

"For practice," Kasami said, without accusation.

"Yes."

"Admirable. Many in your position would not bother."

"Many in my position would already be dead."

Kasami grunted and turned. She leaned against the wall beside the cell, arms crossed. "You sound angry about that."

"Wouldn't you be?"

Kasami nodded. "I would."

"It is not right. I know what must be done. Why not let me do it?"

Kasami did not reply. She heard Ruri get to her feet and begin to pace. A lioness in her cage. "If I could do it with this sword of straw, I would. But it has no edge, no point. I must have a blade."

Kasami heard her stop. Heard the inhalation. But before Ruri could speak, Kasami said, "I will not procure you a blade."

Ruri sighed. "I was not going to ask." She paused. "Why does he do this to me?"

"He was asked."

"I did not ask him."

"No."

"I do not like being a pawn in their games. It is why I… why I…" She trailed off. Another exhalation, softer than the first. "Every day, I awake at dawn. I clean myself as best I can with a bucket of water and straw. I dress, and I practice. I mark the steps and calculate the width and length of my world anew every morning. It does not change. I eat. I sleep. I mark the steps. Over and over again."

Kasami closed her eyes. "At least it is not a complete waste of time," she murmured.

Ruri gave a bitter laugh. "Trust a Crane to say something so asinine."

Kasami stiffened. "And trust a Lion to slap away a friendly hand." She turned and found herself looking into the other woman's eyes. "If you want to die so badly, stop eating. Stop drinking. Slit your throat with a chip of stone, or smash your skull against the wall. There are ways, if one is determined."

"Those are the ways of a heimin," Ruri said, after several moments of shocked silence. "Those are not our ways."

"Our ways? And what are you? A clanless woman. Do you think you deserve any better death than a dog for what you have done?"

"What I've done?" Ruri snarled. "What I've done? I saved my mistress! I did my duty! I do not deserve a peasant's death!" She gripped the bars of the cell. "Give me a warrior's death – I have earned it."

"How?"

Ruri blinked. The question struck her like a dart. "What do you mean?"

"How did you earn it?" Kasami leaned forward. "Tell me about the duel."

"Duel?" Ruri laughed bitterly. "Is that what they are calling it?"

"Was it not a duel?"

"It was not anything," Ruri said, softly. She closed her eyes and leaned her head against the bars. "A red moment, there and gone."

"Tell me."

"He cursed her," Ruri murmured. "Called her… called us such awful names. She is deaf, but she can read lips, and he made sure she knew what he was saying. Swept his sword out. I do not know what he intended, nor did I wait to find out. I saw the sword and – and…" Her hands tightened on the bars, until the knuckles were white and bloodless.

"Acted," Kasami said. She sighed and looked up at the roofbeams. "He was right, you know." The words came grudgingly. She did not like being wrong.

"Who?"

"Shin. Lord Shin, I mean. He said you did not wish to die, and now I have seen it for myself. For if you had, you would have found some way to accomplish it by now."

"I am imprisoned. I have no weapon," Ruri protested.

"As I just pointed out, that is no great impediment." Kasami's gaze bored into the ronin. "You ought to have waited for the magistrate to pass sentence. But you did not. Why?"

Ruri turned away. "Aimi… my mistress forbade me."

Something in the way she said her mistress' name caught Kasami's ear. Her eyes narrowed. She made to speak but paused. She was not Shin, to fill the air to no purpose. So, instead, she bowed her head. "Then you should content yourself with the fact that you have done all you could."

Ruri did not look at her. "Why did you come in here? Curiosity?"

"Lord Shin asked me how I knew you wished to die. I said any samurai would – unless there was a good reason not to. He told me to ask you. And so I came."

Ruri's hands curled into fists. "Give me a blade and I will

show you what I wish." But she spoke without hope.

Kasami turned and walked away. "If I believed that, I just might."

Shin was waiting for her outside, hands clasped behind his back. Kasami stopped, startled by his presence, though she was careful not to let it show on her face. "Well?" he asked. "What do you think?"

"You are right," she said. "She does not wish to die."

Shin scratched his chin and grinned. "Yes, that was my conclusion as well." He looked at her. "If I forbade you from killing yourself, would you?"

She hesitated. "No," she said, finally. "Not if I thought it the only way." A curious expression crossed his face, there and gone before it fully registered. "That she did not means she is either a coward, or…"

"Or she has something – or someone – to live for."

"What do you mean?"

"Twice now it has been intimated that Lady Aimi had a lover, and that knowledge of this is what drove Gen to confront her. Umeko, the matchmaker, voiced a suspicion as to the identity of that lover." He glanced meaningfully at the outbuilding.

"Ruri?" Kasami asked, quietly. "But she is a ronin – unworthy of such a match."

"Love knows no decorum." Shin rubbed the bridge of his nose with a forefinger. "If it is true, it explains the rashness of Gen's actions."

"If you are right, she has double the reason for not speaking up – she is not just defending her mistress' life, but her reputation as well." Kasami shook her head. "It is not that she wishes to die – but she has no choice. If the truth is revealed…"

She trailed off as she considered the repercussions.

"Yes. Unpleasant, at best." He held up a folded piece of paper. "Zeshi Aimi has asked me to meet her at the Shrine of the Small Lord. I'm afraid that means no practice this morning." He attempted a frown, but failed. "So disappointing."

Kasami glared at him, but said only, "When do we leave?"

Sometime later, Shin stood on a wooden walkway, overlooking the steaming fumarole that was supposedly the source of the mountain's hot springs. Looking at the geyser of gas and steam, with the smell of sulfur thick on the air, he could believe it.

The wind turned, and the bells in the trees gave an eerie jangle. He waved his fan, trying to disperse the smell. He would have to change his clothes when he got home. And possibly have a bath. He looked around.

The shrine was a humble thing; a few outbuildings, no real decoration save for the fumarole stone, carved to resemble a miniature palace. Offerings of food had been placed at the foot of the stone by pilgrims. If there was a kami residing here, it was a well-fed one.

The caretakers of the shrine had made themselves scarce. He'd caught sight of them once or twice, but by and large they seemed content to avoid him. Ordinarily, he might have been somewhat insulted, but for the moment, he preferred privacy.

A whistle from nearby caused him to turn. Kasami stood at the far end of the walkway, watching for the arrival of Lady Aimi. She gestured, and Shin raised his fan in acknowledgment. He had been half-afraid that she had changed her mind.

Kasami retreated as the first of Lady Aimi's bodyguards came into view. There were four of them; samurai of the Zeshi household, bearing the colors of the family on their robes. All were armed, but their weapons were peace-bound. Kasami kept her hands well away from her own swords as she stepped respectfully behind Shin.

At the center of the quartet of samurai was Lady Aimi. She was a slight, slim figure, clad in purple, bearing a sunshade against the heat of the day. She folded it and handed it to one of the pair of servants who trailed after the samurai, heads bowed. She gestured, and her guards scattered, moving to take up sentry positions on the walkway. Shin waved Kasami back as he went to meet Aimi.

"Lord Shin," she greeted, her hands moving in time to her words. "I am pleased to meet you at last." Shin detected only the faintest hesitation to her speech, though her voice was largely lacking in nuance. That, and the fact her gaze was fixed on his mouth, were the only real signs that she was deaf.

She was more confident with her hands – her fingers provided the inflection her voice lacked. The Unicorn had developed their own form of sign language during their wanderings, separate from the more standard system devised by the Crane, which most of Rokugan used. Mostly they used it for their horses, or so Batu had claimed. He'd taken it upon himself to learn both in his youth, as well as the particular cant used by some Scorpion courtiers.

"And I you, my lady. Lady Konomi speaks highly of you," he said, bowing respectfully. As he did so, he let his hands fall into the awkward rhythms of the Unicorn cant. The Crane cant was a thing of graceful gestures and circular, sweeping motions. In contrast, the Unicorn version was full of abrupt gesticulations and pointed flicks of the fingertips – rather like the motions of a restive horse. Quite tiring on the fingers. "She considers you favored cousins, and often shares amusing anecdotes of her time spent here."

I wish she were here now, Aimi signed, and then flushed when she realized how such a statement might be construed. Shin laughed gaily.

"Not for nothing, so do I. She is a rare wit, and an adventuresome companion."

Aimi smiled brittlely. Her gestures took on a teasing flutter. *I have heard that you are often seen together.*

"Our friendship is something I treasure most highly," Shin said, signaling pointedly. "A good friend is a rare thing, and one must cultivate friendship the way one would a fragile blossom. That is why I am here now."

I am glad that you are, though the circumstances are unfortunate. She paused, her hands stilling. Then, *You sign well. Hardly a trace of an accent.*

Shin inclined his head. "I take that as a compliment."

"I can read lips, if you prefer," she said, out loud.

"That is appreciated, but unnecessary. I so rarely get the chance to practice." He waggled his fingers flirtatiously and she laughed. But only for a moment.

I wish we had time to speak at length, but I fear this conversation will be quick, she signed. *My cousin doubtless knows that I am here.*

"He did not wish us to speak, though his reasoning was somewhat… sparse."

Her fingers twitched. *He fears that you will upset the negotiations. More than they already are, I mean.*

Shin smiled at that. "Your cousin carries much weight on his shoulders. But I do not think that is what you wanted to talk to me about, is it?"

"Ruri," she said simply. The gesture she made was plaintive – and awkward. As if she had been about to use another sign; one with a more personal meaning.

"Yes." Shin looked at her. She was young, older than her brother but not by much. But old enough to be married, and old enough to know what she wanted. Or didn't want, as the case might be. "Tell me what happened."

She gestured loosely. *By now, you must know the full story.*

"I know the story, but not your version of it. Tell me, please."

She looked out over the fumarole. After a moment, she turned back and signed, *We were walking in the market. We often did that. I liked to look in the storefronts and watch the merchants.*

"I understand. I enjoy it as well."

She smiled at that. It didn't last. *Gen… appeared,* she signed. *With his lickspittles in tow. Drunk, of course. He was often drunk. Celebrating, or commiserating.* Her hands hesitated. *He was drunk the day our engagement was announced. Did you know that?* Her fingers flicked dismissively.

Shin remained silent. She continued to sign. *He accused me of bringing shame to him, to our families, due to my dalliance with a clanless samurai. His sword was in his hand and he was the color of blood, and I… I was afraid.* Her hands twitched uncertainly, as if it was the first time she'd actually thought about it. Maybe it was. She continued. *I'd always considered him a… a lout. A fool. But for the first time, I was frightened of him.* She made a fist and touched it to her stomach – the Crane sign for fear, rather than the Unicorn one.

"And then Ruri stepped between you."

She nodded. *Yes,* she signed. *She demanded that he leave us. He spewed obscenities I will not repeat and attacked her. She was so quick; I never imagined anyone could move so quickly. Her sword was out and sliding home again between one breath and the next. And Gen was dead.*

"He attacked her first. You are certain?"

A sure gesture. *On my honor, I am certain.*

"You told her to run. Why?"

Have you not yet figured it out? Aimi signed, her gesture challenging. *My cousin assured me that you were clever, Lord Shin.*

Shin smiled politely. "I never ask questions I do not already have an answer for. But I like to hear those answers spoken aloud. So tell me, if you would – why?"

Aimi swallowed and hesitated before signing, *I did not wish her to die.*

"No?"

A shake of the head. *No.*

"That is a relief."

Aimi's eyes widened. "It is?" she said, out loud.

"Quite so. I do not wish her to die either. Unfortunately, you and I seem to be the only two who share that hope. So we must work together in order to ensure victory." He leaned forward. "Why did you tell her to run?"

Aimi was silent for long moments. Then, in a small voice, "I love her." Her hands thumped her chest. He saw that they were trembling.

Shin nodded. "Yes. Is that why Gen confronted you both that day?"

Aimi shook her head. *He could not have known,* she signed. *We said nothing, we let nothing slip. I even burned the poetry she wrote me.* Her hands still trembled, making it hard to follow her signing.

After waiting a moment for her to compose herself, he asked, "Poetry?" Ruri did not seem the sort for poetry. Then it was often said that still waters ran deep. A sudden thought occurred to him. "How much of it? And are you certain that you destroyed it all?"

Of course! Her hands fluttered – another hesitation, betraying uncertainty.

"How did you go about burning it?"

Aimi frowned. *I gave the papers to the servants, as we always do,* she signed. She paled, and her hands dropped.

"Yes," Shin said. "It is possible someone in your family intercepted the papers, realized what they were, and decided to tell Gen."

Her fingers cut the air. *But why would anyone do that?*

"I don't know." Shin let his gaze stray as he built the scene in his mind. "No one opposed your marriage to Gen. Not even you."

It was too important. Aimi's hands tightened into fists, before flurrying into motion. *It is still too important.*

Shin felt sympathy for her. He too knew the weight of familial obligation, and how it never lessened – only increased. "If Ruri were to be released, what would you do?" he asked, softly. Aimi's eyes narrowed. "Would you declare your love for your social inferior? Would you flee Hisatu-Kesu in order to be with her?"

Aimi shook her head and signed, *I do not know, my lord. I have not dared hope for her release.*

"That is almost certainly a lie, but an expected one." Shin smiled, so as to lessen the sting of his words. "Hope is no sin, and love is not foolishness. Together, the two are as potent a weapon as any katana."

I would not flee, Aimi signed. She lifted her chin, her expression one of resolve – and her signing even more so. "This is my home and I will not abandon it, or my family. Not for anything or anyone. Nor would Ruri expect me to."

"No, I do not think she would." Shin sighed and smoothed his kimono. "Still, it is a concern for the future. For now we must occupy ourselves by learning the identity of the person who revealed your… affections to Gen."

She made an open palm gesture. *How will you do that?*

"With care and diligence," Shin said. "Rest easy, Lady Aimi. I feel we are on truth's trail at last." He tapped his lips with his fan. "You mentioned lickspittles. Was one of them Totara Ikki, by chance?"

Yes, she signed. *And his cousins, Aito and Giichi. They were always trailing after Gen.* As she gestured, there was a clatter of noise from the direction of the steps. They turned and saw a band of ashigaru, in Zeshi colors, approaching the walkway. Several more samurai were with them, and one called out, gesturing broadly as he spoke.

"Lady Aimi. You are to come with us."

"On whose authority?" she demanded out loud, as her own guards closed ranks. At Shin's nod, Kasami joined them, her hand falling to the hilt of her sword. The newcomers paused, and for a moment it looked as if weapons might be drawn.

"Your cousin, Lord Shijan. He asks that you return home." The spokesman's eyes flicked to Shin. "I apologize for the inconvenience, my lord. But we have our orders."

Shin looked down his nose at the man. "Of course. We all have our orders, and we must obey them. Such is the will of heaven." He turned and bowed low to Aimi. He was not concerned for her safety. Shijan had no reason to harm her, and every reason to keep her safe. If another political marriage was suggested, either Aimi or Reiji would be the logical choice. As such, Shijan could not afford to let either come to harm.

"My lady, it was a great pleasure to finally meet you. Rest assured I shall take all that you have told me into consideration." He gestured sharply, and Kasami fell in behind him as he started towards the steps. The Zeshi ashigaru parted before him, standing respectfully to either side.

He did not look back, but he felt their eyes on him the entire way.

CHAPTER EIGHTEEN
Complications

Batu was in his study when Shin returned. A servant showed Shin into the room, and he knelt on the cushions before Batu, waiting for the other man to acknowledge him. When Batu didn't, Shin cleared his throat. He was forced to do so three more times before Batu finally deigned to look at him.

"And how has your day been?" Shin asked, gaily.

"Troublesome." Batu looked out the window. "While you were annoying people, I was called to arbitrate a dispute between the Zeshi and the Shiko. Another dispute, I should say. An argument between soldiers that spilled over into violence."

Shin's eyes widened. "What happened?"

"A tea house on Six Sparrow Street was wrecked, and several people injured. No one important, thankfully, but now both Shijan and Koji are barking at me to do something about it. I've fined the men in question, but it won't be the last such incident, I fear."

"As the families go, so too does the city," Shin said, idly.

"The families gird themselves for war," Batu said, nodding.

"Neither side wants it, but neither do they wish to be caught out if the other side decides to launch an attack."

"Do you think either are planning such a thing?"

"If it were down to the individuals here? No. But it is not solely up to them. The daimyos of the two families obviously see this as merely another front in their ongoing rivalry, or so I'm told. And it won't be long before individuals within the Iuchi and the Ide decide to exacerbate matters for their own gain."

Shin didn't question this statement. Such things were regrettably common when it came to internecine conflict. Even in times of peace, the clans were a constant stew of status-seeking and glory-hunting. At times of war, every courtier and bushi looking to improve their position came out of the woodwork and tried to insert themselves into matters. That was one of the reasons Shin had attempted to remove himself from the body politic of the Crane. "Then we had best come up with a solution before it reaches that point."

"We have a solution."

"A better solution, then."

Batu shook his head. "Shijan is upset. You spoke to his cousin against his express wishes. He has made a formal protest."

"He would not be the first." Shin studied a point on the wall past Batu's left ear. "I think Shijan is both easily upset and quick to complain when it benefits him. He is a tedious fellow, I will say that for him. And he is hiding something."

"You know this for a fact?" Batu asked, intently.

"I suspect." Shin fussed with the line of his kimono. "Aimi has confirmed what the matchmaker suspected. She and Ruri were – are – lovers."

Batu sighed heavily. "That is... unfortunate."

"Gen knew."

"That is even more unfortunate." Batu paused. "Who told him?"

"She doesn't know. I suspect we won't find the answer to that until we speak to Gen's cronies, if Kitano can manage to locate them." He tapped his knee with his fan, wondering when his servant would return. It was taking him longer than Shin had anticipated. How hard could it be to find three drunken bushi in a city as small as this? "The Totaras are the key, I think. We know what happened, but they might know why."

"So, in conclusion, you have learned nothing of use to us," Batu said.

"On the contrary, I have learned much."

"By insulting members of both families."

"By asking the sorts of questions you should have asked," Shin retorted. "I have clay. I must now build bricks." He snapped open his fan and fluttered it.

"And what does that mean?"

"I have asked the obvious questions, now I must ask the less obvious ones. For instance, what purpose does Gen's death serve?"

"To ruin the negotiations, obviously. As you theorized earlier."

"Yes, but why? What would anyone stand to gain from tensions between the Zeshi and the Shiko?"

"War would interfere with their ability to fulfil their contracts," Batu said, after a moment. "Not at first, but in the long run, their business interests would suffer. Not just here, but everywhere."

"Yes. And who gains by such a breakdown in the order of

things?" Shin shook his head. "That is why I will expand my investigation. I will ask those who know best about such matters. Speaking of which – have you spoken to the merchants yet?"

"I have."

"And?"

"They have reluctantly agreed to speak to you."

"How gracious of them."

Batu snorted. "The local trade association is headed up by a heimin merchant named Yuzu. He's agreed to speak with you on behalf of the rest."

"He serves the Unicorn?"

Batu's smile was hard. "The Ide."

"Ah. Then it may be that he has ulterior motives for speaking with me."

Batu shrugged. "Why you even wish to speak to such a disreputable creature, I do not know. I cannot see what good might come of it."

"Merchants – and more importantly, heimin – talk. They gossip about everything, especially their betters. You could do worse than to listen occasionally."

"I am not an imbecile, Shin. I know the value of informers."

Shin twitched a finger chidingly. "Informers tell you what you wish to know. Listening to gossip will tell you what you need to know, before you wish to know it."

"The wisdom of a courtier."

Shin shrugged elegantly. "Wisdom is wisdom, regardless of its origin."

"Then hear this, O wise one – you are out of time. This arrived while you were out making enemies." Batu held up a folded missive, its seal broken. "From the daimyo of the Shiko family. The Ide representative will be here earlier than we expected. Today, in fact." He tossed the letter onto his writing desk. "They will be here this afternoon, after they have paid a call to the Zeshi."

"That explains why Shijan sent armed men to reclaim his cousin," Shin mused.

"Undoubtedly. The Ide wish to ensure that the Shiko are treated fairly, and do not trust you to arbitrate the matter without bias."

"My word, did they write that in the letter?"

Batu frowned. "No. I was summarizing."

"Ah." Shin extended his hand. "May I?"

Batu sighed and handed the letter over. Shin scanned it quickly and folded it. The Ide had decided to take a hand in things – likely, they simply wanted to pressure Batu into passing the expected sentence. "Well, this complicates matters somewhat, I admit. But perhaps to our advantage. If we could speak to them, make them understand the situation…"

"There is no situation," Batu said. "There is nothing to be done here, except the obvious. The yojimbo will die, and negotiations will resume."

"And then, when the next interruption occurs? Or the one after that?" Shin folded his hands into his lap. "Think, Batu – look at the whole picture, not just your part of it."

"The whole picture is not my concern, Shin." Batu thumped the desk with his hand. "This part is. A magistrate has a duty – I have a duty. If I do not fulfil this duty on behalf of my clan, what good am I?"

"Duty is open to interpretation," Shin countered.

"Not for some of us." Batu set the writing desk aside and rose abruptly. Shin followed suit, though he remained still as Batu began to pace. The look on the other man's face was familiar from their days as students.

"Willow bark might be of help," Shin ventured.

"It is not. Some pain must simply be endured." Batu rubbed his brow, eyes closed. "When the representative arrives, I will have no choice. Surely you understand that."

"Understanding and agreement are two different things." Shin paused. "There is an option – the representative must be delayed, but without causing insult."

"I don't see how."

Shin smiled. "Because you are not a Crane." He tapped his lips with his fan, pondering the situation. "You Unicorns are trained to ride, and we Cranes are trained to prevaricate." Shin hoped he sounded more confident than he felt. The truth was, he wasn't certain that Batu wasn't right. That the only solution available to them at the moment was the most obvious, but he didn't feel like giving up just yet.

Batu seemed convinced, however. He sighed. "I won't pretend that I'm not hoping you're right, Shin. It's just that I doubt the Fortunes are kind enough to let you prove it."

"Nothing ventured, nothing gained," Shin said.

Batu looked away. "It's against my better judgment, but – fine." He slumped. "I will find some matter to occupy me for the next few days and delay my decision as long as possible." He sighed. "Perhaps someone will be murdered by brigands."

"That would be most fortuitous."

Batu peered at him. "I was joking."

"I wasn't." Shin turned as someone tapped gently at the door.

"Enter," Batu called out.

Nozomi slid the door open. "Lord Batu, Lord Shin's man has returned."

"Kitano? Excellent." Shin snapped his fan closed and gestured. "Let's see what he has to say for himself. Show him in." He glanced at Batu. "With your permission, of course."

Batu gestured. "When has that ever stopped you? Bring the man in, Nozomi."

Accompanied by Kasami and Nozomi, Kitano entered the study. He looked somewhat bedraggled and tired. Shin wondered how long the man had been awake. Kitano blinked when he noticed Batu's presence, and he swallowed nervously.

"Well?" Shin said. "I hope you have something to tell me, after being out all night."

Kitano nodded hurriedly. "I did as you asked, my lord. It took some doing, but I found them." He hesitated, cutting his eyes towards Batu.

Shin nodded encouragingly. "Speak freely, Kitano."

"A certain house of… ill repute in Northern Owari. Under the sign of the hare."

"The Jade Hare," Batu said. "I know it."

"Do you now?" Shin looked at him in some surprise. Batu shook his head.

"Don't be a fool. I am magistrate. I know every geisha and gambler in this city, and I know where they ply their trades."

"Did you speak to them?" Shin asked.

Kitano ducked his head. "I tried, my lord. I do not know whether they will show up or not, but…" He rummaged in his clothes and came out with a pouch that clinked pleasingly. "I expect they might, if only to get their money back."

"You stole it from them?" Batu asked, displeased.

Kitano flushed. "No, my lord! I'm no thief. I won it off them in a dice game."

"Fairly?" Shin inquired, smiling slightly.

"Well, no. But they cheated first – and badly, might I add. And they tried to beat me afterwards, when I claimed my winnings." Kitano gestured to his knife. "Luckily, I was quicker than they were."

"I do hope you didn't injure them," Shin said, more for Batu's sake than because he cared.

"Nothing more than a scratch, my lord," Kitano said. He hesitated. "There is one other thing, my lord… Zeshi Reiji was there as well. They – ah – seemed to know each other."

"How curious."

Batu laughed. "I wondered if his name would come up."

Shin frowned. "You knew he was involved?"

"I knew he was often seen in Gen's company. If anyone was placed to murmur gossip about Aimi to him, it was Reiji. But gossip is not a crime, else every courtier in the land would have lost their head by now."

"You did not think to inquire as to whether he might've said something?"

Batu sighed. "It was not pertinent."

"Not…?" Shin shook his head. "You made a mistake."

Batu's eyes narrowed. "I apologize that my foresight was not the equal of yours," he growled. Shin waved his words aside.

"You are forgiven. Aimi claims to have given the poems Ruri wrote her to a servant to burn. Only someone likely intercepted those poems. It had to have been someone in the household… perhaps Reiji."

"Unless the servant sold them," Kitano interjected.

Shin and the others looked at him. Kitano blanched and hastily added, "Some servants do that. Not me!"

"I am sure," Shin said, soothingly. "But keep talking."

Kitano licked his lips. "You… You don't see us, but we see you. Some of them – some of us, we train ourselves to be blind. Others…don't. So they sell what they know. There's always someone looking for information or gossip. You just have to know where to find them. Sometimes they find you, depending." He scratched his cheek and said, "Something like that, there's any number of people who might pay well for such a thing."

"Poems?" Batu asked, in disbelief.

Shin nodded. "Poems are as good a proof as any of illicit attachment. If someone was looking to blackmail Aimi – or Ruri – the poems would be the ideal lever."

From near the door, Kasami said, "Only they didn't blackmail either of them. They showed them to Gen, to provoke him. Why?"

"Because they knew how he would react," Shin said. "They wound him up and aimed him at the object of his ire. He already disliked Ruri, we know that much. Having received this confirmation of his doubts, he did what any half-wit bushi would do."

"He got himself killed is what he did," Batu said. "And made trouble for all of us."

"No, whoever wound him up did that, and I believe they did so knowingly." Shin stared at the ceiling, arranging the facts in his mind. Shaping the framework. "A courtier never wastes a secret. Secrets are currency. You only spend them when you have to. Whoever did this had to know Gen and Aimi personally, else why would Gen have listened to them? They also had to have a reason for exacerbating hostilities between the two families. But would a member of either family gain from such a thing?"

"Maybe they think their side can win," Nozomi said, suddenly. Shin looked at her. She flushed slightly and went on. "Peace most benefits the weaker party. If this person thought that their family might achieve victory in an outright war... then the peace would be an obstacle to that, my lord."

Kasami nodded. "She's right. The war itself might be what they want." She paused and looked at Shin. He nodded.

"It sounds rather familiar, doesn't it?"

Batu peered at them. "What do you mean?"

"It's not important," Shin said. He looked at Batu. "I need to speak to Shijan again, if possible. Tomorrow. Have him come here. In the afternoon, of course. But insist upon it."

"He won't come."

"Tell him I wish to apologize."

Batu snorted. "I've never known you to apologize."

"Nor do I intend to." Shin smiled. "But he doesn't need to know that."

CHAPTER NINETEEN
Ide Sora

As morning wore on into afternoon, Kasami stood outside the house, one hand resting on the hilt of her katana. As a concession to their host, she wore only a kimono – though she refused to part with her swords while outside. Nozomi stood below her, on the steps, similarly attired. Hiro knelt behind them, near the door. He kept his eyes downcast and his mouth shut. Kasami approved of servants who knew their place.

However, she did not approve of those who could not keep to their appointments. "They are late," she said. The Ide had sent word they were coming, and not with the greatest of politeness. Lord Batu had warned that they might be in no mood to be polite, and so she and Nozomi were prepared for any unpleasantness that might ensue. She looked at the other woman. "So what do you think of it all?"

"What do you mean?"

"This business with the ronin – Ruri." Kasami spoke cautiously. Her conversation with Ruri was still bothering her. For as long as she could remember, a life of service had seemed the highest calling a bushi of her rank might aspire to. Duty was to be gloried in, for with it came purpose. When one did not have either, what was left?

"Your master asked me that before," Nozomi said.

"Now I ask you."

Nozomi peered at her, a slight smile curving across her face. "I think I would have done the same as the ronin. You?"

"I have done the same."

"I do not think I would have run."

"Nor I," Kasami said, with some satisfaction. It was good to find another who agreed with her. "She claims her mistress ordered her to flee." She paused. "I think Lord Shin would do the same – he is soft, despite my best efforts."

Nozomi looked away. "It is a rare lord who concerns themselves with the lives of their subordinates. I do not know what Lord Batu would do. I doubt he knows himself."

"He does not strike me as a man given to uncertainty," Kasami said, carefully.

"He is not – but in some ways, he is. I am sure your master is the same."

Kasami gave a bark of laughter. "He is anything but uncertain. Too full of himself, if anything. It gets him into trouble – and me with him."

"So I have heard." Nozomi frowned. "Is it true he once kidnapped a daughter of the Scorpion, and from her own bedchambers?"

Kasami grimaced. "Yes, though it was not as simple as the story claims."

"Were you there?"

"I was. Though I was otherwise occupied at the time."

Nozomi raised an eyebrow, and Kasami shrugged. "Someone had to distract the guards," she said, without elaboration.

Nozomi gave a soft laugh and shook her head. "Trouble indeed. I have a hard time imagining Lord Batu engaging in such... adventures."

"Count yourself lucky." Kasami looked up at the branches of the trees that shaded the front of the house. "Your master has done very well for himself. He does his duty and is respected for it."

It was Nozomi's turn to frown. "That is not entirely accurate."

"No?"

"Sadly, no. When he – when we – arrived, the city had not known the authority of a magistrate for some time."

"There was one here, surely?"

"There was. He was old, and liked his sake and his opium, and he liked to keep his opinions to himself. Many preferred him to a more... active adjudicator."

"You said the city was largely sedate."

"Only because most of the criminal gangs had killed each other by the time we arrived." Nozomi looked down. "There's only one, now. They control every illicit activity in the city, and even a few legitimate ones."

"If you know this, why have you not dealt with them?"

"Why has the imperial governor not dealt with the smuggling gangs in the City of the Rich Frog?" Nozomi asked. She shrugged. "They are useful."

Kasami nodded in understanding. There were some things bushi could not do, or rather, be seen to do; those tasks – illegal, but often necessary – frequently fell to others. Smuggling was one such. Murder was another.

She was spared from having to comment on this by the arrival of their guests. The Ide's appearance was accompanied by the clatter of armor and the stamp of hooves. An escort of two dozen ashigaru in full armor trotted alongside the horses. Nozomi stiffened at the sight of them.

Bodyguards were common enough, as were escorts – but this was something else. A show of force. The Ide were flexing their muscle for all to see. Kasami, used to such displays, was unimpressed. The Lion regularly paraded three times this number of soldiers through the streets of the City of the Rich Frog.

As such, she kept her hands away from her weapons. Nozomi followed suit, though it was clear that it was more of an effort on her part. Then, it was her master who was being threatened, albeit in a roundabout fashion.

Lord Koji was the first to swing down from his saddle. He approached slowly, and seemed unhappy to be there. He looked up at Kasami and Nozomi and said, "The Lady Sora has come to pay her respects to Lord Batu. For their sakes, I hope your masters have something to tell her."

Shin watched the Ide representative seat herself. Ide Sora was a short woman, and stout. Matronly, Shin might have said, were she not somewhat younger than himself and had he not seen the glint in her eye as she entered the receiving room. She presented herself with barely any announcement, and bullied her way in, in defiance of protocol. Proof of her irritation, if not her determination.

She did not come alone. While her bodyguards waited outside, in a polite but wary standoff with Nozomi and Kasami,

Suio Umeko was with her, as were Lord Koji and his wife. The matchmaker had her eyes downcast, and looked as if she would rather be anywhere else. Koji looked nervous, but defiant. Himari just looked concerned.

The introductions did not go well. Though they were of similar rank, Shin would not have known it from Batu's behavior. Deferential was too polite a word for it. Obsequious, perhaps. Servile, even. Sora clearly intimidated him.

"My lady, there was no need for you to come all the way to Hisatu-Kesu," Batu was saying. "The matter of the ronin is in hand, and will be resolved shortly."

"I too regret the necessity of my presence, Iuchi Batu. Would that you had resolved the matter before my arrival, and I could depart, satisfied."

"And miss out on the pleasures of this city?" Shin said, from where he sat to Batu's right. "That would be a shame, I think."

She stiffened and turned to fix him with a steely eye. "My apologies," she said. "I did not notice you there." Umeko made a strangled sound that might have been a laugh, and the Shiko had the good grace to look embarrassed. Shin and Sora ignored them.

"All is forgiven. I am sure you were otherwise preoccupied."

Sora looked him up and down. "You are the Daidoji."

"Daidoji Shin." He bowed. "At your service."

"You are most certainly not." She sniffed. "It is disappointing, but unsurprising, that the Iuchi sent a Crane to do their work for them."

Shin tilted his head. "A little surprising, I should think."

She sniffed again. "The Iuchi are easily distracted by the whispers of spirits. The day-to-day is tedious for them."

"Clearly we have spoken to different Iuchi."

"Clearly." She looked at Batu. "I understand from Lord Koji that the matter is settled to the satisfaction of both families." She indicated Koji with her fan. "Why then is the murderer still alive?"

Batu hesitated. "My lady, it is… complicated."

"Then uncomplicate it. A simple blow from your sword will serve, I think."

Shin laughed softly. When she turned to look at him, her expression one of annoyance, he said, "I was given to understand that Ide emissaries are often practitioners of the peaceful path. Compromise and mutual satisfaction."

"Yes, but here a compromise has already been reached. You stand in its way. So I will do my best to move you aside."

Shin allowed himself a smile. He saw a faint flicker of growing irritation in her eyes, and let the smile widen into something sharp. "I stand in the way of but one aspect of the matter – the unjust death of the yojimbo, Katai Ruri." He gestured airily. "As for the rest, well, as you said. It is done."

"The yojimbo's death is the crux of the matter. Without it, the pattern unravels."

"Then it is not a well-designed pattern, I fear."

"What is your interest in this, Crane? What right have you to interfere with an internal clan matter?"

"I was asked."

"Yet I would expect a Crane to know better than to fly into a roaring fire."

"Hardly roaring. Gently smoldering, I would say." Shin snapped open his fan. "I was asked, and I agreed, and that is all there is to it, my lady."

"Your presence here is an insult," she said, mildly. "A calculated one, I expect."

"If you wish to see it as such, I cannot stop you."

"Nor would you try. If I were to protest, the Iuchi would have no choice but to withdraw you and send a more appropriate representative. If they did not simply wash their hands of the affair."

"That is true. But I do not think you will do so."

"No?"

"No. You can see as well as I that this solution is both inelegant and inefficient."

She smiled mirthlessly. "Trust a Crane to be concerned about elegance."

"But you see my point – this will only solve the problem in the short term. Long term, the underlying hostilities will continue to fester. Soon they will flare up again, and again and again, until someone puts an actual effort towards solving the problem."

"Are you volunteering?"

Shin shook his head. "Perish the thought, my lady. As you said, it is an internal matter. I merely wish to help lance the boil, so to speak. Purge some of the bad feeling."

"By exacerbating the situation," she said, sharply.

"By getting to the bottom of things."

She relaxed slightly "Ah. Your theory that there is a third party involved."

"Yes." He was somewhat surprised that she knew of it, but was careful to let nothing show on his face. From their expressions, Koji and the others had not been informed of this development.

"What do you mean, a third party?" Koji asked.

"It does not matter," Sora said, not looking at him. "A waste of time."

Shin nodded. "Possibly. But are you in such a hurry as to willfully condemn an innocent woman simply for the sake of convenience?"

"For the sake of convenience – no. For the sake of peace? Yes. You would do the same, I think, were you in my place."

Shin let his smile slip. "No. I would not."

"Then you are a fool," she said, simply. She turned to Batu. "As are you, Iuchi Batu. I will make a formal complaint as to your behavior in this matter, when it is concluded. Letting yourself be talked into such needless complications – and by one who is not even of our clan, no less – is shameful, and unworthy of an Iuchi magistrate." She looked down her nose at him. "I was told you were a disappointment to your family, and now I see it to be true. It is sad to me that you have gone to such lengths to cover yourself in false glory."

Batu flushed at her words. He seemed to sink into himself, and he swallowed thickly. Shin saw a vein in his temple swell, and knew that if Batu replied, it would only be to his detriment. Shin cleared his throat.

"I see only one disappointment here."

Sora's gaze flicked to him. "Meaning?"

"You are so eager to be done with this business that you miss the obvious."

"Pray enlighten me."

"What happens when it all comes undone again?"

Sora said nothing. Shin took it as an invitation and pressed on. "If I am correct, this incident was but one of many…" He raised his fan, forestalling an outburst by Koji. "And it will not be the last. Someone is attempting to sabotage relations between the families. That they will continue these efforts is a given."

Sora digested this. "You think you can root them out."

"I do not think – I know."

"Ha! Arrogance."

"Experience," Shin corrected. "I know much of these matters, and, as you pointed out, I am a Crane, and thus predisposed to seeing plots and schemes. I would hazard a guess that I was chosen for the task for that very reason. It would not surprise me to learn that the Iuchi have suspected the same for some time. Is that not right, Lord Batu?"

Batu blinked – but nodded. He cleared his throat. "There has been… some talk on the matter, yes."

Sora looked at them both. "The Ide was not made aware of this."

"The Iuchi thought it best to be certain before such outwardly outlandish theories were put forth. It would not do to claim sabotage when it was only simple human error at work, now would it?"

"But you are certain now."

Shin nodded. "Oh yes, quite certain."

"This is preposterous," Koji said. "You cannot honestly believe that… that there is some conspiracy here? My brother died because he was a fool, and that ronin was quicker on the draw! No other reason."

Shin looked at him. "But who put your brother in that position in the first place, hmm? Who sent him – and why?"

Koji sat back, looking uncomfortable. Shin smiled courteously. "As I have said before, I understand that my investigation is inconvenient. But would it not be worse to allow the true architect of this crime to go unpunished – or worse, emboldened to strike again?"

"What are your intentions, Crane?" Sora asked.

"To find the truth of the matter."

"Truth is what the majority accepts."

"I agree."

Sora smiled thinly. "Very well." She looked at Batu. "I will be overseeing the negotiations from this point. It is my intention to bring the conflict in Hisatu-Kesu between the families to an end. You have until I do so to show me a truth I will accept. If you do not, the ronin will die and we will speak no more of it."

Shin smiled graciously. "It shall be done."

She fixed him with a stern eye. "And you are not to speak to any member of either family without my permission. Is that understood?"

Shin's smile faltered, but only for an instant. "Of course. I would not dream of it."

Sora snorted and bowed her head. "Lord Batu – Lord Shin. It has been a pleasure." She rose without waiting to be dismissed. Koji and Himari followed, leaving only Umeko, who stayed seated, waiting for her betters to leave the room first.

Shin looked at her. "They have kept you on, then."

"In case it is decided another marriage is needed," she said. She glanced at him. "If you're wondering, she's unwed. Her parents are hoping to see her safely married in the next year or two."

"I was not wondering about that at all."

"No?"

"Not a bit."

"Are you sure?" Umeko asked, smiling slightly. "I thought I detected a certain… something there, between you. A spark of interest, perhaps?"

Shin fixed her with a hard stare. "No."

Umeko's smile didn't falter. "I'll ask her, if you like."

"No. Thank you, but no."

Umeko sniffed. "Men. You never know what's good for you." She bowed to Batu, and followed Sora and the others out. Batu looked at Shin.

Shin held up a warning finger. "Not a word."

CHAPTER TWENTY
Cousins

Zeshi Shijan arrived late in the afternoon, but not discourteously so. Shin was taking his exercise in the clearing behind Batu's home, among the outbuildings. Ordinarily, Shin avoided prolonged bouts of exertion when possible. But a faint stiffness in his muscles that morning had warned him that he'd been indolent too long. He also wished to work off some of the frustration he felt after his confrontation with Sora.

So, when Kitano led Shijan and his servant into the clearing, Shin was sparring with Kasami. Wooden swords clacked loudly as they came together and broke apart with fluid speed. Shin was puffing slightly from his efforts to keep up with Kasami. She, on the other hand, seemed almost bored. "You are too slow," she said, swatting his sword aside and laying the edge of hers against his throat.

"I am distracted," he protested. "My mind is on more important matters."

"And that is why you would be dead, if this blade were steel and not wood. Concentrate, or do not waste my time." Kasami drew back and turned. "He's here."

Shin followed her gaze and gave a welcoming smile to Shijan. It was not returned. "Good afternoon, my lord. A fine day, I think."

"I wish to speak to you," Shijan said, brusquely.

"And I you." Shin extended his practice sword to Kitano. "Kitano, prepare me a bath, if you would. Kasami…"

"I will continue my exercises," Kasami said. Shin nodded.

"By all means." He gestured to the trees. "Shijan, walk with me." Shijan hesitated. Then, he signaled for his servant to wait for him. The man bowed low, and seemed to fold into himself as he took up a position near one of the outbuildings.

"She speaks to you with disrespect," Shijan murmured, when they were out of earshot. "If she were my bodyguard, she would know better."

"Then we must be grateful that she is not." Shin smiled. "Your man speaks little. I do not know that I could bear such silence. I find it eases my mind to know what my subordinates are thinking. I encourage them to do so – within limits, of course."

"Of course. Forgive me. I spoke without thinking." Shijan ducked his head, and Shin waved a hand in polite dismissal.

"Nothing to forgive, my friend. In fact it is I who wish to apologize to you." Shin turned to him. "I should not have spoken to Lady Aimi without your permission."

"No, you should not have." Shijan hesitated. "You played host to Ide Sora today, I think. What did you make of her?"

"A forceful presence."

"That is one way of putting it. She is here to help with the negotiations as much as anything else. It is her specialty, apparently."

"So I have heard. When do the negotiations begin?"

"Tomorrow. Early." Shijan shook his head. "I am not supposed to be here."

"Yet here you are."

"Yes." Shijan looked at the trees.

"With the marriage undone, what will you do now?" Shin asked, carefully.

"I am considering several options. Most of them lack the solidity of a marriage, however." He pinched the bridge of his nose. "Still, we will begin anew."

"As easily as that?"

"I did not say it was easy. But it must be done, for the good of both families. With Ide Sora here, perhaps things will move more smoothly."

"You have no objection to letting the Ide guide the negotiations for a new engagement?" As he'd suspected, given Umeko's continued presence, the two families had decided the best way forward was to arrange a new marriage – hopefully between more suitable candidates.

"Not at all. It shows they are taking matters seriously." Shijan paused. "The Unicorn have often fostered rivalries between their forge families in order to elicit better results – I am sure the Crane behave similarly."

"At times."

"That they have decided to put an end to it – at least here – shows that they have realized what is at stake. That violence here will lead to violence elsewhere, and worse, a disruption in the production of armor and leather goods. Without us – without the Shiko – the Unicorn's ability to wage war is significantly reduced."

"Of course, the Unicorn are not currently at war."

Shijan shook his head. "And when has that state of affairs

ever lasted? There are always rumblings – always rumors. War is a constant." He paused, staring into the trees. "The only ones who ever seem to profit from it are the merchants. Sometimes I wish..." He composed himself. "Never mind."

"No, say on," Shin said, invitingly.

Shijan glared at him – an open glare. He had dispensed with his polite mask. "Why? So you can mock me?"

"No. Not today. I merely wish to understand."

Shijan looked away. After a moment, he said, "Do you know what they call me, behind my back? Popinjay. They think me less because I yearn for more." He plucked at his kimono. "Do you know what we are taught here? How to ride, how to fight – and how to make money." His expression turned sour. "The first two, fine. But the last? What sort of thing is that for a bushi to know?"

"I find it comes in handy, myself."

"But it is not the sum total of your knowledge, is it? You learned the courtier's arts – how to talk, how to dance, how to write. Things largely denied me. It was more important that I learn how to hunt down brigands or calculate cargo costs than to converse with my betters." Shijan shook his head. "And because I taught myself those things, they think me a fool. Even that dull-witted lump of a magistrate thinks I have ideas above my station." He gestured vaguely towards Batu's house.

"By itself, ambition is no sin," Shin said. "I have largely avoided it myself, but it is seen as a virtue by some. I am told that a samurai must strive for betterment in all things."

Shijan looked at him. "Maybe you do understand." He sighed. "I did not want to be in this position, my lord. To be head of the family – of this branch of the family. I do not think my shoulders are strong enough to bear the weight."

"Why did you not want Aimi to speak to me?"

The question jolted Shijan, as Shin had hoped it might. Shijan frowned. "She often says too much, or not enough. I did not wish to involve her in this unfortunate business any more than she already is. It is my duty to look out for her welfare now, with her father's... absence."

"Her welfare, and the welfare of the Zeshi."

Shijan nodded. "They are one and the same." He sighed. "If only Gen hadn't died." He looked up, staring past the branches and the leaves to the sky overhead. After a moment, he said, "I was a fool. I knew Aimi did not wish to marry Gen, but I assumed she would do as was needed. But I did not think she would do this."

Shin paused. "What did she do?"

"Isn't it obvious?" Shijan looked at him. "She provoked Gen somehow and set that rogue lion of hers on him. If I'd known that's what she was planning, I'd never have let her go out that day."

"That is not the way she tells it."

"Of course not," Shijan snorted. "She's still a child in many ways. I doubt she truly understands what she's done."

"And what about her brother, Reiji?" Shin asked.

The look on Shijan's face spoke volumes. He paused and said, "What about him?"

Shin nodded. "He is somewhat troublesome, is he not?"

"Hisatu-Kesu holds many temptations for the weak of spirit."

"What did Reiji think of the marriage?"

"He was all for it. Gen and he were... friends, I suppose."

"You suppose?"

"Friendly rivals, let us say. Reiji has ever chosen unsuitable company. Gen and his cousins fit the bill. Reiji strove to emulate them, Gen especially – and to outdo them."

"And what did Gen think of this?"

Shijan shrugged. "You would have to ask him. I rarely considered Gen's thoughts on anything. Or Reiji's, for that matter."

"I would like to speak to him, if I might."

"So would I," Shijan said. "He embarrassed me today. He was not at home when Lady Sora paid her visit." Another hesitation. "I do not know where he is. Likely out making a spectacle of himself in the red lantern district."

"Does he do so often?"

"More than I care to admit." Shijan paused again. "He has debts."

"Many bushi do."

"Foolish bushi. His debts are greater than he can manage on the stipend I allow him. I often fear… Well. It is of no matter."

Shin smiled. "If you thought to mention it, it obviously is. Speak freely." Shijan was clever, but not so clever as he imagined. He was trying to bait Shin into asking questions that he'd no doubt prepared answers for.

Shijan licked his lips. "I believe Reiji might have… taken some of my papers. Records, mostly." The forge families kept meticulous records of every item they crafted, whom it had been sold to and when. Such information could be dangerous in the wrong hands. "And delivery manifests as well. Nor is it the first time."

Shin paused. That was even worse, if it was true. Delivery manifests might allow cunning thieves to intercept deliveries.

The stolen armor could be resold later, or even put to use by the thieves themselves, depending on their intentions. "Why do you believe it was him?"

Shijan shook his head. "You called him troublesome. He is a good deal worse than that. As I said, he owes money to certain parties. I fear he may have taken those papers to pay off his debts." He sighed. "I tell you this only because I wished to warn you that he might not take kindly to being questioned. If you find him."

"Rest assured, we will take care," Shin began. "I... What is that racket?" He turned towards the gate, where a muffled confrontation seemed to be taking place. He could see nothing from where he stood, but it sounded unpleasant. "Kasami," he called out. "See to it, please." He looked back at Shijan. "Forgive me, my lord. It seems we have uninvited guests."

"I have often chastised Lord Batu for choosing to make his home here, where there is little privacy." Shijan shook his head as if disappointed by Batu's intransigence. He looked at Shin. "I have answered your questions. Answer one of mine, if you would."

"Of course."

"Do you... Do you think there is something afoot? Truly, I mean."

Shin considered how best to answer without giving anything away. Something told him Shijan was doing some investigating of his own. Finally, he said, "If I did not, I would not still be here. Now – it might be best if you were to leave by the service entrance, if you wish to avoid whatever is going on at the gate."

As Kasami strode towards the front of the house, the sound

of voices raised in argument grew more strident. She spied Nozomi hurrying towards the gate as well, a look of concern on her face. "It is Totara Ikki and his cronies. They're demanding entrance. Something about a stolen purse." She gave Kasami a meaningful look. "Does your master still wish to see them?"

"Unfortunately. Will they cause trouble? I would hate to have to kill them." Kasami's finger tap-tapped against the hilt of her sword. Nozomi glanced first at her finger, and then at her, expressionless.

"Forgive me for saying so, but I do not think you would hate that at all."

Kasami ceased her tapping and pulled her hand away from her sword. "Perhaps I am a bit hasty. My apologies."

"Do not apologize. I would enjoy watching you remove their swollen heads. But Lord Batu would suffer if you did so, so I ask that you restrain yourself, if possible."

Kasami took the gentle chastisement with good grace. Nozomi was not wrong – she was spoiling for a fight. It had been too long since she'd drawn her blade with any purpose save to sharpen it. And practice with Shin was not the same as a real fight.

At the gate, Batu's men were trying ineffectually to calm the trio of bushi who were demanding entry. The three were dressed well, in rich robes bearing their family crest – though the robes were stained and disheveled. All three were armed, though from the look of them Kasami thought they were more a danger to themselves than anyone else, given the state they were in. Even so, it would not do to give them an excuse to spill blood.

"Let them past," Nozomi called. "We will escort them to the house."

The guards stepped back reluctantly, allowing Ikki and his fellows to spill past. "Make way, make way, we demand to speak to the magistrate," the tallest of the three slurred as he stumbled up the walk. He gestured expansively.

The shortest and broadest spoke up then. "Where is Batu? Is he not brave enough to meet us himself, after having sent a peasant to cheat us?" He gestured with a sake jug at Nozomi. "He sends his woman instead. I am insulted. Are you not insulted, cousin?"

"Deeply," the third replied. He was not as drunk as his fellows, but there was a feral glint in his eye that Kasami did not like. This one wanted to fight, to make trouble. She was starting to understand how Shiko Gen had wound up dead, if these were his companions.

The third one pushed away from the others, swayed slightly, and braced the two women. He pointed at Kasami. "Pretty bird, where is your master? I am Totara Ikki, and I have words for the Crane – and I would have my money back."

Kasami eyed him, noting his unsteadiness and the way his hand fiddled with the hilt of his sword. "Oh? And what money might that be?"

"The money his man stole from us. Step aside now, for your betters." He made a dismissive gesture. "Step aside, I say."

Kasami glanced back at the house and saw that Hiro, Batu's servant, was waiting by the door. The boy was huddled, ready to take their swords. But the look on his face said he'd rather have been without that particular responsibility.

"We will be happy to do so, Master Ikki," Nozomi said.

"Once you and Masters Giichi and Aito have handed over your swords."

Ikki spun, his gaze settling on her. "And why should we do that, then? So that you might slay us, the way an Iuchi yojimbo slew our dear cousin?"

Kasami blinked. Such rudeness could only be explained by Ikki's inebriated state – or perhaps he was simply mad. She'd met many mad bushi in her short life. Shin had a way of bringing that madness out of them; that urge to cut down whatever offended them, with no thought to the consequences.

Ikki continued. "Are you any less an Iuchi dog, woman? Waiting to add more Ide blood to the tally, eh?" He pressed close to Nozomi, stinking of alcohol and stupidity. "Maybe we should even the score, ha? Take your head, the way you took Gen's…"

Kasami's sword flashed from its sheath, and the flat of it tapped against the underside of his chin. He froze, and his companions cursed and scrambled for their own blades. Nozomi stepped away from Ikki and faced them, her hand on the hilt of her weapon.

"Think carefully about the next few moments," Kasami said, not taking her eyes from Ikki. "Think about how this will be spoken of when the blood has dried. Who do you think will be there to tell the story? You – or us?"

Ikki swallowed. "This is outrageous."

"No. It is only to be expected, given your behavior. You insult us, you insult the Iuchi, and you insult yourselves with this shameful display. Now take your feeble fingers from your sword before I remove them."

Ikki did as she bade. Kasami retracted her sword and sheathed it. She looked down at the others. "Leave your swords – and the jug of sake as well. You will be provided refreshment of a more dignified sort inside." She caught Nozomi's eye as the three men sheepishly handed over their swords.

"I trust that was restrained enough?"

CHAPTER TWENTY-ONE
Profit

Shin studied the three bushi as they were shown in to the receiving room. From the sound of it, they'd arrived inebriated, but something – or someone – had sobered them up between the gate and the door. He suspected he knew who. That was good. Newly sober men often had an easier time with the truth.

Batu sat in his accustomed place, glaring at the three. "Idiots, all three of you. If it were within my power, I would have you driven from the city and barred from ever returning." At his curt invitation, they sat in a row before him, eyes properly downcast. "Why are you here?"

Ikki looked up, flushed – angry. "This Crane stole our money!"

"That is a lie," Batu said, bluntly. Ikki flinched, as if struck. "I know it is a lie, for you three have not a koku between you. So it is someone else's money that was stolen."

Ikki rallied. "It was given to us."

"By Lady Nishi, one assumes," Batu said. He shook his head.

"This is how you thank her for her generosity. Shameful."

"Watch your tone, Iuchi," Ikki growled. Batu fixed him with a steady look.

"Or else what, Totara? Will you challenge me? What do you think will happen then?" Batu leaned forward. "Do you imagine some outcome by which you benefit? If so, I would dearly like to hear it."

Ikki fell silent. Batu stared at him a moment longer, then nodded. "I thought not. Since you did not give me an acceptable answer, I shall tell you why you are here. We have questions for you. You will answer them. If you do not, I will put you in a cell until you feel like talking. Is that understood?"

"You cannot do that," Ikki protested. "The Ide – she will not let you!"

"Why would she care? You are not Ide, you are not Shiko – indeed, locking you up is the easiest way to ensure the negotiations are free of the trouble you inevitably cause." Batu let them think on this for a moment before adding, "But I am a generous man. You will answer the Crane's questions, and then you will leave."

"With our money?" Ikki asked.

Shin reached into his kimono and produced the bag of koku he had taken from Kitano. He tossed it onto the floor before them. "I trust it is all there," he said, softly. Ikki glared at him, but only for a moment. He and his companions hurried to gather it up.

When they'd finished, Ikki made to speak, but Shin interrupted. "I appreciate your willingness to speak with me."

"Of course my lord," the short one – Aito – said, in an obsequious tone. The other two nodded, heads bobbing like corks on the water. Aito swallowed and added, "Though, it must be said that we have already given testimony as to what occurred, and the ronin confessed. Surely that is an end to it?"

Shin gave a thin smile. "Ordinarily, yes. Even so, I would like you to tell me what happened that day, to the best of your recollection."

They looked at one another. It was as if they shared a single mind, and any decision had to be agreed upon by all three. Shin hid a smile and waited for them to decide who was going to talk. As he expected, it was Ikki. The lean samurai braced his hands on his knees and cleared his throat. "It is as we told the magistrate, my lord. Cousin Gen wished to confront his intended, and we could not in good conscience let him go alone."

"Why?"

"The bodyguard, my lord. She is vicious."

Shin nodded. "I see. Please continue."

Ikki swallowed. "As we told Lord Batu, we – Gen – confronted them in the market. Gen spoke harshly to Lady Aimi, and her bodyguard attacked him. We were not quick enough to prevent what followed."

"She attacked him. Unprovoked?"

Ikki glanced at the other two and nodded. "Before we knew it, she had drawn her sword and split him open." His face twisted into an expression of frustrated grief. "She never even gave him a chance!"

Shin saw Aito look away, and pounced. "Is that true, Master Aito?"

Aito jolted and turned. "It is as Ikki said, my lord." He swallowed. "Though… Gen may have had his sword in his hand." Ikki glared at him, but said nothing.

"Ah. Would you not consider that provocation?"

"He would not have hurt her," Ikki insisted.

"Was she to know that? Or her bodyguard?" Shin stroked his chin. "Why did Gen see fit to attack his intended in such a manner?"

"Gen claimed someone had told him that she was unfaithful," Ikki said, sullenly. He scratched at his throat. "That she had a lover."

"Was there a name to go with the gossip?"

"It wasn't gossip – it was the truth," Ikki insisted.

"How do you know?"

"She didn't deny it!"

Aito cleared his throat. "To be fair, she did. Several times." He glanced at Shin, shamefaced. "Gen wasn't in the mood to listen."

Shin fixed Aito with a steady stare. "Because you had convinced him to drown his sorrows, I take it?"

Aito's eyes fell. "It seemed the thing to do," he mumbled.

Shin looked at Ikki. "So, you encouraged him to confront her. Why?"

"I just said–" Ikki began, but Shin cut him off with a gesture.

"The real reason, please. There was no satisfaction to be gained from such a confrontation, and you knew it. So why?"

Ikki licked his lips. "The Zeshi are arrogant. They think themselves better than us. I wanted to be there when Gen threw her dowry back in her face." He grimaced. "A bit of fighting would have been good for him. Good for us."

Shin sat back. "What happened after he challenged her with this revelation?"

Ikki fell silent. Aito looked at the floor. Shin switched his gaze to Giichi. The tall man swallowed nervously and his eyes skidded about, as if seeking some escape. Finally, he said, "He… might have threatened her life."

"Might have?"

"He did," Aito sighed. "We all heard him. But it wasn't serious. Gen was all bluster."

"Did she know that?"

The three men were silent. Shin waited. Aito grunted and said, "There was still no call to kill him. That ronin was just waiting for the opportunity."

"Why do you say that?" Shin asked, sharply.

Aito flinched. "You… You could tell, my lord. You can't trust them. Ronin, I mean. Disreputable, clanless – not trustworthy."

"And that is your reasoning?"

"No! No. I mean, she was always watching him. Us. As if we were a threat."

"Did Gen – or you – give her some reason to think of you as such?"

"No," Ikki snapped.

"Yes," Giichi said. He looked at the others, as if daring them to stop him. Then, "Gen paid her a visit one night. He was drunk. He made some… inappropriate comments and she had him thrown out."

"You know this how?" Shin asked. He could imagine what sort of comments they might have been.

"We were there," Aito said. "Outside. We might have… encouraged him a bit before he went in." He swallowed. "A bit of a joke. No harm was meant."

Ikki glared at his cousins in disgust. "It was his right. They were to be married."

"In point of fact, such a thing is not within the rights of a man, married or not. I am surprised he did not perish then and there." Shin paused. "Am I correct in thinking that this incident fueled his eagerness to believe that he had a rival for Aimi's affections?"

The other two looked at Ikki, who flushed. Shin nodded. "Ah. Not just him, then."

"Something was going on," Ikki spat. He shook his head. "Why else would she be so… so cold, eh? Gen was a good man."

"Good at getting into trouble," Aito muttered. He subsided as Ikki glared at him.

"How did Gen feel about his marriage?" Shin asked.

"He was pleased," Ikki said. "And why wouldn't he be? She was a suitable match, even if she was a Zeshi." He met Shin's gaze. "That is why he acted as he did. Her treachery hurt him, and he was right to confront her – what would you have done, my lord?"

"I would not have gone after her with a naked sword in my hand," Shin said, softly. "And I certainly would not have pickled my wits in sake first."

Ikki flushed a deeper hue, and made as if to rise. Batu stirred, and the other two stopped Ikki with looks and gestures. Shin watched them and made no comment. He was certain that they were telling the truth, insofar as they knew it. They were not cunning enough to lie, at least not to him. "I asked earlier if you knew who might have told Gen of this supposed treachery. You never answered me. So I ask again – who told him?"

"He never said," Aito insisted.

"Take a guess," Shin murmured. "Who might have told him?"

The three traded glances. Finally, Ikki said, "Reiji. I think it was Reiji."

"Zeshi Reiji?" Shin raised an eyebrow. "Why do you think that?"

"He… brought Gen something. Something that upset him."

Shin digested this. He needed to speak with Reiji as soon as possible. "And have you spoken to Zeshi Reiji since?"

"No, my lord," Aito said. "We thought it best to keep our distance from the Zeshi, and they from us. No one wanted another… incident."

"Wise," Shin said. He gestured airily. "I thank you for your time, my lords. You may go. Though I may wish to speak to you again in the near future."

But as they made to rise, Shin spoke up. "One more thing, if I might…" They froze, waiting. "On the subject of Zeshi Reiji – I am told he is in debt to certain individuals of low morals. Is this true?"

The three looked at one another. Ikki nodded. "Yes, my lord. The little… fool fancies himself a gambler. He's in it up to his neck, last I heard."

"To whom does he owe money?"

Another pause. What might have been a look of calculation passed across Ikki's face, and he said, "Honesty-sama." Batu hissed in surprise. Shin ignored him.

"Ah. I have heard that name several times since arriving, but have not yet had the pleasure of the man's company. Is he so fearsome, then?"

"I would not know," Ikki said, quickly. "I know only what I hear, and what I hear is that Reiji is desperate to pay off his debts. Honesty-sama isn't the sort of man to care much for a man's status. He'll bury a bushi as quickly as a peasant." He looked uncomfortable as he said it, and Shin gestured.

"Thank you. That is all. You may go."

They went. When they had safely departed, he turned to Batu. "What do you think?"

"I think they told us nothing new."

"Perhaps. Earlier, Shijan implied that Aimi was the one who provoked Gen, so as to get out of the marriage."

Batu frowned. "That's… interesting."

"I was thinking of another word."

"So was I," Batu said. "Convenient."

"Yes." Shin paused. "Shijan was angry, but he was frightened as well. It might have been a ploy to make me more sympathetic to his revelation, but I do not think he is that good an actor." He gestured with his fan. "Something has him worried, and I do not think it is us." He paused. "At least, not us alone."

"Shijan has much to lose if it comes to war, and he knows it," Batu said. "He is not the sort of man to guide his family safely through such a storm. If the worst occurs, the Zeshi will send another to take over operations in the city."

"What of Aimi?" Shin asked.

Batu considered this. "Aimi is too young. Too headstrong. In a few years, with the right teachers, she might make a capable leader. As it stands, neither of them is experienced in such matters." He shrugged. "Then, neither are the Shiko."

"And yet they might be willing to risk it, if the reward is great enough."

"That is what my mind sticks on," Batu said, suddenly. "The reward… What is the reward here? What is to be gained? We still have no answer to that question."

"No, and that worries me. Shijan has given us a neat solution to the conundrum. A headstrong girl, looking to escape an unwelcome situation, engineers the death of her intended. Perhaps she did not mean for Gen to die, but die he did. And Ruri, being the loyal yojimbo, seeks to protect her mistress."

"But what about what she told you? About her and Ruri?"

Shin shook his head. "Nothing she told us contradicts Shijan's revelation. Indeed, it only strengthens the theory."

"But you do not believe it," Batu said.

"Do you?" Shin ran a hand through his hair. "You've known her longer than I; is Aimi capable of such deception?"

Batu slowly shook his head. "No. Or at least, I would have said such, before all this began. She is headstrong, yes. But not cunning – clever, yes, but not cunning. You understand what I mean?"

Shin nodded. "I do. If she had not intended to go through with the marriage, she would never have agreed to it in the first place. That she did implies that she meant to do what was best for her family, whatever the personal consequences might have been." He hesitated. "What about Reiji?"

"What about him?"

"Shijan also mentioned that Reiji might have stolen some papers from him."

"Papers?"

"Forge records."

Batu grunted. "Did he mention anything else while he was being so talkative?"

"Reiji is missing."

"Wonderful."

"If Reiji is looking to pay off his debt to Honesty-sama, selling that sort of information might be the way to do it," Shin said. "And consider this – how hard would it have been to acquire similar records from the Shiko? Especially if he were friends with Gen."

Batu shook his head. "I've met the boy, Shin. He's a petulant fool."

"I've met him as well, however briefly – and I agree. But this is the sort of thing a petulant fool might do. Especially one in debt to someone like the infamous Honesty-sama."

Batu grunted. "Is this a theory, or a fact?"

"That depends on whether you think Shijan and Ikki were telling the truth," Shin said. "I think I shall need to talk to Ruri again – tomorrow morning, perhaps. And you need to start looking for Reiji."

Batu nodded wearily. "Ide Sora will not like this, if she learns of it."

"The more quickly he is found, the less likely she is to find out." Shin rose. "Like good hunters, we can but follow the trails where they lead." He paused at the door.

"Though I will say, this one is proving somewhat crooked, to say the least."

CHAPTER TWENTY-TWO
Bargain

Aimi moved through the house like a ghost, not quite seeing the rooms around her. She wished she had not burned the poems. They were the only thing she had of Ruri's. If the worst were to happen – she would have nothing at all.

Her hands clenched and relaxed. Her father had once said her habit of flexing her hands was akin to muttering to oneself. She did not smile at the thought. Memory of her father did not bring joy – only sorrow.

She stopped. Her feet had taken her to her father's study. She paused outside the door. Shijan had taken it, as he had taken everything. She did not begrudge him such privileges, though it would have been easy to do so.

Her father was gone; someone had to take control. To steer the ship. The thought brought with it another wave of sadness. First her father, then Ruri – it had been too much. She was honest enough with herself to know she was not ready for such challenges. Maybe one day, but not now.

Idly, she peered into the room – and stopped.

"Reiji, what are you doing?" she called out. Her brother was stooped, looking in one of the cabinets that lined the far wall. He shouldn't have been in here. Shijan would be upset.

Reiji turned, startled. "Looking for something," he said, almost too quickly for her to follow. He didn't bother to gesture. He rarely did. "Not that it is any of your business, sister. Shouldn't you be moping somewhere, or have you finally come to terms with it?"

Aimi glowered at him. Reiji had taken a nasty delight in her suffering. He always had, even as a child. As the youngest, he was free to do so, and she had endured it as an older sibling must. But not today. *It is not my fault Gen is dead,* she signed. *He was a fool.*

"Gen was not a fool – save when it came to you," Reiji said. He went through the cabinets one by one. She wondered what he was looking for.

She stepped into the room and stood over him. *What is that supposed to mean?* Her gestures were sharp – combative.

Reiji rounded on her, and she took a step back. "You led him on, and then, when he'd had enough, you had your pet lion kill him."

Aimi shook her head, appalled by his words. Reiji had always lived in his own world – he saw things how he wished, not how they were. Their father had coddled him; he'd been so young when their mother died, barely more than an infant. Her father had not had the heart to discipline him, not in any way that mattered. And Shijan was even worse.

I made my feelings clear in no uncertain terms, she signed, feeling the old anger build. As the youngest, Reiji should have been the one to marry for political reasons, but she had shouldered that responsibility willingly, though not happily.

Reiji snorted. "Say what you like, sister, but I know the truth." He dropped to his knees and lifted a tatami mat. He gave the floorboard a knock. She heard nothing, but he seemed pleased by whatever sound it made. "Ha! I knew it."

She tapped at his shoulder, trying to get him to look at her. When he didn't, she said, "Knew what, brother – what are you doing?"

"Getting what I am owed." He started prying at a floorboard. It came free more quickly that Aimi would have expected. Reiji reached in and removed a pouch that clinked.

You're stealing from Shijan, Aimi signed, her gesture one of disbelief.

Reiji stood, bouncing the pouch on his palm. "No. He stole from me. These are my winnings from my last run at the dice. He confiscated them. Said it was the price I paid for embarrassing him." He beamed at his sister. "He thinks that I do not know about his hiding spots. For a caretaker, he is not very good at taking care."

Aimi frowned at him. Her hands moved slowly. *Are you mad, or just a fool?*

"I told you, I am not stealing! This was mine."

Reiji froze even as the words left his mouth. Aimi turned, realizing someone was behind them. Shijan stood in the doorway, studying them with what she thought might be amusement. "Take it," he said, gesturing for her benefit. "I suggest you use it to pay off a few of your remaining debts." He entered the room, and his cousins stepped aside. Shijan's man waited in the corridor, head bowed.

Aimi covertly observed him. She could not recall when he had come into Shijan's service. She could not recall much about any of the servants, something Ruri used to chide her for. Shijan looked down at the hole in his floor, and then at Reiji. "Were you going to replace the board, or…?"

Reiji sneered. "You do it. It's your floor."

Shijan nodded. "So it is."

"Until Aimi comes of age, at least. Then it will be hers. Or mine."

"Even so. Until then, I am in charge. Which is your bad luck."

Reiji frowned. "What do you mean?"

Shijan fixed him with a stare. "The Ide have suggested, quite charitably, that a new marriage be arranged. For you. A wife from another province, with familial ties to both the Ide and the Shiko. A suitable match, I am told."

"I… I have no wish to marry a Shiko…" Reiji began.

"I am beyond caring about your wishes, Reiji. You will do this thing. But first, you will pay your damned debts. And you will stay out of sight – Batu is looking for you."

Reiji blinked. "What – why?"

"Because he is Batu, and because the Crane has whispered into his ear. It does not matter. You will stay out of sight until the negotiations are finalized. Do you understand me?"

"You… You cannot do this," Reiji blustered. "I do not consent – why don't you do it?"

"Because I am the caretaker, boy," Shijan said, with a mirthless grin. "If you are heir, you must be the one to marry." He paused. "It will do you good, I think. She is supposedly quite plain – but sensible. We could use some common sense in this family."

Reiji turned and fled. That was the only word for it. Aimi

watched him go, not without some sympathy – though, admittedly, very little. She knew what it was to be offered up as a political token. The difference between them was, she had been willing to play the part, and Reiji was – well, a twit.

He might flee the city, you know, she signed.

"You didn't," Shijan said, dropping the floorboard back into place.

Reiji is not as brave as I am.

"True. You have always had more courage than sense." Shijan rolled the mat back and stood. He turned, fingers curling and twitching. "I admire that about you, cousin."

I rather thought the opposite, she signed.

Shijan bowed his head, but did not stop signing. "I must go out. There are things that must be done before tomorrow. The negotiations will be settled then. I would be obliged to you if you would attend. We should show a united front."

"United, but without Reiji?" she asked, out loud.

His hands made the sign for certainty. "Yes. It is better that way, I think."

Tashiro listened to the song of vice, and found it as annoying as ever. The rattle of dice, the murmur of prostitutes – the stale smell of spilled sake and rice wine. The fug of opium and alcoholic fumes dulled his senses and made his eyes water.

He ducked through a curtain and into the back, away from the noise of the common room. The Jade Hare was busy tonight. It was always busy. Too many in this city sought meaningless pleasure as soon as Lady Sun had set. Then, as far as Honesty-sama was concerned, that was as it should be.

No one knew where he'd come from, or why he'd chosen

Hisatu-Kesu as his home. What was known was that within a fortnight of his arrival, he'd begun a bloody takeover of the city's criminal rackets. Bodies had filled the gutters to overflowing before he'd finished. Now, every gang worth the name worked for him. And if you didn't, you soon did, or you came to regret it. Even the Iron Sect trod but lightly on Honesty-sama's shadow, and then only when absolutely necessary.

Tashiro fingered the hilt of his katana as he walked down the wooden corridor, accompanied by the creak of nightingale boards. His employer – he would not call such a man master – was cautious by nature. And, like all cautious men, he was calculating as well. He had many abodes in the city, and each was as much a fortress as its nature allowed. He never resided in one for more than a single night at a time.

Even now, Tashiro knew of only a few of them. Though he was ostensibly Honesty-sama's man, that did not mean his employer trusted him to any great degree. A wise – if somewhat annoying – decision on his part, given Tashiro's true loyalty to the Iron Sect.

The sect had encouraged him to insinuate himself into the cartel, so as to better influence it. So far, however, his influence was limited to the occasional comment – and the altogether too frequent bladework that Honesty-sama required of his favored ronin. Not that he had ever told anyone that; most especially Emiko. It would not do to let the others think there were limits to his usefulness.

At the end of the corridor stood a heavyset man, bare arms crossed over a barrel chest. Tattoos adorned every inch of visible flesh. Tashiro bore similar tattoos, though reluctantly and not on his arms. Honesty-sama believed in branding his property.

The big man looked him over perfunctorily and knocked lightly on the door. A muffled invitation came from within, and he slid the door open for Tashiro. Inside, the office was much like every other office Honesty-sama maintained throughout the city. It was stripped bare of ornamentation and color, with only a few candles for light. There were no windows, and only the one door. He entered – and stopped. Honesty-sama had a guest.

This, in itself, was not unusual. Many sought him out, for Honesty-sama was known to dole out favors and forgiveness – for the right price. But mostly, the pilgrims were heimin; only rarely did the noble-born darken Honesty-sama's doorway.

As the door slid shut behind him, Honesty-sama gestured for Tashiro to approach. He was a big man, round but not soft. He looked like a laborer, but for the fine cut of his kimono. His skin was free of ink, and his scalp was shorn of hair. His face was craggy, worn into flat planes by time spent out of doors and in rough country.

He sat on a plain mat, a bowl of soup and rice by his knee. A cup of tea sat opposite. His guests were allowed no refreshments, not until business was concluded. He smiled as Tashiro knelt a respectful distance to the side and slightly behind him, placing his swords aside. "As courteous as ever, Tashiro," the crime boss murmured.

As always, Tashiro was struck by how surprisingly soft and warm the other man's voice was. Whatever he had been, Honesty-sama had a courtier's voice. Smooth and gentle, even when saying the most terrible of things.

"Do continue, my friend," Honesty-sama said, motioning to his guest. "You may speak freely in front of Tashiro. He is my good right hand."

"If you insist. But I ask that you send your servants away." The voice was familiar enough that Tashiro paused. Only for an instant, and unnoticed by either man. He peered at the guest. The bushi – and he was a bushi, by the way he talked and sat – was clad in fine, dark robes and a cloth mask. The mask was reminiscent of those worn by high-ranking members of the Scorpion Clan, but bore no identifying markings. It was simply a veil of dark cloth with holes for eyes.

Honesty-sama shook his head. "They are both mute and illiterate. They will share nothing of what they see and hear." He smiled. "I am not a man prone to whimsy, as you well know. If they are here, it is because they have purpose. Just like you."

It was a calculated insult, and the masked man bristled visibly. Tashiro hid a smile. He did not know the noble's name. Only a few in the sect did – he was not a member, after all, but their pawn. What he did know was the bushi ought to have been keeping a low profile as Emiko had warned him to do, not seeking an audience with a crime boss. He wondered what had brought the man here, now.

"Now then, to business," Honesty-sama said. "I must say I was surprised by your message. Why did you wish to see me?"

"I wish to make a deal."

"A deal?" Honesty-sama folded his hands over his belly and smiled benignly. "One might say it is hubris to make a deal with a man to whom you owe so much money."

"I can make you more koku than I owe," the bushi said, in acid tones. "The least you could do is hear me out. You owe me that much."

"Tashiro."

Tashiro stood, snatching up his sword as he did so. He

thumbed the blade free of its sheath, ready to draw and slash in a single, smooth motion. The bushi fell back onto his rear, eyes comically wide behind his mask. "Wait – wait!"

Honesty-sama twitched a finger. Tashiro paused. "Why? You have insulted me. And after we have worked so efficiently together these past months." Tashiro cut his eyes to the crime boss. He knew that the bushi had been providing information to the cartel at the behest of the sect. Supposedly he was paying off his debts; in reality, there was no chance he would ever get out from under either party. He was too useful for that.

"Forgive me – I spoke hastily," the bushi babbled. "I… I am overwrought."

"That is no matter to me, little man." Honesty-sama leaned forward. "But you are right – you have done well by me, and so I am inclined to be forgiving. What do you want?"

"M- Men."

"You have men. You are a bushi. You have plenty of little soldiers to play with."

"I need men of a certain… caliber. Men who cannot be traced to me."

Honesty-sama smiled. "Ah. You need killers. How many?"

"As many as you will give me."

Tashiro frowned. Why was the fool hiring men? He must be up to something – but what? He wanted to demand answers, but knew better than to voice any interest. Honesty-sama might wonder why he cared, and that could quickly become awkward.

"Are you up to something then, my friend? Something interesting?" Honesty-sama stroked his neck, his expression curious. He gestured, and Tashiro let his sword settle back into its sheath. "Something profitable, perhaps? Something to do with the negotiations, maybe?"

The bushi hesitated. "Perhaps. Time will tell."

Tashiro wondered if he ought to kill the fool before he did something to endanger the sect. He could always apologize to Honesty-sama. But no – not yet. He had to be careful.

"What do you have for me in return?" Honesty-sama asked. "More papers, more records? They will have to be important ones for something like this."

"I have them. Here." The bushi reached into his kimono, and Tashiro tensed. The bushi withdrew a small leather pouch and handed it over. Tashiro gave it to Honesty-sama, who opened it and perused the contents. He grunted.

"Those are the delivery manifests for the next six weeks. Including shipments from Shiro Iuchi. Any one of those will profit you greatly, especially if you sell them on the other side of the mountains."

"Do not tell me my business." Honesty-sama was silent for a moment. Then, "For what you have offered me, I can supply you two dozen men." Tashiro's eyes widened at the number. He was still not certain how many men Honesty-sama could call on, but two dozen cutthroats was a small army.

"I need men who can hold a blade – not touts and gamblers."

"Oh, they'll be hardened brigands, I assure you. Murderous scum, the lot of them."

The bushi hesitated. "Archers, as well."

Honesty-sama frowned at this. "Archers? Yes. I have a few men good with a bow. A few ex-ashigaru, some poachers. They know how to put an arrow into a target. Does that satisfy you?"

"Yes. So long as they can follow orders."

"They will follow your orders so long as I tell them they must." Honesty-sama smiled and gestured expansively. "Are you certain you won't give me a hint as to what you're planning? Perhaps I can be of some greater help."

The bushi shook his head. "Suffice to say, it will mean great changes for the city. And profit for you, if all goes well."

Tashiro took his seat, wondering what the bushi meant. Whatever he was planning, the others would have to be told – and something would have to be done about him.

"Well, change is a constant, they say." Honesty-sama clapped, and one of his servants rose noiselessly from where she'd knelt by the door. "Food and drink for my guest. And a jug of mare's milk. We shall celebrate our arrangement in the traditional fashion, as our forefathers did in the desert."

CHAPTER TWENTY-THREE
Truth

The morning began with practice. For once, Shin found it soothing rather than annoying. He slipped easily into the rhythm, the practice blade moving like an extension of his arm. As often happened at times like this, his mind turned to Kakita's treatise on swordplay. While the Daidoji favored a more pragmatic approach to swordplay, there was something to be said for the Kakita's more philosophical approach.

"People will lie," he said, as he and Kasami broke apart and lowered their practice swords, "and your eyes will deceive, and your emotions will cloud the path."

"Steel never lies," Kasami said. "In the sword, one finds truth." She paused. As ever, only the barest sheen of perspiration covered her face. Shin, in contrast, was puffing. But not so much as he had earlier in the week. "What of it?" she continued.

"An idle thought, nothing more." He thrust the blade of the practice sword into the soft ground and leaned on the hilt. "I feel as if I am floating on the ocean, and beneath me great shapes glide through the darkness."

"What does that have to do with Kakita?"

"We are missing something. Our eyes deceive us. What we see is not the truth."

"Meaning?" Kasami asked.

"Meaning… I don't know." Shin gestured to a bird pecking at the dirt nearby. "We peck and peck, but so far no worms."

"Maybe there are no worms."

"There are always worms." Shin straightened and tossed her the practice sword. "We just have to dig a little deeper." He ran his hands through his hair. "Enough practice for the day. I would like to speak to our guest and have a bath before I meet this merchant, Yuzu."

"You are free to do as you like."

"I meant you should see to the latter."

"I am not your servant."

"Then please find my servant and have him see to it," Shin said, over his shoulder. He left her fuming and made his way to where the prisoner was being held. The guards stepped aside and allowed him to enter. Light streamed through the barred windows, and he heard soft sounds of effort from Ruri's cell.

The sounds ceased as he approached, and he called out, "You do not have to cease on my account. Kasami informed me that you had found a way to conduct your daily exercises." He picked up a stool sitting near the wall and carried it to her cell.

"I was finished anyway," Ruri said.

"I have come to speak with you again," Shin said, as he set the stool down across from the cell door. He adjusted his kimono and sat. "I hope that you do not mind."

Ruri watched him through the bars. "As before, I do not have any choice in the matter." She hesitated. "You are not unskilled with the blade."

"A compliment?"

"An observation," she said, stiffly. "I have watched your practice these past few days. Initially, I found it amusing. You play at being inept so well that you almost forget that you know better."

Shin paused. "You have a keen eye."

"A warrior must learn to read the story her opponent writes."

"And you have decided we are opponents?"

"What would you call us?"

"Allies. Uneasy ones, perhaps, but we have the same goal in mind, I think. I hope."

"My only goal is to fulfil my oath. You stand in the way of that."

Shin was silent for a moment. "Why do you wish to die now, when earlier you were, by your own admission, reluctant to do so?"

"It is my duty. I killed Gen. Someone must pay. Let it be she who slew him. There can be no ending more appropriate for one so unworthy as myself." She bowed her head, appropriately contrite. Or perhaps stubbornly so.

Impatient, and a touch frustrated, Shin said, "I know about the poems."

Her gaze flicked up, hot and savage. For a moment, he thought she might lunge at him, despite the bars in her path. "You will say nothing of them," she growled. "You will say nothing, or I will–"

"You will what?" he said, sharply. "What will you do from in there? Growl all you like, Lioness, but you have abdicated your authority in this matter. The Crane has chosen to alight in the space you have vacated. You are in the shadow of my wings now."

Ruri glared at him, her fingers wrapped about the bars, knuckles white. "You will say nothing," she said again, and Shin heard the plea in her words. He found his sudden anger snuffed like a candle-flame.

"She told me herself."

Ruri blinked. Her expression became unsettled, and she stepped back. "What?"

"Lady Aimi. She told me herself." Shin stood, hands clasped behind his back. "I should have seen it earlier, of course. The way you reacted when you learned that she had written to the Iuchi, seeking clemency on your behalf – that alone should have told me the whole story." He shook his head. "How did it come to be?"

"It does not matter."

"I will be the judge of that. Tell me."

She peered at him for a long time. So long that he thought she might not speak at all. Then, with a soft exhalation, she said, "I did not mean for it to happen. She is a noblewoman – and I am… what I am. We both knew that it could not be anything more than a passing idyll. A dream, to end at our inevitable waking."

"Yet you succumbed." Shin, who had read no small number of pillow books and wistful poems, felt a shiver of empathy. Though romance was not often a concern of his, he understood it. Like a gardener looking upon a wild flower, something in him longed to see it flourish. "I understand, for she is beautiful."

"It is – was – not that." Ruri gave a thin smile. "Not that alone. She sees me. Do you understand? She sees me, as I am, as I wish to be – not as masterless, but as … as …" She trailed off.

"As a Lion," Shin said, softly. "She sees the truth of you. But what of you? What did you see in her?"

"She is brave," Ruri said. "Headstrong and sometimes foolish. But brave." She paused. "Strong hands. The Unicorn have a saying – 'a woman to ride the plains with.' That is what Zeshi Aimi is, a woman to ride the plains with. She will be a fine wife for whomever is lucky enough to make that match. It will not be me, and I will not allow myself to be used to deny her – or them – that opportunity."

"What are her feelings on the matter?"

Ruri's gaze sharpened. "The same as mine."

Shin tapped his lip with a finger, thinking. "You are certain?"

"Why?"

Shin turned away. "Her cousin, Shijan. He has intimated that she might be responsible for putting you in this situation – intentionally so."

Ruri shook her head slowly. "No. That is not possible."

"It is possible. That is why I ask."

"You think that she told Gen? Why – so that I would be forced to kill him?"

"Yes. Shijan insists that Aimi did not wish to marry Gen."

"She did not. He was unsuitable – a boor and a fool. But she would have married him nonetheless, for the good of her family."

"So she says."

"But you believe Shijan over her?" Ruri scoffed. "I thought you had sense, Crane."

"I have sense enough not to take anything at face value. Having committed myself, I must explore all possibilities. Even those which are somewhat distasteful." Shin turned back and leaned close to the bars. "She has not visited you since your incarceration, save once."

"Because I told her not to."

"Why?"

"It is better she forgets me."

"She does not seem to agree."

"She will learn."

"Shijan certainly seems to hope so. Tell me about him. You speak of observing your foe – what have you observed about Shijan?"

She hesitated. Even now, facing the blade, she had loyalty to the family, not just Aimi. Shin found it simultaneously admirable and irksome. He allowed himself an impatient gesture. "Do not vacillate. Now is not the time."

"Shijan is devoted to himself," she said, finally. "That he identifies himself with his family is to their benefit, but his loyalty to them – to his name – is more tenuous than he would admit. He is – was – the nephew of Aimi's mother, Sachi. It was her wish that he be sent here to learn how to be a true son of the Zeshi, or so Aimi said."

"What happened to their mother?"

"She died young, I think. Aimi barely remembers her, and Reiji not at all."

"And Shijan?"

"He was close to her. More so than anyone else, save Aimi."

"If that is the case, why might he seek to blame Aimi for this?"

"I do not know. He… I think he loves her. Not more than himself, but more than any other. Once, he might have sought to wed her himself."

"And her feelings on that?"

Ruri flashed a smile. "She had none. I doubt she has ever thought of him as anything other than her overbearing cousin." She took a deep breath. "If you are going to ask me if he might have done this – I do not see the gain for him in it. Shijan wishes to be important, to be respected by important people. War with the Shiko gains him none of that."

"That we know of," Shin said, half to himself. "What of Reiji, her brother?"

She laughed. "A callow cub. Shijan, at least, is cunning. Reiji is not."

"No?"

"A fool."

"Like Gen."

She hesitated. "Yes. But Gen was a man grown, and set in his ways. Reiji is a youth. He might learn wisdom some day."

"What do you know of his debts?"

"He had them. Aimi told me of them. Beyond that, I cannot say."

"Is he capable of theft?"

"Most people are, with reason." Ruri frowned, thinking. "Aimi said that things had gone missing – papers and money, mostly. You think he stole them?"

Shin ignored the question. "How long have things been going missing?"

Ruri looked away. "Some months."

"And no one has confronted him?"

"Just before he… vanished, their father, Lord Hisato, spoke to someone. We heard the argument echoing throughout the house. I assumed it was Shijan, but it might well have been Reiji he was yelling at."

"Why assume it was Shijan?"

"They were forever arguing. Shijan thinks of himself as a courtier; he seeks to forget that he is a provincial bushi with not a koku to his name that the family has not granted him." She turned away, looking towards the cell's single window. "Perhaps I have said too much."

"Or not enough." He waved her to silence as she made to reply. He had detected the sound of footsteps in the grass outside. A moment later, Kasami entered.

"Lady Nishi is here."

Shin hesitated. "Did she say what she wanted?"

"To see the prisoner."

Shin looked at Ruri, who shook her head. She went and sat, her back to the door. Shin considered saying something, then decided against it. He left her there and met Lady Nishi outside. She did not seem surprised to see him – though she raised an eyebrow at his clothes. Belatedly, he realized he was still dressed for practice. "Will she not even see me?" she asked without preamble, as they moved a short distance from the guards. Kasami trailed diligently after them.

"Regrettably, no. If you would like me to pass on a message… ?"

"No. It is unimportant."

"I would guess otherwise, else you would not have come here, against Ide Sora's express wishes. She made it very clear to Batu and myself that we were not to speak to any member of either family."

She nodded. "Ide Sora allowed me to come on the promise I would not answer any more of your questions. She said nothing about us having a conversation."

Shin smiled. "In that case, would you care for tea, my lady?"

"I prefer spiced mare's milk, myself. Then, I am something of a traditionalist."

"Traditions have their place. We of the Crane are great believers in the power of tradition." He smiled. "At least when it benefits us."

"So I have heard." She looked away. "I will not stay long enough for tea, I think. I do not know why I came. I did not expect her to see me. I do not know what I would have said, had she done so."

"Uncertainty is the imperfection in the blade," Shin said. "Kakita wrote that. I was thinking of his treatise on swordplay earlier." He glanced at Kasami, and she rolled her eyes. He hid a smile and turned his attentions back to Nishi.

"And do you agree with Kakita?" she asked.

"In this instance, no. Uncertainty is as natural as breathing. Does the water know its route, or does it merely follow the course and hope to reach the sea?"

"I do not think the water wonders about much of anything." She sighed. "It might be easier to be water, I think."

"But less interesting."

She laughed softly. After a moment, she said, "I spoke to Umeko. She told me that she shared her suspicions with you."

"As she must have shared them with you."

"Yes," Nishi looked at the ground. She loosed a slow breath. "Lady Aimi is blameless. And the ronin as well. Gen… liked to fight. He saw challenges everywhere, and my cousins only encouraged him."

"Forgive me, but they did seem as if they might be… unwholesome influences."

She glanced at him. "You spoke to Ikki, then? Is that why he looked so chastened when he returned home yesterday?"

"We did have strong words for him, yes." Again, he glanced at Kasami. This time, Nishi followed his gaze, and she chuckled softly.

"Good. I should not have invited them here, but after my husband's accident I felt in need of family."

"Might I ask… how did your husband come to be injured? Did it have something to do with the Zeshi?"

Nishi shook her head. She gave no sign as to whether so blunt a question shocked her. "Not that we are aware of, though it might be easier if they were responsible. It was an accident – he was out riding in the foothills, not long after we'd moved to the city. Something startled his horse, and the animal fell onto him, breaking its neck and injuring his spine. His bodyguards were helpless to do anything save carry him home and send for a physician."

"There was nothing to be done?"

"Nothing except make him comfortable. It is not well known. We chose not to have it bandied about the sake houses, and swore all who witnessed it to silence."

"A wise precaution." Shin paused. "When we met, he spoke of it as if he did not believe it to be an accident. That is why I assumed the Zeshi played some part in it."

Nishi smiled sourly. "He wishes it to be so, for he seeks reasons to throw us into war – though he knows it would be the ruin of us. If not for the forbearance of Lord Hisato, we might well have gone to war that very day."

"Might that not have been better? Lord Mitsue did mention that he thought open battle might bring an end to the trouble in a decisive fashion."

She gave a soft laugh. "My husband – he thinks that a sword can solve any problem."

"And you think otherwise?"

"I think swords have created more problems than they've solved, traditionally." Her smile turned sad. "Gen thought much the same way."

"Until he met Aimi."

"Yes." Nishi nodded.

"But she did not share his regard."

She hesitated. "Gen had his good points. In time, she might have discovered them. Or learned to live with the rest of him."

"Your cousin insisted that Lady Aimi had been disloyal to Gen."

Nishi frowned. "Where did he hear such a thing?"

"He did not say, though he mentioned Zeshi Reiji."

"Her brother?"

"Apparently he was quite good friends with Gen. At least, according to your cousins."

Her expression was one of puzzlement. "I cannot imagine that. Gen hated the Zeshi." She frowned. "Unless he was using the boy, somehow."

"Using him how?"

"I cannot say." She paused. "Gen liked to gamble. And he was good at it."

"Reiji is said to owe quite a bit of money to various individuals. Might he have told Gen about Aimi's… relationship in return for settling his debt?"

She blanched. "If so…" She put her hands to her mouth. "My poor boy. My poor foolish boy." She looked at Shin, her gaze mournful but decisive. "If it is the truth, then Gen was the author of his own fate. I will speak up – ask that the yojimbo is spared."

Shin felt a sudden flush of relief. "I would be grateful, my lady – as would Lady Aimi, I am certain. I –" He was interrupted by the sudden arrival of Nozomi. She spoke quickly to Kasami, who trotted towards Shin and Nishi.

"My apologies," she said, bowing to Nishi. "Lord Batu has received word – they've found Zeshi Reiji."

CHAPTER TWENTY-FOUR
Reiji

"There," Nozomi murmured, gesturing towards the building across the street from the alley where they stood. Even if he hadn't been there to guide them, the sharp, cloying reek of opium would have told Kasami that they had arrived at their destination.

The whole of the slum stank of it, as well as sake, unwashed bodies, boiling fat and other, less identifiable odors. The buildings here were too close together, the streets piled atop one another as they wound through the rocky terrain. Sluice canals brought hot water from higher up the mountain, dispersing it to the various unlicensed bathhouses that littered this part of the city, before carrying the rest down to the tanneries in the foothills.

The building she had indicated was nondescript, crouching among equally unimpressive fellows. The only point of difference was the tattered sigil – a jade hare – hanging from the doorway, and the disheveled-looking heimin on guard.

"You did not have to come, you know. We are capable of bringing in a suspect on our own." Batu's voice was mild, but Kasami could hear the reproach in his words. She bowed her head, acknowledging his point. He stood behind her, along with Nozomi and two other yoriki. The rest of Batu's contingent – four samurai, all yoriki like Nozomi – and a half dozen heimin soldiers were on the other side of the street, waiting to go in the rear entrance of the Jade Hare.

"Forgive me, but Lord Shin wishes to ensure that nothing goes wrong while he is otherwise occupied." The thought of leaving Shin unsupervised was not one she cared to dwell on. But hers was to obey, even when there was no need for it. Thankfully, she had managed to elicit a promise from him not to go anywhere until she'd returned. He'd sworn to do nothing more strenuous than think on what Lady Nishi had told him.

"And you will see to it, will you?"

Kasami nodded. "I will."

Batu paused. "You do not lack confidence."

"No," Kasami said, simply. Out of the corner of her eye, she saw Nozomi attempting to hide a smile. "I doubt I shall be needed, my lord. But my mother often said that an extra pair of hands rarely goes amiss."

"A wise woman." Batu turned as a heimin, dressed in plain clothes, stepped into the alley, interrupting them. "Well?" Batu asked. The heimin bowed low.

"As you expected, my lord – it's a full house, despite the fact it's only the afternoon." The heimin straightened, smiling. "They have no idea we're here."

"Speed is its own reward," Batu murmured. He looked at

Nozomi. "I want to do this in the usual fashion. We'll cover both entrances. If any try to escape, let them past, otherwise we'll have a bloodbath on our hands. I want no more deaths attached to this matter."

"Do you think he's here?" Nozomi asked, eagerly. "Honesty-sama?"

"I thought we were looking for Zeshi Reiji," Kasami said. Batu glanced at her.

"We are. But the Jade Hare is one of Honesty-sama's establishments. If I were Reiji, looking to sell stolen papers, I would come here. We might be able to catch him in the act. If so, that will be an end to it."

"And if he escapes?"

"As I recall, that is why you are here. To make certain that he does not." Batu gestured. "Nozomi – after you."

Nozomi nodded and smiled. She sauntered across the street, accompanied by the two yoriki. Batu watched her go, and then said, "You will accompany me. Between us, we should be able to spot Reiji."

"As you say, my lord." Kasami wanted to ask how long they would wait, but chose to save her breath. Batu would not enter until the exits had been blocked. Such was the privilege of a magistrate.

"You spoke of wisdom before," he said, studying the street. "Wisdom is something your master sorely lacks, I think."

"My lord?"

"This. All of this. A wise man would have let it be." He looked at her. "He has never been wise. Shin, I mean. Not once, in all the days I have known him. Even as a youth, wisdom was his enemy." His eyes slid away and she shifted her weight, disconcerted by his words. "They tried to beat it into him, you know."

Kasami said nothing. Shin rarely spoke of his youth, save to make some witticism. "They were stern, those Daidoji. Like iron made flesh. And then there was Shin, fluttering about, taking nothing seriously." Batu smiled absently. "He was the first to speak to me, you know. The first to ask my name. The first to care."

"He cares too much," she said, without thinking. Batu looked at her sharply. Rather than admonishing her, he nodded.

"Yes, that has always been his problem. I tried to teach him otherwise, but some lessons do not take. I think you have tried to teach him as well – I wish you more luck than I had." He straightened the fold of his kimono. "He speaks highly of you, you know. I do not think he could function without you."

Kasami, who thought much the same herself, merely nodded. She wondered why Batu was saying these things to her. Maybe it was simply idle speech – Shin did that often. Many samurai spoke only to hear themselves speak; there was no greater meaning to it. But she did not think so. Batu did not seem the sort.

Across the street, Nozomi and her companions had sent the two heimin on guard fleeing. The other group of yoriki had already vanished – likely moving to enter through the rear, as was the plan. "They move quickly," she murmured.

"We have done this a hundred times, if not more." Batu sounded tired rather than pleased. "The longer I am here, the more I understand my predecessors' attitude towards this sort of thing. Our lot is to keep things on an even keel – not to change them."

People were gathering on the corners, obviously expecting

trouble and wanting to enjoy it from a safe distance. Kasami wondered how often this scene had been repeated in this part of the city – a dozen times, maybe, or two dozen – that it had become entertainment. She thought about what Nozomi had said, about the Unicorn tolerating the criminal activity. It did not seem right, and yet it happened. Not just here, but everywhere.

She pushed the thought aside. She'd never used to worry about such things, but of late it was getting harder to ignore the cracks in the surface of what was. She blamed Shin – the way he talked about such things was not worthy of a bushi. Too many thoughts in the head was like too much sake in the belly – it made you sick and stupid.

"Come. Time to make my entrance." Batu started across the street. Kasami followed. He moved with a peculiar rolling gait – not like that of a sailor, but more akin to a horseman who was without a horse. He carried only a wakizashi, leaving the sword work to Nozomi and his men. It showed either supreme confidence or arrogance. Kasami wasn't sure which.

The crowds on the corners had increased. Heimin and hinin alike, watching and perhaps wagering on the outcome. Entertainment. Her eyes narrowed as they lit on a familiar figure – a woman. Small, tattered robes. A bamboo cane in one hand.

The blind woman – the musician.

Kasami paused, wondering at her presence. Why was she here? Batu noticed and glanced at her. "Is something amiss?"

"That woman, the one with the shamisen on her back…" She did not know why she was drawing attention to the other woman. Something Shin had said, perhaps. The woman did not seem a threat, and yet, every instinct Kasami possessed was telling her that there was something wrong.

"What about her?"

Before Kasami could answer, a sudden clamor rose from within the Jade Hare. Shouts echoed from inside, and then, as if a dam had burst, a rush of bodies hit the doors and spilled out into the street. Dozens of people – gamblers, geishas, and drunks – scrambled into the open. Her hand fell to her sword as they swept towards her and Batu. Quickly, she interposed herself, but the wave shivered apart, scattering in all directions.

One of them – a young man, a bushi by his clothing – skidded to a halt at the sight of Batu. He gaped at them, but only for a moment, and sprinted away. Batu snapped around. "There – it's Reiji!"

Kasami was already in motion as the words left his lips. Reiji had a head start, but he wasn't moving as quickly as he might have – inebriated, she thought, though he was sobering up quickly. Adrenaline and terror had a way of doing that.

Reiji dodged around a peddler's cart and sprinted down a side street. Kasami, unfamiliar with the city, considered slowing down, but only for a moment. Instead, she leapt over the cart, causing the peddler to fall onto his rear in shock. She was moving again the moment her feet touched the ground.

As she rounded the corner, she caught the flash of steel and saw Reiji falling backwards, hands raised. Two men stood over him, both dressed like street-roughs. One held a peasant's machete raised over his head as he made to strike at Reiji. Her hand fastened around the hilt of her katana. "Stop," she called.

They did. Three pairs of eyes fixed on her. "This is none of your concern," the one with the sword said, lowering the blade. Even he didn't sound as if he believed what he was saying. The second sidled to the side, a blade in his hand. Kasami ignored him. Instead, she focused on the one who'd spoken.

"He is mine. Leave him be."

Reiji looked back and forth between them. He began to babble. "This… This is all a mistake. Tell… Tell Honesty-sama I have the money."

"Shut up," Kasami and the one with the machete said in unison. The latter glanced at his companion, then back at her. "Walk away, samurai. There might be money in it for you."

Kasami frowned. As if that were a signal, the second one came at her in low rush – a brawler. She drew and struck in one motion, opening him from groin to grin. He whirled, spraying red across the sides of the alley. She turned and caught the blade of the other on her own. He had a bit more skill than his companion, enough to recognize that he was outmatched. He retreated, eyes narrowed. "I told you – this is none of your concern." He sounded desperate, pleading.

"I made it mine." She waited, sword held low, her grip loose. "Why were you trying to kill him?"

"That's our… my business."

She inclined her head. "Run, if you like. I will not chase you." She cut her eyes at Reiji. "I have what I want."

He licked his lips. She read his decision in his eyes, even as he made his play. His form was not entirely absent. With training, he might have made a decent swordsman, for a peasant. Her first sweep removed his sword hand. Her second opened his throat to the bone. Blood spurted, dappling her armor as he collapsed, as if in slow motion. She looked down at the body, struck by his foolishness. Someone must have been paying him well. She twitched the blood from her blade as she turned.

"Why did you run?"

Reiji scrambled to his feet. He ignored her question. "I do not have to answer to you. I… I am a bushi, not a heimin." He turned as if to go – to run, she thought.

"As am I," she said. "Why did you not fight? You are armed." She used her sword to indicate his weapons, still snug in their sheaths. "They were gutter-scum. Are you a coward?" The insult was intentional, and it worked. He spun, hand falling to the hilt of his katana. If he drew it, she would have to kill him.

She slapped his hand with the flat of her blade. He gave a yelp and jerked his hand up and away. She sheathed her sword and got into his face. She caught his wrist and, with a single, smooth motion, flattened him face-first against the wall. Despite his struggles, she pinned his arm behind his back.

Reiji yelped again, and she popped him on the nose with two fingers. "Hush," she said. "Only children bawl. Are you a child?"

"R- Release me, and you will see how much of a man I am!"

She swatted him again. "Only fools threaten. Are you a fool as well?" She paused. "Then, it is said the Fortunes are protective of fools and children. That may explain your continued survival."

"Release me!"

She tightened her grip, and he squealed. "Enough bluster. Calm yourself, or I will break your arm. Would you like that?"

Reiji fell silent. She held him for a moment longer and then released him. The youth turned, rubbing his arm. "No," he said, grudgingly. "I suppose I am most thankful for your timely assistance."

"Good." She paused as a sound reached her ears. A soft, insistent tapping. As of a bamboo cane, feeling its way along the ground. Then the sound faded, and she turned her attention back to her prisoner. "Now come with me. There is someone who wishes to speak to you."

CHAPTER TWENTY-FIVE
Yuzu

Washed and rinsed, Shin stooped to enter the steam bath through the narrow aperture. The room was one of several private areas, available to those willing to pay for the privilege of bathing alone. Due to the lack of windows and the thick clouds of steam, it was all but impossible to see more than a few inches in front of his face.

He coughed politely, to let any other occupants know that he had arrived. When no response came, he realized he was alone. He sighed and sat down, adjusting the towel he wore for modesty's sake accordingly. The heat felt good on his skin, and he closed his eyes to order his thoughts before Yuzu arrived.

As he sat, he listened to the murmur of voices and soft music that drifted through the partition. The Ibusuko Bathhouse on Falling Moon Lane was one of the more popular onsen in the city. Yuzu apparently conducted much of his business in its confines. The warmth and the quiet put people at ease. Shin himself was feeling distinctly relaxed – though he knew he would pay for it later.

He'd sent Kasami with Batu. If push came to shove, he was confident she would not let him down. He'd seen no reason to go himself. Either Reiji would be there, or he would not. Either he would be caught, or he would not. Regardless, she would be angry when she returned and found him gone. He'd promised not to go anywhere without her, but was it his fault that they'd taken too long to return?

He was certain she'd understand. And if not, Kitano would bear the brunt of her wrath. Shin had left him behind to explain things, just in case they got back before he did. He smiled at the thought. It left his face almost as quickly as it had appeared.

He settled back to consider the problem from all angles. He knew that the full picture had not yet revealed itself, though there was, perhaps, enough of one to provide extenuating circumstances, and thus see Ruri spared. Lady Nishi's word alone might settle it. But even with that taken care of, the underlying problem remained. He turned the facts over in his mind and shifted them about like puzzle pieces.

Ruri and Aimi were in love, but neither had wished to endanger the negotiations, so they had resolved to end things. But someone had discovered their entanglement and used it to drive Gen, a notoriously unstable individual, into a murderous frenzy. No matter how that had turned out, the wedding would be off and the burgeoning alliance ended.

Someone was stirring the pot. Keeping tensions high. There were many possible reasons for that, but the most obvious one was that someone, somewhere, wished for war between the Zeshi and the Shiko. But why? Money – perhaps. Money was always involved in these matters, if only tangentially. But no one in either family stood to gain if war broke out.

"I'm missing something," he said, out loud.

"Perhaps I can be of help, then, my lord." The voice came suddenly, and Shin sat up so abruptly he almost slipped off his bench. A slight chuckle followed. "Forgive me, I did not mean to startle you."

Shin peered through the steam and saw a heavyset figure sit down opposite him. "It is I who should apologize, Master Yuzu," he said. "My mind was elsewhere."

"I expect it was." Another chuckle. Shin waved aside a curl of steam and studied the man before him. Yuzu was a thickset man with a heavy beard and wide, dark eyes. His towel was too small to accomplish its task easily, and required constant adjustment. "Still, no apologies necessary, my lord."

"I must thank you for agreeing to meet with me – as well giving me an excuse to partake in one of this city's fine onsen."

"Think nothing of it," Yuzu said. "You wished to speak with me about something? Perhaps the Daidoji think to establish themselves in Hisatu-Kesu. If so, I would gladly give you any help you might require."

Shin leaned forward. "Nothing of that nature, sadly. Rather, I would like to ask you a few questions, if I might."

"Questions, my lord?" Yuzu seemed taken aback. Almost comically so, Shin thought. He was not so surprised as he wished to appear. "Regarding what?"

"Business. Specifically, yours. Or, rather, the business of the merchants' association."

Yuzu's eyes narrowed. The obsequiousness vanished, replaced by wariness. "What do you wish to know, my lord?"

"Lord Batu has explained to me the reasons for founding the merchants' association – in order to protect trade and control pricing. The Daidoji Trade Council was formed for much the same reason. What I would like to know is how you would characterize your association's relationship with the Zeshi and the Shiko. Given their importance in the city's affairs, I can only imagine it is … ?" Shin gestured encouragingly.

Yuzu frowned. "Why do you wish to know this?"

Shin scratched his chin. "Idle curiosity."

Yuzu studied him for a moment. "I will need a better answer than that, my lord." He sounded apologetic as he said it – but firm.

Shin nodded. "As I expected. Very well. Do you know why I am here?"

"Forgive me, but… most of the city knows, my lord."

Shin smiled. "Yes, well. I believe there might be more to Lord Gen's death than is commonly assumed."

"I do not see what that has to do with us…" Yuzu paused. "Unless… the negotiations?" He scowled. "There has been some talk in that regard."

Shin raised an eyebrow. "Oh? Please – illuminate me."

Yuzu settled back and scratched his nose. "These talks between the Zeshi and the Shiko have been going on for years. Recently tensions have increased. Shipments have gone missing. Accusations of sabotage. That sort of thing."

"Business as usual, one might say," Shin murmured, thinking of missing shipment records and schedules.

Yuzu nodded, though he did not smile. "Regrettably. But never as bad as it has been. Almost as if…" He trailed off.

"Someone was deliberately attempting to stoke the fire."

"Naturally, we feared that any suspicion in that regard would naturally fall on us. Our relationship with the Zeshi and the Shiko was… less than convivial."

"I would have thought otherwise, given their need for raw materials."

"Yes, well, they begrudge us every koku. Less so, it must be said, when they are pitted against one another." Yuzu stroked his chin. "In that sense, we've done very well."

"You say we... ? You mean the merchants' association."

"Yes. We act as one, where necessary."

"And the Zeshi and the Shiko have no objection to this?"

Yuzu laughed. "Oh certainly they do, my lord. But what can they do save bully us – and that carries the risk of certain ramifications."

"There is a saying – in war, only merchants profit."

"A pithy saying, my lord, but – forgive me – not wholly accurate. Stability is our friend, and things are not stable at the moment. We have high hopes, but anything we can do to help settle this matter we will, of course, attempt to do. That is why I agreed to this meeting, after all."

"For which I thank you again," Shin said. He sat back, eyes closed, letting the heat work itself into his muscles as Yuzu's words settled on his mind. "What was your opinion of the marriage?"

Yuzu coughed. "I should not like to say, my lord."

Shin opened one eye. "So you had an opinion on it, then?"

Yuzu grinned and tugged at his beard. "Everyone did, my lord. It was a popular topic of discussion among us peasants." There was an undercurrent of bitterness to his words.

"And what did everyone say?"

"Surely it is not important now."

"I expect not. But I would hear it anyway. Specifically, what did you and your fellow merchants think of it – did it please you? Worry you?"

Again, Yuzu hesitated. Shin could almost see him calculating how best to answer. The merchant was hiding something, he thought – but what? Perhaps it was simply the natural reticence of a merchant. "We thought it a bad bargain."

"What do you mean?"

"The Shiko paid an enormous amount of money for that girl," Yuzu said. "Or, should I say, for marriage."

"I thought it was meant to be a political marriage."

"Politics and money often go hand in hand, my lord. Especially up here." Yuzu leaned over and signaled to the servants waiting outside to pour more water onto the coals. "Word is, there was an addendum to the contract – a retainer, if you will. Nonrefundable."

"Paid to the Zeshi?"

"A Zeshi."

"Shijan," Shin said, catching the merchant's meaning. Yuzu tapped the side of his nose to show that Shin's supposition was correct. "Why would he do that? The Zeshi are rich. One of the richest families in these lands."

"The Zeshi are wealthy – but not these Zeshi. Not really. When the trouble began, there were all manner of unfortunate occurrences. Including sabotage. They lost a significant amount of stock – had to pay back customers, that sort of thing. And of course there's the usual gossip."

Shin, well aware of what form the usual gossip took, nodded. "Who are they in debt to? Not the Shiko, I think. One of you?"

"Us as well, but no – debts of a less acceptable sort. You know the sort I mean, I think." Yuzu gave a gap-toothed smile and rubbed two fingers together. Shin sat back.

"That is hard to imagine. I have met Shijan. He does not strike me as the sort."

"Perhaps that is why so few people are aware of it. He goes to great lengths to hide the fact. Or to blame such losses on his cousin, Reiji."

Shin thought of Shijan's admission of Reiji's weaknesses; how easily it had seemed to flow out of him. At the time, Shin had fancied that Shijan had merely been in need of someone to vent to, but now... now it seemed otherwise. "Easy enough to do, given the boy's own proclivities. But if he hides it so well, how do you come to know of it?"

Yuzu's smile was feral. "Well, there, my lord, is a somewhat embarrassing tale. Suffice it to say, I happen to be something of a gambler myself."

"Ah," Shin said in understanding. It would be like Shijan to gamble with his lessers, assuming that they would let him win. "How much did you take him for?"

"Enough that he has yet to play me again." Yuzu laughed and slapped his knee. He peered at the door. "The steam is thinning. I thought I asked them to put more water on the coals." He half-stood as if to peer out the door, when a sudden motion sent him reeling backwards onto the hard wooden floor. Shin shot to his feet. Yuzu squawked and flailed as a third man entered the room. He was fully clothed and hard faced. The red-stained peasant's machete in his hand said he had not come to enjoy the steam.

Acting on instinct, Shin stripped off his towel, rolled it into a tight whip and snapped it at the newcomer's hand. The man gave a bark of shock and dropped his blade. He instinctively stooped to reclaim it, and Shin snapped him again – in the face this time.

The man jerked back as if stung by an insect, but then lunged forward with a bullish roar, hands groping for Shin's throat. Shin flung the towel into his face and deftly avoided the rush.

As his attacker staggered past, Shin drove both elbows down onto the man's side, sending him sprawling against the far wall. "Yuzu – the machete," Shin barked. The merchant gawped at him for a moment before scrambling to reach the fallen weapon. By then Shin's opponent had recovered. He shoved himself up and around, lunging again. Shin wasn't quick enough to avoid him this time, and found himself driven back against the entry partition, a pair of thick hands wrapped around his throat.

"Kill you," the man growled.

"S… So I gathered," Shin wheezed. Blackness clustered at the edges of his vision. He stiffened the fingers of his left hand and drove them up into his opponent's solar plexus, the way he'd been taught by a certain monk of his acquaintance. The pressure on his windpipe relaxed immediately, and he freed himself from his attacker's grip. Dashing the sweat from his eyes, he clapped his hands against the man's ears, eliciting a cry of pain. The fellow staggered back, clutching at his head.

He turned as if to run – and stopped dead. Shin caught hold of him and made to haul him back, but the man toppled onto his side, nearly dragging Shin from his feet. A machete – his own machete – protruded from his belly. Yuzu stood before him, eyes wide, staring at his bloody hands. "I… I didn't mean…"

Shin bent quickly to check on his opponent, but it was clear the man was already dead. He looked up at Yuzu. "Is he…?" the merchant began.

"Unfortunately," Shin said. He stood and retrieved his towel. He could hear shouts of alarm from outside. He wondered whether their attacker had killed anyone on the way in. He hoped not. One dead man was bad enough.

"Unfortunately? He tried to kill us!"

Shin ran his hands through his wet hair. "Yes, but I'd like to know why."

CHAPTER TWENTY-SIX
Revelations

Outside, on the balcony, Shin stared down at the foothills and Northern Owari, daring them to share their secrets. His throat, arms and back still ached from the encounter at the onsen, and he reflected somewhat ruefully that Kasami was right – he did need more practice. He rubbed his shoulder, trying to ease a persistent twinge. Kasami had been angry, of course. Furious, really. Batu as well.

"Hurts?" the latter asked, as he joined Shin on the balcony.

Shin grunted. "A bit."

"Traditionally, a visit to the onsen is supposed to ease aches and pains."

"Yes, well, I shall take it up with the merchants' association." Shin turned to face him. "Who was he?"

"His name is – was – Yacha. He was a bad one. At least two murders to his name, likely more. He mostly worked the peasants' road through the foothills, but lately he's been acting as muscle for Honesty-sama."

Shin perked up at this. "Is he involved, then?"

Batu looked away. "If he is, we'll never know."

"Shame. I was considering the theory that he was behind all of this."

Batu snorted. "No. War is bad for business – at least his businesses." He stretched, clearly tired. Shin knew how he felt. "No, I have no doubt he's trying to keep as far from this as possible. His sort don't like the light."

"Then how do you explain the presence of his men? If this Yacha was one of his, then the ones who attacked Reiji likely were as well."

"Those sorts are available to whoever has the money," Batu said, dismissively. "All it would take would be the promise of a few koku and they'd gut their own mothers."

"A pleasant image." Shin shook his head. "But would they take a job without Honesty-sama's permission?"

Batu looked away. "Maybe." But he didn't sound as if he believed it.

Shin nodded. "Exactly. Northern Owari has been flitting about the edges of this thing since the beginning. You may not like it, but there it is." He paused. "How is Yuzu, by the way?" The merchant had been hurried away by his servants after Batu had arrived at the onsen. He'd looked pale and sick by what had occurred – but angry as well.

"Fine. Shaken, but in one piece. Thanks to you."

"I was simply trying to stay alive."

"I did warn you," Batu said. "I told you that no good would come of this."

Shin waved his words aside. "What about Reiji? Has he talked yet?"

"He was being obstinate, so I had him locked up."

Shin blinked. "A joke?"

Batu leaned on the rail beside Shin. "No. I had him put into a cell opposite Ruri. She might be able to talk some sense into him."

"You haven't released her yet?"

"No. And I'm not going to until this matter is settled." Batu looked up at the night sky. "It's safer that way, I think, and not just for her."

"What do the Zeshi think of you placing Reiji into… protective custody, let's call it?"

"They are not best pleased."

"No, I do not imagine they are."

"Not for the reasons you think. The negotiations are set to conclude tomorrow, and Reiji is the key to the whole thing."

Shin paused. "Another marriage?"

Batu smirked and nodded. "It seems so."

"Who is the unfortunate young woman?"

Batu shrugged. "Some younger daughter from the Garanto Province. Ide Sora and the matchmaker, Umeko, have already made the arrangements. She will be here in a few weeks."

"In chains, I imagine."

"He's not that bad."

"He's not that good, either." Shin sighed. "And what does this mean for Ruri?"

Batu frowned. "The final decision is being left up to me, though I have been strongly encouraged to remove Ruri from the city by whatever means necessary." He looked at Shin. "She cannot stay here. Even though we've saved her life, she will have to be banished."

Shin looked away. "That is unfortunate, as well as unfair."

"I knew you would say that." Batu gave a sour laugh. "Fairness is inconsequential. Harmony must be maintained, and her continued presence will be disharmonious. So she goes – upright, or in a box."

Shin grimaced. "A blunt way of putting it."

"I am a blunt man, as you yourself have pointed out."

"What of the investigation?"

"The Ide are satisfied. The Zeshi and the Shiko – well, it doesn't really matter."

"And the Iuchi?"

"Ide Sora speaks for both families in this. A lasting peace is their only concern. Further grubbing would only complicate the matter." Batu paused. "She is a masterful woman. Proud. Authoritative."

Shin eyed him. "Are you attracted to her?"

A look of panic crossed Batu's face. "What? No. How dare you – this is not the time or the place. Silence!"

Amused, Shin said, "You *are* attracted to her."

"Silence!" Batu sounded almost panicked.

Shin smiled relentlessly. "No. Would you like me to put in a good word for you?"

"No! Cease talking about this." Batu turned away.

"Perhaps we should speak with Umeko. I'm sure something can be arranged."

Batu covered his face with his hands. "Please shut up."

Shin's smile widened. "Honestly, I'm not surprised. She looks like she can carry a horse up a mountain – just your type." He meant it honestly. Sora was a strong woman. Just the sort he could see Batu with. Not someone who would make sport of him, but who would approach life in the same way.

"Do not insult her just to tease me," Batu said, face still covered.

"It wasn't an insult. Strength is appealing. Only a fool finds it otherwise." Shin leaned down. "This one I approve of." He said it softly, quietly.

"Thank you," Batu muttered, sourly.

Shin gave him some room. "I think she'd have this city shipshape in a few months."

"Can we stop talking about this?"

"Yes."

Batu sighed. "Thank you."

"For now. Once this matter is settled I intend to pick up where we left off."

Batu shook his head in disgust. After a moment, he said, "If I tell you to let it be, you will refuse, of course."

"Of course. Are you?"

"I am not. First rule of being a magistrate – never give an order that will not be followed." He sighed and scrubbed his fingers over his scalp. "That said, I do not see where you can go from here. The families no longer have reason to speak to you. Indeed, they have all the reason in the world not to do so. Shijan especially."

Shin waved his words aside. "Do you think Yuzu was telling the truth?"

"Why ask me?" Batu grunted. "You're the one who claimed to be an investigator."

Shin laughed. "Yes, I did say that, didn't I? Thankfully, I no longer require their cooperation." He looked down towards the foothills. "I have learned all I can from them, but I am convinced that this is not settled. Someone tried to have me killed. Even if I did not believe there was something else at play, I would continue. Assassination attempts – especially clumsy ones – irk me."

"I am annoyed as well. Imagine how it would reflect on me if you died."

Shin laughed. "Your sense of humor seems to be returning."

"I wasn't trying to be funny." Batu frowned. "You could have really died, you know."

Shin said nothing. Batu grunted and shook his head. "What now?" he asked.

Shin pushed back from the rail. "Now, I talk to Reiji."

"I hope you have more luck than I did."

Shin made his way out the back, towards the outbuilding where the prisoners were being held. Lanterns had been lit, and armed guards were on duty. Kasami was with them. She had taken it upon herself to make a thorough circuit of the manor grounds, just in case any other assassins were waiting.

When she saw him, she glowered. "You should be inside. What are you doing out here?" She stomped towards him. She was still in full armor, despite the breach of etiquette. "Get back inside immediately!"

"I need to speak to Reiji."

"I don't care. Someone tried to kill you!"

"It's not as if it's the first time," Shin protested. Kasami flushed. Shin continued, quickly. "Come along if you like. I don't think Reiji will prove much of a threat, but you never know." He stepped around her before she could protest further, and continued towards the outbuilding. The guards stepped aside quickly.

The interior was lit tonight, likely for Reiji's benefit. In her cell, Ruri was singing. A soft, lilting song about loves lost and won. She fell silent as they drew close. She gave him a nod, and he returned the gesture. "You will be free soon," he said.

"But not today."

"No, not today." Shin turned. Reiji glared at him from inside his own cell. Shin gestured and Kasami removed the iron bar that kept the door shut. Reiji hesitated, then stepped back. Shin followed him into his cell. "Thank you for agreeing to answer my questions. You have my gratitude."

"I agreed to no such thing," Reiji said.

"You will answer him or I will…" Kasami began. Shin gestured, and she subsided. Reiji licked his lips nervously. Shin smiled.

"You will answer them because it is in your best interests to do so. You will answer them, because if you do not, you will remain here until such time as you do answer them."

"You cannot keep me here forever."

Shin nodded. "That is true. But we can keep you here for several days. Then, you might enjoy that, given what's waiting for you if we return you to your kin."

Reiji stared at him in silence. Shin nodded as if he had spoken. "You have made yourself very difficult to find. Not difficult enough, of course. We found you, as did those men who attacked you. As they might well find you again, and this time Kasami will not be there to save you." Shin peered at him. "Do you know them – the ones who attacked you?"

"I've never seen them before."

"Why might they have wanted you dead?"

Reiji shrugged, as if trying to appear unconcerned. "Perhaps they hoped to rob me. Heimin are all alike. They see a noble and think him wealthy."

"I do not think they intended to rob you. I think they meant to kill you. Indeed, I think they were there specifically to do so."

"Preposterous."

"Someone tried to kill me as well."

"That I believe," Reiji spat.

Shin smiled. "Yes, well, in any event it seems we have both angered the same person. I would like to try and find out who they are, before they try again. To that end, it would be best if you answered my questions."

Reiji hesitated. Then, "Fine. Ask."

"Good. Tell me about Gen."

Reiji glared at him. "We were friends."

"You owed him money."

"Who told you that?" Reiji demanded.

"Is it true?"

"Maybe."

"How much?"

"More than I could ever pay back." Reiji spoke with reluctance. "He loaned me money when I needed it. And I paid him when I could. When he asked."

"If you had no money, how did you pay him?"

Reiji hesitated. "Favors," he said, finally. "Well, just the one, really."

"Which was?"

Reiji looked away. Shin leaned forward. "I cannot help you if you do not talk to me. And you badly need my help, I think. What was the favor?"

"I convinced my father that Aimi ought to marry Gen." Reiji slumped. He slid down the wall of the cell and sat. "It would have solved everyone's problems." His expression twisted. "But of course, Aimi didn't see it that way. She barely gave him the time of day, and for a man like Gen, that was an insult. When I got those poems, I thought… I thought she'd finally come to see reason."

"Why?"

Reiji looked at him as if he'd suddenly sprouted a second head. "Well, she wrote them for him. Who else would she be writing poems about?"

"She didn't write them," Shin said, absently. "I'm surprised you didn't register the difference in handwriting styles. Who told you that she had?"

Another hesitation. Shin could see the wheels turning in the young man's mind. He wasn't a complete fool – just self-centered and inobservant. "Shijan. He… He, well, his man Yo, said that he'd found them, and it was a… a sign that she was thawing. That her intransigence was an act. Shijan told me to tell him, to show him the poems…" He trailed off and looked quizzically at Shin. "Why would he do that, if she hadn't written them?"

"Why indeed. Why did you steal papers from your cousin?"

"I didn't! I'm not a thief!" Reiji's disgust at the accusation was real.

Shin frowned. "No, you didn't, did you?"

Yuzu's words came back to him, and he thought about Shijan's debts and missing papers. And about a missing father. About accidents and sabotage. And then he thought about Shijan himself – ambitious but out of his depth. What might that sort of man do, if he felt he had no choice?

Shin stepped back. "Batu will release you tomorrow into the custody of your family." He closed the cell door. Reiji leapt to his feet.

"Wait – no!"

"Yes. You are safe here. And your safety is paramount." Kasami slid the bar back into place. Shin turned, and she followed him out.

Batu was waiting for them outside. "I've just had a messenger from Ide Sora. Shijan has demanded his cousin's release, and she concurs."

"Did you explain matters to them?"

"I have not yet sent a message in reply." Batu turned, watching the fireflies dance among the trees. "What did he tell you?"

"Enough to know that if that happens, he will be dead within hours, courtesy of his cousin."

Batu looked at him. "Shijan?" he asked, in disbelief.

Shin nodded. "Unfortunately, I believe so. Shijan is the one who gave Ruri's poems to Reiji, and encouraged him to give them to Gen."

"Why? He must have known what would happen."

"I think he was counting on it."

"We must tell someone... Ide Sora – no, I will arrest him. Tonight." Batu made as if to go, but Shin stopped him.

"Wait."

Batu shook his head. "No. We have him. You were right."

"If you accuse Shijan, what do you accomplish?" Shin said, quickly. "His word against yours – you are Iuchi, so you will carry the day. But if Ide Sora speaks up on his behalf?"

Batu frowned. "A stalemate."

"Exactly. And in her favor, given the importance of the negotiations to both families. We must have witnesses – we must drown them in testimony. We must have confessions that repudiate Shijan's claims of innocence."

"What sort of confessions? By whom?"

"Honesty-sama, for one."

Batu stared at him. "Are you mad?"

"No. But Honesty-sama is the one who sent a man to kill me – which he has no reason to do, unless someone had paid him to do so. The same for Reiji's attackers. It would not surprise me if more such assassinations are planned."

Batu shook his head. "But what does he gain from this?"

"A good question." Shin paused. Then, "The negotiations are to be finalized tomorrow?"

"Yes."

"Where?"

"I… I don't know. Presumably the Shiko estate."

"And everyone will be there, yes?"

"Yes. Why?"

"If I were of a mind to disrupt the negotiations, I might see such a gathering as a gift from the Fortunes. What might happen if someone – or several someones – were killed during this celebration?" Shin looked at Batu. "Shijan, if it is him, has already shown a willingness to employ hired killers to do his work for him. What is to stop him from doing so again?"

"They would see the futility of it, obviously. There will be guards–"

"Guards can be bribed, or killed. And there are other methods available to them than storming the front gate. Poison, for instance."

"Poison?"

"In the food. The result is the same whether they approach boldly or subtly – confusion, chaos, and both sides looking for someone to blame." Shin smirked. "Really, this could not have worked out better. How will it look, if, for instance, a high-ranking Ide is killed here?"

Batu went pale. "He wouldn't. No one could be so... so brazen."

"Perhaps not. Perhaps you are right. But what if you are not?" Shin turned away, hands folded before him. "I have a suggestion, if you are willing to hear it."

Batu rubbed his face, eyes closed. "Tell me."

"Suggest that they hold the final meeting here. That way you can keep an eye on Reiji tonight."

"They'll never agree to that."

"What if you tell them that you will pass final judgment on Katai Ruri at the gathering? That way both sides will be able to hear it for themselves, and be satisfied with your decision. They will be unable to resist the drama of it, I think." Shin smiled widely. "I know I would be hard-pressed to do so."

Batu gave him a suspicious look. "What are you up to?"

"I wish only to settle this affair, Batu – and do so in such a way that your status is raised in the eyes of your family." Shin grinned at him. "Really, this is all for your benefit. You might say thank you… though you'll forgive me if I don't hold my breath."

"And what do you intend to do, while I'm doing this?"

Shin smiled. "I intend to visit Honesty-sama and find out why he tried to kill me."

CHAPTER TWENTY-SEVEN
Gamble

"He tried to kill me!"

Yuzu was incensed. Emiko had never heard the normally unflappable merchant so aggrieved. "It is unacceptable," he barked, slapping a partition wall with his hand.

They were meeting in the back room of an onsen this time. Emiko could smell the sulfur and taste the damp on the air. She heard boards creak from somewhere close by as bathers made their way to the water.

It was not her favorite meeting place, for there were too many smells and sensations. But they could not meet in the same place twice in a row. It was too dangerous, especially now.

The city was abuzz with word of what had occurred, and the magistrate's deputies were on every street corner, rousting anyone even remotely suspicious looking. That included blind musicians. She knew who was ultimately responsible, and felt a flicker of annoyance at herself for not dealing with them when she'd had the opportunity. Now, everything they'd worked towards was in danger. All because one man couldn't do what he was told.

"The Crane was the target, not you," Fumihiro said, chiding Yuzu. She could hear the smile in the noble merchant's voice as he spoke. Fumihiro had been most amused by Yuzu's brush with death. Emiko had not. She could not see, but she was not blind in the ways that mattered.

Tashiro had brought word that Shijan was up to something. Why else would he have hired men to kill the Crane and his own cousin? These were not the actions of someone planning to lay low until things settled down. She wondered if it might not have been better to kill him at the shrine.

"I do not think hired killers make such distinctions. I was a witness. He would have happily butchered me, had the Crane not intervened." Yuzu paused to catch his breath. "This has gone on long enough. Action must be taken."

"What do you propose?" Eiji growled. "You're the one who counselled us to do nothing. To let him play out his string. You cannot moan about it now."

"And yet here I am – moaning. As for what I propose, it's simple… We kill him. Now. Make him vanish, the way we have made others vanish."

In the silence that followed, Emiko knew that she had become the center of attention. She smiled thinly and shook her head. "There are too many eyes on him now, with the negotiations largely settled. For him to vanish would only be to invite more attention. Something we still wish to avoid, yes?"

"She is right," Fumihiro said.

"And so is Yuzu," another voice interjected. Ichika. The geisha spoke softly, her voice lilting and gentle. "Our friend is no longer our friend. He is a stone, threatening to drag us under. We must cut him loose."

"As I said – kill him," Yuzu said.

"It would be easy enough. We have someone in the household who can accomplish the deed. We could ensure that evidence of his debts and other unsavory practices made it into the hands of the magistrate, making it appear as if it were a retaliatory killing." Emiko sighed and shook her head in mock sadness. "Everyone knows that the criminals of Northern Owari will kill anyone, regardless of status."

"A good idea," Yuzu said, approvingly.

"And what if he escapes?" Eiji grumbled. "What then, eh? Will we hunt him down – or let him go?"

Another long pause followed this question. Emiko listened to the murmurs and whispers of her fellow travelers. If it were left to them, they would argue the matter unto death. She considered saying nothing else. As far as she was concerned, she had done enough. Still – the great work was unending, and all must contribute.

She tapped the floor with her cane. The noise echoed through the room. Silence fell. She lifted her head. "There is danger here, but also opportunity."

"Say on," Ichika said. She sounded amused. Emiko wondered if she had seen it herself. The others clearly hadn't.

"If he is no longer our friend, he will be desperate to hide his complicity," Emiko said. "In attempting to do so, he may well further our ends despite himself. So let him scheme and twist himself into knots. Whatever he does, we will profit by it. Then, when he has made his move – we strike. We cut the cord and let the weight of their justice fall upon him, and him alone."

Someone cleared their throat – Tashiro. He had been the last to arrive. "There is another complication. The Crane… he has made it known in the last few hours that he wishes to speak to Honesty-sama."

"And?" Yuzu asked.

"Honesty-sama is not inclined to listen; in fact, I rather think he intends to kill the Crane – as a warning to others, if nothing else."

"That would be unfortunate," Yuzu said, quickly. "The Crane's death would prompt further investigation, not least from his clan."

"Blame would surely fall on the Unicorn," Eiji said. He sounded pleased. "His death would be to their detriment."

"Or to ours," Yuzu said. "Especially if it is somehow tied to our tame – or should I say formerly tame – bushi."

Fumihiro snorted. "And how would that happen? Planning to tell them yourself?"

"I am simply saying that the Crane's death would open us up to further danger." Yuzu grunted. "And, too, it seems a waste."

"What do you mean?" Ichika asked.

"He means that the Crane might be a candidate for recruitment," Emiko said.

Silence fell. Recruitment was a serious concern – it was necessary, but dangerous. The sect could not thrive without it, but every new recruit had the potential to endanger all that they had worked for. They had to be observed closely; vetted and tested; and finally, the other members had to unanimously agree to allow them to join. If at any point they failed, they would be disposed of.

"Why not just buy him, the way we bought the Zeshi?" Fumihiro asked. "Simpler by far, and more efficient."

"Except look where that's gotten us," Yuzu said, acidly. "No, the Crane has potential – but only if he survives whatever Shi – our friend – has planned."

"Or maybe you're feeling sentimental because he saved your fat neck," Fumihiro shot back. "You're the one who told us how dangerous the Crane is. He's the real threat here, not that fool, Shijan." A muffled murmur followed this, and Fumihiro snorted. "Oh please. We've as good as washed our hands of the Zeshi. We may as well say his name."

"The Crane is a threat," Ichika said. Emiko heard Yuzu make a sound of protest, hastily stifled. She went on. "But as Emiko said, in danger is opportunity. And great danger makes for great opportunity."

Emiko smiled.

Shijan stared out the window at the lights down below. The city. His city, soon. If his gamble paid off. He was due a win, he thought. Hopefully the Fortunes agreed. It was a shame his opening gambit had failed, of course. But one could not expect everything to go one's way in games of deceit and death.

He heard Yo enter the room behind him, and sighed softly. "Any word?"

"No, my lord. Your cousin remains in custody."

"Fine. It is just as well. He would only get in the way." Shijan turned. "Aimi?"

"Lady Aimi is in her room."

"Good. She will accompany us tomorrow." Batu's request for the negotiations to be concluded at his home had proven momentarily concerning. A change of venue meant a change of plan, but one had to know how to adapt.

"Are you certain that is wise, my lord?"

"It is necessary," Shijan said, not without some regret. But victory could not be achieved without cost – and great victories often had great costs. "Are the men ready?"

"As ready as such men ever can be."

"They know what is to be done?"

"If they do not, we will know of it soon enough." A rare flash of humor from the normally humorless Yo. Shijan frowned.

"That is not good enough. Things must go perfectly, else we risk everything coming undone. That will not do."

"No. It will not." Yo paused. "Tell me, my lord – what is the point of this?"

Shijan laughed. "You, of all people, ask me that?"

Yo paused. A brief look of puzzlement crossed his face. Shijan smirked. "Come, come. Do not play the fool. I know whom you serve. I know that you are here not for my benefit, but that of your unseen masters."

Yo bowed his head. "Then perhaps you will see fit to answer my question."

Shijan snorted. "What do you think the point is, fool? To serve your ends and mine."

"Your ends, perhaps," Yo said, softly. "Not ours, I think. We asked you to be quiet. To wait. This is not waiting and it most certainly will not be quiet."

Shijan did not meet his servant's bland gaze. "No. It will not be. But it will serve your purpose nonetheless. When it is done, I will be more useful to your compatriots than ever, and you will thank me for it."

"I do not think we will," Yo said. Even now, he spoke respectfully. He tilted his head, his open, honest eyes fixed on

Shijan. "We have done so much for you, Zeshi Shijan, and ask for so little in return. And you cannot even give us that."

The anger came back – in truth, it had never really gone away. He recalled his humiliation as he realized that Yuzu had beaten him in a game of dice. The heimin merchant had forced him into servitude, as if he were no better than a peasant.

Then had come the worst of it – the threat to reveal his humiliation unless he sold information to Honesty-sama; and not just information relating to Zeshi deliveries, but that of the Shiko as well. He did not know how Yuzu had gotten it, and he did not ask.

He had been caught between two tigers, forced to feed both lest he be devoured himself. Forced to sabotage his own family, as well as the Shiko, all to save himself – not his life, but from the shame of it all. Or so he told himself.

Then had come the command to disrupt the engagement, to further exacerbate the hostility between the families. Only now, it seemed, his mysterious enslavers were worried by what he'd done. More, they were afraid. And finally, he had an opportunity to turn his servitude to his advantage.

"What have you ever done for me?" Shijan demanded, letting the anger he felt creep into his voice. "You rig a game of chance, put me in debt to a criminal, make me your puppet… these are not the gifts you imagine."

"You say we have given you nothing." Yo's expression did not change. "But we removed your uncle, did we not?"

Shijan paused. He had always suspected that such was the case, but had not been sure. Even now, he wondered if it were a lie – a convenient story, meant to bind him even more tightly to them. "I did not ask that of you."

"And yet you wished for it. You hoped for it. Like all your kind, you would happily climb a ladder of bodies if it meant one more day at the top of the dung heap you've made of this land." Yo took a step towards him.

"Who are you to speak to me so?"

"A free man. One no longer bound by false courtesy." Yo took a second step towards him, and Shijan backed away instinctively. "I was told to watch and listen and I have. I know now that the Blind Woman should have killed you when she had the chance."

"Step back, Yo. Leave the room, and we will speak of this no more."

Yo sighed. "That cannot be done, I'm afraid. You have outlived your usefulness, my lord. I am sorry for you, though I expect that you do not appreciate it at this moment. Perhaps in the next life." His hand darted into his robe and reappeared with a knife.

Yo swept the blade up and came at Shijan in a rush. Acting on instinct, Shijan drew his wakizashi and intercepted a blow meant for his head. Yo stumbled slightly, but recovered more swiftly than Shijan expected. They circled one another.

Shijan held his sword awkwardly, but the lessons were coming back to him. Yo was fast – but without the element of surprise, he was just a commoner. He could not hope to match a bushi with a sword. At least, Shijan hoped that was the case.

He gritted his teeth and tried to focus. Yo slid forward on light feet, face set in that same damnably bland expression he'd always had. As if he were undertaking no more arduous a task than walking down the street. Shijan met him, desperation lending him speed, if not accuracy.

Their blades met, and slid away. Shijan rolled his shoulders, riding the momentum as his teachers had taught him, and pivoted at the last moment. His stroke opened Yo's back to the bone, and the servant gave a little gasp as the force of the blow knocked him to the floor. His blade clattered from his grip.

Somewhat startled by the suddenness of his victory, Shijan could only stare at the fallen man as he groped weakly for his weapon. Then, the cold calculus of the moment reasserted itself. Shijan lifted his sword and sent Yo's head tumbling away with a single, ragged stroke.

Breathing heavily, he lifted his sword and studied the blood running down its short length. He'd never killed anyone before, a fact which had always secretly embarrassed him.

It wasn't as difficult as he'd imagined.

As he wiped the blade clean, he felt strangely relieved. It was said that there was clarity in death, though he suspected that this was not what was meant.

There was no going back now. It had all come down to a final roll of the dice.

Win or lose, the game would end tomorrow.

CHAPTER TWENTY-EIGHT
Meetings

"This is perhaps the most idiotic thing you have ever done," Kasami said. Shin nodded cheerfully.

"Yet," he corrected. "That I have done yet." He looked up. Lady Sun was riding high in the sky. "Let us not be hasty. The day is still young, after all."

Batu had been against it, of course, but they had only a limited window in which to find something useful. Otherwise Shijan might well get away – at least with his reputation intact. Shin had considered several other options for bringing him low, including a vicious campaign of gossip, but he felt this would be more satisfying in the long run.

Shijan had tried to use the sword of Rokugani justice for his own ends – now they would use it to cut him down. What better end to this particular story than that?

To that end, Shin had made it known about the city – through the use of Batu's surprisingly extensive network of informants – that he wished to speak to Honesty-sama on an urgent matter. "There are worse ways I could spend my time," he said. "We could be listening to Shijan and Koji drone on at one another instead of enjoying a brisk constitutional."

Kasami grunted and looked around. They stood in an alleyway in Northern Owari, not far from the Jade Hare. The message had come in the morning, via certain routes known only to Batu's informants – Honesty-sama was happy to entertain a visit from Lord Shin. If the honored Crane would be so good as to meet a representative at a prearranged location, he would be escorted to Honesty-sama forthwith.

"It's a trap."

"Yes," Shin said, with a sniff. "And an obvious one. Clever, in a parochial sort of way. If I show up, I will be taken like a piglet to slaughter. If I do not, then the point is still made. Honesty-sama is not to be trifled with."

"Then why are we here?"

"Because I intend to trifle with him."

Kasami shook her head and looked away. "Foolishness."

"No. Curiosity. It's what I'm counting on. Honesty-sama knows something, but so do I. Like any good criminal, he'll want to know how much I know, and who I told."

"Or maybe he'll just kill you out of hand, just in case."

"Well, that's why you're here."

Kasami frowned and looked away. "You make me very tired sometimes."

"Exhaustion is good for the soul."

She glanced at him. "Something you read in one of your books?"

"Yes, why?"

"You only get that sort of nonsense from them."

Shin smiled. "Yes, well, not all of us can subsist on rice and duty. Some of us need more substantial meals – both literal and figurative." Shin caught sight of the ronin lurking at the opposite end of the street – he could be nothing else, given his kimono and the blades he wore. Shin nudged Kasami, and she nodded.

"I saw him a few moments ago. You should pay more attention to your surroundings." Kasami pushed past him and interposed herself between him and the approaching ronin. "That's far enough."

The ronin stopped. He was tall and saturnine. His kimono bore no sigil, and was the color of dust. "You are the Crane?"

Shin looked down at his blue kimono, as if to check. "I believe so."

"Good. Come." The tall ronin jerked his head. "This way."

"Where are we going?"

"You wanted to see Honesty-sama." The ronin was already moving away, down the street. "I will take you to him."

"And what is your name?" Shin asked, as he followed.

"Unimportant."

"I beg to differ."

The ronin glanced at him. "Tashiro," he said, somewhat grudgingly.

"A pleasure to meet you, Tashiro."

Tashiro grunted also, but did not reply. Shin looked at Kasami. "Not very talkative, is he?"

Kasami grunted, her eyes fixed on Tashiro's back. Shin sighed.

Tashiro led them along a circuitous route of alleys and side streets, away from the main flow of traffic. It put Shin in mind of walking backstage at the Foxfire Theater. He saw children pursuing one another through the dusty streets. Beggars congregated in the lee of tall buildings, and nightsoil carts rattled along.

They came at last to one of the low, sturdy warehouses that marked where the city began to slide into the foothills. The warehouses were unlike those he was familiar with, being little more than enclosed sheds, meant to protect their contents until they could be moved down into the foothills. Tashiro gestured. "Here."

"Inside?"

Tashiro nodded. As they entered, Shin saw that he had misjudged the size of the place – it had been built into the rockface of the slope, and extended back a good deal farther than he'd imagined. The warehouse was empty, save piles of canvas and wood, left behind by some previous owner. He presumed that Honesty-sama owned the building; according to Batu, he owned many such properties.

"I do not like this," Kasami murmured. "This is a good place for an ambush."

Shin shrugged. "So was the street, or the alleys."

Tashiro led them to the back of the building, where a heavy door of wood had been set into the rockface. The ronin knocked once and hauled the door open. The room beyond was dark, and smelled of dust and damp. Shin glanced at their escort. "In there?" he asked, doubtfully.

"Where else?"

"Somewhere with a bit of light, perhaps? A chance for a spot of tea?"

The ronin snorted. "This is a hideout for a criminal conspiracy, not a receiving room. Inside. Or else be on your way."

Shin frowned. He glanced at Kasami. She nodded wordlessly,

her hand resting on the hilt of her katana. Tashiro had one eye on her, as if calculating how much trouble she might be. Shin was confident that whatever answer he came to would be the wrong one. He sighed and stepped inside.

Despite the lack of light, he knew he was not alone in the room. There were at least four people standing in the shadows – maybe more. He felt a thrill of uncertainty. Perhaps this truly was a bad idea. The door slammed shut behind him, cutting off all sight of Tashiro and Kasami, and he resisted the urge to turn, as he was plunged into absolute darkness. "Well, Honesty-sama, I presume," he called out.

A soft laugh greeted him. Then the hiss of a flame, as a taper was touched to a wick. Illuminated by the soft glow of a single candle was a familiar face.

The blind woman smiled.

"Hello again, my lord."

Batu sighed as the negotiations entered their third hour. He sat in his accustomed place, trying very hard not to slump or slouch as the interminable wrangling gnawed at his frayed patience. He'd thought the matter settled, but it seemed otherwise. It seemed there was not one bone of contention but a whole skeleton.

He'd had a low table set out so that his guests might sit around it, thus implying an equality of status and esteem – Shin's suggestion, of course. Ide Sora sat near him, fanning herself against the heat. She watched the argument between Shijan and Koji with a look of bemused satisfaction. Umeko, the matchmaker, sat just below her.

There were others in attendance – Himari, ever at her

husband's side; Aimi and Reiji, both looking impatient; Lady Nishi and Lord Mitsue; as well as the usual profusion of servants, seeing to the needs of their masters. Lady Sora had brought her own clerks – who knelt at a respectful distance, busily recording all that was said.

Both parties had brought only the minimum escort allowed, as a sign of good faith. Ashigaru, mostly – all waiting outside, a safe distance from one another and in sight of the house. Bushi retainers stood on the steps, just outside the main doors, under the watchful eyes of his yoriki. There was less tension than he'd imagined.

Looking to distract himself, he ran over his preparations; Nozomi was making a circuit of the grounds with several other yoriki. The doshin were scattered about, guarding entrances as well as the prisoner. When the negotiations had concluded, he would order Ruri brought in so that he might pass judgment before the assembled parties.

After that – well. It all depended on Shin. He'd argued against visiting Honesty-sama. He feared there was nothing to be gained there, but Shin was adamant. Whatever he learned could be offered up as evidential testimony. Batu's eyes strayed again to Shijan.

The Zeshi did not seem nervous, or upset. Indeed, he seemed calm – collected. As if some great weight had been lifted off his shoulders. Even so, there was an air of anticipation about him. It might have been related to the negotiations, but somehow Batu didn't think so. Shijan was up to something – that much he was certain of.

His eyes flicked to one of the servants, kneeling behind Shijan. Something about the man seemed familiar – where had he seen him before? He wasn't Shijan's usual servant, that was for sure. He wondered what had happened to the bland-faced heimin.

"You are frowning," Ide Sora said, from behind her fan.

Batu leaned over. "I thought it was all over bar the formalities. Was I mistaken?"

She didn't look at him. "These are the formalities. All of the details have been arranged – all that remains is naming a time and a place."

"So they're arguing about who gets to hold the wedding?"

"Yes. Weren't you listening?"

"No."

She glanced at him. "You seem distracted."

Batu hesitated. How to explain? So he said nothing. Sora's smile was cool. "I was surprised when you offered your home as neutral territory. I thought you well out of it."

"Shin convinced me otherwise."

"Ah, the Crane. Now it makes sense. Hoping to shore up your flagging reputation?"

Batu grunted distractedly. "I have never been much concerned with my reputation." The words left his mouth before he'd thought about them, and he flushed. Sora looked away.

"No, I did not think so. From all that I had heard of you, I expected a brusquer welcome. I was surprised by your... effusive agreeableness earlier."

"This is an important matter. I do not intend to be the one to ruin it."

Sora nodded. "Even though you have continued to allow the Crane to peck about."

Batu almost laughed. "If you'd like to try and stop him, be my guest."

Sora frowned. "Where is he, anyway? I expected him to be here."

"Oh, he's pecking about somewhere."

"Was that a joke?"

Batu paused. "That depends entirely on how you wish to take it, I suppose."

Sora shook her head. "Iuchi humor." She turned her attention back to the negotiations. "I am glad that you chose to free Reiji, especially given you had no cause to hold him."

"I am magistrate. That is all the cause I need."

"The more you lean upon that authority, the weaker it becomes."

"Do you still intend to make a formal complaint?" he asked the question bluntly, hoping to startle her. He succeeded, for she gave him a curious look.

"No," she said, finally.

"Why?"

"It would serve no purpose now."

Batu nodded and straightened. "Good. I have enough problems."

She made a sound that might have been a stifled laugh, and he felt a moment's satisfaction. Shin wasn't the only one who could flirt. "What of the bodyguard?" she asked, after regaining her composure.

"I will release her, when this is done."

"And banish her, I hope."

Batu frowned. "Yes."

Sora nodded. "It is best." Her gaze strayed to Aimi. "The girl will not be happy."

"She has not been happy for a long time," Batu said, not without pity.

"Happiness is a gift, not a right," Sora murmured. Batu looked at her.

"My thoughts exactly." He was going to elaborate, when he heard a shout from outside. Just one – and cut off suddenly. He stiffened – and saw Shijan do the same.

"What is it?" Sora asked.

"I don't know." He half-rose from his dais, and detected the scent of smoke on the air. Something was burning, somewhere close.

"Stay here."

He circled the room, moving to the doors. Outside, smoke filled the corridor. Bodies on the floor. And two men, in the livery of Zeshi servants, approached him, blades in their hands. He whirled to shout a warning, and felt something tear through his side. As he fell, he saw Shijan's servant rise from behind his master, knife in hand.

The last thing he heard was Lady Sora screaming.

CHAPTER TWENTY-NINE
Agreement

"You are not Honesty-sama, I think," Shin said. The light of the candle did not stretch far beyond their immediate vicinity. He could not determine the number or faces of the others in the room with them, as they no doubt intended.

"Why? Because I am blind – or a woman?"

"No. You are too short."

She paused, face wrinkling in an expression of confusion. "What?"

"Exactly. You were in Two Step when our boat docked. I remember you now. And then at my welcome dinner. Kasami mentioned seeing you as well." He glanced in the direction of the door. "I trust your companion will not try to harm her."

Emiko inclined her head. "Most impressive. And she is perfectly safe."

Shin frowned, but accepted her statement. He could do little else at the moment. "I don't believe I caught your name last time."

She frowned. "Emiko."

"A lovely name. Who are your friends?" He peered past her into the dark. "Will they not share their names?"

"No," a woman's voice said, so softly that Shin almost missed it. "It is not for you to know our names. But it is for us to know yours, Daidoji Shin."

"That is not very impressive. My fame precedes me." Shin looked at Emiko. "What is going on?"

"We are saving your life. Honesty-sama would have killed you."

"I am aware that he would have made the attempt."

Another pause from Emiko. "Then why did you come here?"

"Because of what he might have said before attempting such foolishness." Shin sighed theatrically. "All you have saved me from is acquiring a last bit of evidence against the one responsible for a good deal of trouble." He clapped softly. "Well done, you."

"He insults us," a polished voice said. Courtly tones, but with a hint of provincial roughness. Shin followed the sound of the voice.

"Is it an insult to state fact? I think not. But I dislike muttering in the dark. Show me your faces, and let us converse as civilized folk."

Emiko shook her head. "No."

"Why?"

"Because you are who you are, and we are who we are."

Shin pondered this. "But you are not afraid of showing your face?"

"I am not important," she said. "Merely a part of the greater whole. You need not fear. We mean you no harm."

Shin snorted, annoyed with the melodrama of it all but

nonetheless pleased that death was not on the agenda. "Wonderful. A conspiracy, then. And what do you want?"

A new voice, muffled, but still somewhat familiar, spoke up. "To tell you what you want to know. The name of the party responsible."

"Zeshi Shijan," Shin said. He smiled as a startled silence followed his words. "I am aware of Shijan's perfidy. But I require proof – testimony, a confession, something." He narrowed his eyes. "Again, I ask – who are you?"

"Our identities are not important," the unseen woman said.

"I beg to differ. They are of the utmost importance, I think. How do you know anything of this matter?" He looked around. "Unless you are somehow involved."

"We are concerned citizens," Emiko said.

Shin shook his head. "No, I think not. There is something else going on here. A mystery beneath the mystery."

A man's voice this time, rough and stolid. "All you need to know is that Shijan is your quarry, and we can help you bring him to bay."

"I do not require your help for that. I have already made arrangements in that regard."

"The magistrate?" Emiko asked, head tilted.

"What of it?"

"He will not be enough."

Shin paused. "What do you know?"

Someone cleared their throat. "It appears we do know something that you do not."

Shin frowned. "Perhaps."

"Then maybe we have something to discuss after all."

"Did you bring me here to bargain?" Shin asked, and laughed.

"You should know that I do not haggle with those whose faces I cannot see."

The muffled voice again. "In this instance, you must."

"Possibly." Shin stared into the darkness. He hesitated, then said, "If you know of Shijan, then you must be involved somehow. I know that Shijan is in debt, and I suspect that he has been selling information to pay off those debts. What I do not know is to whom he has been selling it. I assumed it was to Honesty-sama."

"You would be correct," the muffled voice said.

"And how do you know that?"

"Because it is what we told him to do," Emiko said. Shin looked at her. He'd expected something like that. Things began to click into place. Who better than someone placed as highly as Shijan to disrupt the negotiations?

"What? Why?"

"You do not need to know that," the woman's voice purred. "All you need to know is that your suspicions were correct. Shijan is the culprit."

Shin looked around, taking in the darkened room, the lit candle, Emiko. He laughed softly. "Of course. Of course!"

"Why are you laughing?" Emiko asked.

"Because it all makes sense now. I could not see the motive for any of this – even Shijan's motive was suspect. Selling information to get out of debt – possible, but there are other ways for a bushi to get money if he needs it. Unless he had no option. Unless someone forced him to do so. Under threat of exposure, perhaps." He shook his head. "I wondered what I was not seeing, and here you are. Tell me, are you the reason Shiko Gen is dead?"

Another moment of silence. He could almost feel them looking at one another. Then, the polished voice spoke up. "We did not intend for Shiko Gen to die. We merely wished for the tensions between the families to continue – Gen was good at causing trouble, both for his family and the Zeshi. He was worth more to us alive than dead."

"His death was Shijan's fault," the muffled voice added.

"But you are the ones pulling Shijan's strings." Shin smiled thinly. "And now you intend to cut them – why?" He held up a hand, forestalling any reply. "Let me guess, my investigation endangers you somehow. Or maybe you are simply cautious. Either way, why bring me here? Why not let Honesty-sama handle the problem for you, if he could?"

"It has gone beyond that now," the muffled voice said. "Shijan wished to have you killed. We forbade it."

"He defied you," Shin said.

"He has gone his own way."

"Perhaps he realized that you no longer had use for him." Shin could feel their tension, though he could not see their faces. Shijan had not just angered them – he had scared them. That was why they were here, now.

"All the more reason to bring him to heel," the muffled voice said.

"Then do so," Shin said, flatly. He gestured. "You clearly have resources. Employ them. Make him vanish, as you no doubt did to Lord Hisato."

"How did you know that?" the polished voice hissed, after a moment's hesitation.

"I didn't," Shin said. "It was a guess, but thank you for confirming it. A tidy little scheme – remove Hisato, elevate

Shijan, then blackmail him. Worthy of a courtier." He looked at the shadowy figures. "Unfortunately for you, you are amateurs. You did not see all the variables – and so now you must scramble."

"Not all of us are born with the crooked mind of a Crane," Emiko said. Shin looked at her. She was smiling, but the expression was not a pleasant one. He was reminded of a tiger he'd once seen, as it gnawed on the leg of a goat.

"No, but you try your best regardless, for which I congratulate you." He straightened his kimono. "I think you brought me here because you are afraid that Shijan is planning something else – something that will reflect poorly on you. Am I correct?"

"You are," the muffled voice said.

"Then tell me."

Silence. Then, "Shijan has more men in his employ than you realize. A small army, in fact. Two dozen men, at least. Killers – brigands and bandits."

Shin blinked. "Why would he need so many? What targets other than myself and Reiji might he… Wait." He felt a cold chill sweep through him. "The end of the negotiations. The Ide envoy, the Shiko, the Zeshi, Batu – they will all be in attendance."

"He has nothing to gain by killing them," Emiko said.

"He has everything to gain. Now, at least." He laughed softly. "His only options are success – or death." He stroked his chin, trying to see it from Shijan's perspective. Ambition, fear, need – what might they drive a man to do?

Shin looked up. "Imagine, if you will," he began, "a conspiracy to undermine the families of the Unicorn." He gestured, indicating the shadowy figures. They shifted uneasily, and he smiled. He cleared his throat and went on.

"This conspiracy launches a deadly attack on two vassal families, even as they make peace with one another," he said. "All present are killed – save one miraculous survivor, who, with the aid of the vengeful Iuchi and Ide, hunts down the culprits behind the deaths of his family. The conspiracy is shattered, and the hero of the hour rises to his rightful place in the esteem of the Unicorn."

It was a good story – but only a story. There was no way to tell if that was Shijan's plan, or merely fanciful thinking. But a good courtier knew that the truth was often shaped to fit the audience. They already suspected Shijan – all he had to do was give them reason to fear him. "Only a fool would think he could pull off such a deceit," one of the masked figures spluttered, but unconvincingly. Shin laughed.

"Who will gainsay him? You? Or will you scatter and hide, hoping that he does not know more about you than you knew about him?" He laughed again. "He is a schemer and a gambler. This is his last throw of the dice. If he loses, he is finished. But if he wins – ah, if he wins, his fortune is assured."

A murmur passed through them as they looked at one another. Shin gave Emiko a surreptitious glance, and saw that she, at least, did not seem unduly troubled. "You are not worried?" he murmured.

"Shijan is weak. He was always going to break. The only question was how much trouble he would cause when he did so. I am gratified to find that I was correct in my estimation."

Shin blinked. "Well, I am glad you are glad." He looked back at the others. They were arguing, albeit in hushed voices. "Enough – *Enough!*" he said, raising his voice. They fell silent. "It might be that I am wrong. That Shijan will simply flee.

But I do not think so. So, what now?"

A throat was cleared. "What do you mean?"

"I mean, what now? You brought me here to tell me that Shijan was the culprit. Why? Because you have lost control of the situation, and you wish to sever the thread that connects you to him. Perhaps you have already tried to do it yourself, and failed. Either way, you now expect me to do it for you. Very well, I will do so."

"And what then?" someone asked.

"That depends on him. I hope to turn him over to the magistrate."

"Unacceptable."

Shin's smile was hard and cold. "Now we come to it. This was always to be the bargain, wasn't it? What do you want?"

"Shijan."

"If you can find him, by all means take him."

"We want your word that if you catch him, you will give him to us."

Shin gave a bark of laughter. "I will make no such promise."

"You have no choice," Emiko said, softly. She tossed the candle into the air and he caught it, instinctively. There was a hiss of steel, and he froze as the edge of a blade nestled against the hollow of his throat. Emiko, head cocked, held her blade steady.

"Good catch," she said, a slight smile on her face. "You will not leave here unless we come to an accord, Crane."

He was glad Kasami was safely on the other side of the door. If she'd been in here with him, things would have turned very nasty, very quickly. "The same sort of accord you had with Shijan?"

"He is a fool," the muffled voice said. "You are not. You are a clever man, and we can use clever men. Men who see the truth of the world. You are right – about all of it. We made a mistake, and compounded it through ignorance and arrogance. We shall rectify that mistake, but in our own way. Surely you understand why."

"I do. If he talks, there is a risk he will be believed. His confession will go into a file that someone with an open mind might read some day, and decide to investigate." Shin looked in the direction of the muffled voice. "And that would be bad for you, wouldn't it, Master Yuzu?"

A sharp inhalation greeted his words. After a moment, Yuzu stepped forward into the candlelight. "How did you know?"

"You told me yourself, remember? You're the one he was in debt to. Who else would be able to exert such power over him?"

Yuzu laughed. "I told you he was smart."

"Or maybe you were just a fool," the polished voice remarked.

Yuzu gestured irritably. "Either way, we must come to an agreement." He looked at Shin. "I owe you my life."

"You have a funny way of repaying debts," Shin said. He reached up and with a finger he gently, slowly, eased Emiko's blade away from his throat.

"You help us, we help you," Yuzu said, clasping his hands behind his back. "Surely you see the sense in it. We want the same thing." He smiled. "Decide quickly. If I know Shijan, you don't have much time."

"If he is harmed, I will kill you – and then whoever is hiding in that room," Kasami said lazily, as she stared at the door that had separated her from Shin. She tapped rhythmically at the hilts of her swords. The ronin tensed, and his hand drifted towards his own sword.

She wished he would go for his weapon. Taking out her frustrations on the ronin would have made her feel somewhat better. To her annoyance, he looked away. "You might find that more difficult than you imagine," he said.

Kasami stared at him in silent challenge. "No. I won't."

The ronin frowned, still not meeting her eyes. "If we wanted you dead, you would be dead. I could have brought a dozen men to that alleyway."

"That is not my concern. I am merely stating fact." As she spoke, she wondered who "we" were. Not Honesty-sama, she thought. She'd dealt with enough criminals on Shin's behalf to know that this was something different. She didn't like it.

She didn't like anything about any of this. A simple matter had become something sprawling and messy, thanks to Shin's insistence on meddling.

The ronin grimaced and scratched at his neck. He was unshaven and unkempt; the sort of ronin that gave all the rest a bad name. Kasami looked around. The warehouse was small and empty, save for the detritus of more profitable times.

"What is this place?"

"One of Honesty-sama's properties."

Kasami raised an eyebrow. "How do you know this?"

The ronin grunted and looked away. Kasami snorted. She could hear voices inside the room. Shin was doing most of the talking, as was to be expected. She'd half expected it to be some form of ambush. That such did not seem to be the case was almost disappointing.

Again the old frustration welled up. Once again, Shin had

nearly died and she had been elsewhere. Memory of the fire at the Foxfire Theater still brought a flush of shame to her face. What sort of bodyguard was she, that she could not keep one Crane out of the fox's jaws? She frowned. Of course, it would be easier if Shin didn't insist on crawling into said fox's mouth at every available opportunity.

The door opened suddenly, and Shin stepped out. His face was pale – as if he were angry. He was followed by the blind woman. Without a word, Shin caught the ronin's arm. "You work for Honesty-sama, yes?"

The ronin blinked in surprise. "What?"

"The tattoos on your neck and chest. I caught a glimpse of them. They're similar to the ones on the man who tried to kill me."

"Yacha," the ronin grunted and tugged at his kimono, as if to hide the offending tattoos. "He was a fool."

"So you knew him."

"I know them all."

"Good." Shin gestured to the blind woman. "Emiko here tells me that you have some authority over the thugs Shijan has hired. That you might be able to call them off."

"Not without good reason," the ronin protested.

"Tashiro," Emiko said, softly.

The ronin looked at her, and a strange look passed across his face. Kasami wondered at it, and at the way the blind woman touched his arm. Shin was too preoccupied to notice. She knew the look on his face well enough. His mind was focused on the problem at hand. The ronin – Tashiro – nodded. "I can do it, yes."

"Good. Then you will come with us."

"As will I," Emiko said.

"No," Tashiro said.

"A blind woman is more hindrance than help," Kasami began. She heard a hiss of steel and barely interposed her own blade in time to deflect a blow that would have opened her jugular. Emiko smiled and stepped back, sheathing her blade.

"I do not need eyes to cut," she said.

Kasami glared at her, though she could not see it. She raised her blade. "But you do need a head to live," she growled, as she took a step forward. The blind woman frowned and stepped back, lifting her cane.

Shin stepped between them. "No."

"Step aside. She nearly killed me."

"We have no time for this. They have offered to help, and I have accepted that offer. That means you will leave her head attached to her neck where you found it." Shin turned to the blind woman. "And you will keep that blade of yours sheathed until I tell you otherwise."

"You do not command me, bushi…" Emiko began.

Shin spun and leaned close to her, causing her to take an involuntary step back. "For the moment, I do. That is the bargain we made. If you do not like it, take it up with your comrades back there." He gestured to the door. "Otherwise, cease upsetting my bodyguard, or I shall let her have your head."

Kasami looked at Shin. "We cannot trust them," she said, but it was half-hearted. He had already made up his mind. She wondered at the nature of the bargain he'd mentioned. She wanted to ask, but now wasn't the time.

"No. We cannot. But we must." He started towards the doors.

"We do not have time for anything else. Now come – we must make haste."

Kasami hurried after him. "Why? What is going on?"

"Shijan is planning to attack the negotiations. Our... friends here are going to help us stop him."

"Why?" she asked, suspiciously. "Who are they?"

"Concerned citizens," Shin said, tersely. He stopped at the doors. "We will never make it in time if we have to walk. Not even you can run that far, that fast."

"Horses," Tashiro grunted.

Shin turned. "Nearby?"

Tashiro smiled tightly. "This is a Unicorn city, Crane. There are horses everywhere. You just have to know where to look."

"You hate horses," Kasami murmured.

"Yes." Shin attempted a smile. "But I hate losing more."

CHAPTER THIRTY
Gambit

Shijan could smell smoke and hear the clangor of weapons. It did not sound as frightful as he had imagined. He took a deep breath, though he knew it was inadvisable. He felt a sense of relief that the clarity he'd gained the night before was still there. No more hesitation. No more fear. Only action.

The bodies of several servants lay against the walls, huddled in death. The survivors – including the useless pair who served Batu – had been left tied up in the kitchen, where they would undoubtedly perish, either from the smoke or the fire.

He felt a faint flicker of guilt for that. It seemed a waste of good servants. But needs must when necessity drove. Besides himself, three men stood over the still-seated representatives of the families. Though these men wore Zeshi colors, they were not servants – at least not his servants. Not really.

They belonged to Honesty-sama, body and soul. Hard men, killers and thieves. Idly, Shijan wondered if this was how it had begun for the great families, so long ago. A baptism of blood, and killers who would be remembered as heroic warriors, if they were remembered at all. He looked at the closest of the three – the one who'd stabbed Batu. "Well?"

The man nodded. His name was Kota and he spoke calmly, but with the rough accent of one born in the foothills. "It's working. Taka and his bunch are raining fire on this place. Chiko and the rest are seeing to the guards – they'll keep them distracted, if nothing else."

"Good." The plan was a simple one – divide and conquer. Honesty-sama's men had split into three groups. One, composed of those who knew how to use a bow, had set themselves a safe distance from the grounds and sent a volley of fire-arrows to distract the guards and draw them into the open. A second – and third – volley had cut their numbers and sent the survivors scrambling for cover.

With the guards thus distracted, the second group had gone over the walls, or through the main gate. In the confusion, they were to kill anyone they came across. Between the occasional arrow, efforts to fight the spreading fire, and Chiko's armed killers, both the families' escorts and Batu's deputies were scattered and overwhelmed.

The third group had been given the most onerous task – pretending to be servants. They'd snuck in weapons, and had killed any real servants who put up a fight. It was they who were the most important part of his plan.

It had all been so easy – surprisingly so, in fact. He'd wondered, even as he did it, whether there had been some value in learning the arts of war after all. Though perhaps his family had not intended that he put those lessons to use in this fashion.

Kota grunted. "We couldn't stop them from sounding the

alarm, though. We should leave soon, before anyone comes to see what's going on."

"We will. But not yet." Shijan looked down at Batu. The magistrate wasn't dead, but he was hurt. Kota's knife had taken him in the side, and there was a substantial amount of blood on the floor. Once, the sight might have repulsed him. Now he felt only satisfaction.

Shijan sank to his haunches and looked down at the injured man. "You almost had me, you know… you and the Crane. And for that, I thank you. I might never have conceived of this – any of it – if you hadn't pushed me."

Batu groaned and tried to rise. Shijan stood and stepped on him, forcing him down. "Stay down. I do not wish to make this any more painful than it has to be." He turned, looking at the others. "Not for any of you."

"What… What have you done?" Koji demanded. He made to rise, but one of Shijan's men gestured with a knife, and the Shiko sank back down. "What is this?"

"The end of the war," Shijan said. "I won, by the way."

"The Crane was right about you," Reiji said, his voice hoarse. "You sent someone to kill me." He looked so much like a child that Shijan almost felt pity for him.

"Yes, Reiji," Shijan said. "And even there, you disappointed me. If you'd had the good grace to die when I wanted, this all would have been so much easier."

Easier for you, you mean, Aimi signed furiously, her hands shaking. She was staring at him as if he were some species of venomous serpent.

"Yes, well, you only have yourselves to blame." He forced a smile. "None of this would have been necessary if you had simply listened to me. But you didn't, and now here we are. I told you that ronin would be nothing but trouble, but you didn't listen."

"Why kill Gen?" Reiji croaked, staring in befuddlement. "Why argue for marriage and then… and then kill him?"

"I didn't kill him. I didn't intend for him to die. That he did is not my fault. I merely wanted to stoke the fire a bit – not burn down the house." He chuckled. "And now look where we are. A man makes plans, and the Fortunes laugh."

"This is unacceptable," Ide Sora said, as she gathered herself and stood from where she'd been kneeling. She'd lost her composure only briefly, when Batu had been stabbed. Before anyone could stop her she had made her way to Batu, and was kneeling beside him. Kota made to grab her, but Shijan held him back.

"Don't touch her. Whatever else, she is still a lady of the Ide."

She gave him a cutting look. "Good manners do not make you a man, Shijan." She began to tear strips from the hem of her kimono. "What do you hope to accomplish with this… this idiocy?" As she spoke, she began to bind Batu's injury.

Shijan looked down at her in bemusement. "Idiocy? This took quite a bit of thought." He gestured, and Kota placed a knife in his hand. "Days of planning, of debate and consideration. At first, I feared I might not have the courage for it."

"Courage?" Mitsue said. "This is not courage. This is…" He fell silent as Nishi took his arm. Shijan ignored them. He turned to Kota.

"What about the ronin?"

"What about her?"

"We must make sure she is dead. No one can be allowed to survive – save myself, obviously. Else the whole plan is for nothing. Go – see to her yourself."

No, Aimi signed, getting to her feet as Kota made for the door.

"Sit down, cousin." Shijan gestured with his knife. "If you truly love her, I am certain your souls will meet again." He smiled, sadly. "I hope so, at least, for your sake." He motioned, and his two men moved towards the others. "I ask that you do not struggle. The easier you make this, the easier your deaths will be. That is the only mercy I can offer you."

Sora glared up at him. "Mercy? Is that what you call it?"

Shijan grabbed a handful of her hair and jerked her head back, exposing her throat. He raised his knife. "Better than burning to death, I should think."

Kitano leapt back as another flaming arrow thudded home into the wooden frame of the outbuilding. He'd been trying to get a game going with some of the Shiko soldiers, but dice were the last thing on his mind now. He and three soldiers now crouched, trying to avoid the deadly rain that fell across the grounds.

The arrows had come from seemingly nowhere. They arced over the trees and the walls, punching into the dry grass, the branches of the trees and the outbuildings. All of them were alight, and the fire had caught in too many places to count. Smoke filled the air. Someone was ringing an alarm bell, but Kitano doubted anyone would respond. He could hear the clash of weapons from somewhere back among the trees, as well as out front.

"What's going on?" one of the ashigaru asked, ducking back as another arrow sank into the side of the outbuilding.

"What does it look like?" Kitano said. He reached for his knife. "We're under attack."

"Who'd be mad enough to attack this place?" the ashigaru demanded.

"Whoever they are, there are a lot of them." Kitano peered towards the house. The smoke made it hard to see anything, but he thought he saw shapes moving towards the building. He glanced at the soldiers. "We need to get to the house."

"I'm not going out there," one of the men said.

"Your lord is in danger," Kitano said.

"Our lord is behind big thick walls, and surrounded by the magistrate's men."

Kitano paused. The man had a point. Even so, he had to go. He shook his head. "Suit yourself. I'm going."

"What? Why?"

"Better than burning up in here." Without waiting for a reply, Kitano ducked out into the smoke. His eyes immediately began to water, but he kept moving. The grass had caught quickly, and the crackle of fire was loud in his ears. Whoever had planned the attack had been smart. Fire was a criminal's best friend. It was bright and loud and inevitably attracted everyone's attention. Some of Kitano's best scams had involved fire. And firefighters were always good for a game or two, especially when they had a protection racket going.

He headed for the house, sleeve pressed tight to his hand and nose. Eyes stinging, he spied bodies laying on the ground. Some had arrows in them – but not all. He could hear the clash of steel – someone, somewhere, was fighting.

Coughing, he reached the back of the house. He still wasn't sure what he was going to do once he got inside. He wasn't a soldier, or a samurai. Just a gambler. But if he didn't try to do… something, anything, he'd never hear the end of it. Knife in hand, he slid the door open. There was no smoke inside. The house hadn't caught fire yet, but it wouldn't be long before that happened unless someone put it out.

On instinct, he headed for the kitchen. He heard muffled cries, and saw a huddled group of servants, bound together by torn rags. Quickly, he stooped and began to cut them free. As he did, Hiro told him what had happened. They'd been left to die, Kitano knew, though he didn't say it. No sense frightening anyone more than they already were.

When he'd finished, Yuki clutched at him, weeping. Gratifying as that was, now wasn't the time. He gently pushed her aside. The others milled about, frightened – at a loss. Kitano caught Hiro's attention. "Someone needs to get these people out of here. Can you lead them to the service entrance?"

"What about you?" the boy asked, face pale, save for a bruise purpling on one cheek. He'd fought back and paid for it. Kitano smiled.

"Someone has to rescue the bushi, eh?" He paused. "Once you're out on the street, send someone for the firefighters. And alert the neighbors. Can you do that?" The boy nodded, and Kitano patted him on the shoulder. "Good lad. I–"

The door slid open, interrupting him. A man in Zeshi colors stood in the doorway, a puzzled look on his face and a knife in his hand. "What's going on in here? Who are you?"

Kitano stood and let the man see his own knife. "Nobody important." He glanced at Hiro. "Everyone out – now!"

As he spoke, the Zeshi servant – who was not a servant – came at him in a rush, knife held low. Kitano, no stranger to back-alley knife-fights, lunged to meet him. They scuffled, trading slashes and curses. Kitano got in a lucky cut, and his opponent dropped his blade. Kitano made sure he didn't pick it up again.

He looked around and saw, with some relief, that Hiro had done as he asked. The servants were gone. Hopefully they'd make it. But he couldn't worry about that now. Puffing slightly, bleeding from several shallow cuts, he staggered out of the kitchen – and nearly lost his head. He fell back, hands up. "I'm on your side!"

Nozomi glared down at him. "What are you doing here?" The yoriki was bleeding, one hand pressed to her side. Arrows jutted from her armor. But her sword was steady in her hand and her expression was deadly serious.

"I was… coming to help?"

She snorted – and spun, her sword opening up the man who'd crept up on her. Kitano blinked. He hadn't even seen him. "W-Who are they?" he asked.

"Zeshi."

"No," Kitano said, looking at the dead man. "What sort of household servant has tattoos like that?" He picked up the dead man's blade. "This is something else." Lord Shin would know what was going on, Kitano was sure of it. Only Lord Shin wasn't here. He thought quickly. "Have you seen the magistrate?"

"No," Nozomi said.

"They had the servants tied up. They might have Lord Batu and the others in the receiving room." Kitano licked his lips. "We should probably hurry."

Nozomi hesitated, visibly surprised. "You will come with me?"

Kitano gave a weak smile. "If I didn't, Kasami would take off the rest of my fingers."

CHAPTER THIRTY-ONE
Out of Luck

Three horses galloped through the crooked streets of Hisatu-Kesu. Tashiro, in the lead, bent low over his steed's neck. Kasami, on the one behind, did the same. Shin brought up the rear, Emiko clinging to him. The blind woman had insisted on riding with him, likely to ensure his compliance. He hadn't argued.

"You ride well, Crane," Emiko said, leaning against him. He couldn't tell whether she was trying to compliment him – or reassure him.

"How can you tell?" Shin shot back. He hated horses, but like all bushi knew how to ride. But knowing something, and doing it, were two different things.

"I haven't fallen off yet."

The main gate of Batu's home came into sight. Smoke rose in thick columns from behind the stone walls, and an alarm bell was ringing. A quartet of men in rough clothing stood near the gate, loosing arrows over the wall. One turned as the horses approached and, eyes wide, raised his bow.

Tashiro thundered towards them, shouting. The arrow went wide, thudding into a nearby building. Thankfully, it had not been lit. Tashiro's horse reared as he berated the men, and they retreated in apparent confusion. Shin galloped past, Emiko holding tight to his midsection. The gates were open, and his steed shot through them without slowing. "Do you have a plan?" the blind woman shouted. "Or are we just going to gallop about?"

"The plan is to stop Shijan – and the best way to do that is to interrupt whatever he's planning! Now hold on!" Shin bent low over his horse's neck as he urged the beast on. Tashiro and Kasami fell in behind him as he rode through the gates and into the inferno that had been made of Batu's grounds.

"I'll find Chiko and the others," Tashiro shouted. Shin acknowledged his words with a nod. The ronin would send away as many of Honesty-sama's men as he could. Anything to even the numbers. Shin urged his horse on towards the house. Kasami followed.

There were bodies on the ground, arrows jutting from them. Others had been cut down in the midst of running somewhere or seeking cover. The smoke was thick, clogging the air. Shin's horse whinnied nervously as it picked its way over the dead. He felt a coldness settle in him as the house came into view.

He slid from the saddle and helped Emiko down. Kasami climbed out of the saddle as well. She drew her sword, and after a moment's hesitation, he did the same. The doors were open. They stopped. The blind woman paused. "I hear nothing," she said.

"We might be too late," Kasami said, softly.

Shin shook his head and stepped inside. He hurried towards

the receiving room, ignoring Kasami's attempts to get ahead of him. He stopped as two figures suddenly appeared from the opposite direction. He blinked, startled, as he recognized Nozomi and Kitano. The yoriki had looked better – pale, obviously injured. Kitano was bleeding as well, but not as badly.

"My lord," Kitano began. Shin silenced him with a gesture. The doors to the receiving room were shut. He made to open them, but a light touch on his arm stopped him. Emiko stepped past him, unsheathing her blade as she drew near the door. Before he could say anything, she paused, head tilted – and then drew and slashed, parting the partition in two places. A body collapsed through and crashed to the floor, dragging most of the door with it.

The dead man twitched, and died without a sound. He was dressed in Zeshi raiment, but bore the tattoos of a criminal. Emiko stepped back, head bowed. Shin and the others stepped into the room.

A frozen tableau greeted them. No one was moving. Whatever had been about to happen had been interrupted by their arrival. Shijan stared at them, mouth open. He held Ide Sora by her hair, a knife in his other hand. Beside him, another man in Zeshi colors raised a sword over Lord Koji's head.

"Kasami," Shin snapped.

The command hadn't been necessary. Kasami was already moving, and the swordsman, startled, backpedaled away from his intended victim. He put up a half-hearted defense, and tried to dart past her – but Nozomi was waiting. The yoriki's sword flashed, and the unlucky man fell with a choked grunt.

"Put the knife down," Shin said. His eyes found Batu – lying on the floor, injured. Still alive, though. And his eyes were open.

He looked relieved. Also angry, which Shin somehow found more comforting.

Shijan hesitated. He licked his lips. "No. No, I think not. I think–"

Whatever he'd been about to say was interrupted by Batu's roar of anger. The magistrate heaved himself up onto one knee and clawed for Shijan's wrist. Sora went sprawling, and the knife clattered to the floor. Shijan shoved Batu back with a curse, and dove for the sword his man had dropped. He snatched it up before anyone could stop him, and was out the door a moment later, heading for the back.

"I think he's going after Ruri," Aimi said. She was pale, but had a knife in her hand. Shin hesitated, looking at Batu.

"Go, Shin – catch him," Batu said, wincing in pain. Sora was trying to help him to his feet. "Do what you came here to do."

Shin nodded. "Kitano – help get everyone out." Shin was already at the door as his servant made to reply. He raced for the outside, Kasami and Aimi hurrying after him. He wanted to tell the young woman to wait, but there was no time to argue.

Outside, flames clawed at the sky. Smoke prowled thick among the outbuildings. He could hear shouts and alarm bells. Someone was trying to put the fire out, but there was no way to tell who. It didn't matter. Through the smoke he saw Shijan, hurrying towards the outbuildings. He was shouting for someone – a man, in the livery of the Zeshi.

The latter had hauled the doors of the outbuilding open. He turned, eyes widening slightly as Shijan hurried towards him. "Kasami," Shin said, coughing as the smoke rolled over them. Kasami put on a burst of speed and raced for the man at the door. He fell back, startled, and Shijan leapt aside.

The man bore a long blade – a peasant's blade – and he had some skill, but not enough. Kasami cut him down without a word, dropping him to the ground. She was forced to fall back as Shijan slashed out at her. Shijan retreated into the outbuilding.

"There's no way out of there," she said, as Shin reached her.

"There's one way," Shin said. He waved Kasami and Aimi back, and stepped inside. Shijan was waiting for him at the far end near Ruri's cell. He'd opened the door, and she stood, the tip of his sword pressed to her throat.

Shin sheathed his own sword and folded his hands. "Hello, Shijan. Funny seeing you here." He looked up. "Strange weather we're having."

"Shut up," Shijan growled.

Shin forced a smile. "Now is that any way to talk to the man who's going to save your life? One would think you might be able to muster a bit of courtesy, even now."

Shijan gave a bark of laughter. "Save my life? You're the one who's ruined it – and all for a worthless ronin." He turned his blade, digging the tip into Ruri's throat. She made no sound, her soot-smudged expression one of calm.

Aimi was not so composed. She ignored Shin's attempt to wave her back. "Let her go, Shijan. Take me instead. I am a better hostage." Her hands moved frantically, belying the monotone calm of her voice.

Shijan frowned, as if considering this. Shin spoke up quickly, before the other man could come to a decision. "All things considered, I am a better option," he said. "There is a greater risk to all concerned if I should die."

Shijan glared at him. "I do not know that I could trust myself not to cut your throat." He gestured to his cousin. "Get over here – now!"

Aimi started forward, but Shin caught her arm. "No, I think not."

"I will kill the ronin," Shijan insisted.

"I am aware," Shin said, softly. He met Ruri's gaze and she nodded, ever so slightly. "But you must know that this is a trade I will not allow."

Shijan snorted. "After all the trouble you went to to save her?"

"Even so."

Aimi clutched at his arm and gave a soft, inarticulate cry. Shin ignored her and kept his eyes on Shijan. "Kill her, and I will still have Kasami take you alive. Minus a hand, perhaps – or a leg. There is no way out for you."

Shijan was silent for a moment. Then, "Tell me – where did you go today? I expected you to be here, but you weren't. You went somewhere, talked to someone – who?"

Shin said nothing. Shijan nodded. "Yes, I thought so. You talked to them, didn't you? My silent partners in all of this. They tried to kill me, you know. This is all because of them – they set me on this path, and then had the gall to complain when they at least felt the heat of the flames they'd helped kindle."

"Yes. They did seem an ungrateful bunch."

Shijan laughed shakily. "You have no idea. I was not the first they have used so, nor will I be the last."

Shin took a step towards him. "Then let me help you. Together, we might be able to see that they are brought into the light. You will not escape justice – so why should they?"

Shijan gave a sickly smile. "A good point. But I do not need you to help me repay them. I will do so in my own time, in my own way, I assure you."

"Be that as it may, you will not do so today. Let Ruri go, put down your sword, and surrender. There is still a chance to survive this."

Shijan's eyes narrowed. He hesitated – Shin saw the tip of his sword slide away from Ruri's neck. As it did so, she leapt forward, out of the cell and away. Aimi cried out and lunged to meet her. Shijan cursed and made to follow, but Shin interposed himself. Without turning, he said, "Kasami, see them to the house. I will be along shortly."

"No," she said.

"It was not a request," Shin said, flatly. He lifted his sword, and Shijan's expression wilted. His confidence had evaporated, but his defiance remained. He lowered his sword. The gesture seemed to satisfy Kasami, and Shin heard her usher the other two out. "That's better," Shin murmured. "Now we can talk in private."

"I have nothing to say to you," Shijan said, hoarsely.

"Not yet. But maybe later. Later, when you've had a chance to think on things." Shin took another step towards him. "These friends of yours – ex-friends, I should say – they are dangerous. So are you, but they are more so, I think."

"You have no idea. But you will. You'll find out soon enough, if you were foolish enough to make a bargain with them. Even if not. They have a way of getting their hooks into you, whatever your intentions." Shijan raised his sword.

Shin tensed. "Do not do this."

"I will not surrender. I will not be shamed by you, or anyone." Shijan made to say something else when there came a distinctive tap-tap from the direction of the doors. Shin turned. The smoke parted – and there was Emiko. The blind woman had her head cocked, listening. Her cane was held tight across her body.

"It is too late for that, I think," she said.

Shijan made a strangled sound, deep in his throat. He took a step forward. Shin fancied that he could see the frayed strands of Shijan's courage finally snap.

"Shijan – listen to me. Surrender and I will do what I can to–"

Shijan wasn't listening. He charged forward, face stretched in a silent snarl. Shin stepped aside, narrowly avoiding a wild blow. He drew his sword, but Shijan did not stop. He barreled towards Emiko – and past her, into the smoke.

Shin considered pursuing him, but stopped as Emiko turned to follow the fleeing noble. "Do not concern yourself, Crane," she said. "As we promised, we shall clean up our mistakes." She paused. "Thank you for your help."

Shin lowered his sword and turned away. He felt sick at heart, but he had made a bargain, and he would not – could not – back away from it.

He did not look back, until the tapping of her cane had faded to silence.

CHAPTER THIRTY-TWO
Departures

"Well. This has been fun."

Shin stood on the steps, looking up at Batu. His luggage was already loaded atop a horse, ready to be carried back to Two Step and the waiting boat. Behind him, Kasami stood watching as Kitano checked the bags.

"It has not," Batu said. He looked up as a worker yelled something to one of his fellows. The house was crawling with them, as were the grounds. "But it has been interesting, I will say that." He winced and pressed a hand to his side. "Too interesting."

Shin nodded. "What now?"

Batu shrugged. "The negotiations are over." He paused. "Ide Sora is staying for a few days. To make certain everything goes as it should."

"Is that the only reason?"

"What other reason would there be?"

Shin laughed. "Never mind. Forget I asked." He looked

towards the horses. "What of Ruri? Has anything changed there?"

Batu shook his head. "The Zeshi are still arguing over the matter. I never passed a sentence on her and … well, for the time being, Aimi is in charge of the Zeshi fortunes here. If she wishes to retain the services of a ronin – or even formally adopt her into the family – who is to gainsay her?"

Shin smiled. "Who indeed?" He paused. "Any sign of Shijan?"

Batu frowned. "No. And I cannot say I am not glad of it. Better for everyone that he should disappear, I think."

"Still – a man like that, I might prefer to have proof of death," Shin said.

"Even if he is not dead, there is little harm he can do now. The Zeshi have disowned him, and from what I hear, Honesty-sama is unhappy with him as well. If one side doesn't catch him, the other will. No, in all likelihood, he's resting somewhere in a shallow grave." Batu sighed and smiled. "You were right."

"About what?"

"All of it. If you hadn't pressed the matter, there's no telling what might have happened. Shijan might have gotten away with everything."

"Or maybe he would have done nothing at all."

Batu shrugged. "I'm trying to be nice, Shin."

"It is appreciated, Batu." Shin looked up at the sky. "Time to go, I think." He snapped open his fan and made to turn, but stopped. "I meant what I said earlier. You should come visit, time and tide permitting. It would be good to see more of you."

Batu nodded. "Perhaps I will. Goodbye, Shin."

"Goodbye, Batu."

The ride back down into the foothills was as uncomfortable

as the ride up had been, but Shin bore it with stoic grace. He thought about all that had occurred over the last few days, since the fire. The negotiations had been completed, insomuch as those things could ever truly be completed.

Fifteen people had died altogether in the attack. Many others had been injured, both Zeshi and Shiko. He wasn't certain how many of Honesty-sama's men had been injured, though at least eight had been killed. He was certain that more would have died, had they not managed to stop Shijan.

He'd written letters to both the Ide and the Iuchi, detailing his findings. He'd left out all mention of the blind woman and her compatriots. It would only muddy the waters and raise unanswerable questions. He was not certain what would come of it all. Thankfully, it was not up to him.

His mind turned again to the bargain he'd made with Emiko and her lot. The thought of it still brought a twist of nausea. It had been necessary, but that did not make it sit better on his stomach. As a boy, he'd been taught time and again to never forsake his personal honor – but this wasn't the first time he'd found a flaw in the iron of his code.

"Necessary," he murmured to himself. The Daidoji did what was necessary, always. Even a reluctant Daidoji, such as himself.

Two Step was much as he remembered. Bustling, but quietly. Lun's boat was waiting for them where they'd left it. Her crew was loading a cargo of leather goods for sale in the City of the Rich Frog, and she seemed pleased. Watching them load, he wondered whether Kenzō had finished going through his finances. He was almost looking forward to the conversation. After the last few days it would be something of a relief.

He was thinking of the theater when he heard the sound of

a shamisen. He turned and saw her. Emiko. The blind woman stood on the shady side of a sake house, her face tilted towards the river. She sniffed the air, and Shin wondered if it smelled different to one who could not see. He strode towards her, and her dead eyes swung to meet him. He realized that she could hear his movements even amid the clamor of morning traffic. The thought was unsettling. "Good morning, my lord," she said, in a clear, calm voice.

"Good morning, Emiko," Shin said, politely.

The beginnings of a smile quirked at her lips. In the light, she was lovely – but it was the loveliness of a viper, all colorful scales and graceful movements. "You are going home," she said. It wasn't a question.

"We are."

"I wish you a safe journey."

Shin heard something in her voice – it put him in mind of the twitch of a cat's tail. He studied the narrow figure, in her plain robes and bamboo cane, her eyes dull and unfocused. But the mind behind them was as sharp and as lethal as a blade. "Is that a warning?"

"You may take it as such, if you like."

Shin glanced at Kasami. She was speaking to Nozomi. He took a quick step towards the blind woman and saw her twitch her cane, as if in preparation for a fight. "I would advise caution on your part, my lord. I am not undefended."

"Yes. Did you know, I spotted it the first time we met."

Emiko cocked her head. "Oh?"

"The way you carry it attests to its weight – it is somewhat heavier than a normal cane, isn't it? Also, the bamboo rattles slightly against the metal, a common flaw in concealed weapons."

She smiled thinly. "You are very observant."

"Yes. Would you like to know what else I have observed?"

"If you wish to tell me."

"I do. You are worried."

"Concerned, merely. We wish to be your friends, Lord Shin. We hope you will not forget our arrangement when you are safely back in that fine city of yours."

"Another warning."

"Take it as you like," she said.

"Perhaps I shall not take it at all." Shin gave his surroundings a surreptitious glance. He saw no obvious threat, but that did not mean that it was not there. "Perhaps I shall wipe you from my mind as soon as I leave Unicorn lands."

"That would be unfortunate. We can be of such help to one another."

"As you were of help to Shijan?"

She paused. "Shijan… Shijan chose his path. We tried to show him another, but he preferred to make his own way."

"He will never be caught, will he?"

"Do you wish him to be?"

Shin smiled grimly. "Do not offer the impossible. I fear he is already dead, his body buried in a shallow grave next to that of Zeshi Hisato."

Emiko gave no sign that she recognized the name. Then, Shin had not expected her to. "It could be. Brigands and worse are a constant threat to travelers in these mountains. If he fled alone into the wilderness, any number of unfortunate fates might have befallen him."

"A regrettable truth." Shin looked towards the river. "The river is beautiful this time of morning. I am sorry you cannot see it."

"Beautiful things are often dangerous."

"Are you describing yourself, Emiko?"

She smiled prettily, revealing her crimson-stained teeth. "You flatter me, my lord. I am but a humble musician – a hinin, of no worth or importance."

"And yet here you are, delivering a warning on behalf of a society which may or may not exist, save in the fevered delusions of a few."

"One might ask if there is a difference between an empire and its hypothetical equivalent." Emiko tilted her face up, and her eyes fluttered against the heat of the sun. "I do not think so, myself. Then I am but a poor, uneducated creature, barely fit to speak to one such as you."

"Enough," Shin said, softly. She paused.

"My lord?"

"Enough," he repeated. "Spare me the false courtesies and get to the point."

"Have I angered you, my lord?"

"If you had, you would not have to ask." Shin sighed. "Let us not play these games. I am not Shijan. Do not treat me as if I am."

She frowned – the first crack in her mask he had observed. "No, my lord. You are not him. Shijan was a little man with little dreams."

"And what am I?"

She fell silent. Then, "We do not yet know. You are a samurai, but you do not act as a samurai ought to. You are clever, and clever men are dangerous."

"I'll take that as a compliment."

"That cleverness is why we wish to be friends. As Yuzu said, we have use for clever men – men with the ear of governors and aristocrats."

"And if I choose not to be of use?"

Emiko smiled again – a pretty viper, baring crimson fangs. "That would be unfortunate."

Shin digested this as he considered how to reply. Finally, he said, "Did you threaten Shijan as well?"

"We do not make threats."

"And yet, I feel distinctly threatened." He snapped his fan open and gave it a flutter. "Let us put aside courtesy for the moment. You chose to help me because it served your purposes."

"And you accepted our help because it served yours."

Shin nodded. "So I did. We have helped one another. And now you think to make me a catspaw, as you did Shijan. But as we have both acknowledged, I am not Shijan. Therefore I will not be a catspaw. I will not be bullied or flattered into serving your purposes."

"I thought the Crane were known for paying their debts."

"And so I will. At a time and place of my choosing – not yours." A dangerous game, but one Shin was willing to play, until such time as he could work out how best to deal with Emiko and her friends.

Emiko frowned. "That is not how this works."

"No? A shame. For that is the only way it will work, with me." Shin leaned close, staring into her sightless eyes. "I do not know the extent of your reach, but I know the extent of mine, and I think I have you beat."

"Are you willing to test that, my lord?"

He laughed softly. "Yes, I am."

Her smile vanished, wiped away by his laughter. Red teeth bared, she said, "You samurai, always so full of yourselves. So certain of your invulnerability. I might not be able to see, but you are the one who is blind!" She fell silent and her grip on her cane was white and tense as she raised it to the level of her face. Shin saw her thumb twitch, and heard the soft scrape of steel against bamboo.

He tensed, his hand falling to his own sword. Then he paused. "I see more than you think," he said, and she hesitated. He closed his fan with a click. "Your anger is but another mask. You have many of them, I think. This one is less attractive than the others, but perhaps that is intentional."

At his words, she relaxed immediately, and he sighed in satisfaction. She straightened and lowered her cane. "Any other bushi might have struck me down."

"You said yourself that I am not as other bushi. Your attempt at provocation was crude. You would not last a moment in the Winter Court."

"That is the finest compliment a man has ever paid me," she said, and Shin almost laughed. He was not sure why she had attempted to provoke him, though he suspected it had been a test of sorts.

"Yes, well." He stepped back, putting a small distance between them. "I am not one to deny the talents of another." He took a slow breath. "Nor am I one to make promises I cannot keep. I owe you a favor, and it will be repaid, but at my discretion. If that is not good enough, then you may as well attempt to cut my throat now."

"With your bodyguard so close? I am not a fool."

"I am glad to hear it."

She smiled and turned away without replying. Cane before her, she made her way into the crowd, and in a few moments was lost to sight. Shin sighed and made his way back to the boat. Kasami was waiting, her expression thunderous.

"Was that the blind woman I saw scurrying away?"

"It was."

"What did she want?"

"To thank me for my efforts."

Kasami frowned, but let it pass. She fell into step with him. "It is time to board. Are you ready, or are there other criminals you wish to bid farewell?"

"No. No, just the one." He looked up at the sky and then at Kasami.

"I think it's time we headed home, don't you?"

CAST LIST

Crane	
Daidoji Shin	*wastrel, layabout, detective*
Hiramori Kasami	*yojimbo in service to Shin, easily annoyed*
Junichi Kenzō	*courtier, good with numbers*

Unicorn	
Iuchi Konomi	*noblewoman, meddler*
Iuchi Batu	*magistrate, very tired*
Kenshin Nozomi	*yojimbo in service to Batu*
Ide Sora	*noblewoman, problem-solver*
Suio Umeko	*matchmaker for the Ide daimyo*
Zeshi Shijan	*nobleman, cousin to Aimi*
Zeshi Aimi	*noblewoman, fiancée of Gen*
Zeshi Reiji	*nobleman, brother to Aimi*
Shiko Gen	*corpse, fiancé of Aimi*
Shiko Mitsue	*nobleman, father of Gen*
Shiko Nishi	*noblewoman, wife of Mitsue*
Shiko Koji	*nobleman, son of Mitsue and Nishi*
Shiko Himari	*noblewoman, wife of Koji*
Totara Ikki	*nobleman, cousin to Nishi*
Totara Giichi	*nobleman, cousin to Nishi*
Totara Aito	*nobleman, cousin to Nishi*

Other

Ito	*merchant, spy*
Wada Sanemon	*master of the Three Flower Troupe*
Nao	*actor, flirt*
Lun	*ship's captain, former pirate*
Kitano Daichi	*servant to Shin, gambler*
Yo	*servant to Shijan, very bland*
Katai Ruri	*ronin, yojimbo in service to Aimi*
Honesty-sama	*crime lord, scary*
Gozen Emiko	*musician, assassin, member of the Iron Sect*
Tashiro	*ronin, in service to Honesty-sama, member of the Iron Sect*
Natsuo	*herbalist, member of the Iron Sect*
Yuzu	*merchant, member of the Iron Sect*
Fumihiro	*merchant, member of the Iron Sect*
Eiji	*blacksmith, member of the Iron Sect*
Ichika	*geisha, member of the Iron Sect*

ABOUT THE AUTHOR

JOSH REYNOLDS is a writer, editor and semi-professional monster movie enthusiast. He has been a professional author since 2007, writing over thirty novels and numerous short stories, including *Arkham Horror, Warhammer: Age of Sigmar, Warhammer 40,000,* and the occasional audio script. He grew up in South Carolina and now lives in Sheffield, UK.

joshuamreynolds.co.uk
twitter.com/jmreynolds

DESCENT
JOURNEYS IN THE DARK™

Epic fantasy of heroes and monsters in the perilous realms of Terrinoth.

A trio of legendary figures reunite to solve a mystery but instead uncover treachery and dark sorcery, and a holy warrior is the only hope of salvation from a brutal demonic invasion... adventure comes at a high price in this astonishing world.